Praise for Dee Davis

After Twilight

"Dee Davis pours on the atmosphere and cranks up the danger in this terrific new thriller. Perfect pulse-pounding reading for a cold winter's night."
—*Romantic Times*

"Dee Davis provides her fans with a powerful romantic suspense. *After Twilight* is an entertaining tale that works because the characters seem real and their interactions quite genuine."
—*Affaire de Coeur*

Just Breathe

"Rising star Dee Davis returns with a new story of sizzling romance and danger. *Just Breathe* is sure to please Ms. Davis's growing list of admirers."
—*Romantic Times*

"A wonderful, not-to-be-missed, stay-up-late read."
—*The Philadelphia Inquirer*

P9-BYA-012

Dark of the Night

"Intrigue, deception, and murder make *Dark of the Night* a great way to spend your entertainment hours. Author Dee Davis is making quite a name for herself in the romantic suspense field."

—*Romantic Times*

"*Dark of the Night* is a compelling, thoroughly entertaining tale of romantic suspense. Fans of the genre should add Dee Davis to their list of 'don't miss' authors."

—America Online's Romance Fiction Forum

Also by Dee Davis
Published by Ivy Books:

AFTER TWILIGHT
JUST BREATHE
DARK OF THE NIGHT
DANCING IN THE DARK

Books published by The Ballantine Publishing Group are
available at quantity discounts on bulk purchases for pre-
mium, educational, fund-raising, and special sales use. For
details, please call 1-800-733-3000.

MIDNIGHT RAIN

DEE DAVIS

IVY BOOKS • NEW YORK

Sale of this book without a front cover may be unauthorized. If this book is coverless, it may have been reported to the publisher as "unsold or destroyed" and neither the author nor the publisher may have received payment for it.

This book contains an excerpt from the forthcoming paperback edition of *Dancing in the Dark* by Dee Davis. This excerpt has been set for this edition only and may not reflect the final content of the forthcoming edition.

An Ivy Book
Published by The Ballantine Publishing Group

Copyright © 2002 by Dee Davis Oberwetter
Excerpt from *Dancing in the Dark* copyright © 2002 by Dee Davis Oberwetter

All rights reserved under International and Pan-American Copyright Conventions. Published in the United States by The Ballantine Publishing Group, a division of Random House, Inc., New York, and simultaneously in Canada by Random House of Canada Limited, Toronto.

Ivy Books and colophon are trademarks of Random House, Inc.

www.ballantinebooks.com

ISBN 0-8041-1977-5

Manufactured in the United States of America

First Edition: December 2002

10   9   8   7   6   5   4   3   2   1

For Lexie,
the light of my life

Acknowledgments

Without the input of the following people, this story would not have been possible. Although I have worked to portray the characters in an accurate way, there are bound to be errors, and for those, I take full responsibility.

Thank you to Diana Hunter, Ph.D., PT, and Myrna Ward, RN-C, for helping me understand traumatic brain injury and its repercussions; Laura McCanlies, who made sure my Spanish was accurate; Julie Kenner and Kathleen O'Reilly, who put up with my inane worries and questions at all hours of the night; Charlotte Herscher, who, as always, pushed me to be my best; and a wonderful FBI agent, who, by request, shall remain nameless.

Prologue

Choahuila, Mexico

What he needed was a little excitement.

Jonathan Brighton shook his head, trying to clear it, to stop the slow incessant onslaught of fatigue, forcing himself to concentrate instead on the road ahead. It was the sameness that was getting to him. The lack of anything remotely entertaining.

The hazy mountains shimmered in the distance, taunting him, the diametric opposite of the arid hellhole he was driving across. As if in testament to his thoughts, a swirling cone of dust chased a tumbleweed across the road, dissipating when it reached the other side.

What in God's name had possessed him to come here? He'd needed a break from the headaches of running Guardian, but surely a nice beach located next to a five-star hotel would have been a better choice of getaway. Instead, he was heading for a mountain retreat that was apparently located in the middle of nowhere. Somewhere remote.

Isolated.

He'd lost his fucking mind.

Or rather his brother had. He'd been the one to insist that Jonathan needed something different. Something quiet. And of course, his partners had jumped right up on the bandwagon, offering their sage advice. Go here. Go there. Take this road. Take that one.

And he'd listened.

So here he was, in the middle of nowhere, in a rental car that shook if he accelerated past fifty, with a radio that only worked some of the time and an air conditioner that had stopped before he'd gone a hundred miles. Another of his partners' brilliant ideas. "Don't drive your own car in Mexico, Jonathan. Just rent one. It's cheap, it's . . ." *Crap.* The goddamned thing was crap.

Oh yeah, this was the life.

Based on the way things were going he sincerely doubted there'd be anything redeeming about the trip at all. He did not feel refreshed. He didn't even feel like he was on vacation—more like he was exiled in hell. Angrily he punched at the fan button, pushing it to high. Sun-heated air blasted out of the vent, and he gritted his teeth, reaching over to roll down the window. Nothing was worth this kind of torture.

Truth was, he wasn't the rough-it-out-in-the-wilds type. He smiled at the thought, glancing down at his pressed jeans and polo shirt. Even they felt odd. He spent his days dressed for success, Armani his uniform of choice. The rest of the world might believe in dress-down Fridays but Jonathan thought it was bullshit. A way for people who couldn't afford the best to justify their situation. And he wasn't falling for it.

With a murmured curse, he pressed down on the accelerator. The little car shook, but held its course. It was turning into a hell of a day. Hopefully things were going better in Austin. Derek's email had certainly made it sound that way. Although with his cryptic ramblings it was hard to tell for certain. Still, John was glad he'd stopped before crossing the border to check on things.

Between Danny and Derek, everything would be handled properly. It was tempting under the circumstances to go home and deal with it himself, but his brother was totally competent, and Derek had as much as said that things were fine. He just needed to have a little faith.

And call the office the minute he arrived.

He sighed, leaning back against the headrest. He'd put everything he had into Guardian. It was like a child. And he wouldn't—couldn't—allow anything to happen to it. If it died, so did he.

A horn sounded behind him, breaking into his reverie. He hadn't even heard the truck coming up behind him. Three hours in the desert and he was already losing his edge. With a frown, he pulled the rental over onto the shoulder.

The truck, its red paint faded to orangey-brown, started to pass, then slowed, matching its pace to Jonathan's car. A stocky man in the passenger seat smiled, gesturing for him to stop. Jonathan held his speed steady, concentrating on the rutted shoulder. The truck stayed with him.

Just what he needed to top off an already perfect day—a couple of crazy Mexicans in a beat-up pickup truck. Jonathan accelerated, the car protesting its mistreatment. The pickup followed suit, the man waving his hand now in agitation, his smile fading.

Something glinted in the man's hand. A badge. The son of a bitch was waving a badge. Jonathan blew out a breath, relief mixing with anger. Where the hell was his siren? Pulling the car to a stop, he turned off the ignition, already reaching for his wallet.

The cop walked up to the car and leaned down, his beefy face glistening with sweat. *"Salga del coche."* Jonathan's beleaguered brain struggled to translate as the man repeated himself. *"Salga del coche."* Get out of the car.

Jonathan reached for the car handle, but before he could open it, the door jerked outward, the man's beefy hand closing on Jonathan's shoulder.

"¡Ahora mismo!"

He nodded and stepped from the car. The big man's partner joined them, his eyes hidden behind the mirrored lenses of his sunglasses.

"*Su licencia, por favor.*" Despite the word *please*, Jonathan recognized that the request was in fact an order.

He opened his wallet, digging for his license. "*Yo no hablo español.*" He actually did speak the language, but it had been a long time, and until he understood what was happening, he thought it best to keep the fact to himself.

The two men conferred for a moment, and then the second man handed the license back, his fat friend heading for their truck. "Where are you headed?" Jonathan returned his attention to the policeman in sunglasses. He was speaking English now, his words heavily accented.

"I'm on my way to the mountains. A place just outside of Satillo." He was actually heading for a little village near Torreon, but again it seemed prudent to keep his destination private.

The man nodded. "You are on vacation here in our country?"

"Yeah. I needed a little peace and quiet." Which was turning out to be a whole lot less soothing than advertised.

The policeman smiled, revealing a gold front tooth. "You have come to the right place, my friend. I think we can guarantee you nothing but peace and quiet from now on."

Jonathan smiled back, but the hairs on his neck rose as some part of his body responded to a thread of something else in the man's voice. For the first time he realized that neither of the men was wearing a uniform. Laughter off to his left signaled that fatty had moved, and Jonathan turned, his heart pounding as adrenaline pumped through his body.

The heavyset man was standing a few feet away, the hot sunshine highlighting the pistol in his hand.

There was a flash, and before Jonathan had time to think, let alone act, the sound of the gun's report filled his ears. Then for a moment everything was quiet, the world seeming to move in slow motion. He watched as a bead of sweat dropped from the shooter's heavily jowled face, waiting for the inevitable, and it came—an explosion of heat and light that obliterated all other thoughts.

He struggled to hold on, fighting to maintain consciousness. There was still so much he wanted to do. Somewhere amidst the pain in his head, he heard tires squealing as his assailants' truck pulled back onto the highway, leaving him alone on the side of the road.

If he could have, he'd have laughed. It was an inglorious way to die, ironic really. The complete opposite of the life he'd led. Always pushing for more. As the darkness swirled up to swallow him, his last thoughts were of all that had been left undone. What he could have been. But nothing—not his money, not his connections, and certainly not his company—could save him now.

With a sigh, Jonathan Brighton gave in to the dark.

Chapter I

Austin, Texas—Six months later

All he had to do was lift the goddamned pen.

John Brighton concentrated on the writing implement, willing his right hand to move. He was halfway there. He'd managed to get his fingers to close around the thing. Now all he had to do was lift it up.

His hand quivered and for a moment rose off the table. He closed his eyes, trying to visualize the action. How could something so seemingly inconsequential be so difficult? Six months of rehab and he was no better than a newborn. Weak and untried.

He swallowed, concentrating on the pen. This might be the biggest challenge he'd ever faced, but he wasn't about to go down for the count. A couple of low-life Mexican thugs were not going to get the best of him.

The pen lifted, his fingers shaking with the effort.

"Hey, bro. Ready to blow this pop stand?"

The pen dropped to the bed, then rolled to the floor. "Danny." John looked up, trying to conceal his annoyance. Maybe he was jealous of the fact that his brother had full use of his faculties, or maybe he was just in a generally crappy mood. Either way, there was no point in taking it out on Danny.

His brother hung a garment bag on a hook, and dropped into a chair by the hospital bed. "Having a little trouble signing out?" He bent down to retrieve the pen.

"I could have done it." John sounded petulant and he knew it. "You surprised me. That's all."

"Look, Jonathan, there's no need to push yourself like this. Your recovery is nothing short of miraculous as it is. What you need is a little downtime. Let your body come back at its own pace."

"I've had six months of downtime, and believe me when I tell you it isn't what it's cracked up to be." He wasn't surprised to hear bitterness in his voice. So much had been lost. Things he might never recover. Gaping holes in his memory. A darkness that sometimes threatened to swallow him whole.

Danny held up a hand in apology. "I didn't mean to ruffle your feathers. I just want you to take a breath. Maybe move a little slower. The mind's a funny thing. You shouldn't push it."

"There's nothing to push, Danny. What's gone is gone. My memories aren't coming back. The only thing I can do now is try and pick through what's left. Get on with my life."

"So let me help you. It's about time I got the chance to be the big brother." His expression belied the lightness in his voice.

"And how exactly do you propose to do that?" John swung his legs carefully out of the bed, using his left leg to propel his right.

"Well, to start with I can sign these." Danny reached for the dismissal papers. "I doubt anyone will look too closely." His grin was contagious and John felt his mood lightening. Maybe things would feel more normal once he was home.

"Whatever it takes to get me out of here." He watched as his brother signed the release papers, envying the ease with which he wielded the pen. "So what'd you bring me to wear?"

"Armani." Danny smiled. "What else? I made a special trip to get it." He unzipped the bag and pulled out the beautifully tailored suit.

John swallowed back a wave of frustration. The suit had enough closures to keep him occupied for a century. All hundred years. He forced a smile. "Thanks. But I think I might have preferred something a little simpler."

Danny frowned. "Yeah, right. This coming from a guy whose friends wager about whether he wears a tie to bed at night."

John winced at the reference. It wasn't the first time he'd heard it. But repetition didn't make it seem any more real. He remembered the need for things like Armani, but the idea just didn't fit anymore. It was as though that part of him had been damaged, twisted— the mirror image of what he'd once been. And no one seemed to understand.

He *was* Jonathan Brighton. And he *wasn't*.

All at the same time.

Hell, he didn't really understand it himself. He only knew he no longer wanted to wear Armani, even if he did have an entire closet full of it.

He looked up at his brother, striving for levity he simply didn't feel. "I hope I'm not an odds-on favorite, because I don't think I'll be tying ties anytime soon." He fought to close his hand, frustration combining with anger. Even the simple act of making a fist eluded him.

"Which brings me back to my original point. You're pushing yourself too fast." Danny reached for the suit coat, sliding it off of the hanger. "Flo said you were even thinking of coming back to work."

"It's time. I've been out of commission too long as it is." With his good hand he levered himself up, careful to center his weight, slightly favoring his good leg.

"You were shot in the head, Jonathan. It's going to take more than a few months to recover."

He frowned at his brother, fighting to keep his irritation from showing. "I've asked you to call me John."

"I know that, but after thirty-three years of calling you Jonathan, you can't expect me to just instantly switch."

"I expect you to try." He knew he was being unreasonable, but he couldn't seem to help himself.

"Honest to God, *John,* what kind of man changes his name at thirty-five?" His brother's tone bordered on exasperation.

"The kind whose life has been turned inside out." He met his brother's gaze, the tension in the room almost palpable. "The simple truth is that part of Jonathan Brighton died on that highway in Mexico, and it's never coming back." He shrugged, a left-sided affair that still managed to convey his misery. "John is all that's left."

"You're talking nonsense." Danny's voice was earnest, worried. "You're going to be fine. It may take time, but everything will be like before, you'll see."

"Nothing will ever be the same, Danny. I've accepted that fact. And you'd do well to accept it, too." He blew out a breath, suddenly feeling tired.

"I'm working on it." Danny dropped his gaze to study his wingtips. "But in the meantime, I can't help worrying about you."

"I understand that. And I appreciate your concern." John closed his eyes, massaging his temple. "But the fact remains that it's my call. And I say I'm ready to come back." Anger, hot and heavy, swelled through him. "What I need now is work. And the work I choose is at Guardian." He banged his good hand down on the table. "At *my* company. Do I make myself clear?"

Some part of him, deep inside, was appalled at his tone of voice, surprised at the depth of his anger, but it held no sway. He glared at his brother, waiting for an answer.

Danny sighed, obviously working to contain his emotions. "I just want you to be yourself again."

"I know that." John dropped heavily back onto the bed. "I didn't mean to lose my temper. It's just that right now, Guardian is all I have. And for the time being I need to be there. I need to try and make it all work again."

"Then I'll be there to help you." Danny's troubled gaze met his. "Look, one way or the other, we'll find a way to make it all right. I swear it."

Tears pricked the back of John's eyes. He was so fucking emotional these days. He tried to smile, certain that it was, at best, lopsided. "I hope so, Danny. I really hope so."

His brother's smile was artificially bright. "All right, then, what do you say we start by getting you dressed."

"I think a suit might be overkill for a casual afternoon of recovery." The voice was decidedly feminine, deep and smoky. Like aged whiskey, it washed over him, deceptively smooth, ending with a swift kick. He liked it.

A lot.

He swung around, curious to see the woman behind the words. He wasn't disappointed.

She stood in the doorway, dressed in faded green scrubs, the cotton hugging every sweet curve. Neither tall nor short, she simply was. Inhabiting space as if it belonged to her.

A single braid hung casually over her shoulder, her hair brown with golden highlights. *Sun-kissed* was the word that popped into his head. He smiled at the imagery, wondering if he'd lost his mind, and then ruefully accepted the fact that, regardless of the situation, he was no longer playing with a full deck. Still, he was in the game, and that had to count for something.

"So you guys want to quit staring, or shall I give you a runway turn?" She smiled slowly, green eyes sparkling, and stepped into the room, breaking the spell.

He shot a glance at his brother, whose eyes were also

riveted on the new arrival, his smile predatory. Jealousy surged through John, surprising him with its force. Yet another emotion out of control. Hell, he didn't even know the woman. He pulled to his feet again, fighting to keep his balance. His leg was much better, but standing required his full attention, distraction almost certainly spelling disaster.

And this woman was definitely a distraction.

She moved before he had a chance to think about her intent, steadying him with gentle hands, the soft smell of her surrounding him with tantalizing hints of vanilla.

He reached up with his good hand, planning to push her back, to protect his space, but she'd already moved, standing again in the doorway, one shoulder propped against the door frame.

"Who the hell are you?" His words came out sharper than he'd intended. The woman's scrubs marked her as a hospital employee. A nurse of some kind, no doubt. He shouldn't have snapped, but he wasn't a man who liked to be coddled and he was more than capable of standing on his own two feet.

"Apparently your dresser." She held up a pair of sweats and a T-shirt. "Can you lift your arm?"

Shooting her what he hoped was an indignant look, he slowly raised his arm, stopping when it reached shoulder height, the effort costing him more than he wanted to admit. "How's this?"

"It's a good start. Can you get it any higher?" She watched him dispassionately, but he could see a spark of something in her eyes. Pity or maybe compassion. It didn't really matter. Either sentiment was abhorrent. And he wasn't about to tolerate it from a stranger—hospital staff or no.

He let his arm drop. "I don't see that it matters."

She shrugged. "It doesn't—to me. But I'd think sometime in your life you'd like to be able to pull something off the top shelf, or hang the star on the Christmas tree."

He studied her through narrowed eyes, responding to the challenge in her voice. "And you care about this because . . ."

She smiled, the gesture changing her from formidable to impish in an instant. "I get paid if you touch the stars."

There was a world of meaning in her words, but only in John's imagination.

"Does that go for me, too?" Danny's tone was a cross between wistful and wolfish.

John shook his head, pulling himself back to reality. The woman was a witch. He'd completely forgotten his brother was in the room.

"Only if you've suffered major head trauma." Her gaze brushed over Danny, dismissing him. "I'm John's physical therapist."

Nonplussed by the brush-off, Danny grinned. "Hey, I'm the patient's brother. Surely that gives me the right for consults or something."

John took a hesitant step forward, pleased when his right foot obeyed. "You have a name?" His voice was still brusque. A combination of irritation and embarrassment.

"My name is Kathleen." Her words tickled his ear, and he realized she'd moved again, this time flanking his bad side. "Kathleen Cavanaugh."

"Irish?" The word popped from his mouth before he had time to think about it.

"Boston Irish." Her eyes crinkled at the corners, and his heart rate ratcheted up a notch.

"That explains the accent." Danny moved to his other side, and together they helped him toward the bathroom.

"Take these." She handed him the sweats when they

reached the door. "You ought to be able to get them on yourself."

His eyes met hers, and it felt as if they were locked together in a world all their own, the soft intake of her breath assuring him that he wasn't alone in the feeling. "And if I can't manage?"

Her smile was slow and sure. "Then I'll just have to come in and help you."

She'd lost her freaking mind. Katie stared at the closed bathroom door, trying to ignore Danny Brighton's blatant stare. It bored into her back. But he wasn't the source of her discomfort.

No, indeed. It was much worse than that. She was having less than pure thoughts about Jonathan Brighton. And she wasn't supposed to be thinking about him like that. Heavens, she wasn't supposed to be thinking about him at all.

She was a professional. And this was a routine situation. All she had to do was observe the man, and based on what she saw make recommendations to her superiors. Simple as that.

The door opened and he stepped out of the bathroom, every muscle outlined by the T-shirt she'd provided. His dark hair curled against the neckline, his face shadowed with the hint of a beard.

He looked unkempt. And dangerous. A far cry from the button-down workaholic she'd been briefed about. This was a man with an edge.

And she'd always liked men who walked the line.

"You're staring." His tone was mild, but the current running between them was reflected in his eyes.

"I wasn't actually. I was just thinking about where we ought to begin."

"On the bed?" His smile sent shivers trailing down her back.

She swallowed, struggling for composure. "I beg your pardon?"

Danny laughed behind her, a hint of something protective in his voice. "I think he means that he needs to sit down."

She pulled her mind out of the gutter and focused on the man in front of her. Really focused. He was holding himself together by sheer willpower, but a sheen of sweat glazed his face, and his jaw was twitching with the effort to look at ease.

"Oh God, I'm sorry. What was I thinking?" Five minutes and she'd compromised his health. Her training had been rushed, but it had been thorough. She wasn't here to hurt him. On the contrary, she needed Mr. Brighton fully operational. Again her overeager mind flooded her brain with vivid images having nothing to do with her job or Jonathan Brighton's recovery.

Danny joined her, and they helped Jonathan to the bed. He sat down with a sigh. "I'm the one who should be sorry. Getting dressed never used to be an all-day affair. Although this getup," he gestured to the faded sweats, "beats the hell out of that." He tipped his head toward the suit, shooting her a grateful smile.

"I thought Jonathan already had a therapist."

Katie regretfully pulled her attention away from Jonathan, turning to face Danny's skeptical gaze. "He does. Or rather, he did. Linda Osborne was his PT here at the rehab clinic, but now that he's being released, he needs someone at home. Someone to watch over him, to work with him to continue to improve his mobility."

"And that would be you." His eyes narrowed as he studied her. This time there was no hint of playfulness. Danny Brighton was all business. And the business was protecting his brother. For all their physical differences—the one dark as sin and the other almost angelic—the brothers obviously had a deep bond. And right now Danny Brighton was assessing her.

"Exactly. Linda doesn't do home care." She met his gaze square on, unflinching. "I do."

"And you're good at what you do?"

"So I've been told." She fought to keep her tone level. She'd never responded well to unspoken threats. And there was no question that Jonathan's brother was baiting her.

"Give the woman a break, Danny. She's just trying to do her job." Jonathan's voice was laced with laughter, but there was an underlying note of authority.

Danny studied her for a moment longer, then relaxed. "I'm sure you can understand my concern, Ms. Cavanaugh. My brother has been through quite an ordeal. And I just want to be certain that he has the best of everything."

"What he means, Kathleen," the name tumbled off his lips like warm wine, caressing her from the inside out, "is that he likes to think he's running the show. And you were a curve he hadn't expected." He smiled at his brother, then returned his attention to her. "I assume you were assigned by my doctor?"

"Your insurance company actually." She shrugged, leaning over him to straighten his pillow. "Your doctor orders in-home care, but your insurance company is responsible for assigning someone."

"I see." He nodded, his expression thoughtful. "So you're with me for the duration."

"Duration?" She straightened, trying to read the subtext of his words.

"Yeah. I need to know that whoever I'm working with will be around to see things through to the end."

"You mean a full recovery." He was testing her again, but she wasn't exactly sure how.

He shrugged. "Or as full a recovery as I'm likely to get."

"You get what you work for, Mr. Brighton."

"John." He smiled again, the tension dissipating with

the gesture. "And I always work for what I want, Ms. Cavanaugh. Always."

"Now, there's an understatement." Danny's words were mumbled, but there was a wealth of information in his tone.

"Looks like I'll fit in just fine, then. I expect my patients to work hard. But I assure you, in the end it's more than worth the effort." She shot a look at first one brother and then the other, noting again the contrast between them.

Women were more likely to respond to Danny's pretty-boy looks than to John's dark mystery. There was something off-putting about the older Brighton boy. Something that she had absolutely no intention of investigating. She was here to do a job.

Period.

"So where do we start?" John's question pulled her out of her musings.

"I'd think the first thing to do is get you home." Danny's voice was proprietary again.

"Sounds like a plan." John's smile included her as well as his brother, and warmed her all the way to her toes. "I suppose I have to wait for a wheelchair?"

It was Katie's turn to smile. "Actually, if you're up to it, you can walk. Since this is rehab, and not a hospital per se, we like for our patients to feel like they're leaving in better shape than they've arrived. I'd say you've earned the right to walk out of here." She was babbling. But it was better than letting her mind wander free. "Of course, if you'd rather have the wheelchair . . ." She trailed off, already certain of his response.

She wasn't disappointed. He held up a hand, shaking his head. "Not on your life. They wheeled me in here. They're sure as hell not wheeling me out." To illustrate his point he pushed himself off of the bed, wincing with the effort. Without thinking, she slid an arm around his waist, feeling his muscles bunch in rebuff.

"I can do it myself." His words vibrated through her, his body warm against hers.

"I know you can." She tightened her grip, steadying him. "But sometimes it's all right to ask for a little help." She told herself that she needed to gain his confidence, and prove to him she knew what she was doing, but the truth was, she just wanted to touch him.

And the thought scared her to death.

"Thank goodness I caught you before you left." A redheaded whirlwind blew into the room, almost upsetting their forward progress in the process. "I tried the phone, but they said you'd been discharged." The woman stopped, eyes narrowing at the sight of Katie. "Who're you?"

John took a deliberate step closer, his arm tightening around her, his eyes bright with mischief. "This is Kathleen Cavanaugh, Flo. She's coming to live with me."

The woman's eyebrows disappeared into the tumble of hair as she glared up at John. "I hardly think now is the time—" She cut herself off, her face flaming. "Oh. You're with the hospital." John and Danny's laughter provided a backdrop for the woman's obvious embarrassment. "I'm sorry." Her face was as red as her hair. "I sometimes don't stop to think."

"It's okay," Katie reassured the older woman, pulling away from John. "I can see where you'd get the wrong idea." She shot a look at the Brighton brothers, her narrow-eyed gaze ending on John.

He shrugged, grinning. There was something a little wicked about Jonathan Brighton. Which of course was an understatement. The thought made her sober.

"I'm Florence Tedesky. Flo to my friends." The older woman held out her hand. "I have the misfortune of working for these brats." Her tone of voice belied her words. It was obvious there was shared affection among the three of them.

"More like we work for you," Danny said. "Flo

worked for our father for years. And when he died, she sort of adopted us."

"The truth is, I wasn't ready to hang up the towel, and John was kind enough to let me come to work at Guardian." Flo shot a grateful look at John.

"She's pulling your leg. I had to beg her to help me out. Flo has more business sense in her little finger than Danny and I have put together."

"Speak for yourself, bro," Danny said, pretending to be wounded.

"Come on, boys, you're confusing Kathleen." Flo smiled fondly at the two men, and then turned her attention to Katie. "You'll have to keep an eye out for these two. But I expect you've already figured that out."

Katie nodded, her mind spinning. With every revelation it seemed that Jonathan Brighton moved farther away from the profile she'd been given. "If I hadn't, I have now."

"So what brought you over here like a house on fire?" John asked. "I gather it wasn't concern for me."

"Oh my, no." Flo immediately brought her hand to her mouth. "That didn't come out right, surely. What I meant to say was that I got a phone call from the police."

The lighthearted air evaporated in an instant, both brothers' attention immediately on the redhead.

"They found Derek Miller." Flo drew in a breath, her eyes darkening with concern. "He's dead."

Chapter 2

Eric D'Angelo stared at the open police file on his desk, hoping for divine revelation. But of course nothing came. Not a damn thing.

"I thought the FBI was handling the Miller case?" Tony Haskins popped the last bite of sandwich into his mouth and leaned back in his chair, propping his feet on his desk, letting go with a satisfied belch. Etiquette wasn't exactly his strong point. But then, that wasn't a quality Eric valued in a partner. And as partners went, Tony was the best.

"Not officially. At least not yet." He turned the page, skimming the contents of the medical examiner's preliminary report.

"But you said they were at the scene. Fucking Edmund Roswell was there. You know that's gotta mean something big."

D'Angelo nodded. "Probably. But until I hear otherwise—officially—I'm going to keep investigating the case."

Haskins reached over for the file, flipping through it. "According to this, he was reported missing six months ago."

D'Angelo shrugged. "If it hadn't been for the drought, he'd probably still be missing. There was a preliminary investigation, but when they came up cold, it was shoved to a back burner. A guy like Miller's not exactly a priority."

"Looks to me like a deal gone south. Based on his drug record, I'd say it's a miracle he stayed alive this long."

"Yeah, but he only took one shot to the head, clean as a whistle."

"So, what, you're thinking a hit?" Tony frowned.

"I'm not thinking anything, except that the whole thing feels off somehow. I mean, if this is about drugs, then why aren't we dealing with DEA?"

"So what did Roswell say?"

"Not a hell of a lot. Just that Miller had been in touch. Something heavy hanging on his heart."

"But before he can talk," Haskins shaped his fingers like a gun, "boom."

"Exactly."

"Still could have been drugs. Maybe something involving the border. That'd bring in the Feds."

"It's a possibility. Although I still think it's odd that two FBI guys show up at the scene almost before the body is out of the water. It's almost like they knew."

Tony shrugged. "It wouldn't surprise me if they're wired into dispatch, they're listening in everywhere else. It's like fucking Big Brother." Tony wasn't a fan of the FBI, particularly Edmund Roswell.

Roswell was the antithesis of the stereotype of an agent. Paunchy and balding, the man had seen better days, but he was still a mean son of a bitch, and when he was on a case, he'd use anything and everything, legal and otherwise, to solve it. Eric kind of admired the old bastard, although he shared Tony's dislike of the man.

"Well, they can listen in all they want, but until we hear otherwise, the case stays in homicide."

"So where do we start?"

Eric sighed, running his hands through his hair. "I don't know. The guy worked for a company called Guardian. Ever hear of it?"

Tony frowned, staring down at the file, sorting through the data in his brain. On the outside Tony resembled a rumpled teddy bear, but inside he was solid steel, and sharper than a tack. He carried more information around in his brain than most computers. "Yeah. Something to do with security. Computers, I think." He looked up. "Remember the corporate type who got mugged in Mexico? I think he was with Guardian."

"You're talking about the guy they thought was dead?" Eric perked up, his senses buzzing.

Tony nodded. "Jonathan Brighton. They found him in some backwater Mexican hospital."

"That's right. He'd been carjacked. Shot in the head. I remember."

"Don't see a connection to Miller, other than the fact they worked at the same place."

"Well, for starters, Jonathan Brighton owns Guardian. And if nothing else it's an interesting coincidence."

Tony smiled, his eyes knowing. "Yeah, but you don't believe in coincidence."

It was Eric's turn to smile. "No, as a matter of fact, I don't."

John stood in the doorway of his apartment, wondering if he'd ever considered it home. Everything was perfect. Like a magazine ad. If home was really where the heart resided, then this wasn't exactly a glowing endorsement of his personal life. But he'd take what he could get. The fact that he had a life at all was pretty damn amazing, all things considered.

He closed his eyes, fighting for composure.

"I thought I might find you here."

He jerked up, startled out of his thoughts. "Jesus, Flo, you want to put me back in the hospital?"

The older woman shook her head, her smile tolerant. "No sense standing here regretting what's done, John."

She'd always been able to read his mind. His father's right-hand man for many years, Flo Tedesky was a special part of the family. She'd stepped in to help raise him and Danny when their mother had died, and she'd been there when their father passed away as well. He honestly couldn't imagine not having her as a part of his life.

Suddenly the apartment didn't seem so empty.

"Come on." She moved to his side. "Let's get you inside." Together they moved over to the sofa and he sank gratefully down onto the cushions.

"I don't remember living here."

"Well, you wouldn't." She sat beside him, still holding his hand. "We'd only just moved in."

He lifted an eyebrow, confused. "We?"

She laughed. "This place is huge. It covers the whole top floor of the building. I have my own suite of rooms. Believe me, we won't get in each other's way. Besides, it just seemed easier, with Guardian downstairs."

"Makes perfect sense." He smiled slowly. "I'm glad you're here."

She squeezed his hand. "Me, too."

He let his gaze wander around the room, trying to force some kind of memory. " Does Danny . . ."

"Live here?" she finished for him. "No. I think he'd have felt a little too confined."

"Living under my thumb." Danny's need for independence was something he hadn't forgotten. His brother liked doing things in his own way—and in his own time.

"Something like that. I also think all this was a bit too austere for him." She swept her arm around the room.

"Frankly, I'm not sure that I don't agree. Did I pick all this out?" He let his gaze encompass the room, taking in the sleek lines and dark upholstery. A funeral home was peppier.

Flo shook her head, and relief flooded through him. "You've never cared about where you lived. A decorator did this. The same one who did your last apartment."

He frowned. "So why the move?"

"As I said, the office is downstairs." Her eyebrows rose, underscoring her words.

"I see." He should have guessed. Hell, he should have known.

"What do you say we do something to lighten things up?" Flo's tone brooked no argument as she walked over to the heavy drapes and pulled them aside.

Sunlight flooded into the room, the golden light a perfect backdrop to the skyline of Austin. The sparkling buildings provided a panoramic view anyone would envy. A view he'd bought and then chosen to hide away behind yards of horrendous gray fabric.

The contradiction was confusing, to say the least, and definitely more than he wanted to deal with just now. So, pushing his morbid musings aside, he turned his thoughts to more pleasant prospects.

"Where's Nurse Ratched?" He worked to keep his voice casual, purposefully avoiding the use of her name.

Kathleen.

He liked it. He liked her. Which was odd considering he hadn't met her until a couple of hours ago. Still, there was something about her that seemed real. Something that stood out among all the doubt and confusion shrouding his life.

Truth was, it was more than that. She made him feel powerful—masculine. Without any conscious effort on her part, she enhanced the very part of him he thought he'd lost. A notion that was at once equally ridiculous and intoxicating.

"I'm expecting her any time now. I readied the guest

room. I assumed you'd want her close by." Flo nodded toward the doorway, her eyes knowing.

He felt heat on the back of his neck, and ducked his head, feeling all of about thirteen. "I'm not certain I want her at all. I'm doing pretty well on my own. I mean, they let me out of the hospital. That has to count for something, right?"

"It counts, certainly. But that doesn't mean you don't still need some help."

He ran his good hand through his hair. "I just like standing on my own two feet."

"Of course you do, but sometimes the best way to do that is to lean a little on someone else. You've come a long way, John, and Kathleen Cavanaugh is here to help you go the rest of the way. You want your life back, right?"

He nodded, already knowing what she was going to say.

"Then you have to let her help you."

The thought was more than enticing; it was down-right pleasurable. And it had been a hell of a long time since he'd felt anything close to pleasurable. Still, he prided himself on the fact that he'd never really *needed* anyone.

Loved people certainly, but never needed them. His attraction to Kathleen Cavanaugh was undeniable, but the idea that he might actually have to lean on her was another matter altogether. He released his breath, fighting against his conflicting emotions.

"John?" Flo's gaze met his, her eyes dark with worry. "Honey, you just can't do this on your own."

He nodded, the pain in his chest more emotional than physical. "I know."

"So you'll give Kathleen a chance?"

He desperately wanted to, but it wasn't easy to step out on the limb. Still, there was something exciting about the prospect of letting her in. Of testing the potency of the chemistry between them.

Maybe he did need Kathleen Cavanaugh. The thought was fascinating and frightening all at the same time, the contradiction making him feel more alive than he'd felt in years. "Yeah," he said, looking up at Flo, surprised to find himself smiling. "I'll give her a chance."

And for the first time in six long months, he felt a stirring of hope.

It was too damn hot to be outside. Which mimicked the turmoil inside her completely. She'd been totally unprepared for her meeting with John Brighton. On the surface, it had gone perfectly. But underneath—underneath it had been a disaster.

She jogged along the wooded path, the soft pounding of her feet a counterpoint to the steady beat of her heart. Just because she was drawn to the man didn't mean she couldn't do her job. She was a professional.

Besides, it wasn't as if she really knew him. He was a stranger. Anything she felt for him was strictly chemical. She ducked to avoid a low-hanging branch. He wasn't even her type. Dark and brooding was taxing. And there was seldom a happy ending. Look at Heathcliffe and Cathy. She blew out an angry breath, wondering what in hell she was thinking, comparing her life to a gothic romance.

Wuthering Heights be damned.

This wasn't about some romantic meeting on the moors. It was a professionally orchestrated operation, and she had obligations to far bigger things than her hormones. She'd just let her imagination get carried away, that's all. The next time she saw him, she'd realize she'd been mistaken.

He was a means to an end. Nothing more. And she'd

do well to remember it. There was a lot riding on her doing her job properly.

She sprinted around a corner, and recognizing the spot, slowed to a stop. The trees were thick here, their leaves blotting out the daylight. She leaned over, hands braced against her thighs, sucking tepid air into her lungs. Despite the fact that the running trail was in the heart of the city, the vegetation gave it a hushed feeling of isolation.

Over the cadence of her heart, she listened to the silence, automatically checking for anything out of the ordinary, constant vigilance fitting her like a second skin. A twig snapped behind her and on instinct she spun, adrenaline pumping, muscles tightening.

Branches moved as something pushed through the bushes. Without thinking, she struck out, the force of her foot eliciting a sharp groan from the big black man entering the clearing. She stepped back, crouching slightly, arms raised, ready for a rematch.

The man straightened, stepping into the dappled light. Her stomach dropped three stories. Jerome Wilcox. *Her contact.* Great, she'd just attacked the home team.

"Shit, Cavanaugh, you trying to kill me?" His dark eyes narrowed in an odd combination of anger and mirth, and she felt her cheeks flame.

"If I'd wanted to kill you, I would have." Chagrin made her words sound sharper than she'd intended. "I don't like it when people sneak up on me."

"I can tell." He frowned, rubbing his rib cage.

"Sorry." She wasn't, and he probably knew it, but the words still seemed necessary. He was a decent-enough-looking guy. Tall and clean-cut, his features chiseled and strong. The perfect FBI agent. Everything she wasn't. But then, UC agents weren't meant to be poster children for the agency. That was the point. "Why didn't you use the track?"

"I took a shortcut." He nodded toward the under-growth, and dropped down on a park bench, eyeing her expectantly. "You been waiting long?"

She sat at the far end of the bench, shifting against the splintery surface so that she was facing him. "Long enough to get jumpy."

"Comes with the territory, I guess." He leaned back against the bench, studying her. It was almost as if he expected to see an alien. But then, Katie, was used to the look. No one really understood why someone would willingly go undercover. Not even another agent. "How you dealing with the heat?"

She forced a smile, trying to lighten the moment. "I honestly don't see how you guys stand it. And I sure as hell don't understand why you'd choose it for a meet."

"I didn't." He smiled, dark eyes full of laughter. "Roswell did."

She reached out to twirl a strand of ivy. "That explains a lot. He probably hoped I'd drop dead. The old buzzard doesn't like me very much."

Jerome's smile widened. "He doesn't like anyone very much. Especially UC."

"*Female* undercover in particular, if I had to call it."

"You got it. He's been around a long time. Seen almost everything. But he's definitely an old-school kind of guy."

"And you?" She kept her tone bland, but she was baiting him, curious to see whether he and Roswell were cut from the same cloth.

"I give respect when it's warranted. And despite his faults, Roswell has more than earned it." He leaned back, stretching an arm out along the bench. "You have any trouble this morning?"

There'd been trouble, but not the kind he was thinking of, and she could see absolutely no reason to discuss hormones with Jerome Wilcox. "Everything went fine.

He bought into it completely. The brother, too. I'm set to move into his apartment later today."

"So what are your first impressions?"

"Of Brighton?" Intriguing, magnetic, discombobulating. Again not impressions for public consumption. She frowned, as much at herself as at the question. "He wasn't what I expected. From the background information, I assumed he'd be a pasty-faced computer geek." Which was about as far away from Jonathan Brighton as one could possibly get.

"You saw his picture."

"Yeah. But I guess I rearranged my mental image to fit the facts."

"Don't beat yourself up about it. The important point is that you're safely in place. Now all we have to do is connect the dots."

"Which may not be as easy as we'd thought. I've read his charts. The memory loss is the real deal." It was heartbreaking actually. He seemed so alive, so vibrant. She just couldn't imagine what it would be like to wake up with black holes inside your head.

"Then you'll just have to find another way. Use what we know to elicit what we don't."

"Yeah, but what do we really know? Miller had information. Brighton knew Miller. Miller disappears. Seems like a real stretch."

Or maybe she just wanted it to be a stretch. She'd never been in a situation like this before. Never, in six years with the bureau, had she been attracted to a target. She tipped back her head, centering her thoughts on the here and now.

"Not when you consider that the ME places Miller's death right around the time he disappeared. That means Brighton was probably the last person to see him alive." Jerome's smile was patient, and she had the sense that he was seeing far more than she wanted him to, but the notion was ridiculous. Masking her feelings was one of the

things she did best. "Couple that with the fact that
Brighton left the country at an opportune moment with
a hell of a lot of money . . ." He broke off with a shrug.

"And you're left with a lot of supposition and no
motive. Or is there something else?" She studied the
other agent, trying to assess whether he was holding
something back.

"You know what I know. Miller called us. Conceivably with information about Brighton's company. Next
thing we know Miller is dead, and Brighton's left the
building. Seems a logical leap. Bottom line—the big
brass thinks Brighton popped Miller."

All of which meant that she and John were playing
opposite sides of the street, and no matter what she may
have felt upon meeting him, her job was to establish a
link between Miller's death and Jonathan Brighton. Period.

She frowned, shoving her weaknesses deep inside.
There was no room for emotion in undercover work.
She'd learned that only too well. "Don't worry, Wilcox.
If Brighton's behind Miller's death, I'll find a way to
prove it."

Brave words. The only problem was that to live up to
them, she had to get close to John Brighton. And in
doing so, she had the feeling that, like the moth to the
flame, she was the one who was going to get burned.

Chapter 3

"So what's the bottom line here?" Valerie Alejo looked over the top of her glasses at the group assembled around the boardroom table.

"Christ, Valerie, a man died. Couldn't you at least drum up a little sympathy?" Danny tipped back his head, rubbing the bridge of his nose.

"The guy was a drug addict." She waved her hand dismissively. "You were expecting me to do the eulogy?"

"Come on, now. The least we can do is try to show a little respect." John's tone was stronger than he'd intended, his frustration evident. But an employee was dead and the ramifications of the fact had yet to be ascertained. Just when he thought things were looking up, he had to face reality again.

"Wonderful, we have a dead employee, and the dictator's back." Valerie walked to the window, her anger reflected in the set of her shoulders.

"She didn't mean that." Frank Jacoby fidgeted with the pile of papers in front of him. "It's just that it's been rough around here. First Derek disappearing, and then you hurt, and now this."

"It's not like I got hurt on purpose, Frank. Sorry if it inconvenienced you."

The other man's head shot up, his eyes reflecting confusion and regret. Mild-mannered at best, Frank would never knowingly hurt someone. John had been out of line to snap at him.

"I'm sorry, Frank. This is all just a little more than I bargained for."

"Now you know how we feel." Frank sighed, his expression grim.

"Hang on, everybody." Danny held up a hand, ever the peacemaker. "This isn't getting us anywhere. I know we're all sorry that Miller died."

Valerie's hands tightened on the windowsill.

"All right." Danny shrugged. "Maybe we're not sorry. But I don't think anyone here wished the man dead."

"Someone did." Frank's voice was soft, his face inscrutable.

"A drug dealer." Valerie spun around, eyes glittering behind her glasses.

"Possibly." John reached for a pencil with his good hand, twirling it absently between his fingers, watching his partners.

"Look, as callous as it sounds, *who* killed him isn't relevant to our discussion." Frank's gaze encompassed them all. "What matters now is how it's going to affect Guardian."

"Hopefully not at all." Danny leaned back in his chair, crossing his arms over his chest. "I'm with Val. The guy had a definite problem. So it's totally possible he pissed off a dealer, got whacked, and wound up in Lake Travis. It's a sad story, but other than the fact he worked for us, I don't see how it affects us one way or the other."

"Maybe it doesn't, but even so, I think we need to think about damage control." Jason Pollock was a man of few words. The head of public relations, he was a latecomer to the Guardian team. He'd been with the company only a couple of years, but in that time he'd more than earned his way into the inner sanctum.

"But there isn't any damage." Frank's look was almost comical.

"Yet." Jason raised an eyebrow, the single word telling.

"So give us the worst-case scenario." John dropped the pencil, fighting fatigue. All in all it had turned into a hell of a day.

"In the wake of Jonathan's injuries, Miller's disappearance may have been pushed aside, but his death will certainly raise questions." Jason stood up, clearly in his element. "The police will ask if we knew he had problems. If we know of anyone who might have wanted him dead."

"Great, we've dropped into the middle of a *Law & Order* episode." Valerie didn't even try to contain her sarcasm.

"The point is," Jason continued, ignoring Valerie's outburst, "that it's all routine. And assuming none of you know anything," he paused, eyeing each person in turn, "then that should be the end of it. We'll all profess our sorrow at Miller's death, but business will go on."

"That's worst case?" Frank asked.

"No. Worst case is if the police don't find the killer, and this thing drags out. That's when the press will start to get interested. And even if there's nothing to connect Miller's death to Guardian, our clients may start to get edgy."

"So what do we do?" Valerie sat down at the table, her attention on Jason.

"We strike first. Make sure our clients know that while Miller's death is regrettable, it has nothing to do with us or with the company. We make it clear that although we were supportive of his efforts at recovery, had we known he was still involved with drugs, he would have been fired."

John dropped the pencil, trying to keep his focus, voices blending together into a cacophony of sound, each indistinguishable from the other. The doctors assured him the effect would fade with time, but so far it hadn't, and every time it happened he had to fight his own fear to maintain control.

"John, are you all right?" His brother's voice filtered through the haze.

He shook his head, struggling for clarity, relieved when the voices separated. "I'm fine." He opened his eyes, dismayed to find everyone staring at him. "I'm just a little tired."

"Why don't we wrap this up and let John get out of here." Danny's eyes conveyed his concern, and John found himself torn between anger and gratitude. Anger won. Still another sign that he wasn't in full control of his emotions.

"I just said I'm fine." All things considered, he *was* fine. Everything was relative, after all. The mere fact that he was sitting here in the boardroom spoke volumes about his recovery. If sheer willpower could make him whole again, then he was on the right track. "Val, you draft a letter and have it on my desk in the morning. We'll send it to all our clients." He struggled to his feet, pushing away Danny's helping hands. "In the meantime, Jason will come up with guidelines on how to handle the police."

"What about the press?" Frank stood, too, still fidgeting with the papers.

"Hopefully, they won't be overly interested. But if they start nosing around, send them to Jason." He frowned at the PR man. "Why don't you come up with a nonstatement. Some sort of one-liner that expresses our regret over Miller's death. That way, if any of us are caught off guard we'll have something prepared."

"That it?"

"For now. We can talk again tomorrow."

Valerie exchanged a glance with Frank, and stood up. "Jona . . . *John,* I know I speak for everyone when I welcome you back. But we're all concerned that you're pushing things too fast, and in light of everything that's happened, don't you think it might be better to let us continue handling things?" She paused, glancing over at his brother for support. "With D.E.S. on board, we can't afford any mistakes."

John fought another wave of anger. They were treating him like an invalid. "Wilson Harris brought his company to Guardian because of me, Valerie. And I can't help but think that my resuming control of *my* company will only serve to reassure him, as well as our other clients."

Frank stood up, holding out his hands. "We're well aware that most of Guardian's clients wouldn't be here if it weren't for you. That's not the point."

"No. The point is that you all believe I'm incapable of running my company. But you're wrong. It's just that simple. I'm back. And I'm staying. So if anyone has a problem with that, then you can take it up with the un-employment office."

He would have loved to spin around and storm from the office, but spinning wasn't on his menu these days. Instead, he garnered all his strength and walked slowly toward the door, the silence behind him telling in more ways than he wanted to examine.

He was back, all right.

But at what cost?

John sank down on the sofa, grateful for the peace and quiet. As if things weren't bad enough, now he had to contend with the fallout from Miller's death. He leaned back, eyes closed, trying to force himself to relax. He'd had a little biofeedback in rehab, but he'd never really gotten the hang of it. All that visualization left him more tense than when he'd begun.

Which left him with a pounding headache and a racing brain. Not exactly the stuff relaxation was made of. What he needed was a miracle.

"You don't look so good."

Then again, a man should be careful what he prayed for. Kathleen stood in the doorway, clad in shorts and a T-shirt. Every curve outlined in cotton-hugging clarity. He swallowed reflexively, his heart rate ratcheting up to match the tempo in his head.

"If this is a bad time, I can come back later. Flo sent me up here." She held up a duffel bag. "I thought I'd settle in."

Just at the moment, settling in forever wouldn't have disturbed him in the slightest. Whatever his worries, they seemed to disappear in the wake of her presence. Even his head seemed to throb less ardently.

"It's fine. Come on in. I could use some company actually."

She crossed the room to settle on the arm of the sofa, her expression full of concern. "Flo said you'd been in a meeting. Looks to me like you overdid it."

"Miller's death has hit everybody pretty hard."

"Yeah, but *everybody* didn't spend the last six months recovering from a near-fatal shooting. You can't expect to hit the ground at full steam, John. You've got to take it slowly."

Somehow, coming from her, the sentiment failed to make him angry. He should have been surprised by the fact, but he wasn't. Nothing about Kathleen Cavanaugh elicited a rational reaction.

"So everyone keeps telling me." He laughed, the sound rusty. "I'm afraid sitting still isn't something I'm good at."

"Well, it's something you're going to have to get used to." She swung her legs around so that she was sitting on the arm with her feet on the cushions. "No matter how much you want to hurry it, recovery comes at its own pace."

"And I suppose you're here to ride roughshod over me?"

"Someone's obviously got to do it." Her smile was infectious. "It might as well be me."

"All right, then, let's examine your qualifications, shall we?" He shifted slightly, on the pretense of getting comfortable, but in truth he just wanted to be closer to her. "How long have you been doing this?"

"Six years." She slid down onto the cushions, sitting cross-legged in front of him. "Five of them in the field."

"I'm assuming fieldwork is the same as home care?"

"One-on-one, so to speak." Her smile was slow, and just a trifle wicked. "I do better in a more intimate situation."

He decided to let that one pass, although it was tempting to just forgo niceties and pull her into his arms. Better to stick to conversation for the time being. It seemed the better part of social valor. "So what's your specific area of expertise?"

"Besides being very good at what I do, I suppose I'm known for listening. Sometimes the key to physical health is mental."

"Spoken like a true therapist. But surely you have more to offer than that?" He leaned even closer, trying not to stare at the soft rise and fall of her breasts. He couldn't remember the last time he'd simply engaged in the art of innocent banter. No games to play, no hidden agenda.

"Hmm . . ." She tilted her head, pretending to contemplate the question. "I make an excellent grilled cheese, I play passable guitar, and my brothers would tell you I pack a mean punch."

"Brothers?"

"Two. Both of them older than me."

It was his turn to grin. "So you really had no choice. About the punch, I mean."

"None at all. It was survival of the fittest."

"Sounds like a wonderful childhood."

She sobered, her face looking almost wistful. "It was. I don't see enough of them." She flipped her braid behind her shoulder, her face clearing with the motion. "But you know all about brothers. You've got Danny."

"Yes. And you've seen what a handful he is." He gave her his best pathetic look, but it obviously fell on deaf ears.

"From what I've seen, you're well matched."

He shrugged. "I suppose you're right. And I am lucky to have him here. He's been a godsend over the last few months. I couldn't have handled any of this without him." The thought brought reality crashing down around him again.

"It'll all come right in the end, you'll see." Kathleen reached for his hand, the warmth of her touch reaching soul deep. "All you have to do is have a little faith."

He turned his hand in hers, wishing he could capture the moment, trotting it out when things looked bleak again. But if the last few months had taught him anything, it was that nothing lasted forever, and there was no sense wishing it so.

Instead, he'd simply have to revel in the moment. They sat quietly, still touching, neither saying anything, and then despite himself he yawned.

She leapt to her feet, her green eyes lighting with concern. "Some professional I'm turning out to be. Here I am supposed to be helping you, and all I've done is tire you out."

"Actually, it's quite the opposite. I don't know when I last felt this good." It sounded trite, but he meant it. Really meant it.

Just for a moment, he'd actually been able to put his troubles aside, and for that alone he owed her an enormous debt.

Now if only he could find a way to convince her to collect.

Have a little faith?
She'd sounded like freaking Mother Teresa. John

Brighton brought out a part of her she thought she'd left behind in childhood, along with Pop-Tarts and wishing on a star. If Roswell could have seen her this afternoon, he'd have had more than enough ammunition to have her ass sent back to Boston on the next plane.

She'd been flirting. Flirting. And worse still, she'd been enjoying herself. There was something about John Brighton that put her off guard. Made her feel safe, comfortable. And neither of those words should ever be used in concert with an undercover agent.

Ever.

Damn it all to hell.

Katie lay on the bed, trying to absorb the cool comfort of the sheets, to banish John from her thoughts, but neither seemed to be a possibility. The heat was still cloying, even with the air conditioner blasting at sub-zero levels.

Maybe that's why she'd acted the way she had. Heat made people overemotional, surely. There was really no other explanation. It wasn't as if this were an over-whelming assignment. She'd been on a lot worse.

And she'd never acted like this. Jumpy as a cat in heat. And just as dangerous. She'd even hit Wilcox. Not that he hadn't been asking for it. Sneaking up on her like that.

She hadn't been kidding John. Two older brothers with a penchant for surprise attacks had taught her the rudiments of self-defense at an early age, and what she hadn't already figured out, she'd learned at Quantico. In her line of work, she needed to keep her reactions honed.

Sometimes a split second was all you had.

She shuddered, her thoughts turning to Walker Priestly. Despite the passage of time, the memory still ran just below the surface. A constant reminder of how quickly things could turn ugly. Going after him had almost cost her her life. Five years in undercover obviously hadn't been enough to engrain the concept of backup firmly enough. She'd felt invincible. But all that had changed with the flick of a knife. . . .

She shook her head, clearing her mind. No sense in dwelling on the past. She'd survived and the bastard was dead. She traced the ridge of scar beneath her T-shirt, a tribute to the fact that good had won the day.

And so here she was, fighting other battles. Lesser battles. Finding out the truth about Jonathan Brighton ought to be a walk in the park. Her first active duty in three months, she was determined to prove that she still had her edge.

But with a look, a touch, he'd managed to slide right past her carefully erected barriers. Which just wouldn't do. Not if she was going to prove herself to Roswell.

Roswell.

Now, there was a piece of work. A chauvinist's chauvinist. She'd only met him a couple of times and he'd already driven her to violent thoughts. The asshole might be her superior by title, but he was nothing more than a reptilian throwback.

And that was putting it mildly.

Thank God she had Wilcox as a buffer.

She looked around the room at the artfully arranged bric-a-brac in what was supposed to pass for a guest room. There was nothing personal at all. No photographs, no individual touches. Just a decorator's feast of chrome and gray.

Either John Brighton had no taste, or he simply didn't care. Neither of which seemed to jibe with the man. An enigma. That's what he was. On the surface one thing, and underneath . . . well, time would tell.

She reached for the half-empty soda glass, wishing it were tomorrow already. It was like she'd told Wilcox, waiting always made her edgy. She got off the bed, pacing the floor, thinking about John Brighton. There'd definitely been a connection between them. Something she hadn't expected.

Her senses were tingling. Warning her of danger she couldn't define. Not physical, certainly. Not even danger in the true sense of the word. Nothing she could actually put a name to, really. Just an unease. A sense of something more to come. Something personal. She shivered again, this time not from fear.

God, it would be so much easier if she could just go to John, lay her cards on the table, get the goods, and get the hell out of here. But rushing things never accomplished anything. Her father had always said that police work was like fishing. It required a good line and a lot of patience. She had both.

She pushed back her hair, perspiration making it stick to the back of her neck. Whatever it was between them, it was strong. And it would take every ounce of willpower she had to resist it. Which sounded a bit melodramatic.

She was a professional. Surely she could manage to smother whatever it was she was feeling. If necessary, she'd rely on cold showers. The perfect remedy for everything that ailed you.

She shook her head, and grabbed a book off the bed, flipping to a bookmark about halfway through. She'd read it twice already, but it never hurt to bone up on the facts. One slip and it was all over. And they didn't pay her to slip up.

Tomorrow, everything she'd learned would be put to the test, and even though she knew her stuff, she couldn't afford a mistake. There was a lot riding on it. Not the least being a man's recovery. Enigma or no, she had no intention of harming him. At least not in a physical way.

The rest of it, well, either he was guilty or he wasn't, only time would tell. Time—and despite any impulses to the contrary, a helpful little nudge from her.

Chapter 4

"So how well did you know the deceased?" D'Angelo watched as Jason Pollock shifted nervously in his chair. The conference room at Guardian was more than plush, it was elegant, in that quiet understated way that spoke of money. Lots of money.

Not that Eric had a great deal of personal experience with that sort of thing. Still, he'd seen his fair share of corporate boardrooms and this one was right up there on the opulence meter.

"He had a name, you know." The man narrowed his eyes, looking first at Haskins and then back at D'Angelo.

"All right, then, how well did you know Derek Miller?" Eric repeated the question, using the guy's name, resisting the urge to roll his eyes.

Tony, who was seated slightly behind Pollock, didn't show the same restraint. He struggled with a smile, his eyes telegraphing his thoughts. *God save them from stupid people.*

D'Angelo suppressed his own smile, forcing his concentration back to Pollock.

"I didn't know him all that well. We saw each other in passing from time to time. That's about it."

"So you can't think of any reason why someone would want him dead." Haskins finished writing something in his notebook and then looked up to meet Pollock's gaze.

"He had a problem with drugs. Or at least that's what everyone says. I didn't actually see him or anything." Jason looked down at his hands.

D'Angelo studied the man, wondering why he was lying. Pollock had practically bitten his head off for not using the man's name, and now he was claiming not to know anything about him.

"According to Valerie Alejo, you had lunch with Miller on a regular basis. Is that what you meant by 'in passing'?" Haskins made a play of looking back in his notes, obviously thinking along the same lines.

The other man shifted again, his eyes locked on the table in front of him. "I had lunch with Derek. We all did. It's a small shop. And it's natural to go out with colleagues. Valerie and Frank had lunch with us, too. Sometimes even Danny would come along."

"What about Jonathan Brighton?"

"No, he never came." Jason's answer came quickly. "He's not a get-down-in-the-trenches kind of guy."

"A loner?" Haskins looked up from his notes, interested.

Pollock shrugged. "I think that's probably overstating it. Jonathan lives for business. He's a classic workaholic. Hanging out with us would have been a colossal waste of time."

"I see." Haskins scribbled something, then looked up. "But *you* did hang out—with the others, I mean."

"At work."

"And lunch." Haskins was beginning to push and it looked like Pollock was pushing back.

"I don't spend my private time with any of these people, if that's what you're getting at. I work with them. Nothing more." He stood up, walking to the window, turning his back on them. "I can't believe any of this is happening. First Jonathan and now Derek."

"So is there a relationship?" D'Angelo leaned back in his chair, waiting.

Pollock spun around. "I don't see how there could be. I mean, a carjacking in Mexico is a far cry from an execution."

"Who said it was an execution?"

Pollock shrugged. "A murder, an execution, is there a difference? The man is dead."

Haskins closed his notebook. "In our business, Mr. Pollock, there's a hell of a difference."

Jason held up a hand. "I'm sorry if I said something wrong. I've never had to deal with this sort of thing before." He sucked in a breath, obviously seeking fortification. "It makes you realize just how fragile life really is. It could've just as easily been me." The last was an after-thought, almost mumbled, but D'Angelo heard him loud and clear.

Jason Pollock was hiding something. The sixty-four-thousand-dollar question was—what?

John looked at the weight machine, torn between laughter and anger. How was he supposed to manage all this? In the hospital it had been easy. Go here. Do this. But now, everything bordered on overwhelming. He had to make decisions about everything, and what had once been relatively simple had become excruciatingly painful. Virtually impossible.

"It's not as hard as it looks." Just as before, her voice washed over him, soothing in its complexity.

"Easy for you to say." He was surprised when he smiled. "You've got the use of all of your appendages."

"So do you." Her answering smile was warm, as she efficiently adjusted the weights. "You're just a little out of practice using them, that's all." She definitely had a way about her. A manner that made him feel comfortable and off guard all at the same time.

Dangerous.

He almost laughed. Most people wouldn't think of a physical therapist in that light. But then again, maybe they just hadn't met Kathleen Cavanaugh. "And you're going to help me." He looked up, his breath catching as her soft scent caressed him.

"If I can. But a lot of it is about you." She helped him adjust the padded bar on the weight machine, and then stepped back, waiting. "You've got to want to get better."

Taking a deep breath, he concentrated on lifting the bar, using both legs. Good and bad. Trying to keep a balance. "And you think I don't?"

"It doesn't matter what I think, John. It's what you think that matters."

"Mind over body?" He pushed upward again, muscles burning with the effort. "What if you're asking too much? What if I can't go any farther? Maybe I just don't have it in me."

She leaned across him, to adjust the padding, her hair brushing against his chest. "That's when you've got to dig deeper. Find the strength inside you." She straightened up, her eyes locking with his. "I know it's hard, but you're a fighter. You can do this. You've come too far to quit now."

He lifted the bar for another rep, pushing against the weight, forcing the muscles in his right leg to respond.

"You're doing great." There was a note of sincerity in her eyes. A camaraderie that he hadn't experienced in a long while.

"So does it hurt a lot?"

"The weights?" he asked, surprised. Surely she was familiar with the pain of a workout. Especially considering her occupation.

She smiled, reading his thoughts. "No. Your head. Does it still hurt?"

"Not in the way you're thinking. I can't even feel the bullet. Sometimes I imagine I can. But there's no actual feeling. Just a hunk of metal lodged against my skull."

"Nice conversation piece." She spoke lightly as she

adjusted the weights, but he could hear the underlying sorrow in her voice. Not pity. Just honest sympathy. As if she'd been there herself.

Which of course she hadn't.

"Oh yeah," he strove to match her lightness, but missed, coming off sounding sarcastic and bitter instead. "I'm sure to be the hit of the cocktail circuit."

"I didn't mean it like that."

He finished the set and reached over to cover her hand with his. "I know you didn't. It's just that sometimes I wish—I don't know, that it had been somebody else."

"Or that you hadn't survived?" Her somber gaze met his, the hint of a shadow darkening her eyes. Secrets. Kathleen had secrets.

The idea almost came as a relief, putting them on the same footing somehow.

"Sometimes," he admitted. "On the worst days. But not so much anymore."

"Which is good." The shadows passed, her eyes clearing, and she reached across him again to adjust the machine. He liked the proximity, and felt foolishly disappointed when she moved back. "Let's do ten more. This time try and gradually shift the weight so that the right side is working harder than the left."

"No rest for the weary?" Despite his aching muscles, he smiled up at her, determined to rise to the challenge.

"None at all." She shook her head, her smile at odds with her words. "Besides, you haven't been working long enough to be weary." She leaned back against a massage table. "So tell me about Guardian."

"It started in college." He couldn't decide if she was really interested, or just talking to keep his mind off the pain. He supposed it didn't matter, although if he were honest, he'd have to say that, at least at some level, he wanted her to be interested in him. "I was a computer geek. A real nerd. I thought—and still think, to some extent—that the world begins and ends with bits and bytes. But like most people I have another side."

"The dangerous one."

It was all he could do not to roll his eyes. "I think *rebellious* might be a better word. Anyway, I got interested in hacking."

She frowned. "You're telling me you broke into other people's computers."

"As often as possible. You've got to understand, it didn't have anything to do with what was on their computers. It was all about the challenge of getting inside. Of beating the system, so to speak." He lowered his legs, letting the weights drop as well.

"And that makes it all right?" Her expression was a mix of curiosity and censure.

"Of course not. But it does make it fun."

"I'm not sure I see how any of this ties in with your company."

"That's the beauty of it. You see, I figured out a way to make hacking a profitable, *legal* enterprise." He lifted the weights again. "Guardian specializes in protecting computer systems from people like me."

"And to do that, you still get to hack."

"Exactly. Someone has to make certain there isn't a way in." He gritted his teeth against the resistance of the weights. "And that seems to be an area where I excel."

"So you founded the company."

"*Founded* seems a bit formal, and I'd be lying if I said I did it all by myself. Guardian was a team effort from the beginning."

"You're talking about Danny and Derek."

"Yeah. And Frank and Valerie. We all started out in the business school together. Derek, Valerie, and I were into computers in a serious way. Derek was a natural programmer. So it was all innate for him, and Valerie has never failed at anything she's set out to do. I'll admit she's a little bit self-involved, but her computer skills more than make up for it."

"What about Frank?"

"He's an odd duck, but he's a hell of a worker bee, and he's incredibly loyal. They all are, really. I can't imagine having done any of this without them."

"Was Danny into computers, too?"

"No, that came later." He finished the last rep, surprised at how quickly he'd accomplished the task. "I think he hung around in the beginning mainly because he wanted to get into Valerie's pants."

She smiled, her eyes crinkling at the corners with laughter. "And did it work?"

"Only for a little while. Valerie goes through men almost as fast as Danny goes through women. But they parted friends." And had remained so. In fact, they'd all remained friends. Which was sort of amazing when one considered the ups and downs of the past ten years. "Anyway, when I came up with the idea for Guardian, it just seemed logical to bring my friends in on it."

She helped him stand and they moved to a different station, just the touch of her hands sending his senses reeling. He wanted to write it off as the effect of the workout. Endorphins and all that. But if he was being completely honest, he'd have to admit that it was more than that. Sort of a man-woman thing.

Which sounded really stupid. So he kept the thought to himself, concentrating instead on the workout. After adjusting the weights, he began to pull upward, the motion designed to strengthen his weak arm.

"So what kind of clients do you have?"

"All kinds really. We started with mostly financial companies. Banks, brokerage houses, that sort of thing. But we've branched out a lot since then. Our newest client, D.E.S. makes jet engines, among other things."

"Sounds lucrative."

"It is. And challenging, which is more important to me."

She glanced around the Guardian gym. "But money doesn't hurt, surely."

"It gives me more freedom, I guess." He concentrated on keeping his arm straight. "So come on, turnabout's fair play. Tell me about you. You said you were from Boston."

"Actually," she smiled, "I said I was Boston *Irish*." The mischievous glint was back in her eyes.

He lifted an eyebrow, playing along. "And that's not the same?"

She shook her head, eyes sparkling. "I'm from Medfield, a little town outside of Boston."

"A sleepy New England village?"

"Only in the tourism brochures." She increased the weight slightly. "One more set."

"Still, you're a long way from home." He started the new set, but kept his eyes on her, fascinated with the curve of her eyebrows, the tiny mole at the hollow of her cheek. Mentally shaking his head, he turned his attention back to the weights. "What brought you to Austin? UT?"

"No, I went to a liberal arts school in northwest Mass. About two and a half hours from Boston."

"Liberal arts, huh? I'll bet you majored in history."

She smiled, shaking her head. "Nope. English. Applicable degree, don't you think?"

"I don't know," he said, enjoying the banter, "I, for one, have always preferred a physical therapist with a good command of the English language."

"Lift thy weights, O noble son?" Her laughter was contagious.

"Well, maybe something a bit less erudite." He grinned up at her. "So you never said what brought you here."

"I, ah—" She waited a beat, and he wondered for a

moment if he'd hit on the source of the shadows. "I followed a boyfriend."

"Past tense?" The words came out a question and he waited, fervently wishing it so.

"Very." Her nod was emphatic, and relief washed through him. "Turned out he was more in love with my ability to support him than anything else, and the moment a bigger meal ticket came along he was out the door."

He listened for a hint of regret or anger, but there was nothing. Whatever this man had meant to her, he was not the cause of her shadows. "But you're still here."

She shrugged. "I have a good job. I like what I do. So here I am."

"Living with me." Even though the words were meant innocently, they hung between them, creating distance where there had been at least a sense of intimacy. He wanted to reach out, to stop her from pulling away, but he hadn't the right.

She made a play of adjusting the machine, her hair hiding her eyes. "Only temporarily."

"Temporarily?" he repeated, dropping the weight, worried suddenly that she would disappear as quickly as she'd come.

She must have heard the panic in his voice, because she closed the distance in an instant, her gaze locking with his, her breath caressing his hair. "I only meant that you're going to get better. Then you won't need me anymore."

He'd only just met her, and yet he suspected this was a woman a man would have trouble getting over. He reached up, laying his hand against her cheek, searching her eyes for something he wasn't even clear on himself.

Truth was, just at the moment he'd like nothing more than to find out exactly what she felt like lying underneath him, their bodies joined together in a heated

dance. Of course, the thought was not only inappropri-
ate, it was probably impossible. No woman wanted to
sleep with half a man.

He dropped his hand, forcing a smile, praying his
thoughts weren't reflected in his eyes. "I can't argue
with that."

She licked her lips, looking every bit as uncomfortable as he felt, but she didn't move away, and he admired the way she held her ground. He took a step
forward, so close now, he could see the flecks of green
in her eyes, count the freckles on her cheeks.

He felt her intake of breath, heard the sweet sound of
capitulation deep in her throat. Blindly he reached for
her, forgetting all the reasons why he shouldn't. There
was only now, and the fact that she made him feel so
desperately alive.

"Are we interrupting something?"

They jerked apart, the fantasy evaporating in an instant. Kathleen retreated to the table, her eyes too wide,
her breathing jerky. He shifted to stand between her and
the men in the doorway, two of them, in ill-fitting suits.
Cops, if he had to call it. He scrambled to shift gears,
knowing he needed his wits about him.

The younger man stepped forward. A hardened army
type with straight dark hair and piercing gray eyes. John
was instantly on alert. "Eric D'Angelo, Austin PD."

The detective held out his left hand, and despite his
initial response John found himself relaxing. "John
Brighton." He nodded at his injured right hand. "But I
assume you knew that. This is my physical therapist,
Kathleen Cavanaugh."

D'Angelo raised an eyebrow, the gesture the silent
equivalent of a whistle. John suppressed a smile.

"I should leave you guys on your own." Kathleen
had either missed the exchange or was ignoring it. From
what he knew of her, he suspected the latter. She was
coolly in control now, completely professional, no sign

of the passion that had shimmered between them only moments before. He wasn't certain if he should be relieved or disappointed.

Perversely, he put a hand on hers, a silent request for her to stay. He needed the moral support. "You're fine. I'm sure these gentlemen won't be long."

D'Angelo shook his head. "We've only got a few questions." He motioned the other man into the room. "This is my partner. Tony Haskins."

John tipped his head in the direction of the older man. "What can I do for you?"

"As I'm sure you've guessed," D'Angelo picked up a hand weight, absently lifting it up and down, "we have some questions about Derek Miller."

John moved to sit on the edge of the table. "What exactly can I help you with?"

"We're trying to understand more about Miller. Hopefully find a reason why someone would want him dead."

"Seems the obvious choice would be his drug problem. You're thinking there's something more?" John studied the other man, liking what he saw, but recognizing that at least for the moment the man was an adversary.

"That's what we're here to find out." Haskins spoke this time, pulling a little notebook out of his pocket. "You knew about Miller's problems. So why would you continue to employ him?"

John fought to keep focus. He was getting tired, and that meant it was harder to maintain control. "A couple of reasons." He braced his good hand on the table, and was grateful to feel Kathleen move closer, her body slightly behind him, supporting his bad side. "First off, he was a good man, despite his bad habits. And second, he was one of the best programmers I've ever worked with. With talent like his, you can overlook a lot of problems."

"But you didn't encourage his bad habits." D'Angelo took over the questioning.

"Quite the contrary, we paid for his rehab. Twice."

"Second time being the charm."

John shrugged. "As far as I know."

"Right." D'Angelo straddled the workout bench. "Well, here's what *we* know. A couple of days before you went to Mexico, Miller was arrested for possession. We also know that you bailed him out. What we don't know is what happened to Miller after that. You were evidently the last person to see Derek Miller alive. Can you help us with that, Mr. Brighton?"

John turned inward, trying to pull something—anything—out of the tumbled darkness of his mind. He'd liked Derek Miller, even wanted to help him. Truth be told, he still did. But there simply wasn't anything left to remember. "I'm sorry. I don't remember bailing him out. I don't even remember his being in jail. If he told me anything that could help, I'm afraid it's gone."

D'Angelo exchanged another look with his partner, then turned to Kathleen. "I'm not up on amnesia. But I gather his memories aren't coming back?"

Kathleen's eyes met the detective's, her gaze unflinching. "It isn't a matter of it coming back, Detective. When a bullet enters the brain it destroys everything in its path. Leaving a gooey mess in its wake. The brain is a marvelous thing, it can compensate for almost anything. But it can't re-create memories that don't exist anymore. It just can't."

"So I guess that leaves us at square one." Haskins closed his notebook.

"I'm sorry," John said, and he was. He'd give anything to be able to remember. Not just for Miller, but for himself. "The good news is that I doubt I knew anything helpful anyway. I liked Derek, but we weren't close. I sincerely doubt he'd have confided anything useful to me."

"Well, call if you think of anything." D'Angelo's face was blank, all emotion effectively masked.

"Of course. And conversely, you'll let us know what you find out."

"You can count on it." D'Angelo stood up, their gazes locking, and John wondered what the detective knew that he didn't.

Everything—and hopefully nothing.

Taking John's side had just been part of the cover. Which was all well and good, but that didn't even come close to explaining why she'd almost kissed him. Without the detectives' timely intervention, there was no telling what would have happened.

Hopefully better sense would have prevailed. But she wasn't so certain. She watched as he moved through the last of his exercises. There was a vulnerability about him. And it called to her. Speaking on some deep inner level that she frankly hadn't even been aware existed.

All of which made her completely insane. Crazy.

Certifiably nuts.

And if she was honest, disappointed. She'd wanted to kiss him. Wanted it with a fervor that had surprised her with its intensity. Fortunately, neither of them had mentioned it again, the detectives' discussion bringing reality slamming down around them both.

And since they'd left, John had been all business, preoccupied no doubt with the death of his colleague and the implication that he might have known something about it. A heavy burden for anyone to bear, but especially for John, considering the circumstances.

She blew out a breath, pushing her thoughts away. No matter what lay between them, it wouldn't—couldn't—come to anything. She was here to do a job, and that's exactly what she intended to do.

Resolutely, she crossed the room. "I think you've had enough for today." She purposely kept her voice just this side of brusque, determined to maintain control. "It won't help you to push too hard." She reached out and took the hand weight from him.

"So everyone keeps telling me." His tone was argumentative, but he handed her the other weight, and she noticed he was favoring his left arm.

"They're saying it because it's the truth. Recovery is a slow process. You're literally building your body again. Muscle by muscle."

"I take it you're not here with magic fairy dust. Or maybe Oscar Goldman. I'd make a hell of a bionic man." There was wry humor mixed with bitter regret, and she fought against the urge to offer comfort.

That's not why she was here. "I'm afraid you'll have to do it the old-fashioned way."

"Right, I have to earn it." He attempted a smile, the effort obviously costing him.

"The detectives upset you."

He studied his hands. "No. Not really. Derek Miller's death upsets me."

"I thought you said you weren't close?" She wondered if there was something he'd kept from the police. Something maybe he'd tell her.

"I wasn't. But he was a decent man. He'd just had a run of bad luck."

"Of his own making, to hear people talk about it."

"He was trying to get clean. Or at least that's my last memory of him." He struggled to stand up, holding a hand out to stop her from helping. "The problem with my head is that I can't trust anything I remember. So many things have shifted. Changed. It's like I'm seeing everything through a warped window. And no matter how much I want it, I can't make my head whole again. I can't make my hand respond on command." Reflexively he tightened his fingers, trying to make a fist.

She was fairly certain that if anyone could will their body to mend, it would be this man, but she knew that anything she said would be meaningless. Empty promises. And besides, she was supposed to be uncovering his weaknesses, not helping to build his strengths.

Still, she needed to say something, the need to offer comfort almost overwhelming now. "It will get better."

He watched her through narrowed eyes, the irises almost black. "Maybe not. Maybe it'll never be better again. Do you know that I can't even remember the guy who blew my head apart? You'd think that would have made a hell of a memory."

"I'm sorry. I didn't mean . . ." She stepped back, a calculated move to allow him space, to let her breathe.

"No, *I'm* sorry." He closed the distance between them, his gaze colliding with hers. "I didn't mean to snap. You can't imagine how nice it is to have someone to talk to. Someone without a vested interest in my remembering."

Guilt flooded through her. "But I do have an interest."

He frowned, eyes still locked on her. "And that would be?"

"It's my job to make you better, remember?"

He moved closer, his breath hot against her cheek. "But we're talking physically, not mentally."

She fought the urge to retreat, and held her ground. "One goes hand in hand with the other, surely."

His smile was slow, traveling up his face to light his eyes. "If you say so, Ms. Cavanaugh."

"Katie," she whispered, forgetting all about keeping her distance.

"Katie," he repeated, his face only inches from hers. "I've got a feeling you're going to be really good for me."

With a sharp intake of breath, she stepped back, breaking the spell, reality returning with a vengeance.

He had no idea how wrong he was.

* * *

"So are you in or out, Frank?" Valerie sat on the edge of his desk, the hem of her skirt rising up, showing more thigh than he'd a right to be looking at.

He swallowed, forcing his eyes to her face. "I don't know, Val. I feel like I should stand with Jonathan."

"Even if he brings down Guardian?" She shifted, the skirt inching a tad higher. "Surely you don't want that to happen."

"Of course not." Almost against his will, his eyes dropped back to her satiny skin. "But aren't you assuming a lot in thinking he'll just lay down at your feet and resign?"

"I'm not assuming anything, Frank. I know that Jonathan won't go down without a fight, but maybe with Miller dead, he'll rethink things. He's not a fool. He's got to know that Miller's murder will impact our business."

"Maybe. Maybe not." Frank tried to concentrate on the conversation, but it was hard. Valerie's perfume was tantalizing and he felt as if he were drowning in the scent. "Jason seems to think he can contain the damage."

"Jason doesn't know anything. He's not as astute as you are." She licked her lips provocatively, sexuality practically oozing out of her. "Which is why I need you on my side."

Despite the fact that he was married, Frank found her hard to resist. Not only did she have an amazing body, she had a mind to match, and the fact that she was coming on to him gave him a heady sense of power.

And having spent the bulk of his adult life following other people's dictates, power wasn't something he was intimately acquainted with. Of course, siding with Valerie was not exactly a bid for freedom, but at least with her there was an opportunity for something more than what he had now. If he helped her obtain the presidency of Guardian, there'd certainly be a payoff for

him. A payoff that would go a long way toward making
Jessica realize his worth.

Making his wife happy, and spending more time with
Valerie. There was a certain appeal. Still, John was a
good friend, and the idea of hurting him didn't sit well
at all.

"You're not listening." Anger darkened the smooth
lines of her face, the emotion only making her appear
more sensual.

He pulled himself from his thoughts, and forced a
smile. "Of course I am. You were talking about taking
over the company."

"Exactly." Her smile was slow, the gesture contrived,
but it heated his blood nevertheless. "And we can use
Miller's death to do it."

Frank swallowed again, his mouth suddenly dry. "I
don't see how. It's not like Miller was a big player in the
grand scheme of things. How is his death a threat to the
company?"

"You never see the big picture, Frank. In and of itself
maybe his death isn't a problem. But with the right spin,
it's possible that it could mean trouble."

He eyed her speculatively. "And you're going to help
with the spin."

She shrugged, a tiny smile playing at her lips. "If I
have to."

Frank studied her, considering his options. Valerie
Alejo had a way of getting what she wanted. And with
Jonathan playing at less than full capacity, he figured
now was the time for her to make a move.

The question was whether he wanted to join the
team.

Chapter 5

"You were conveniently missing in action today." John looked up as his brother walked into the study.

"Someone has to keep the company running." Danny's voice was light, but there was an undercurrent of something more.

John leaned back in his chair, every muscle in his body aching. He had no idea if it was the morning's workout, or the afternoon at his desk, but either way he felt as though he'd been run over by a very long freight train. "Well, you missed all the excitement."

"I heard the police were here, nosing around about Derek." Danny crossed to a closed cupboard and opened it to reveal a little refrigerator. He opened it and pulled out a beer. "Want one?"

John shook his head. "Alcohol isn't exactly on my approved food list these days."

"Sorry." Danny didn't look anything of the sort. But then, that was Danny. Anything that didn't directly affect him tended to sail right over his head. It was part of his charm. And the bane of John's existence. He contained a smile, watching as his brother dropped down into a chair with an exaggerated sigh.

"So who were you meeting with?" John reached for the little statue he'd made in occupational therapy. It wasn't much to look at. A blob of clay that was supposed to resemble a bird. But despite its less than aesthetic appearance, he'd found that rubbing the smooth surface helped relieve some of his stress.

"Traylor from First Federal. They've just upgraded their software and are angling for some free modifications from us."

John's fingers tightened around the statue as he struggled to remember Traylor. "The terms in the contract are clear."

"I told him that. But he says you'd mentioned the updates." Danny sipped his beer, waiting.

John released the statue, afraid he might break it, his stomach clenching. Why the hell couldn't he just remember? "I might have said something, I honestly don't know. But even if I did, I wouldn't have overstepped the boundaries laid out in the agreement."

"I know that." Despite his words, there was doubt in Danny's voice. "And that's what I told him. But this kind of thing can't continue. Guardian can't operate like this, and you know it."

"Everything is going to be fine." A muscle in John's jaw started to pulse as anger surged through him.

It wasn't Danny's fault. He was absolutely right. Maybe that's what hurt the most. All John's life he'd been the reliable one. Danny had been the one who'd floated through on charm and good looks. And to see Danny taking over for him, behaving like him, it was like watching a movie with the lead actor miscast.

"It's not fine. Look at you." Danny tipped his head toward John's right arm, lax on the desk. "This isn't working."

"I've only been back a day. For God's sake, give me a chance. So I don't remember one conversation. I'd wager there's a lot of conversations you've forgotten. Particularly when you're drinking." He glanced pointedly at the beer bottle.

"This isn't about me. And I'm not the enemy. I'm

your brother, Jonathan. And I'm just trying to look out for you."

John leaned back, his anger deflating. "I know that. And I'm doing better. Honestly. I just need a little time. And until I'm at a hundred percent, I'll just have to count on you to fill in the blanks." Literally.

"All right. I'll cover your back. But I want you to promise you'll quit if it gets to be too much." He put the beer on the table, his eyes darkening with worry. "Deal?"

"Deal. I told you, I have no intention of doing anything that could harm Guardian. We just have to work a little harder to get things back on track. Together we can accomplish anything."

"The Brighton brothers ride again." Danny grinned and raised his bottle, lightening the moment. "So tell me about Kathleen Cavanaugh."

"She's nice." Now, there was an understatement.

"Nice?" Danny's brows rose in amazement. "I'd say she's a lot more than *nice. Hot* is actually the word that comes to mind. Sizzling, actually."

"Come on, Danny, she's my physical therapist." The truth was, he wasn't ready to share his thoughts about Katie with his brother. Not yet. Hell, maybe never.

"So touching is allowed." Danny's smile turned positively lascivious, and John had to resist the urge to wipe it off his face.

"No, it's not." He frowned at his brother, his emotions running rampant. He might not be certain about his feelings for Katie, but he was positive sharing wasn't on the list. "And that goes for you, too."

Danny held his hands up in mock defense. "Hey, bro, I've never been the poaching type. I can get my own women. I don't need to steal yours."

"She's not *mine.*" His frown changed to a glare. "Come on, I've only known the woman for a day." And almost kissed her twice, but Danny had no way of knowing that.

"So maybe you should do something about it." Danny's grin widened. "In the old days, you'd have had her in bed by now."

John stared at his hands, the left one clenched tightly. "This isn't the old days, Danny, and it never will be again. Some bastard with a gun made damn sure of it."

"Oh God, Jonathan." Danny rose from the chair, reaching out beseechingly. "I didn't mean that. Not the way it sounded anyway. I was just yanking your chain."

John pointedly ignored his brother's obvious discomfort. He hated himself for it, but couldn't seem to force any other reaction. He wanted to be whole again. To be able to laugh and joke with his brother. To bed a woman he wanted, just because he desired her.

But he couldn't—he just couldn't.

His life was changed forever, the bullet's path crippling his body and his mind. The sooner he accepted the fact, the sooner he could get on with his life.

Such that it was.

"So how long you want to do this?" Tony Haskins closed his eyes, rubbing the bridge of his nose. "Unlike you, I have a wife to go home to."

Eric suppressed a smile. It was a long-standing argument and there were times when he truly envied his partner's happiness. Bess was a hell of a lady, the perfect match for Tony. But Eric had been the marriage route and learned the hard way it wasn't for everyone.

Especially not a cop. His kind of cop.

"So go already. I can handle this on my own." He waved at the stacks of paper littering their desks.

Tony sighed. "Nah. I'll stay. No sense letting you have all the fun." He picked up another folder. "So what are we looking for?"

"I don't know for sure. Something out of place." He

riffled the edge of a file. "Something that links one of these people to Miller."

"They worked with him, Eric. They all have a connection."

D'Angelo ran his hand through his hair. "I know that. But maybe there's something more. I just don't see this as a drug thing. It doesn't play right."

Tony nodded, opening the file. "I agree with that. And the atmosphere at Guardian is definitely tense. Of course, that could be because their chief has been missing in action."

"Maybe." Eric leaned back in his chair, propping his feet on his desk, a pile of bank records in his lap. "Time will tell."

"And in the meantime, we dig."

"That's what they pay us for." He scanned a sheet and tossed it aside.

"Shit, I thought they were paying us to chase the bad guys."

"They are. We're just doing it one page at a time." He laughed, and turned to the next record, scanning the contents, his eyes coming to an abrupt halt about halfway down the page. "Well, I'll be damned."

Tony looked up, his interest piqued.

"Looks like Derek Miller had an influx of good luck, to the tune of about thirty-five thousand dollars."

"Does it say from where?" Tony's eyes narrowed as he considered the possibilities.

"No. It just says 'deposit.'" He flipped through the rest of the statement, frustrated. "Is there a checkbook?" He motioned toward the boxes of Miller's papers they'd taken from his house.

"Not that I've seen, but there's a lot of crap here. Anyway, the bank should have a record."

"Yeah, we can give them a call tomorrow. Based on what I've seen so far, this would have pumped up Miller's bank account significantly."

"And whoever paid him just might have had something to do with his death."

"It's a start." Eric shrugged. "We'll know more tomorrow." He glanced over at the boxes. "In the meantime, what'd you say we call in for pizza? I've got a
feeling it's going to be a long night."

John stood in the doorway looking at what had been
Derek Miller's office. The blinds were drawn and the
only light came from a small lamp on the desk. It spilled
innocently over the scattered papers and pictures, ball-
point pens and paper clips.

Things Derek Miller would never use again.

John stepped into the room, trying to remember
what he knew about Miller's family. Nothing really. A
mother in the panhandle somewhere. Lubbock maybe.
Derek still had the telltale West Texas drawl. He shivered, mentally correcting himself. He'd *had* a drawl.

Despite Derek's talent with computers, John had
thought long and hard about bringing him into the
company. Especially as a partner. But even with his continued battle with drugs, Derek had been a hell of an
asset over the years.

Until now.

John tipped back his head, realizing suddenly just
how tired he was. Maybe he should have waited until
tomorrow to go through Miller's things, but there was
always the possibility that the police would subpoena
his effects, and so this might be his only chance.

He took another step toward the desk, his mind's eye
picturing Miller sitting there, back turned, the chair
slowly spinning around. Reality obediently complied
with his imagination.

"Son of a bitch." John took an involuntary step
backward, almost losing his balance. "What the hell are
you doing here?"

Jason Pollock steepled his hands as the chair came to a stop, his gaze dispassionate. "Same thing as you."

John dropped down into the chair in front of the desk, trying to control his wildly careening heart. "You scared me half to death."

"Sorry." It was hard to tell if he really meant it. Jason was a master at hiding his feelings. That's what made him so valuable to the company. But it could also be unnerving at times.

They sat in silence for a moment, each waiting for the other to blink. John forced himself to break the silence. "So did you find anything?"

"That would explain Derek's death?" Jason opened his hands as he shrugged. "No. I've been through his calendar and his personal files and didn't find a thing." He gestured toward the papers on the desk. "Danny said you don't remember anything about bailing him out of jail."

"You guys are making it a practice to discuss my business now?"

"It wasn't exactly a secret, John. The police even know about it. I just wondered if you really don't remember anything or if . . ." His words trailed off as his gaze met John's.

"Or if I'm using my head injury to cover something up? Come on, Jason, that's a bit far-fetched."

"Hey, I didn't mean to imply anything. It's just that you look so—*normal*." Jason shrugged again, this time with obvious embarrassment.

"This," John slowly raised his right arm, lax fingers a testament to his words, "is not normal. And neither is having a hole in my brain."

"I'm sorry. I didn't mean to doubt you."

John relaxed, allowing his hand to drop back into his lap. "It's totally understandable. I mean, look at the circumstances. I meet with Derek, bail him out of jail, and then conveniently waltz out of town just when Derek disappears. I can see how it looks."

Jason stood up and walked around to the front of the desk, leaning back against the edge. "Maybe it was a fluke. You were scheduled for your vacation long before Derek wound up in jail. And of all of us, you're the only one who would have bailed him out. Derek had his good points, but face it, he was trouble from beginning to end. If it hadn't been for you giving him second chances, he wouldn't have been with Guardian as long as he was."

John frowned. "So if you're not questioning me, then why are you here?"

"I don't know really. Morbid curiosity?" He stared down at his shoes, lips pursed as he thought about the question. "I guess the truth is, I wanted to protect Guardian. I mean, part of my job is to try and control spin. And this sort of thing can easily be blown out of proportion."

John nodded, waiting.

"So I figured if there was something here, something that might explain what happened, then better we find it than the police."

"You'd suppress information?"

Jason smiled. "Not suppress it, no. But I'd delay it if I thought it would help the company." He pushed away from the desk. "Look, we're talking about conjecture here. The fact is, I didn't find anything. Which is just as well, because with you out of commission, we've got more than enough to deal with. Our business is built on clients trusting in our ability to keep their businesses safe. And most of that trust has been based on your competence."

John clenched his good fist, trying to keep his emotions under tight rein. "And you're saying I'm not competent."

"I'm not saying that at all. I'm simply saying that the

perception, would be understandable under the circumstances. And if we're going to combat that perception, one of two things has to happen."

Their gazes met and held.

"Either you have to prove to everyone that you're back. One hundred percent."

"Or?" He felt the muscles in his jaw contract, knowing full well what Jason was going to say next.

"You're going to have to step down."

Katie jerked awake, sweat trickling between her breasts. She wasn't certain what had awakened her. The nightmare, or something in the night. But either way, she wasn't taking chances. She swung out of bed onto silent feet, automatically reaching for the bedside table and her gun.

When her hand met nothing, she swore under her breath, reality crashing in. She wasn't in her apartment, she was halfway across the country in a suspected killer's guest bedroom. And that meant no gun.

Damn it all to hell.

She strained into the darkness, all five senses on alert. From somewhere beyond the door, she thought she heard breathing. Or maybe it was the hiss of the air conditioner. Hard to say. Moving cautiously, she edged toward the door, careful to keep her balance as she crouched to avoid being in someone's direct line of sight.

Another noise, this one low and unidentifiable, filtered through the open doorway, setting the hairs on the back of her neck on end. She sucked in a breath, and moved into the living room, balancing on the balls of her feet, ready for whatever she found.

A slash of moonlight cut across the living room, highlighting the emptiness. If someone had been here, they'd obviously withdrawn. The apartment was silent now. The only sound the steady ticking of the grandfather clock in the foyer.

Katie drew in another breath, this one cleansing, and let her gaze sweep over the apartment. The word *apartment* was a bit of an understatement actually. It was larger than most people's houses.

Again with the enigma. On the surface, John Brighton seemed to be a man who liked living large. Armani suits, oversized apartments, and monochromatic furniture. A successful company and money to burn. And yet there was nothing personal about any of it. Nothing to identify the man.

Not that she should be thinking of him in that light. She'd gone far enough with that already. She squared her shoulders and took another cautious step into the room. What she needed was to find something that cemented the facts. Something that proved beyond a shadow of a doubt that John was exactly the man the FBI believed him to be.

A man capable of murder and cover-up.

She froze as another sound broke through the silence. Muffled and low. Pivoting slightly, she surveyed the room, her eyes lighting on a hallway off to her right. The sound had come from there. She reached down, fingers closing around a pewter candlestick. The sound came again, clearer now, and she released the candleholder, her breath coming more easily as she recognized the sound.

Someone was in pain.

John.

Her mind shifted from intruders instantly, instinct telling her to return to the safety of her room. But another part of her, the part she kept submerged, was calling for compassion. John needed help, and she could give it. It was as simple as that.

Without stopping to examine her motives further, she made her way down the hallway, toward his room. Her training as a physical therapist might have been rushed, but it had been thorough. There had to be something she could do.

Besides, she rationalized, people were less guarded in the night. Maybe if she was lucky she'd break through his barriers.

A tiny voice in her brain continued to call for caution. The feeling of danger was back. Danger and inevitability. She shook her head, dispelling the notion. This was a case. Nothing more. All she had to do was keep things in perspective.

Easy enough in the abstract, but as her past bore out, not so easily achieved in reality. She tended to lead with her heart—a definite occupational hazard. One that she was not going to allow to bring her down.

Not this time.

There was too much at stake. She'd learned the hard way that if she was going to excel in her career, she had to keep her eye on the ball. Nothing ahead and nothing behind. If anything, dancing with death had only strengthened that resolve.

And right now, what she needed to do was coax the truth from John Brighton, and to do that she needed to transform herself into whatever it was he needed. Katie the chameleon. Whatever anyone wanted to see, that's what she gave them.

And the fact that no one knew the real Katie didn't matter at all. In truth, she'd lost sight of that particular reality herself. Or maybe it was just that she didn't want to know. Facing demons required a courage she simply didn't have.

She sighed and started down the hallway, forcing herself into her role—locking Katie somewhere deep inside, ignoring the part of her that yearned for something more.

His right side ached. Bone-deep throbbing that threatened to unman him. He wanted to scream, to throw something, but the irony was, he couldn't use his damn hand to do it. He shifted in the bed, trying to find a comfortable position.

He supposed in some awful, tortured way the pain was a good thing. It meant he was alive. That his nerves were working, his muscles responding. But it also hurt like hell, sometimes making his nights unbearable.

The doctors said in time the pain would go away. Well, he was ready.

Now.

A shadow in the doorway shifted, his synapses firing a warning. Someone was there. Using his good hand, he pushed himself upward, looking around for something with which to defend himself. Ever since the shooting he'd been on edge, waiting for the other shoe to drop. Perhaps the time had come.

Adrenaline pumped though him, anger mixing with trepidation.

The shadow shifted again. "Are you all right?"

Her voice was better than a tonic, his body relaxing as it washed over him. His mind, however, was slower to recover. "I'm fine." It was a lie. But then, he'd been lying a lot lately. And the thought only served to make him angrier. He valued honesty above all else. But his need to protect his dignity was stronger.

She stepped into the room, her face still in shadow. "I heard you cry out."

He swallowed a sigh. The woman obviously wasn't going to let it go. "Sometimes at night my leg aches." God, he hated being incapacitated. What he wouldn't give to be whole again. Mind and body.

"Maybe I can help."

He thought for a moment she'd read his thoughts. Somehow it would have suited her. But when she moved to the side of the bed, he knew she meant the pain.

"Got anything on under there?"

It occurred to him to lie, to tell her he was stark

naked. Just to see how she'd react. But his mouth was evidently having nothing to do with the idea. "Gym shorts."

She pulled back the sheet, the slight breeze from the ceiling fan sending cool air chasing across his skin. "Roll over onto your stomach." Her voice was husky, the timbre rich like honey. Obediently he turned over, his neurons primed and ready, waiting for the touch of her hands.

He closed his eyes, tensing with anticipation. It was almost as if the very air they breathed was charged and waiting. He heard her sigh, the release of breath warm against his back, and then her hands circled his calf, her fingers moving softly across his skin, as if she was learning the feel of him.

"Just let yourself relax."

"It's not as easy as it sounds."

"I know." Her fingers tightened, rhythmically stroking, sure and strong, sensation washing through him, eroding his pain. "But you have to try. It's the only way you'll get through it."

"Day by day?"

She leaned closer, the smell of her skin intoxicating. "Minute by minute, if necessary." There was something in her voice. Resolution mixed with certainty. As if she was empathizing rather than just sympathizing. "It will get better, John. I promise."

"Sounds to me like you're speaking from personal experience." He waited, wondering if he'd been mistaken.

Her hands stilled, and silence mingled with the darkness. It was only a second, but it felt like an eternity and he wished he'd never spoken.

"I've just had a lot of patients in the same boat." It was an attempt to end the conversation, but he wasn't letting her off that easily.

"There's more to it." He rolled over, his eyes seeking hers. "I hear it in your voice. Talk to me, Katie."

She sat on the side of the bed, fingers nervously laced together, moonlight playing in her hair. "My mother was sick when I was young. She had cancer."

The word hung between them, hideous in all that it represented, and his heart went out to her. "How old were you?"

"A teenager." She stared down at her hands. "I don't talk about it much."

"I'm sorry. I . . . I didn't mean to overstep the boundaries." He reached over to cover her hand with his, wanting to turn the tables, to give her comfort.

Her fingers fluttered under his. "You didn't. Not really. I was the one who opened the door." She hesitated for a moment, then continued. "There's nothing much to tell really. She fought it as hard as she could, but in the end it won. It was particularly painful at the last, and I often spent the night with her, trying to ease the pain."

"Like this." The intimacy was back. "In the dark."

"The dark is freeing. It allows the soul to wander. I think my mother liked that. To be free from it all. At least for a little while." She looked so fragile, sitting there in the moonlight, his heart ached for her.

"You helped her with that. The escaping, I mean." He reached up to touch her cheek, surprised to find it wet with tears.

"I hope so." The words were soft, forlorn, and she turned her hand in his, their palms barely touching, her fingers caressing his skin.

And for a moment, in the darkness, he felt a connection—something deep and tangible. Without thinking about consequences, he pulled her closer, her breath sweet against his face, the silky softness of her nightshirt grazing his chest.

Time seemed to hang frozen. Even in the shadows he

could see the curve of her throat, the thrust of her lower lip as her tongue darted out to moisten it.

He reached up to push the hair from her face, reveling in the soft silky feel of it. Her breath caught, and just for a moment he thought he saw something flare in her eyes—a hint of passion building deep inside.

"I can't. . . ." She pulled away, stumbling as she rose to her feet. He tried to reach out, to come to her aid, but his body refused the call, his injured leg responding only after she'd righted herself, moving farther back into the shadows. "I'm sorry. . . ."

The last was only a whisper and he knew without looking that she was gone, the spell broken, leaving him alone again with the shadows of the night.

What in the world had she been thinking?

Katie paced the confines of her room, trying to figure out exactly what had just happened. One minute she'd been in charge of the situation, and the next she was babbling on about her mother as if she shared that kind of thing with strangers every day.

And then to make matters worse, she'd all but climbed into bed with the man.

She'd obviously gone round the bend in the worst way. Which of course wasn't true at all. And frankly, that's what scared her. She'd wanted him. Wanted him with a hunger she hadn't even realized she was capable of. Granted, she didn't have a lot of experience. In her line of work, dating could be a little awkward.

But she wasn't a gangly teenager either. She'd had her share of physical encounters. *Physical encounters.* Now, there was a telling statement. She stopped pacing and sat on the bed. Maybe that was the problem. She'd never allowed herself to feel anything, knowing before it started that it would have to end.

Relationships and undercover work were like oil and water. Which until a few minutes ago had never posed a problem. She stood up, anger flashing through her. There was no problem. Just a strange combination of pheromones and darkness. The man was the object of her investigation. Nothing more.

Chemistry be damned.

She sighed, and walked over to the window. The glass was still warm to the touch, even though the sun had long gone to bed. *Bed.* With a flash of memory, all she could see was John stretched out on the sheets, his muscles tight and hard. His skin . . .

She clenched her fist, her nails digging into her palm.

What in the hell had prompted this adolescent display of hormones? That's what it was, of course. Hormones. Her brothers would have a field day with this one. Katie Cavanaugh kisses the perp.

But she hadn't kissed him. That was the key. Despite her desire to do so, she'd walked away. That had to count for something. Didn't it?

She turned around to face the room, leaning back against the windowsill. What was it about John Brighton that was so damn compelling? She'd worked with other suspects. Some of them far more handsome. And some of them a damned sight more charismatic. But she'd never once thought of them as anything but an adversary.

Undercover work required walking a fine line, but she'd never been tempted to cross it.

Until now.

Wrapping her arms around herself, she fought against feelings of inadequacy. That's what Priestly had done to her. Made her doubt herself. Maybe her attraction to John was some kind of delayed reaction to everything that had happened.

Except that it made no sense at all.

Priestly had been repulsive. A predator to the core. And John . . . John was gentle, and lost, and somehow, despite the circumstances, she had felt a connection to him. A kindred moment in the dark.

How stupid was that?

She crossed back to the bed, lying back against the pillows, the soft whooshing of the ceiling fan underscoring her tumultuous thoughts. There were people in the bureau who doubted her abilities. Who honestly believed she'd never be as good as she had been.

This was her chance. Her shot at jumping back into the action. And she couldn't afford to blow it. Not for loneliness, not for hormones, not even for honest-to-God attraction.

And certainly not for a single moment in the dark.

Chapter 6

It was early. Guardian's office complex was empty, silent. The morning sunlight filtered through the window at the end of the hall, a stark contrast to the dark last night. Katie sighed. There was no question about it, darkness was seductive. She made her way down the corridor, carefully checking each office for personnel. So far she was alone.

Which was exactly how she wanted it.

Now and always.

At least in the morning light she was sure of that. And overall there hadn't been any real harm done. She'd talked more than she should have, certainly. But nothing could damage her cover. She'd managed to hold on to that one little bit of sanity.

Which surely counted for something.

She checked the hallway again, and then certain she was alone, slipped into Jonathan Brighton's office. Although it didn't seem likely, she had to admit she was hoping she'd find something here. Something to positively incriminate the man.

Then she'd be on her way back to Boston and last night would just be a memory.

If even that.

The office was austere at best. Black on gray with nothing that looked even remotely personal. This room made the man's apartment look positively warm and fuzzy. Katie carefully closed the door and walked over to the desk.

A big mahogany affair, it filled the space, diminishing everything else with its sheer presence. But like the rest of the office it looked unused. Puzzled, she sat down in the executive chair and pulled open a drawer.

Empty.

Frowning, she pulled open another. This one held the remnants of office supplies. A broken pencil, a half-empty tape dispenser, and a couple of paper clips. She swiveled the chair and opened the credenza behind her. Again, nothing but leftovers. The odd paper or report. Nothing that could possibly help her.

It was as if the man had left in a hurry.

But he hadn't. He was upstairs this very moment. Alone and, at least in the dark of the night, vulnerable.

Or had she been the vulnerable one?

She closed the door to the credenza, using the motion to close the door on her thoughts. There had to be a logical explanation. She just needed to find it. The sound of footfalls in the hallway set her blood racing, and she moved to the opposite side of the desk, reaching the other chair just as the door swung open.

Danny Brighton stood at the threshold, his expression carefully masked. "I thought I heard someone in here." His words were neutral; his tone, however, was not.

She forced a smile. "I was trying to find John. I thought maybe he'd be in his office, but . . ." She let the words trail off, waving a hand to indicate the empty room.

"He's probably upstairs." His lips parted in an answering smile, but his eyes still held questions. "We moved his things up to his study. I thought it would be better if he didn't have to come down here except when absolutely necessary."

Katie nodded. That explained the empty office. She

should have thought of it herself. "I didn't know. And when he wasn't in his room, I just came down here. We have a session scheduled this morning." She started for the door, but he held up a hand to stop her.

"How's he doing?" Danny's expression turned serious. "I mean, how is he really doing?"

"As well as can be expected, I guess. Better, actually. He was lucky there wasn't more damage."

"I suppose he was." There was an awkward pause, Danny avoiding her gaze. "It's just so hard to see him like this. Struggling to remember, to walk—hell, to pick up a fucking pen."

"It takes time, Danny."

His eyes mirrored his anguish. "But will it be enough?"

"You'll have your brother. In some capacity or another. He may not be the same as before. But he's here. That has to mean something."

Danny purposefully cleared his face. "Of course it does. I don't know what I was saying. There's something about you, Kathleen. You make a man want to spill his soul." The smile was back.

"I don't think it's me at all. It's just that you're dealing with some difficult issues. The truth about head injuries is that they change people. Sometimes forever."

"What if I don't want things to change?" His gaze connected with hers.

"You don't have that choice. Things have changed. And the only way any of you are going to move forward is to let go of the past."

"Good advice." His smile was crooked, endearing. "But damned hard to follow." He sobered, his eyes suddenly looking old, and tired. "You have to understand something. My brother is the heart and soul of this business. Without him at the helm, I'm not sure it can continue to exist. At least not in its present state."

"There's no reason to believe that John won't be able

to run his business. His mind isn't gone, Danny. It's just been rearranged here and there. Reprogrammed, so to speak. But I haven't seen anything that makes me question his ability to handle things cognitively."

"Well, I'm glad to hear that." John's deep voice startled her, and she jumped away from Danny, feeling foolishly guilty. "Am I interrupting something?"

"Would that you were." Danny's grin turned rakish. "But I'm afraid it's a lost cause. Our Kathleen was looking for you." He did everything but put a hand to his head, and despite herself, Katie smiled. Danny Brighton was a charmer, all right.

So why was it she felt this insane connection to his brother?

She made a play of looking at her watch, fighting for control over her emotions. "It's time for your session." She glanced up, her gaze colliding with his. There were questions in his eyes, questions and something more, an intensity that took her breath away, and for just a moment the world seemed to stand still. Time losing all meaning.

And then, just as quickly, it was gone, his expression shuttered, the fragile connection between them broken. "I haven't got time for a workout." He turned his attention to his brother. "Harris called. He wants to meet."

Danny's eyebrows shot up in surprise. "Problems?"

"I don't know. He didn't give any reason. Just said he needed to see me as soon as possible."

"Do you want me to come with you?"

"No. I'll be fine." John's answer was quick and resolute. "Besides, Frank will be there."

"Frank?" The word was like a curse.

"He's been in charge of the D.E.S. project in my absence."

"It should have been me."

"You had your hands full with other things." John shrugged. "And Frank has a relationship with Harris."

"His wife's mother's cousin, or something like that. Hardly kissing kin. I have seniority, I should be handling the big accounts."

"You are. Hexagon, Hobson Enterprises, the Brantley holdings. You're doing more than your fair share." John's tone was just this side of patronizing.

Danny heard him, and looked up, eyes flashing. "I am far more capable of running this company than Frank Jacoby, and you know it."

"I just said that I did." John's voice was placating now, and Katie got the feeling that this sort of confrontation was not unusual between the brothers. "And I think anything else you need to say should be said in private." He tipped his head toward her, his eyes sending a separate message. One that Katie couldn't read.

"You're right." Danny blew out a breath, and turned to Katie. "Excuse my rudeness. It's that magic of yours at work again." He smiled, the gesture moving up his face to his eyes. "I totally forgot you were here."

"Not an easy thing to do." John's eyes were darker than his brother's, smoldering with promises of things she didn't dare let herself think about.

Things that could never be.

"I have some concerns." Wilson Harris stood at the window in the conference room, his hands tense against the sill.

"I'm sure you do. But I'm also certain that we can work it out." John glanced over at Frank, who shook his head with a shrug. No help from that quarter. "Why don't you clarify a little."

"All right." Harris turned around, his eyes hard. "The truth is, I'm not sure Guardian is up to handling our business anymore."

"I've done a good job for you." Frank held out his

hands, almost plaintively. That was the problem with Frank. He had no social skills. Or next to none. But he was a hell of a programmer, and that's what they were paying him to do.

Still, maybe it had been a mistake to put him in charge of the D.E.S. account. Maybe Danny would have done a better job.

Then again, maybe not.

"I think Wilson's referring to me, Frank."

Frank dropped his hands back to the table, looking decidedly uncomfortable.

John almost felt sorry for him.

Almost.

He turned his attention back to Harris. "I'm right, aren't I? You meant that you don't think that *I'm* capable of handling it." He'd expected to feel angry, but oddly enough he only felt numb.

Harris shot a look at Frank, obviously considering his answer.

"Just say it." Here came the anger. At least something was predictable.

"Fine." Harris met his gaze, unflinching. "I don't think you're up to it."

"Guardian is more than just Jonathan, Wilson." Frank's voice rose defensively with each word. "I think I've taken pretty good care of you without his input."

"Maintenance." Harris waved a hand, dismissing him, his gaze still locked with John's. "But what happens when we need something new?"

"Then you get me." John had played blink with tougher men than Harris. The key was not to break eye contact. And not to give in. No weakness. He excelled at the game—or had excelled. Now he wasn't so sure.

"At full capacity?" Harris frowned, his focus still on the game.

"Half of me is better than most men, Wilson. You

know that." He waited a beat. "But yes, when you need me, you'll get me at full capacity."

"And you can promise that."

"There are no guarantees in this world. I just spent six months in the hospital learning that lesson. But barring further catastrophe, yes. You have my word."

Harris studied him, and evidently liking what he saw, blinked. He held out his hand. "Your word's good enough for me."

"So we're back in business?" Frank stood up, his attempt to reenter the conversation awkward at best.

Both men looked at him, and Harris smiled. "I think you can safely say that." He glanced back at John. "But I'll be watching."

John forced an answering smile. "I wouldn't expect it any other way." There had been a time in his life when he wouldn't have let anyone say something like that to him. A time when he had been riding high. The top of the heap.

But those days were gone.

There were new rules. And he intended to master them the way he'd done everything else in his life.

One fucking step at a time.

"You shouldn't be doing that on your own. You're not strong enough yet." Katie was leaning against the doorway, arms crossed, eyes narrowed, looking like some sort of demented guardian angel.

John continued to lift the weights, ignoring her comment. He needed the physical strain. Needed to work off his frustration. It hadn't exactly been a stellar morning. First seeing Danny and Katie together, thick as thieves, and then the meeting with Harris.

He wasn't sure which upset him more.

"I thought you were working this morning."

"I was. But the meeting's over and I needed the break." He needed more than that, but there was no discussing it with her. There was an awkwardness. A tension that hadn't existed before last night.

And it was all his fault. He'd moved too quickly. Taking advantage of her vulnerability. But he'd wanted her so badly. Wanted the chance to lose himself in something good. Something far removed from Miller, and Guardian, and gunshots on the side of a Mexican highway.

"We need to talk, John." There was just a hint of hesitation in her voice, enough to make him feel guilty all over again. He never should have put her in this position.

"There's nothing to say." He bit out the words, concentrating on doing his reps.

"Of course there is." She reached over to take the weight from him. "What happened last night was a mistake."

His heart sank. In his mind the only mistake had been her leaving. "I see."

"No. You don't." She straddled the end of the bench, facing him, her gaze reflecting her concern. "Being with you would be amazing. I'm certain of it. But I'm here in a professional capacity and it isn't right for me to let myself get involved with you." She paused, her breath coming out on a sigh. "No matter how much I want to."

"So we just pretend it never happened? Pretend there's nothing between us?"

"There isn't anything between us."

"Yet." He mumbled the word underneath his breath, but she heard him, her eyes darkening with regret.

"John, I'm here to help you. It's my job, remember? And there's no way I can keep professional objectivity if I'm emotionally involved."

"Then I'll get a new physical therapist." He was being obstinate and he knew it, but he wasn't letting this go without a fight.

"Fine. I'll leave if that's what you want." She started to rise, and he reached for her hand, pulling her back down beside him.

"That's not what I want, and you know it. I want you. But if it's professionalism you want, then that's how we'll play it—for now. But mark my words, this thing between us won't lie dormant forever. And I, for one, have no intention of fighting it when it surfaces." He tightened his grip on her hands. "There aren't that many chances in life, Katie, and when something special comes along, you have to grab on to it with both hands, or run the risk of letting it slip away."

"Easy to say. But much harder to do. Following your heart has a price, and sometimes it's just too much to pay."

He forced a smile, squeezing her hands then letting her go. "Some things, Katie, are worth any price."

"I find it hard to believe that a man could work somewhere for nearly ten years and yet all of his coworkers deny knowing him on anything but a purely surface level." D'Angelo watched Danny Brighton, waiting. There was just something about the man that he didn't like. Maybe it was the fact that he was overly solicitous, or maybe it was the fact that he was a pretty-boy. A purebred southern pretty-boy.

There were two kinds of Texans. The ones who worked hard and got the job done, and the kind that came along to enjoy the spoils. Danny Brighton was definitely a latecomer to the party.

"What can I say? Derek kept to himself. You know he had problems." Hell, the man couldn't even say the word *drugs*. "And to be honest, none of us really wanted to get involved."

"Except your brother." Again he watched the younger man, forcing his expression to remain noncommittal. "According to police records it was your brother who bailed Miller out of jail."

"Doesn't surprise me. Miller was his latest cause. Jonathan fancies himself a do-gooder."

D'Angelo frowned, trying to decide if there was a rift between the brothers, or if the younger Brighton simply didn't understand the concept of generosity. "And I take it you don't feel the same way."

"I just think business has to come first. If we'd fired Miller when he started having trouble, his death wouldn't be affecting Guardian."

"And it's affecting it now?"

"Hell, yes, we've been fielding calls all morning. You have to understand that Guardian was headline news for months after Jonathan was shot. Now, when things are finally getting back to normal, this happens." He gestured at the newspaper on the desk. The headline about Miller.

"Getting to the bottom of things is only going to help the situation, Mr. Brighton." D'Angelo purposely made his voice soothing, conciliatory.

"Look, Detective." Danny spread his hands wide, the gesture almost apologetic. "I wish I could help you, but the truth is, I don't keep tabs on my brother. If he bailed Miller out, he didn't discuss it with me."

"I see." He made a play of searching through his notes. Whatever was between the two brothers, they were obviously united against outsiders. Time to take a different tack. "So tell me about your brother's vacation."

Danny looked up, surprised. "Not much to tell. Jonathan doesn't routinely go on vacation, so this one was a big deal. He was scheduled to spend some time in the Mexican mountains. A client has a home up there, and he offered it to Jonathan."

"You said he didn't like vacations."

"I didn't say that. I said that he didn't usually go. My

brother is a one-note man, Detective. He lives and breathes for Guardian. He created it, and basically, he made it what it is today. And to do that, he's sacrificed everything else."

"Everything?" Eric frowned.

"He has no social life. No extracurricular activities, if you know what I mean." Danny's eyebrows waggled to underscore his meaning. "And, until Mexico, he rarely even took time off."

"So why did he go?"

It was Danny's turn to frown. "You know, I don't really know. It was sort of sudden actually. He just came in and announced that Andy Martin had offered him the villa, and that he was going."

"Didn't you think that was a little strange?"

"I didn't stop to think. I just remember thinking that it was about time he got away." His expression turned sheepish. "And I was delighted he finally trusted me enough to leave the company in my hands."

"But you're partners."

"Of a sort. But in many ways, no matter how long we work together, I'll always be the little brother. That's the way Jonathan's always treated me—until now."

"With his injury."

"Yes. As awful as it is, one good thing has come out of it. Jonathan had to let me take care of things for a change. Both at home and at Guardian."

"It must be hard on him."

"Probably." Danny considered the statement. "But in the end, he'll be glad he trusted me."

D'Angelo closed his notebook, nodding. "One more question, Mr. Brighton." Danny looked up expectantly—confident, no doubt, that he'd handled the detective. D'Angelo almost smiled. "Were you aware of the fact that your brother paid Derek Miller thirty-five thousand dollars the day before he left for Mexico?"

Chapter 7

"Why didn't you tell me you gave money to Derek Miller?" Danny's face was flushed with anger as he strode into the gym.

With Katie's help, John released the weights he was holding, and sat up to face his brother. "I have no idea what you're talking about."

"I just got out of a meeting with Detective D'Angelo, and according to Miller's bank records, you gave him thirty-five thousand dollars the day before you left for Mexico. So do you want to tell me what's going on?"

"Once again I seem to be in the middle of private affairs. Why don't I leave you guys alone to talk." Katie's gaze met John's, her eyes questioning.

"I think that would be best." It was tempting to ask her to stay. He felt more grounded when she was in the room, as if somehow she anchored him in reality. But it was probably better to face his brother on his own. "We're finished here anyway."

"All right." She frowned at him, as if she wasn't certain she was doing the right thing, and then, with a little sigh, turned and walked away.

Danny watched until the gym door closed behind her, then turned to face John, his jaw working in anger. "So are you going to tell me what the hell is going on, Jonathan?"

"John." The correction came automatically as he scrambled to make sense of his brother's tirade.

"John, Jonathan—whatever." Danny waved a hand through the air. "Just tell me about the goddamned money."

"There's nothing to tell." Frustration coated with anger laced through him. "If I gave money to Derek, I have no memory of it. You're sure D'Angelo wasn't just yanking your chain?"

"Oh, he was yanking, all right, but not about this. He had proof. You gave the money to Derek. The big question here is, why." Danny sat down on a bench, his anger dissipating somewhat.

John walked over to the watercooler, taking his time to fill a cup, trying to sort through his cascading emotions. Everything was askew. Nothing as it seemed. First Katie, now this.

With a slow exhale of breath, he turned to face his brother. "Maybe the money was for Miller's bail?"

"Not likely." Danny's voice was calmer now. "You'd have posted bail directly to the bondsman. What about rehab?"

John shook his head. "That doesn't fly either. I might have agreed to help him, but I'd never have given him the money directly. That'd be like handing him the drugs."

"D'Angelo seems to think it might have been a payoff."

"For what?" John wadded the paper cup up in his good hand, ignoring the water still inside.

"I don't know, Jonathan, but I think you'd better figure it out. This D'Angelo fellow is determined to find out what happened to Miller, and unless I'm off my game, you're on his short list of suspects."

"For what? Killing Derek? In case you've forgotten, I was in Mexico at the time, facing the wrong end of a gun."

"Maybe." Danny's eyes narrowed in thought. "Then again, maybe not."

"What the hell do you mean by that?" John threw the cup at the wastepaper basket in disgust.

Danny held up a hand. "Not what you think. I only meant that according to D'Angelo, Derek could have been killed the day before you left."

"So what? I paid him thirty-five thousand dollars and then killed him? That makes absolutely no sense at all. If I did pay Miller money—and I'm not saying I did—I'll bet my life on the fact that it was for a legitimate reason. And no matter why I did it, I sure as hell didn't kill the man. I fucking liked him."

"Hey, take it easy. I'm just telling you what the guy said."

Danny was right, spinning out of control wasn't going to help anything. He pulled in a slow breath. "I'm sorry. I didn't mean to go off like that."

"It's all right. You're entitled to a little anger." Danny shrugged. "Besides, I'm fairly certain D'Angelo was just fishing. If they had anything concrete, they'd be taking action."

"Hopefully you're right." He rubbed his eyes, his head suddenly full of cotton wool. "But just in case, I want you to see if you can find records from our end. Something to explain why I would have given the money to Derek. Or maybe something to show that I didn't." The last was said in a pathetic attempt to make his memories match with reality.

They weren't going to do that, of course. But he couldn't seem to stop himself from trying. Derek Miller was dead, and if Detective D'Angelo was to be believed, he just might have had something to do with it.

Or at least it was a possibility.

Which was something an hour ago he would have sworn was impossible.

Katz's Deli was the last thing Katie had expected to find in Austin. A strange combination of New York and

Texas, it definitely leaned toward the Big Apple side of things. And she had to admit the corned beef wasn't half bad.

Jerome hadn't arrived yet. Which was just as well. She needed the time to pull herself together. Her meeting with John hadn't gone exactly as planned. She'd said her peace. Made it perfectly clear that they couldn't have any kind of relationship.

But somehow, despite all that, he'd managed to deflect it all with the turn of a phrase, and to be honest, she wasn't sure where they stood. It should all be so simple. But it wasn't. What had seemed clear and logical in the cold light of her room became clouded with emotion the minute she was within three feet of him.

It was as if her pheromones had revolted, taking control of what was usually her very rational brain. Sighing, she took a sip of tea, the cold liquid soothing her frazzled nerves. One thing was for certain, she couldn't go on like this much longer. The more contact she had with John, the more likely she was to give in to her feelings.

Which of course was the dilemma. In order to do her job, she had to get close to him. But if she got close to him, she wasn't going to be able to do her job.

Damned if she did, damned if she didn't.

A comforting thought.

"Cavanaugh."

The voice came from the booth directly behind her. And she recognized it in an instant, distaste filling her gut. Roswell. Where the hell was Jerome?

"I'm here." She leaned back, keeping her voice pitched low. The setup was perfect. The booths were on a platform against a wall and Roswell's was the last one, which put him in a corner, his back to the rest of the crowd. She could hear him, and respond, and no one could see them conversing.

Not bad. Maybe she was underestimating Roswell.

"So, sugar, you find anything helpful?"

Or maybe not.

She fought against a wave of resentment. "It's only been two days, Roswell. I'm not a miracle worker."

"That's not what I heard. Word from Boston is that you're fucking amazing. Take on anything that stands in your way." There was a lurid tone to his voice that made Katie want to take a swing at him. Chauvinistic son of a bitch.

"Where's Jerome? I thought I was meeting him."

"He's close to a bust on another case. So for the moment you got me."

Wonderful. "Whatever. I honestly don't have a lot to report. No one suspects me. And I've pretty much got access to the whole of Guardian. Which helps." She took a sip of her tea, smiling at a passing waitress. "Anyway, John definitely doesn't remember anything. I've seen his medical charts and they're irrefutable."

"I know that, Cavanaugh. We're not paying you the big bucks to find out things we already know."

She ground her teeth together, biting back a retort. "I'm working as fast as I can. Undercover work takes time."

"So speed things along. Surely you can get to him the old-fashioned way. Men love to talk postcoital."

Sheer red-hot rage roiled through her. "You're a real piece of work, Roswell."

"At least I've got the cojones to get the job done."

She sucked in a breath, striving for calm. "My record stands on its own."

"Until recently."

She sputtered into her drink. Leave it to Roswell to point out her weaknesses. "I did what I thought was right."

"I'm sure you did. But the fact remains that you risked not only your life but the other operatives involved as well. And all for the sake of some two-bit floozy."

"She was a human being, Roswell."

"She was a whore." He spit the words out. "And if you hadn't gone on some wild vendetta to avenge her, you'd have saved yourself and the bureau a hell of a lot of trouble." She could hear the disdain in his voice. Southern style. But it wasn't all that different from what she'd heard in Boston.

So be it.

Narrowing her eyes, she centered her thoughts on business. She'd be damned if she'd rise to the bait. What was done was done. Besides, she could deal with Roswell. She'd dealt with his kind before. And just because he was playing on her side of the street didn't make him any different from the others. "I did find out something that might interest you. Seems Brighton gave Miller a large sum of money the day before Miller bought it."

She could hear Roswell scooting closer. "Say again?"

"John evidently paid Miller thirty-five thousand just after he bailed the man out."

"He told you this?" Roswell asked, his voice a whisper.

"Yeah, right. He miraculously regained his memory and confessed it all to me. Give me a break. Eric D'Angelo found the bank record among Miller's things. From there he managed to put two and two together."

"D'Angelo is still nosing around?"

"It's his job." She laid her head back against the seat, wondering if the left hand did in fact know what the right hand was doing.

"Not if it interferes with our investigation." Roswell's tone brooked no argument.

But Katie had always led with her mouth. "Looks like this time it helps us. Kinda nice to have the locals doing our work for us."

"I'll deal with D'Angelo. You just keep your focus on Brighton."

Now, there was an unneeded directive. She couldn't seem to think about anyone else.

"You napping, Cavanaugh?"

"No. Just thinking about the case."

"Well, think on your own time, sugar. When you're with me, you listen. Am I making myself clear?"

God, she wanted to plant one right between his eyes. Or maybe another part of his anatomy. "You're clear. Anything new I need to know from your end?"

"Nothing substantial. We're trying to trace things from Miller's end."

"So basically you have nada."

She could almost hear him shrug. "We're doing the best we can. And yeah, if you want to quantify it, we got nothing. A bunch of circumstantial evidence that adds up to bubkis. But I've got a feeling about this one, Cavanaugh. And you're our best hope." He said the last as if it were a tragic thing.

Bastard. She'd just have to show him what she could do.

Of course, to do it, she'd have to find something that tied John to Derek Miller's death. Something that proved he was guilty. No matter how she felt about him.

But then, that was the name of the game.

John slammed the study door with his good hand, and walked over to his desk. Everything was spinning out of control, and he couldn't seem to do a damn thing to stop it. When the hell was life going to get back to normal? He sat down, realizing the irony of his words. When had it ever been normal?

He'd worked for everything he had. It would have been easy to have rested on his father's laurels. Let the old man's money take him for a ride on easy street. But John hadn't wanted it that way. And neither had his father.

Buck Brighton hadn't given his sons a thing. Except

a college education. The rest had been up to them, the
bulk of their father's fortune passing on to his favorite
charities. He'd loved them, of course. But in a tough-
love, make-you-into-a-man kind of way.

John had been challenged.

Danny had just been pissed. He'd rebelled against
their father from the start, certain that the old man had
a mean streak a mile wide. And maybe he had. But it
had worked to make John the success that he was.

And truth be told, neither he nor Danny had needed
a dime of their father's money. Not a dime. Still, John
had spent the better part of his adult life making sure
that other people did get the chance they needed.
Money, jobs, whatever. Part of Buck's legacy had been
to make John more cognizant of others and their needs.

It was all done in a hands-off kind of way. Checks
were a hell of a lot easier to write than relationships
were to maintain. So he helped mankind in his own
way, following in his father's footsteps.

All of which meant that it wasn't out of the realm of
possibility for him to have given money to Derek. There
had to be a logical reason he'd done so. Something that
would clearly show that he wasn't involved in Miller's
death.

The alternative was unthinkable. And irrational. He
was letting his fears get the better of him. Just because
he'd forgotten part of his life didn't mean that part was
worth forgetting. Did it?

He tried to remember what the doctors had told him.
Something about the mind covering up incidents that
caused overwhelming stress. Like the shooting. Now,
there was a logical reason for a mind to go blank.
Who'd want to remember something like that?

But what if there was something else? Something
he'd done that had so horrified his mind, it had erased
the memory?

He banged his good hand down on the desk. He was

being paranoid. Minds didn't just go around erasing themselves. His memory loss had been caused by physical trauma. The trauma of almost getting his head blown off.

There was nothing more to it.

Nothing at all.

There was a knock at the door and John rose, careful to keep his balance slightly to the left. "Come in."

Florence Tedesky poked her head around the door, her face lined with worry. "You're supposed to be resting."

"I'm not going to break, Flo."

She frowned, but refrained from comment. "Danny wanted me to tell you that he didn't find anything."

John couldn't decide if he was disappointed or elated. Something in between, no doubt. Still, he doubted Detective D'Angelo would lie. "Then we're not looking in the right place."

"I had a feeling you'd say that." Flo sat down in a chair in front of the desk. "But we looked through all the ledgers and there was nothing."

"You looked at both hard and soft copies?"

"Of course."

John sat down again, leaning back in his chair, a vein in his forehead throbbing. "Then you must have missed something."

"Or you didn't write the check." Flo met his gaze square on.

He blew out a long breath, trying to ease his welling frustration. "I don't know if I did or I didn't. But as far as the police are concerned, I did. So there must be something here to explain it." He swiveled his chair so that he could better see the computer screen. "I've been doing a little hunting myself."

"Why doesn't that surprise me?" Flo stood up, moving so that she could look over his shoulder. "Did you find anything?"

"Nothing definitive. But there are some irregularities in the way these accounts have been filed."

Flo frowned at the screen. "What do you mean?"

"Well, look at this." He pointed to one of the listed accounts. "This account is supposed to be inactive. This one, too. And yet when I sort for accounts with activity around the time of Miller's death, they both come up."

"Well, it was six months ago. Maybe they were active then."

"No. They weren't. See?"

She leaned closer, peering at the screen. "You're right. We haven't used any of these in years. They should have been purged from the system." She leaned back, obviously perplexed. "What happens when you try to open them?"

"Nothing." He hit a button and the computer beeped indignantly. "I assume you didn't see them at all?"

Flo scrunched her forehead, still looking at the monitor. "They weren't on my computer. How come you found them?"

John smiled at her. "I still know a few things about these systems you don't. Truth is, I was getting frustrated with the accounting program, so I tweaked it a bit here and there."

"Hence your list." She waved a hand toward the computer screen. "But I'd say it backfired this time, since these accounts don't exist." Her expression fell somewhere between smug and confused. "At least not on the computer."

"What about the ledgers?"

"We went through them with a fine-tooth comb. And I didn't see anything out of the ordinary. But if you'll wait a minute, I've got the journals outside."

"Just in case." He grinned.

She smiled in return. "I thought you'd probably want to look at them."

"Am I that predictable?" There was something actually comforting in the fact.

She shrugged, heading for the door. "I've known you since you were a little boy."

John held back a laugh, turning to study the computer. If the files appeared on the list, then there had been activity. And that meant they were on the computer—somewhere.

He entered a few keystrokes, waiting as the computer buzzed with activity, a new screen appearing.

Flo walked back into the office carrying two ledger books. "According to these, neither account has been active in years. The first one for almost five and the second one for more like eight."

John nodded, his attention still on the computer screen. He tapped out some additional commands, his progress slower than he'd have liked since he was typing one-handed. "I think maybe I've got something here."

Flo dropped into the chair. "You found the files."

"Looks like it." A column of numbers filled the screen. "Son of a bitch." He let out a low whistle.

"What?" Flo leaned forward and he turned the monitor for her to see.

"This account is far from inactive." There was a series of deposits, the amounts varying. A couple of transfers and withdrawals spaced out over a period of months. But it was the bottom of the list that held his attention, the last recorded withdrawal. A check.

For thirty-five thousand dollars.

Chapter 8

"I talked to someone from the bank. It was definitely your signature on the check." Flo stood in the doorway, leaning against the frame. "So D'Angelo was right."

John felt a surge of disappointment. Part of him had hoped that the whole thing was a mistake. Something that would be laughed about and forgotten. But another part of him, the part that faced reality head-on, had known it wouldn't be so. "Did I make the deposits?" He waited, holding his breath, almost afraid to hear the answer.

"They weren't actually deposits." Flo shook her head. "Looks like they were transfers from other Guardian accounts. According to bank records, they were authorized by you."

He slammed his hand down on the desk. "What about the withdrawals—any record of those?" There had been three other withdrawals besides the check to Miller. All in five-digit amounts.

"Only the one check. The rest was withdrawn in cash." Her worried gaze met his. "The authorization came by fax."

"My signature." It was a statement, not a question.

"Yes." Flo looked away, obviously troubled.

"Great." He ran a hand through his hair, trying to assimilate the information. "So now instead of one problem, we have two."

She nodded her head resolutely. "Well, I'm certain there's a reasonable explanation."

John wanted to believe her. Wanted to make things go back to the way they had been before he'd been shot. But then again, maybe he didn't. In the space of forty-eight hours he'd discovered things about himself he wasn't sure he liked. Things that made him wonder about his own integrity.

Things that frightened the hell out of him.

He drew in a breath, reining in his fear. It wouldn't do to lose control. "So we still have no idea why I gave Derek the money, or why I used this account to do it."

"It was a business account." She laced her fingers together, resting them on her knee. "Maybe he was working on a special project of some kind."

"For thirty-five thousand dollars?" He tried but couldn't keep the skepticism from his voice.

"Look, whatever it was, I can't imagine you doing anything that would have caused another person harm."

"I wish I were as certain as you. I mean, in my heart it makes sense. But Detective D'Angelo thinks there's more to it than just me writing a check, and there's evidence here to support that."

"Detective D'Angelo doesn't know squat." Leave it to Flo to call it as she saw it. "He's on a fishing expedition. Probably getting all kinds of pressure from higher-ups to solve the case. He's got to follow up on anything he finds. And now he has. End of the road."

She sounded so certain. So sure that he wasn't involved in anything suspicious. But he couldn't stop the little thread of doubt that was pounding at his brain. "I hope you're right. But in the meantime, I want to look at all the books. There's got to be something that explains my involvement with Derek."

"I'm telling you, it's the result of nothing more than a good heart. But I know you, and you aren't going to rest until you find out what happened." She stood up, her expression resolute. "Which accounts do you want to start with?"

He smiled at her, his uncertainty replaced with love. She was a hell of a lady, Flo Tedesky, and he was damn lucky to have her in his life. "Let's start with mine. Maybe there's a reason why I used Guardian's money and not my own."

"You guys look like you could use a break." Katie stood at the door to the study, holding a tray of iced tea, hoping she looked more casual than she felt. John and Florence had been holed up in his study since she'd returned from lunch, and from the grim expressions on their faces, she doubted they were enjoying the work much.

Flo immediately closed the ledger she was examining, a slow flush indicating she was hiding something. Protecting John. Katie'd always admired loyalty. Even if it was misplaced.

"It's okay, Flo." He raised a hand. "I think we can trust Katie." John's solemn gaze met hers, the look assessing.

She fought to maintain her composure. He had a way of seeing inside her, beyond her carefully constructed persona, but despite what he saw or didn't see, the truth was she wasn't to be trusted, and yet everything depended on his believing the opposite.

And, for the moment, he did.

She ought to be feeling elated, but she wasn't. She set the tray carefully on the desk, pausing to look over John's shoulder at the computer screen. "So what's going on?"

It was a silly question really, but she couldn't think of anything else to say. All she seemed to be able to concentrate on was the rise and fall of his shoulders as he breathed in and out, the rhythm somehow hypnotic, pulling her in, daring her to believe in him.

"I'm looking for an explanation actually." He reached for a glass at the same time that she did, his hand warm against hers, an internal conversation going on between them that had nothing whatsoever to do with ledgers and bank accounts.

She jerked back, just stopping herself from pulling her hand all the way to her chest. "An explanation for what?"

Flo opened her mouth to protest, and then closed it again, instead taking a frosted glass from the tray, her expression guarded.

"We found the check. It was written on a Guardian account—with my signature. So we're looking through my financial records to try and find a clue as to why I saw fit to give someone with a drug addiction that kind of money."

"You aren't guilty of anything, John." Florence's voice was tight, colored with emotion.

"I appreciate your faith. But the only way we can be certain is to try and figure out what's going on. And since I can't remember, we'll just have to find the answers some other way." His injured hand closed awkwardly around an oddly shaped lump of clay.

"You make that?" Katie forced a smile, gesturing to the object in his hand. It was a complete non sequitur, but her thoughts were tangled, and she needed a moment to think.

"Yeah." He looked down at the clay figure in his hand. "I made it in OT. It's supposed to be a phoenix, but I'm afraid it looks more like a blob."

"I think it's beautiful," Flo added loyally.

John's smile was brilliant as he turned to Flo, and Katie found herself wishing she'd been the beneficiary of the gesture. "It's symbolic, isn't it?"

"Yeah," he turned the statue, rubbing a thumb along

what looked to be the wing of the phoenix. "I couldn't get the image out of my head."

Flo looked puzzled for a moment and then broke into a smile. "I get it. You're like the phoenix rising from the ashes. The bird is meant to be a symbol of your recovery."

John shrugged, looking embarrassed now. "Something like that. Not that it's done me a bit of good." He pushed the statue away from him, leaving it sitting forlornly on the corner of the desk.

Katie watched him from under lowered lashes, her heart going out to him. He seemed so sincere. So honest. Incapable of hurting anyone. And yet, the evidence seemed to support Roswell's accusations. So where was the truth?

She bit the side of her lip, studying the pile of ledgers. "How much of this have you been through?"

"About half of it." He rubbed the side of his face with his hand, his eyes heavy-lidded as he struggled to contain a yawn.

"You're pushing it again," Flo insisted maternally. "You need to rest."

"I'm fine." This time his smile missed reaching his eyes. "I just need to get to the bottom of this."

"And you're certain the answer is here?" Katie watched as he considered her question.

"No, but it's a logical place to start."

"Not if it puts you back in the hospital." She met his gaze, knowing her face reflected her concern.

Florence nodded her agreement, her expression determined. "We'll finish this later."

Their words bounced off him like water on a hot griddle. "We'll finish it now."

Once he'd made up his mind, there was apparently no stopping him. Again Katie found herself admiring the man. Despite the situation. Or maybe because of it.

Either way, she was treading on thin ice, but at least she was cognizant enough to recognize the fact.

"Then I'll help." The statement was matter-of-fact, leaving no room for discussion, and he accepted it without a fight.

"Here." He reached to the pile and handed her a ledger.

The thing she didn't know for certain was if she was helping him to expose him, or helping him to clear his name. Philosophically, she told herself, it didn't matter, but for reasons that didn't make a bit of sense, her heart was singing a different tune.

Which meant that it did matter.

A lot.

Frank paced the confines of his office, trying to decide what to do. If he made the wrong decision he could easily wind up worse off than he was now. Of course, Jessica would throw the old adage "nothing ventured, nothing gained" at him. And he supposed in some ways she'd be right.

Except that he wasn't very good at taking risks.

He sighed, staring out the window at the evening traffic. The rush was already beginning. Cars moving at a snail's pace, people locked inside metal boxes. Trapped for the duration. A lot like him.

But then, he'd made his bed. Married above his station, and then somehow managed to disappoint her. No matter what he tried, what he accomplished, he was never good enough. Which was the biggest reason why siding with Valerie was so tempting.

As long as he worked for Jonathan, there wouldn't be any grand promotions. No spotlight. He'd always be an underling. Well, maybe not an underling, but certainly not the kind of man that could hold on to a woman like Jessica.

He picked up a photograph of his vivacious wife. It

might not be much of a marriage, but it was all he had. And that meant that he had to do everything in his power to stop it from slipping away. Truth be told, Valerie's proposal was looking more alluring by the moment.

"Hey, Frank, you good for a drink?"

Frank pulled out of his reverie to meet Danny's gaze. "Of course, come in." He gestured to a visitor's chair and then turned to the small credenza that served as a bar. "The usual?"

"Yeah." Danny sounded preoccupied.

Frank poured a stout whiskey and turned to hand it to Jonathan's brother. "Something wrong?"

Danny smiled wanly. "Nothing I can't handle."

"Doesn't sound like it to me." Frank poured his own drink and sat down in his chair, propping his feet on the desk.

"It's just everything. Jonathan, Miller, all of it. I guess I'm not certain this is the right time for him to be coming back."

"Have you thought about asking him to step down?" Frank studied the younger man's face, trying to read his thoughts. Danny Brighton might look like an open book, but Frank had known him a long time. Danny only showed people what he wanted them to see. The rest he kept locked inside him, only occasionally giving a hint to his true feelings about things.

"Yes. But I don't think he'll do it." He stared into his whiskey, watching the amber liquid swirl against the glass.

"Well, it wouldn't have to be permanent. Just a continuation of status quo. We've done a good job for Guardian over the last six months. Jonathan has to see that."

"He does, Frank. But that doesn't mean he isn't ready to resume control."

Frank dropped his feet, leaning forward. "You saw

him. He's obviously in pain. And then there's the whole memory thing. For all we know, he's still losing bits and pieces. That can't be good for business."

"I don't know, Frank. I can't make that kind of call. I'll admit that Jonathan isn't the man he used to be. But that doesn't mean he can't handle his job."

"What about the cop? He's still snooping around, and it's pretty obvious it's because he believes Jonathan had something to do with Miller's death."

"Maybe. Or maybe the man is just playing the angles." Danny took a long sip of whiskey, his face a polite mask. "Whatever he's doing, I don't see how getting Jonathan to step down will help things."

"It insulates us from the fallout, Danny."

Danny frowned, obviously considering his words. "You're talking about more than a leave of absence, aren't you?"

Frank took a deep breath, realizing he was walking a fine line between committing to Val's scheme, and his loyalty to Jonathan. Still, it couldn't hurt to test the waters. "It's possible. If we all stand together."

Danny set his drink down on the edge of the desk. "But Jonathan has controlling interest."

"What about Derek's shares?"

"You already know the answer to that. They're divided up proportionally between the remaining partners. Status quo preserved. So even if all of us were to get on board, the best we could hope for is a tie. And Flo has enough shares to break that tie."

"She cares more about your brother than anyone. Surely she'd want what's best for him."

"I think you're whistling in the dark. John isn't going to resign. And Flo will support whatever decision he makes. Besides, the point is moot, I'm not about to join in a coup against my brother."

Frank made a play of pouring Danny another drink. He was blowing it. "I'm not suggesting a coup, Danny.

I was merely exploring our options. I just want what's best for Jonathan. It's at least worth thinking about."

"I suppose so. I just don't want to see my brother hurt. He's been through enough."

"I agree." He handed Danny the new drink, forcing what he hoped was a casual smile. "I wouldn't be where I am today if it hadn't been for Jonathan, Danny. I'm not about to bite the hand that feeds me."

But Valerie would. Which meant he couldn't sit on the fence any longer.

It was time to get in the game.

John stared at the computer screen, his mind refusing to contemplate the implications of the entry he was staring at.

"Is something wrong?" Katie's voice intruded on his thoughts and without thinking he reached over and turned off the computer.

"Nothing at all." He forced a smile, hoping to hell the horror he felt wasn't reflected in his face. He needed time to think. And he needed to do it alone. "I'm just tired."

"I should think so." Flo's eyes narrowed with concern and a touch of I-told-you-so. "You've been at it all day, without a break."

Katie frowned, her gaze assessing. "You sure that's all there is?"

He nodded, pushing back from the desk. The woman saw too damn much. "I think I'll just take a breather. We've basically finished anyway. I can go over the rest in the morning." He stood up, rubbing his eyes, fighting against a headache. He was tired. Bone tired. And confused as all get out. First the check to Miller and now this.

"John?" Katie had moved to stand beside him, her eyes worried.

"I'm fine. Really. You don't have to mother me."

"I know that. It's just that—" She broke off, her gaze locking with his, something decidedly unmotherlike passing between them. She stepped back, swallowing nervously, her eyes still dark with emotion. "It's my job, remember?"

"How could I possibly forget?" He moved closer, their breath mingling, energy crackling between them.

Flo cleared her throat, short-circuiting the moment. "Maybe you should continue this conversation over dinner?"

"I don't think that would be appropriate." Katie backed up again, her expression inscrutable.

"Nonsense," Flo said, ignoring the undercurrents, "I think it's a marvelous idea. John hasn't been out of this building since he came home. A nice dinner out would be just the thing."

"I hardly think he needs his therapist along." She was obviously flustered, her tongue darting out to trace the line of her bottom lip.

"Oh, come on, Katie, it'd do us both good. The perfect therapy." He stressed the last word, surprised to find he was holding his breath. He needed to be with her. Needed to forget about his problems for a while. After all, they'd still be waiting when he got back.

"He's right." Flo beamed at Katie, her look cajoling. "It's just what the doctor ordered."

"When you put it like that, how can I refuse?" Katie sighed, accepting defeat, her slow smile warming him in places he hadn't even realized he'd been cold.

He held out a hand, grateful when she took it. "It'll be good to get out of here."

At least for a meal.

And then—then he'd have to deal with the fact that he'd liquidated half a million dollars in assets just before leaving for Mexico.

Which seemed like a hell of a lot of cash for a vacation in the sticks.

Chapter 9

"Isn't it a little late for a house call?" D'Angelo frowned up at Roswell, realizing with a sigh that his dinner was going to get cold.

"The desk sergeant said you were working late." Roswell shrugged, perching on the edge of the desk opposite Eric's. "And I thought we might have a few things to talk about."

"Derek Miller's murder being at the top of the list?" He pushed his burger out of the way, and sat back so that he could see the man. Roswell was obviously trying to maintain the upper hand. Height advantage and all that. What he failed to understand was that D'Angelo wasn't intimidated easily. Even by a man with Roswell's reputation.

"We're concerned that your nosing around might be interfering with our investigation." Roswell's carefully modulated voice took on the tone of a schoolteacher. A teacher talking to a truant.

Irritation surged through him. "I'm more concerned that we won't find Miller's murderer."

"I'm aware of that fact, but sometimes there's more at stake than is readily apparent."

"You're talking in riddles, Roswell, and frankly I don't have time for them. So why don't you just cut to the chase." With more nonchalance than he was feeling, he reached for a french fry.

"I'm talking about all the questions you're asking over at Guardian."

His resentment ratcheted up a notch, and he fought to keep his tone civil. "I'm a detective, Roswell, that's what I do."

"Not when it might endanger an ongoing FBI investigation."

"Which you can't tell me about." He reached for another french fry, considering what he'd do with it if it were capable of inflicting pain.

Roswell shrugged, the gesture laced with superiority. Fucking bastard. "It's need to know."

"Fine." Eric leaned forward, eyes narrowed, just barely hanging on to his temper. "Until you decide I *need* to know, or until someone pulls me off of the case, I'm going to continue to ask questions."

Roswell leaned forward, too, his face just inches away from D'Angelo's. "I came here as a courtesy, but if I have to go to your superior, I will. I want you to back off. And I want it now."

"So you're taking over the case?" He held his position, even though it was an effort to do so. Not for all the beer in Milwaukee would he let the bastard think he'd gained ground.

"No." Roswell sat back. Score one for the APD. "It's still your case."

Which meant Roswell was here without authority. Eric frowned. "Then I don't understand what you're asking me."

Roswell stood up. "I just want you to proceed with caution. There's a lot at stake."

"I'm always careful, Roswell. That's why I'm good at what I do. Now, if you're finished . . ." He gestured to his now cold hamburger.

The man fixed him with a stare meant to intimidate. "Just watch your step."

D'Angelo raised an eyebrow, holding back a spurt of

laughter. He'd used the same technique on suspects. He hoped he was better. He picked up a fry, ignoring the fact that it was greasy and cold. "No problem."

Roswell narrowed his eyes, obviously doubting Eric's sincerity—smart guy—then with a curt nod he turned and strode from the squad room.

"What the hell was that about?" Haskins walked up to the desk Roswell had vacated, dropping down into the chair.

"Damned if I know." D'Angelo threw the hamburger at the trash can. It landed with a satisfactory thwack.

"Looked like a pissing match to me." Tony leaned back, propping his feet on the desk. "So who won?"

"Let's just say I did the department proud." Eric grinned, then sobered. "Seriously, I don't know what the fuck was going on. He told me to back off the Miller case, but then when I wouldn't back off, he did."

"The great Roswell?" Haskin's sarcasm was thicker than the squad room coffee.

"Yeah. Go figure." D'Angelo leaned back in his chair, trying to sort through the conversation. "One thing is for certain, though. This is about something a whole lot bigger than a drug addict with a big mouth. Whatever Miller had to sell, the FBI wanted it bad. And unless I miss my guess, Jonathan Brighton is involved in it up to his memory-impaired ass."

"Are you all right?" Katie wasn't sure exactly why she asked the question. It's just that he'd seemed so determined to get her to come, and now that they were actually out, he hadn't said more than three words.

"I'm sorry." John stared down at his pizza, toying with the edge of his paper plate. "I'm afraid I'm not very good company tonight."

"That's a bit of an understatement actually." She reached across the table to cover his hand with hers. "Why don't you tell me what's wrong."

He studied her face for a moment, obviously debating the wisdom of revealing himself, then, with a sigh, he leaned back in his chair, his expression shuttered. "According to my bank records, I liquidated about half a million dollars worth of assets before leaving for Mexico."

"That's a lot of money." She sat back, frowning. "You've no idea why you liquidated it?"

He shook his head. "None at all. There's nothing to indicate where I put it or what I might have wanted with it."

She toyed with her pizza, trying to order her thoughts. "Have you told anyone else what you found?"

He shook his head, carefully reaching for his iced tea. "I wanted to sort through it first."

"And you wound up taking me out to dinner instead." She met his gaze, surprised to see honesty there. Honesty and hope.

God, he believed she was going to help him. Guilt washed through her. Guilt colored with emotions she wasn't about to examine.

At least not now.

"Believe me, it was a much-needed distraction." His smile was slow, his eyes still worried. "Look, I didn't mean to drag you into my problems."

"You didn't drag me. I volunteered. Remember? Besides, sometimes it's nice to be able to talk to someone with no ulterior motives."

"Everyone has ulterior motives, Katie."

She was silent for a moment, considering his statement. "I suppose that's probably true—if you want to be that literal. But that's not what I meant. I just thought it might be nice to talk to someone who wasn't a part of your life before you were injured."

"I'm sorry." He turned the glass absently in his good

hand. "I know you're trying to help. It's just that without memories, I'm not sure how to proceed."

She shifted so that she could see him better. "Maybe it'll help if we look at it sequentially, beginning with the trip to Mexico."

"Conceivably a vacation. But with half a million dollars missing, it's certainly possible something else was going on."

"Is there anything in Mexico that could have meant you'd need that kind of cash?"

"Nothing that makes any sense. Certainly not on a vacation. Hell, I'm having trouble with the idea that I went on a vacation at all, money or no. Especially somewhere like Mexico."

"More a Riviera kinda guy?" She'd meant it as a joke, something to lighten the moment, but it came out an insult, and she immediately regretted the words.

"Maybe before. But now," he laughed, the sound without humor, "now . . . I don't know."

"Well, we know you went, despite your past preferences. Which could mean something in and of itself."

"You mean because I normally wouldn't have gone there, there must have been a nefarious reason?" His voice held a note of sarcasm at odds with the resignation reflected in the lines of his face.

"Not nefarious, necessarily. You're jumping to conclusions. But it is possible there was a reason beyond just a vacation. Danny told me you borrowed a place from a friend?"

"A client actually. Hobson Enterprises. The account manager offered me the place. The problem is, I don't remember accepting."

"Have you talked to this man?"

"Andy? No, I haven't, but it's a good idea. I'll call him in the morning. And I can talk to my broker about the asset liquidation. Maybe I told him what it was all about. At the very least I'd have had to authorize the transactions."

"It's a good beginning." She leaned forward, wanting to reassure him. "One way or the other, you'll get to the bottom of this. You've just got to take it step by step. And if you'll let me, I want to help."

"You're a special person, Katie Cavanaugh." His gaze connected with hers, his gratitude almost palpable.

The guilt was back. "You're making a judgment without really knowing me."

"I already told you, I trust my instincts."

"So," she said, knowing that her smile was a little too bright, "is Cozzoli's local?"

John released her hand, considering the question, accepting the change of subject. "I don't know. I never really thought about it. I just like the pizza."

"Is this where you usually take your dates?" It came out before she had the time to think about how it sounded.

There was a moment's hesitation, a beat when their eyes met and words ceased to matter. But it was gone almost before she was cognizant of its existence.

"No. I usually try to be a little more impressive. Something more upscale." He waved an arm at the plastic-molded booths.

"So I didn't rate?" Again with the mouth. She bit her lower lip, trying to force her brain to take control. She'd meant it as a joke, but somehow it came out sounding like she was hurt. Or petulant. Or something.

He looked down at his empty paper plate, the fingers on his right hand twitching, tightening, trying to form a fist. "I couldn't manage anywhere else."

The statement had cost him a lot, and she recognized it, and was ashamed. She hadn't thought about his injuries. About how difficult handling cutlery and glasses must be for him. Dinner, no matter where it was, would be difficult. And a meal out was like putting it all under a microscope for everyone to see.

"I'm sorry. I never stopped to think about how you might feel about eating out. I never should have agreed to this."

"I'm the one who wanted to come, remember?" He held her gaze for a moment, and then looked down again. "So have you had enough?" He tipped his head toward the pizza, changing the mood with just a sentence.

She couldn't decide if she should be insulted or relieved. Relieved probably. "More than enough. This place could be addictive." They stood up and Katie was careful to flank him as they walked toward the door.

"I'm not going to fall down, you know." His tone was wry, but there was an undernote of frustration. This was a man used to being in control, and the shooting had robbed him of some of his self-confidence. He tried hard to mask the feelings, but she could see it there, just below the surface.

"I know." She casually linked arms with him. "But I can't help reacting. Write it off as an occupational hazard." Which of course wasn't true. Quite honestly, she couldn't explain her need to help him even to herself. It was automatic. Almost like breathing. And about as uncharacteristic as if she'd suddenly taken to following the edifications of Martha Stewart.

"Feel like walking?"

They'd come out onto Congress Avenue, the downtown streetlights seeming to radiate heat. Even with the sun down, it was still hot. "Sure." She fell into stride beside him, adjusting her natural pace to his slower gait.

The state capitol lay in front of them, resplendent against the night sky, stars twinkling around the figure of lady liberty.

"It's taller than the one in Washington."

"I beg your pardon?" She glanced over at him.

"The dome." He pointed toward the capitol. "When Texas joined the union they built their capitol so that it would be taller than the one in DC."

"Everything's bigger in Texas?"

He laughed, his face shadowed in the half-light, his profile strong. A shiver of something primal ran down her spine. This man was dangerous.

She tripped on a bump in the pavement, and his hand tightened on her arm, keeping her upright. They stopped, standing face-to-face, their breath mingling together beneath the hazy light of the street lamp. "Maybe I'm not the only one who needs to be taken care of," he whispered, his voice caressing.

She licked her lips nervously, wanting to step back. To move away. But she couldn't.

She couldn't.

Almost against her will, she leaned closer, until his mouth was just centimeters from hers. He closed the distance between them, his good arm sliding around her waist, pulling her against him, his lips brushing hers, lightly at first, then harder, more insistently. As if he couldn't get enough of her.

It had been a long time since anyone had made her feel like this. Free. Uninhibited.

Crazy.

She pushed back, gulping for air, her eyes searching his.

His grin was slow, almost lazy, and it made the nerves along her skin dance. "It's about time we did that, don't you think?"

"I . . . I don't—" She was actually stuttering.

He covered her lips with a finger, his touch gentle, yet sensual. "It's late. We should go."

She nodded mutely, and let him lead her back toward the car, wondering what the hell was happening to her. Her lips were tingling. Her head was spinning. And she felt all of about fourteen. The rational side of her brain was screaming that she take charge of the situation, put him in his place once and for all, but the other side of her, the side she kept locked deep inside, was awake and demanding a rematch.

She was caught between the proverbial rock and hard place.

And quite frankly, it hurt like hell.

Jason Pollock watched as the computer screen flashed a series of files, arranged by date.

"Shit." The word rang out in the stillness of his study, the dates on the computer indicating that someone had accessed the files only a few hours before.

"Jason?" Valerie's voice was sleep-clouded. "Is that you?"

"Yeah, I dropped something." He closed the lid on his laptop as she walked into the living room. "I didn't mean to wake you."

"Work?" She tilted her head toward the computer, smothering a yawn.

He nodded with a sigh, reopening the computer, canceling the screen with the files. "I couldn't sleep. Too much on my mind, I guess."

She nodded, and sat down on the sofa. Even tousled from sleep, Valerie was a looker. And it constantly amazed him that she deigned to grace his bed. "I know what you mean. Between Derek's death and John's return, it's hardly been business as usual."

"I had three calls today."

"About John?" Her perfectly sculpted brows drew together in a frown.

"Two about him, one about Derek and the police. Not that I blame them. It's all over the papers. Even if there's nothing to any of this, we look like we're involved up to our necks." He abandoned the computer to come and sit beside her. "So what happened with Frank?"

"He hasn't committed yet. But he will." Her smile held a touch of malice. "Frank's easy to manipulate. He's hungry for attention. All I have to do is make him believe I'm interested in him, and he'll follow me like a puppy."

"You're seducing him." He frowned, the idea repugnant in and of itself, but even more so when he factored in his feelings for Valerie.

"Something like that." She ran a finger up his thigh. "But there's nothing for you to worry about. Just a means to an end."

"One more step toward taking Guardian away from Jonathan."

"Exactly. Although you make it sound so calculated." Valerie shrugged, the gesture just a little too practiced. "I care a great deal about Guardian, Jason. You know that. And Jonathan would be the first one to admit that anything that created a liability to the company should be exorcized. So can you fault me for thinking that now is the time to make our move? Jonathan is down for the count, the troops are restless, and to top that off, some of the clients are beginning to make noises about all the attention we're getting. All of that adds up to leverage."

"Against Jonathan."

"Look," she reached over to lay a hand on his knee, "if it bothers you so much, think about it as if we're doing the man a favor. He's not well, Jason. You've seen that. He'd be better off starting over."

"Do you really believe that?"

"Does it matter?"

He blew out a long breath. "I suppose not."

"Then you're with me?"

"I'm not sure what it is exactly you think you're going to do. But yes, I'm with you."

"Good." She stood up, extending a hand. "Then come to bed."

He wanted to go with her. To put all this out of his mind for a moment or two. But he couldn't. He had to figure out where he stood. And then he had to figure out what he was going to do about it. The play was in motion and it was past time for him to make his move.

The question was, what the hell was he going to do?

Katie stood at the window looking at the lights of the city, her stomach tied in knots. She was in over her head. And being a pragmatic person she was the first to admit it. But that didn't mean there was an easy way out.

She couldn't quit. That would be tantamount to admitting that Roswell was right and that a woman couldn't handle the job. But she couldn't continue deceiving John. Not after that kiss.

Lightning flashed against the horizon, the broad band of light giving a momentary illusion of daylight. She sighed. It was classic really. An undercover agent getting too close to the mark. It was always a fine line, but given the chemistry between the two of them, she shouldn't be surprised. The question was, what to do about it.

And the answer to that was obvious. She had to get her hormones in order. Get the information she needed. And then get the hell out of Dodge. She was a professional. Everyone probably had a brush with something like this. It was a test. And she was determined to pass with flying colors. Nothing had happened between them.

They'd talked. And he'd kissed her. That was the pertinent fact. *He'd* kissed her. Not the other way around. Granted, she'd let it go on a little longer than necessary. But all things considered, she had stayed in character. That had to count for something.

Besides, the only one who was ever going to know about it was her. . . .

And John Brighton.

John.

She sighed and leaned her head against the window glass. There was something so elemental about him. Something that touched her at a level she hadn't even known existed. She shook her head, her hands tightening on the windowsill.

But none of it was real.

None of it. This was all an elaborate charade. The woman John had kissed didn't exist. She was a creation of the situation. A pretend woman that Katie was using to get what she needed. So he wasn't interested in the real woman. He was interested in a chameleon. A shadow.

She watched as the lightning flashed again in the distance. Rain would be nice. Anything to break the heat. She tipped back her head, trying to clear her thoughts. She'd been in worse spots than this and she'd always landed on her feet. There was no reason to believe that this one would be any different.

The trick was to keep part of her, the real part of her, walled off somewhere deep inside. To keep herself separate from the person she was pretending to be. That was the only way she could be certain to keep things straight in her head. To clarify between reality and fantasy. And anything she felt about John Brighton was fantasy.

She tightened the belt on her robe, twirling it absently. There were lines one just didn't cross. Even in undercover work. And quite honestly, she was dangerously close to jumping over them with total abandon.

Damn it all to hell.

The lightning flashed again, the light bright even against the neon of the city.

"Heat lightning."

His voice was gruff with sleep, washing over her with the softness of velvet—deep, dark velvet. He was standing in the doorway, wearing nothing but a pair of sweats, the moonlight playing off the angular planes of his chest.

She shivered despite her earlier resolve. Whatever game they were playing, it was for real, and just at the moment she wasn't certain she stood a chance of winning.

But then, perhaps the term was relative.

Chapter 10

"It's not going to rain?" She sounded so disappointed, he almost wished he could conjure up a storm. Of course, he wasn't a sorcerer. He was just a man. Half a man, at that.

"No. It's just heat lightning. Nature's idea of a practical joke." He came up to stand behind her, not touching her, but still close enough to feel the rise and fall of her breathing.

He'd stood in the doorway watching her for longer than he cared to admit. She'd looked so lost somehow, swallowed up by the dark of his apartment. Hell, the dark of his life. He hated the thought that any of what was happening to him could touch her.

The sensible thing to do was dismiss her.

Send her packing. Back to Boston. As far away from this nightmare of a life as possible. But he knew that he wasn't going to do it. He needed her here. In some insane way she had become his lifeline.

Which probably showed just how screwed up his thinking had become. She'd been here for less than three days and already he was making her into a touchstone of sorts. Maybe he *was* crazy. He'd certainly been through more than enough to qualify him for a breakdown.

"Does it ever rain here?" She'd turned to face him, her green eyes bright in the light from the city below.

"Yes. But this is tough country. Around here, it's all or nothing."

"I'm not sure I understand."

"It's dry here for months at a time. Hot beyond belief. And then suddenly it rains. Not just a gentle shower, mind you, but a full-blown storm that washes out roads, trees, sometimes even houses. When it rains here, it's not long before people are wishing for a drought again."

There were words being spoken beyond the mundane. Promises being made by primal instincts beyond his control. He blew out a breath, realizing that he wasn't up to fighting nature. Whatever their course, he wasn't capable of staying it. So he'd just have to go for the ride, and pray that they survived the tempest.

"All or nothing." Her words were soft, less than a whisper. "And then?"

"Then it rains some more."

She searched his face, looking for answers he knew he couldn't provide. "You make it sound so feral."

"It is. We forget sometimes that we're only here on borrowed time. With all our accomplishments, all our posturing for superiority, we're fragile beings. One big swat from nature and we're gone. Just like that. Any security we think we have is nothing more than an illusion."

"We're back to Miller again, aren't we?"

"It's hard to think of anything else."

She chewed on her lower lip for a moment, the gesture reflective of her thoughts, but also incredibly sexy. He wondered idly if she was aware of the fact, then dismissed the thought. Katie Cavanaugh was exactly what she appeared to be.

Unlike everything else in his life.

"I wish I could say something that would help." She reached up to push the hair back from his face, and he covered her hand with his.

"It's enough that you're here."

She turned her hand in his so that their palms were touching, the contact sensual in its simplicity, her gaze still locked with his. "I don't think people can change that fundamentally, John. Not even when they go through something as traumatic as you have."

"So who we are is cast in stone from birth?"

"Well, that's oversimplifying. What I mean is that there's a balance inside all of us. A continuum of good and evil. And once we find our place on that continuum, I think it's pretty difficult to move to a different position."

"So good is good and evil is evil. That's a pretty naive way to look at the world, don't you think?"

"I said it was a continuum."

"Shades of gray."

"Something like that. Look, you're missing the point. What I'm trying to say is that I don't believe you could have done something before you were injured that you wouldn't do now."

"So you're saying that there's a reasonable explanation for the things I've been discovering."

"I'm saying there's an explanation, and that if you look deep inside yourself, you'll know in what direction that explanation lies. You're still fundamentally you, John, despite everything that's happened."

He pulled away from her, his eyes drawn to the skyline out the window. Lightning still flashed intermittently along the horizon, but it was waning, the encroaching night taking away its power, the promise of rain dying with each fading flash.

Was he the same?

His memories seemed to mesh with the man he was now. More or less. But it was the part that he couldn't remember that was haunting him. The part that had him skimming money from his own company and writing checks to drug-addict employees. The part that liquidated assets to the tune of half a million dollars. The part that seemed for all practical purposes to have run away to Mexico.

Which left a frightening question.

If he hadn't been shot, would he have ever come back?

She watched the pain cross his face. Not physical pain. But something even worse. Self-doubt. And the sight almost broke her heart. He was such a strong man. And he'd survived so much. It seemed almost criminal to let someone like Miller bring him down.

She ignored the tiny voice in her brain, the one saying that she was the one who was going to bring him down. It was too much to handle. Especially right now.

Without meaning to, she reached out for him, her hand closing around the fingers of his lame hand. He lifted his head, his gaze seeking hers, emotions laid bare.

"Katie, I—"

She shook her head, bringing his hand to her mouth, kissing first one finger and then the rest, her touch almost reverent, her eyes never leaving his. With a low groan, he pulled her to him, his lips slanting over hers, his kiss at once gentle and hard. She twined her fingers through his hair, pressing closer, opening to him, their tongues dueling, dancing—following steps that seemed preordained. As if somehow they had always known each other.

His good hand found the opening to her robe, and impatiently he pushed inside, his fingers brushing against the crest of her breast, the nipple tightening immediately in anticipation. She dropped her hands, letting them slide over the powerful muscles of his chest, reveling in the feel of him.

His kiss deepened and his hand slipped behind her, pulling her tight against him. Body to body. Skin to skin. The fingers of his injured hand tracing the planes of her face as his lips dipped lower, following the line of her neck to the tender hollow at its base.

She closed her eyes, allowing sensation to wash over her in hypnotic waves of heat, filling her, touching her deep inside, the power of his touch almost more than she could bear. His mouth closed over her nipple, the wet suction sending fire spreading through her. Threatening to consume her. Her hands cupped his head, holding him, urging him on. She wanted more. Wanted him.

John.

The man she was here to trap.

She pushed back, gulping for air, her eyes searching his, guilt replacing passion. "We shouldn't be doing this."

"I know." He stepped away, a shadow crossing his face. "I'm sorry."

She reached for him, her hand closing around his arm, scrambling for an explanation. Anything but the truth. "I didn't mean it like that. It's just that, indirectly at least, I work for you, and—"

"And I overstepped the boundary." He walked over to the window, his voice still rough with emotion.

"No." She followed him, forcing him to stop, to turn and look at her. "I wanted to kiss you. But I can't. *We* can't. I tried to explain it before. I'm your therapist."

"*Physical* therapist, Katie. It isn't like you're my shrink. There aren't rules against it."

"Actually, there are." Serious rules. Career-impeding rules. Rules against agents fraternizing with criminals. "But that wasn't what I meant." She reached up to run the back of her hand along the strong line of his jaw. "You're in a vulnerable place right now."

"Damn it, you make me sound like a freak." He pulled away, turning back to the window.

"I didn't say that at all. You've been through a lot, John. And you can't pretend that it didn't affect you. I'm just saying I don't want to take advantage of that."

His laugh was bitter. "Watch out for the emotional cripple, is that it?"

"No. You're not listening to me."

He turned around to face her, anger burning in his eyes. "All right, then. Explain it to me. Explain how I don't know my own feelings."

Despite her resolve to maintain her professional equilibrium, his words sparked anger. "I am not placating you. I loved kissing you. All right? Loved it enough to have let it go farther. But I don't think that's a good idea for either of us. And I, for one, don't want to wind up getting hurt."

He reached out to pull the edges of her robe together, tying the silk belt firmly around her waist. The simple gesture somehow more intimate than if he'd stripped her naked. "I'm not going to hurt you, Katie."

"You can't say that unequivocally. No one can. You, of all people, know there are no givens in life."

"Everything is subject to change?" He reached for her hand. "Well, I know my own feelings. And I'm a man who goes after what he wants."

She sucked in a breath, heat pooling somewhere deep inside her. "I understand that. I'm just saying it's possible you don't know what it is you want."

He shrugged, but didn't release her hand. "What do you say we agree to disagree."

Despite herself, she smiled. "I suppose I can live with that."

Which was, of course, an understatement. She was treading on ice so thin now that she could almost feel the rushing waters underneath. Never in her years undercover had she felt anything at all for the people she'd been hunting. *Never.* And yet here she was arguing with a man that moved her beyond anything she could possibly have imagined. A man who was quite possibly a killer—among other things.

She'd danced with the devil more than once. So it ought to be second nature.

But then, she'd never met a devil like this one.

Katie watched as the sun shot pale pink fingers into the sky, curling over the horizon and into the clouds. High above the city, she felt insulated. Separate from the early-morning commuters with Starbucks coffee cups balanced on their knees.

But separate wasn't always good. And she wasn't living in a fairy tale. Reality waited for her. The hot summer sun ready to burn through all illusions. The magic of his kiss vanishing with the night.

She sighed, wondering when she'd become so damn poetic. It was just a ball of hydrogen and helium. She turned from the view, rubbing the back of her neck with one hand. She hadn't slept at all. A fact that would have been providential had she used the time to dig deeper, find something incriminating.

But instead she'd passed the night mooning like a schoolgirl over something she couldn't have. And she wasn't a schoolgirl. Not by a long shot.

"I brought you some tea."

Katie started guiltily. Flo Tedesky's voice held a hint of something just beneath the surface. As if she knew what Katie had been thinking. Or worse, as if she knew what had passed between Katie and John last night.

But of course she didn't know anything. Katie was just tilting at windmills. Making problems where none existed.

She forced a smile. "Thank you. I'm afraid I couldn't sleep."

Flo nodded, her expression nothing more than companionable. "I know the feeling. It's the heat. Even with the air-conditioning, I can't seem to relax." She set the tray on the table, the smell of bergamot filling the air.

Katie sat down on the sofa and took the cup Flo offered. "*Hot* tea?"

Flo shrugged. "Sounds crazy, doesn't it? But it actually works somehow. Something to do with the pores. Or so say the English. Even in the hottest climate we still drink hot tea."

Katie sipped the scalding liquid, studying Flo as she poured milk into her tea. "You said 'we.'"

The older woman laughed. "I realize you'd never be able to tell it from my accent, I've been in Texas way too long, but I was born in Manchester. A lifetime ago."

"So how did you wind up here?"

"I met George in a pub." Flo smiled. "He was in England on holiday. A big, strapping Yank. There was something exotic about him. Bigger than life." She shrugged. "I was lost from the moment I saw him."

"You must have loved him very much."

Flo met her gaze, her eyes brimming with tears. "More than you can imagine."

Katie held up a hand. "I'm sorry. I didn't mean to pry."

The redhead reached over to take Katie's hand in hers. "Honey, not a day goes by that I don't think of him. It's lovely, really, to have someone ask."

"Has he been gone long?"

"Seems like forever. But we had twenty-two wonderful years together."

"Sounds magical."

Flo's smile widened. "It was."

Katie stood up, walking to the window, feeling irrationally jealous. "How did you meet John's father?"

"He and George were old friends. So it seemed natural to settle in Houston, to begin our married life with Buck and Crystal as a part of it."

Katie resisted the urge to smile. Buck and Crystal sounded so . . . well, Texan. "And Danny and John."

She nodded. "We didn't have children of our own.

And when Crystal died—" She broke off, her voice quivering.

"You were there to help." Katie's tone was gentle, as she turned to face the woman John considered a mother.

"It was the right thing to do. And I loved those boys as if they were my own." She reached for the teapot, pouring more tea into her cup. "And then when George died, working for Buck seemed like a godsend. He and John and Danny were the only family I had left."

"Well, they're lucky to have you. And luckier still that you decided to come to work for Guardian." Katie put her empty cup back on the tray, and sat down on the ottoman, facing Flo.

"I don't know about that. I mean, look around you. I have a lovely home and my boys underfoot all the time. The truly lucky one is me."

"Until John was shot." Katie waited, studying the older woman's face.

"They thought he was going to die, you know. Were certain of it actually." The woman's anguish was mirrored in Katie's gut. "But John's a fighter."

"I see that in him."

It was Flo's turn to study her. "I think that maybe you do. But he's more than that. John feels things that others don't. He was sensitive as a child, and that sensitivity has matured into a depth of character that most people don't see. There's so much of John that he keeps hidden away. Especially now."

Katie understood the need to hide away part of oneself, understood it at a soul-deep level. But she wasn't about to share that fact with Florence Tedesky. "I'm not surprised that he keeps part of himself separate. Guardian seems to be his lifeblood, and unfortunately it also seems to have the potential to suck him dry."

"An astute comment. You care about him, don't you?"

Katie was startled, wondering how much the older

woman could see. "He's my patient, Flo. Of course I care about him. It would be impossible to work with someone so closely and not care. But it's purely professional."

The older woman smiled, nodding her acceptance, her eyes signaling just the opposite. Flo Tedesky definitely saw too damn much.

Katie stood up again, suddenly restless. "Why do you think John gave all that money to Derek Miller?"

Flo's expression was immediately guarded. The mother hen protecting her chick. "It could be for any number of reasons. You have to understand something about John. He's generous to a fault. And if Derek came to him in trouble, I wouldn't put it past John to help him out. No matter the personal cost."

"But that's just it. It wasn't personal. It was Guardian money."

Flo nodded, her brows drawn together in a frown. "I've thought about that. But it's entirely possible that John simply used that account because he had access to it. He certainly would have had no problems paying it back." She obviously wasn't aware of the money John had taken to Mexico. Flo's gaze met hers. "Even with the money he took to Mexico, Katie. He still had more than enough to repay the Guardian account."

The woman was fast moving into the realm of mind-reader. She met Flo's gaze head-on. "It was my understanding John hadn't told anyone else about the money."

The best defense was always a good offense. How many times had her father told her that?

"He hasn't." Guilt washed over her face, guilt followed by regret. "I found the withdrawal myself." Flo nervously fingered the thin edge of the teacup. "I found it four months ago."

"And you didn't tell anyone?" Katie tried but

couldn't keep the surprise from her voice. "Not even John?"

Flo put down the cup on the tray, the china clattering as it landed. "He wasn't in any shape to find out. As I said, the doctors didn't expect him to live. And when he did, it was still touch and go. They weren't certain he'd ever walk. Not to mention the memory thing. I'd hoped that there'd never be a need to explain it."

"But sooner or later someone was bound to find it, Flo."

"I know. I thought about doing away with the evidence, but that seemed to be going too far. I mean, it was his money, after all. I guess I just wanted to protect him. Is that so wrong?" The woman looked at her in askance. As if somehow Katie had the power to make everything all right.

If only she knew just how wrong she was. The guilt Katie had been fighting for the last few days surfaced again, surprising her with its force. What the hell was happening to her?

"I'm not the person to say, Flo. I wasn't there when he was in the hospital. So I don't know what he could have handled. But I do know that he has a right to know everything. He's not the sort of man who likes playing from a blind deck. And there are enough holes in his memory without you complicating the fact by withholding information from him."

"Oh God." Flo sank onto the sofa, burying her face in her hands.

Katie moved to sit beside her, sliding her arm around the older woman's shoulders. "It's all right. He knows about it now. And your motives were good ones. He'll understand."

She looked up, her eyes filled with tears. "I'd never do anything to hurt him. I just wanted to protect him from it all. For as long as I could."

"And you did." Katie patted her back, wishing she

could magically make the pain go away. But she couldn't. And these people, despite her growing attachment, were strangers. Strangers who'd made a bed that they must now lie in.

"I'd do it again." The tears were gone, Flo's chin lifting in a stubborn tilt. "He's been through too much. It's not fair for him to have to go through this now. He didn't kill Derek Miller. And whatever reason he had for taking that money with him, it was solid. I'm sure of it."

"Then we'll just have to find out what it was all about. Maybe John can't remember, but there were other people involved. His broker. The man who lent him the cabin. Someone will know something." Flo's certainty was catching. "We will get to the bottom of this, Flo. I promise."

Good or bad. Incriminating or not. She *was* here to find answers.

At least that much wasn't a lie.

Chapter 11

"Get to the bottom of what?"

Katie and Flo both jumped at the sound of another voice, and John almost regretted the intrusion. Almost. It was early. Too early for civilities. He stood in the doorway, his gaze moving first to Flo and then to Katie. "Does one of you want to tell me what this little tea party is all about?"

He already knew. He'd heard enough to know that they'd been discussing him. But it wasn't clear exactly what they'd been talking about. Although he had a feeling. And if he was right, his trust in Katie had been a mistake.

"We were talking about the money you took to Mexico." Katie's voice was soft and melodic—caring. But it meant nothing. Nothing at all. Disappointment washed through him, clouding his anger with a pain almost physical.

He'd been so certain that she was different. Magical.

Maybe he really was addled. More than just missing synapses.

"You told her." The three words came out on a harsh whisper, his anger crescendoing inside him. He tightened his good hand into a fist, trying to control the riot of emotion, his eyes locked on Katie.

She shook her head, her eyes still soft, and a little sad.

He'd trusted her. Trusted her. He took a step forward,

intent on reaching her, but Flo stood up, blocking his path, the concern on her face almost worse than Katie's betrayal. He didn't need anyone to take care of him. He didn't need anyone. Period. He'd been lying to himself to think anything different.

Flo's hand closed on his arm. "She didn't tell me, John. I already knew about the money."

And as quickly as it had come the anger departed. His mind spinning from the overload of endorphins and adrenaline. He stared down at his hands, relief warring with acute embarrassment. She hadn't betrayed him.

Katie seemed to materialize at his side, her touch separate from Flo's, warmer, her energy seeping into him, giving him strength. "You had no way of knowing. If I'd have overheard our conversation I'd have thought the same thing."

"I shouldn't have jumped to conclusions. I'm sorry." He didn't use those words often and they had never seemed more important. He waited, holding his breath, praying that she'd understand.

Her answering smile wiped the last of his confusion away. Warmth spread through him, cleansing in its heat. "I already said it's okay."

Flo sat down across from John, her face still torn with regret. "I should have told you."

He pulled his bedazzled mind away from Katie to focus on Flo. "How did you find out?"

"I was trying to keep your private affairs in order. You'd given me the passwords, so I was reconciling some of your accounts. I found it that way."

He nodded, trying to order his thoughts. "But you didn't think you should tell me?"

"You were in the hospital, John. I didn't think it was the most opportune time to ask about the money. And you have to understand that I didn't think much of it. In isolation it was odd maybe that you'd liquidate that many assets. But it certainly wasn't sinister. I figured it could wait."

"And now? In light of everything else we know, why didn't you tell me?"

"I was afraid. Things were spinning out of control so rapidly. And I wasn't sure how you'd take the news. I still don't believe it means anything, John. You've got to believe that. It's just that—" She broke off, chewing the side of her lip, her gaze locked on his.

"You thought it was the final straw."

"No. I just thought it might be more than you could handle."

"Better I hear it from you than the police, Flo."

"How would they know?" Flo's brows drew together, her eyes narrowing with worry.

"They can access bank records. Probably already have. The check to Miller was enough to give them cause.

"It's still only circumstantial," Katie said. "There's no motive, and some of the evidence is contradictory. I mean, why would you pay the man and then kill him?"

"I don't know. Maybe I was involved in something really off-color. Something that would justify a payoff to Miller. Something that ultimately got him killed."

"There's no point in speculating. It doesn't accomplish anything." Katie's matter-of-fact tone did a lot to help him control his careening emotions. She was right. There was nothing to be gained by giving in to panic. "What you've got to do is concentrate on gathering facts. You still have things you need to follow up on. Like the check, and you said you were going to talk to this Andy fellow."

"Andy Martin?" Flo asked. "What's he got to do with any of this?"

John shrugged. "Probably nothing. But he's the one who mentioned the cabin. So I figure maybe he remembers more about it than I do."

"It's worth a shot, I guess." Flo sounded doubtful.

"Of course it is," Katie was quick to reassure. "The idea is to turn up every loose stone. The majority of them will be worthless, but you never know when one of them will yield gold."

John smiled at her. "You're sounding like an expert again."

She shrugged. "My father was in security. Anyway, I think you should exhaust all avenues and then take what you know to the police."

"And hope they don't come to me first?"

"Well, that would be a bonus." She leaned back against the windowsill. "But if they do, you tell them what you do know then, and it goes from there. I don't think sitting on it a few more hours is going to change anything one way or the other."

"Except if they think he was trying to hide what he's found." Flo sounded unconvinced.

"Katie is right, Flo. I need to find out what I can, and then present it to D'Angelo. Anything I tell him now is only going to confuse the issue. I have facts but no explanation. Maybe after talking to some of these people, I can get a better understanding of why I did what I did. And who knows," he tried for a smile but knew he didn't quite make it, "maybe I'll find something that clears it up once and for all."

"Fine, then, we'll see what turns up." Flo started to gather the tea things, placing cups on the tray.

He turned to face Katie, worried suddenly that he was asking too much. "And how do you feel about being dragged into all of this?"

"It's my job to see to your well-being, and finding out what happened would be the best possible remedy. So you can count me in."

There was a message in her eyes. One he didn't want to read. *Yet.* But it gave him hope. Hope that there would be another day—another time—when all this was behind him. And maybe, just maybe, there'd be a chance for something more between them. Something he hardly dared to imagine.

But not now.

All things considered, definitely not now.

"You're looking well." Andy Martin sat back in his chair, the dim lighting of the Texas Chili Parlor combining with the smoky haze to mask his expression. "To hear the talk, I thought you were this side of death's door."

"I was." John shrugged and reached for his burger. There was something obscenely normal about a burger at the Texas Chili Parlor, despite his reasons for being here, or maybe because of them. "But I'm better now."

"I'll say. You look almost normal. No scar. I expected a shaved head or something."

John's hand went involuntarily to the tender ridge of scar tissue above his ear. The hair was shorter there, but not noticeably. Time, it seemed, did heal all wounds. Or at least hid them. "You just can't see it."

"So is the bullet really still in there?" Andy leaned forward, eyes glistening with morbid curiosity, and John remembered why he hadn't liked the man.

"Yeah. Lodged somewhere in my frontal lobe, a perpetual memory." Which was ironic in and of itself. He forced a smile. "But I can't feel it."

"Cool." Andy immediately looked regretful. "I didn't mean it like that. It's just that the brain is an amazing thing."

"Believe it or not, I actually agree with you. Although I'd much prefer it was your brain being amazing."

Andy made a great play of opening a sugar packet, obviously embarrassed by his insensitivity. "Why did you want to have lunch? On the phone you sounded sort of intense."

Intense seemed to be the word of the moment where he was concerned. His whole life had taken on a level of intensity he'd never have thought possible preshooting. But then, he'd never thought he'd be using the word *preshooting* in context to himself either. So that explained a hell of a lot.

"I need to know about Mexico. About the villa." He hated admitting he didn't remember. Even if it was common knowledge, it was still hard to face it head-on, to talk about it. "I know you offered it. But unfortunately that's about all I remember. I'm hoping to maybe clarify things a bit."

"There's nothing to clarify really. I mean, I offered you the retreat and you turned me down cold." Andy shrugged. "Said you didn't believe in those kinds of perks."

"I remember that. But didn't I come back later and accept the offer?"

Andy reached for a tortilla chip, his confusion more than apparent. "You didn't. At least not from me. As far as I know, you never agreed to use the place. In fact, I was surprised when the news broke that you were in Mexico."

John frowned, trying to place the new information in some kind of logical context. "So as far as you know I wasn't heading for Torreon?"

Andy dropped the chip on his plate, holding up both hands. "Look, as far as I knew, you weren't even in Mexico. You told me in no uncertain terms your opinion on vacations. When news of the shooting broke, you could have knocked me over with a feather. But hey," he shrugged, "everyone's got a right to change his mind."

"Is it possible I asked someone else about using the retreat?"

Andy shrugged again, reaching for another chip.

"Anything is possible. But if you did, I sure haven't heard anything about it. I can ask around, if you want."

"Thanks. That'd be great." John resisted the urge to rub his temple. His head was pounding, but he hated public signs of weakness—and somehow, revealing his pain to Andy was more than he could bear.

"Why do you want to know? Surely under the circumstances it doesn't matter anymore." Andy's expression had changed to speculative.

"I'm just trying to piece things together. You know, fill in the gaps. It's about peace of mind, I guess. Closure of some kind." It seemed he was making a practice of lying, and the prospect didn't sit well at all. But he couldn't risk telling someone like Andy Martin the truth.

Whatever the hell that was.

"I guess I can understand that." Andy drained the last of his iced tea. "Sorry I didn't help."

John pulled out his wallet, and then reached for the bill. "I appreciate your meeting with me."

"No problem. Got a free meal out of the deal." He stood up, obviously ready to end their conversation. "And hey, I wouldn't worry about the trip. So you didn't use the Hobson retreat. It's not that big a deal. You probably just got a better offer."

Which was, of course, the question of the hour.

With the real issue being the kind of offer he'd accepted, and whether it was something that had cost Derek Miller his life.

It was past time for John's workout, and despite the fact that Katie was merely a stand-in, she wanted to be certain he kept at it. No matter what else was happening. She walked through the living room toward the study, the thought of seeing him igniting fires she'd best be keeping tamped down. Not that there was any controlling pheromones.

She stopped short in the doorway, realizing that he

was not alone. Three men sat in front of the desk. She recognized Detective D'Angelo and his partner Tony Haskins, but the third man had his back to her, his face blocked by the back of a chair.

John saw her and motioned her forward just as she was about to beat a hasty retreat. The last thing she wanted was to interrupt. Or worse still, do something to make the detectives curious about her. But there was no graceful way out.

"I was just coming to see if you'd forgotten your workout, but I can see you're busy."

John's smile was for her alone, and despite herself she shivered, the result of little explosions of electricity dancing along her spine. "I'm almost finished." Underneath his smile he looked tired. Really tired.

A muscle in his cheek twitched, the only physical indication of his stress. But Katie was getting to know him better, and part of that was learning to recognize when he was fighting fatigue. "I've just been discussing my financial activities with these gentlemen."

D'Angelo stood up, offering her his chair, and despite the situation, Katie was struck by his gentlemanly conduct. Surely a rarity in law enforcement.

She walked farther into the room, and stopped as suddenly as if there had been a barrier of some kind. The third man in the room was standing as well, smiling politely at her with the expression of a curious stranger.

Except Edmund Roswell was not a stranger.

She forced herself to move, to sit in the chair, wondering what in hell he was doing here, risking her operation with just his presence. "I didn't mean to interrupt." She sought John's gaze and was reassured to see that he hadn't noticed anything awkward about her entrance.

"We're almost finished. You know the detectives, but I don't think you've met Edmund Roswell." He gestured toward Roswell, his eyes narrowed speculatively. "Agent Roswell is with the FBI. Evidently they've taken an interest in Miller's death as well."

Roswell smiled absently in her direction, his attention centered on John. "We're just following up some loose ends on a related investigation, and D'Angelo here was kind enough to invite me along for the ride."

Based on the look passing between the two detectives, Katie was fairly certain that Roswell's intervention was anything but welcome. She kept her attention on John. "Why don't I just wait for you in the gym."

"Katie is my physical therapist." John's remarks were addressed to Roswell, his smile still for her.

She stood up, her intention to get the hell out of there, before Roswell said or did something to further threaten her position.

"Ms. Cavanaugh, right?" Roswell turned to look at her, his interest obviously feigned. "If you don't mind, now that you're here, I have a couple of questions. Maybe you can help me."

She shot a glance at John, who nodded almost imperceptibly. With a sigh, she sank back into the chair. "I'm happy to help any way I can."

Roswell smiled, his eyes not reflecting any mirth at all. The guy was good, she had to give him that. "We were just discussing the convenience of Mr. Brighton's missing memories." She could almost feel John's frown. "Maybe you can explain to me how it is this sort of thing happens."

"You get shot in the head." John's voice was low, the line meant as a throwaway, but somehow in the quiet of the study that only made it more pointed.

"Beyond that." Roswell was still smiling.

Tony Haskins was looking out the window, but Katie knew he was listening. D'Angelo was watching her, his look speculative. Or maybe it was just her imagination. Damn Roswell.

She took a deep breath, forcing a smile. "It's pretty straightforward actually. In John's case, when the bullet entered his head it carved a path upward until it hit his skull. The force of the impact caused a ricochet that sent the bullet forward, stopping just before it reached the front of his skull." She paused, her eyes seeking John's. Again he nodded. "Basically, as the bullet plowed through his gray matter, it obliterated everything in its path." Haskins flinched, his eyes on John's head. "So anything in that path—memories, knowledge, emotions, anything—they're gone." She met Roswell's gaze, her own narrowed in anger. "Forever."

"I see." He nodded, apparently satisfied with her answer.

D'Angelo, however, wasn't as certain. "Then it's your professional opinion that Mr. Brighton is telling the truth when he says he doesn't remember."

"I'm not a neurologist, Detective. But yes, within the scope of my knowledge I'd say he's telling the truth. I've read his chart, and the opinions there are based on the sizable body of knowledge of an entire battery of physicians." She sounded defensive and hated herself for it, but she'd been caught off guard by her own damn people.

"I didn't mean to put you on the spot." The detective's smile was meant to be disarming, but then, she knew all the tricks. "You explained it to me before, I know. But it's a difficult concept to accept."

"For a layperson maybe. But the fact remains that John isn't going to remember anything. So questioning him is useless."

"I don't know that I'd go that far." This from Haskins, who was still staring at John's head. "I think we've learned quite a bit today." He snapped out of his reverie, his gaze seeking his partner's. "We done?"

D'Angelo rose, extending his hand to John. Again the left one in deference to his injury. "Thank you for your help. I appreciate the fact that you were honest with us."

"As honest as I can be." John's smile was strained but genuine. In spite of everything, he hadn't lost his sense of humor. Whatever else was happening here, John Brighton was a strong-willed man.

"Well, I thank you for seeing us on such short notice." D'Angelo nodded to her, and with his partner left the office, leaving Roswell alone with them.

"Thanks for your time." He held out his hand as well, the right one, and for a moment Katie felt a rush of anger. Internally she shook her head, wondering exactly whose side she was playing on.

Sometimes the line was so damn fine.

"Ms. Cavanaugh." Roswell nodded in her direction, the twinkle in his eye unmistakable. The bastard was actually enjoying this. He turned his attention back to John. "I'll be in touch if I have any more questions. And in the meantime, you have my card. Call me if you remember anything."

John flinched, but kept the polite look of indifference plastered on his face. "I will."

Katie couldn't decide if Roswell was being obtuse in general or on purpose, but either way it was uncalled for. And just at the moment she was certain she was playing for the wrong team.

Which should have scared the hell out of her.

But it didn't.

Chapter 12

"So what's the big news?" Jason set his beer on the table and sat down across from Frank. "I had to walk out of an appointment at the *Statesmen*."

"Oh, give me a break, Jason. It's not like you were meeting with the publisher himself." Valerie pulled a chair up to the end of the table, pint in hand. The Dog and Duck was Austin's answer to the British invasion. Complete with pub grub and dartboards, it was almost authentic. Except that it was in Texas.

"Advertisements are important, Valerie. Especially now. You of all people should know that." Jason's voice was mild, but there was a spark of something in his eyes that Frank suspected was anger. He turned his attention to Frank. "I take it you're with us."

Frank shot a questioning look at Valerie. He'd thought Jason was only a periphery player.

Valerie's hand found his leg under the table, her touch soothing and arousing all at the same time. "Of course he's with us. Frank and I always stand together, Jason. You should know that by now." Her tone was condescending, as if she couldn't be bothered with Jason's opinions.

Frank bit back a smile, basking in her favor.

"Is Danny coming?" Valerie asked, bringing his thoughts back to the matter at hand.

He shook his head. "He couldn't make it."

"But you said you talked to him."

"I did. And as I told you, he's on the fence. I think he's amenable to helping us, but he doesn't want to hurt his brother."

"Fat lot of good that's going to do us when Jonathan drags the company down the toilet." Valerie's eyes sparkled behind her glasses. No hidden anger with her. She wore her feelings right out front for anyone to see.

"Look, I didn't call you here to discuss Danny. We can deal with him when the time comes. Right now we have bigger problems. D'Angelo is back at the office, holed up with Jonathan." He waited, enjoying his moment of suspense.

Jason frowned. "So what? He's been in and out of the office practically since they pulled Derek out of the lake."

"True." Frank made a play of adjusting his cardboard coaster. "But not with the FBI."

"Shit." Jason almost spilled his beer. "How do you know it was the FBI?"

"I eavesdropped. At least on part of the conversation. Enough to know that Edmund Roswell was in the room." He waited for a reaction, and was disappointed when he didn't get one. Didn't these people read the papers? "Roswell was the lead agent on the Travis Heights murders."

Valerie's face paled, and Frank nodded with approval. The murders had been headline news for months. A state representative's family had been massacred, with practically no leads at all. Roswell had been the one to make the link to the representative and ultimately put the man on death row.

"The point is that if he's involved you can bet there's a lot more going on than just the death of an addict."

"I think you might be right." Jason stared down at the glass in his hands, obviously considering his words carefully. "There's something you all don't know. A few months after the carjacking, I picked up Jonathan's mail

for Flo. And among other things there was a bank statement. It was already open. The envelope was mangled,
and half the pages were hanging out."

Valerie held up her hand. "Enough with the excuses.
Just tell us what you found."

Jason sighed. "Jonathan liquidated a half-million
dollars in assets just before he left for Mexico."

Frank sat back, trying to assimilate this newest information. "Why didn't you tell us?"

"Because, at the time, it didn't seem important
enough to share."

"But you've known about this since they found
Miller's body. Surely that made it worth our knowing."
Two bright spots of red stained Valerie's cheeks, a sure
sign that she was close to losing control.

"Hang on a minute." Frank raised a hand, his gaze
locking with Val's. "Don't go jumping to conclusions."

"Why the hell not?" Valerie pushed away from the
table, her anger almost a physical thing.

"This isn't getting us anywhere," Jason said, his
voice harsh. He might be under tighter control, but his
concern was more than apparent. "What I did or didn't
tell you isn't the issue. The bottom line here is that if we
want to protect our livelihood, we've got to take the of-
fensive. And we've got to do it now."

"But we have to have Danny." Frank fought a wave
of nausea. He honestly didn't like confrontation, and
the thrill of imparting his news had worn off with
Jason's disclosure.

"I'll make it happen." Valerie shot them a tight-
lipped smile. "Trust me."

"There's one other little problem." Frank was loath
to make things worse, but there was really no way
around it. "Flo has shares. And if she votes with
Jonathan . . ." He trailed off with a shrug.

"Which she will." Jason's tone reflected defeat.

"Maybe there's a way around it." Frank met each of their gazes, working to hold his steady.

"What?" Valerie and Jason asked almost in unison.

"Not yet. Let me work on it first." His smile was only a shadow. In truth, he hadn't a plan at all, but that didn't mean he couldn't think of one. If he was going to be a player he had to show his worth, and this was the perfect way to do it.

He'd worry about the details later.

"What the hell were you doing at Guardian?" Katie fought to keep her voice to a normal level but it was hard, damn hard. She glared at Roswell across a bin of oranges. Central Market was teeming with activity, evening shoppers hurrying to get dinner bought.

"Your job, evidently."

"And just what do you mean by that?" She barely managed to avoid a hiss.

"I mean that if you'd get the information we need to convict Brighton, we'd have him just where we want him."

"Spewing information about Guardian? Whatever secret it is you think Miller was selling?"

"Something like that." He made a play of inspecting the oranges.

"Well, I think you're severely underestimating the man. He doesn't hit me as the type to cave so easily."

"It's amazing what the threat of a needle in the arm can do, even to the most stalwart of holdouts."

"And what if he's innocent?"

"He's not."

"Look, I'm not here to argue the merits of the case. You could have compromised the operation by showing up like that. The least you could have done is give me a heads-up."

"There wasn't time. I went to see D'Angelo, and they were on the way to talk with Brighton. He asked me to come along. Considering we haven't exactly been seeing eye to eye, I figured it was a show of good faith."

"Did you tell him about me?" She reached for an orange, sniffing for effect.

"No, I didn't. In fact, I'd assumed we wouldn't even run into you. I was as surprised as you when you walked through the door. And all things considered, I thought I was the model of civility."

"On the surface maybe." She fought for an even tone. "But what about the questions?"

"What about them?" He shrugged, dropping a couple of oranges into a plastic sack.

"What would have happened if I hadn't known the answers?"

His smile was slow and reeked of testosterone. "You told me yourself, you're good at what you do. So it didn't seem that much of a risk."

"Next time either tell me you're coming or stay the hell out. I don't like surprises."

"Well, neither do I. Let's just say I wanted to see how the wind was blowing." He wasn't talking about John anymore, and she released a breath, trying to maintain control.

"I'm not going to do anything to jeopardize this operation." She glared at him, her nails digging into the soft skin of an orange, grateful that he couldn't see into her soul—particularly the part that was drawn to John Brighton. "Stop worrying about it."

"No dice, sugar. They pay me to make sure you stay out of trouble. And I'm not having your girly bullshit stand in the way of my getting to the bottom of this case. Jonathan Brighton is the key. And I'm not letting the bastard slip out of my grip. You understand me?" He'd moved toward her, his sheer bulk dwarfing her, his stance meant to be menacing.

But he'd clearly underestimated her. She'd stood up to someone a hell of a lot more frightening and lived to tell the tale. Edmund Roswell was a pansy in comparison.

"I hear you. But that doesn't mean I'm listening."

His face flushed deep red, and she knew she'd scored a point. He made a play of adding more oranges to the sack, and then twisted the bag shut. "Look, Cavanaugh, as long as we're in this thing together, we're a team. You might not like it, and I sure as shit don't like it, but that doesn't change the way it is."

"You're right." And he was. Despite their feelings for each other, they were on the same side. And she'd do well to remember it. She pulled a plastic sack off of the spindle, some of her anger evaporating. "But it goes two ways, Roswell. You have to let me do my job. And I can't do that unless you stay out of my way."

"All right." The words were grudgingly spoken, but it was a truce of sorts. "I'll back off. But we need Brighton. If we're right, he's got a hell of a lot to tell us. And nailing him for Miller's death is a surefire way to get him to spill his guts."

"About Guardian?" According to the file, Miller had called the FBI intimating that he knew something about the company, something that had marked him for dead long before he could talk. Roswell obviously believed that John had the answers. And she had to admit that from a certain perspective the speculation made sense.

But then, Roswell didn't know the man.

"Look, Cavanaugh, your job isn't to try and break the guy. We just need you to tie him to the murder. Nice and simple. You deliver the package, and then I'll take it from there. You think you can manage that?"

Their gazes met and held, animosity almost as thick as the Texas heat. So much for the truce. She opened her mouth to retort, the words acidic on her lips, but he was already walking away, carrying his oranges, one more harried shopper hurrying home for dinner.

Only he wasn't a shopper.

But then, neither was she.

"So basically you're telling me we're in deep shit." Danny paced the living room carpet, his restless energy filling the room. John wondered if he'd ever be able to pace like that again. And then immediately quashed the train of thought. There wasn't any point in borrowing problems. He already had more than enough.

"I think you're in the clear. It's me that's looking guilty as sin." He closed his good hand reflexively, wishing for a beer, knowing it wouldn't help anything.

Danny studied him for a moment and then walked over to the mantel to pick up a picture. It was a photograph of the two of them standing on the side of the highway in front of a "Welcome to Colorado" sign— testament to a long-forgotten summer vacation.

John loved the picture.

"We were so goofy-looking." Danny rubbed his thumb across the smiling faces.

"We were kids." John was surprised to hear longing in his voice.

"Yeah. And then we grew up." Danny put the picture back on the mantel, turning his back on it. "This money you took, was it from Guardian accounts?"

John shook his head. "No. It was my money."

"Then I don't see whose business it is that you took it." Danny plopped down in an overstuffed chair. "Everything so far is circumstantial. It doesn't add up to anything." He looked up, his eyes narrowing. "Unless you killed him."

"I didn't." The words exploded out of him, fueled by anger and frustration. "At least I don't think I did." And just as quickly as the emotion had come, it was gone, leaving him feeling empty inside—and full of self-doubt.

"Therein lies the rub." Danny's expression was an

odd mixture of compassion and concern. "And in order for this nightmare to be over, we're just going to have to find a way to prove it. Did you talk to Kendall?"

Kendall Richardson had been his broker for years. "I tried. But he's on vacation. I left a voice mail and emailed. So hopefully with all that, he'll get word and call back. In the meantime, I'm trying to explore other avenues. I talked to Andy today."

Danny frowned. "Andy?"

"Martin. From Hobson. He's the one who offered me the house."

"Oh yeah. I'd forgotten. Did he shed any light on things?"

"No. In fact, he only managed to make it worse." John stared down at his injured hand, concentrating on making his fingers curl into his palm. The gesture seemed easier than before. Although only slightly. A tiny light in the midst of incredible darkness. "According to Andy, I never agreed to use the house in Mexico. Evidently I turned him down flat."

"But you didn't. Because you definitely told me that you'd taken the Hobson retreat. In fact, now that you mention it, I think you specifically said it was Martin who offered it."

"Which means I lied to you." He slammed his good hand down on the coffee table.

"Hey." Danny's voice was soft, cajoling. "Don't jump to conclusions. Maybe you just talked to someone else. I could be mistaken about Martin. I didn't even remember him until you mentioned his name."

John sighed, struggling to stay focused. His head was throbbing, the pain almost unbearable. "Hopefully you're right. Andy is going to ask around. Although I didn't get the idea he thought it was a priority."

"Who else knows about this?" Danny stood up, crossing restlessly to the window.

"The police and the FBI know about everything but

my conversation with Andy. I didn't think it was worth telling them about the retreat until I had more information."

"Makes sense." He leaned back against the windowsill, his somber gaze meeting John's. "What did the FBI fellow have to say?"

"Not much. He asked Katie about my memory, but other than that he mainly listened."

"Katie was present when you talked to the police?" His head snapped forward, his eyes flashing anger. "What the hell were you thinking?"

"She came in at the end of the interview. D'Angelo is the one who asked her to stay. What was I going to do, argue with him?" He leaned back against the cushions, the pounding ratcheting up another level. "Besides, she's on our side."

"Maybe." Danny didn't sound convinced. "But it wouldn't hurt to have her checked out. If she's on the level, it won't matter. So tell me what you know about her."

The truth was, he didn't know all that much. Bits and pieces. "She came here from Boston. Followed a boyfriend."

Danny raised his eyebrows. "He still in the picture?"

"No. She just stayed for the job."

"Well, that's something we can check out. What else do you know?"

"Her mother died of cancer. Her father is in security, I think. And she has two brothers."

Danny frowned. "Lovely family picture, but that's not likely to help. Did she say anything more specific? Where she's from, that sort of thing."

Again he realized how very little she'd said. "She went to a liberal arts school. English major. Somewhere in Massachusetts. She said it was a couple of hours from Boston." He frowned, trying to remember their conversations. "And I think she said she was from Med something. I don't know. But it's not far from Boston."

"That's it?"

It was John's turn to frown. "It's not like I was interviewing her."

"Well, it wouldn't have hurt. We've got a lot riding on your situation resolving itself peacefully. And I, for one, think we're better off with too much information than not enough. Especially when it concerns someone who just sort of dropped into our lives and is occupying a rather large part of your time."

"Fine," he said, purposefully ignoring his brother's pointed inference. "Do what you have to."

He wasn't completely comfortable with the idea of investigating Katie. But he was equally certain that there was nothing to find. Besides, once Danny got something in his head, he wasn't likely to drop it.

"Look, Jonathan, I doubt your Katie has anything to hide."

"She's not *my* Katie." His response was automatic, but even as he said it, he realized he didn't mean it. Not on his side anyway. He did want her. More than he could say. But she'd made her thoughts on the matter perfectly clear.

Although her body had certainly been singing a different tune.

Which just might mean there was hope after all.

Jason stood in the hallway, listening to the quiet. A building had a way of breathing. Almost as if it had its own life. He'd always been able to sense things. Unease, disquiet. But now everything seemed absurdly normal. Guardian's employees were gone for the day. Nestled safely in their little beds.

All except the janitor. Light from a doorway at the end of the hall cut a swath across the floor, the sound of the vacuum cleaner white noise. Cover.

Just what he needed.

With a last look over his shoulder, Jason walked into Derek Miller's office. The light from the window cast an eerie glow over the room, and despite himself, he shivered. There was an energy here he didn't like. As if someone was watching.

He shook his head at his own foolishness. No one was here to watch, and he had more important things to do than to stand here jumping at shadows. Miller was dead, and nothing was going to bring him back. Besides, Jason didn't believe in ghosts.

He reached around to close the door, then crossed the room to the desk. There wasn't much here. Certainly nothing personal. Derek hadn't been a memento kind of guy. Most of the things here belonged to the company. But not everything.

With a smile, he dropped down into the chair, swiveling so that he was facing the credenza. The offices at Guardian were mostly alike. Desk, chairs, computers. No frills. Economy over personality. Except for Jonathan's office, which resembled a well-appointed suite. Of course, he wasn't able to use it. And if things went as planned, he soon wouldn't have an office at Guardian at all. Empty or otherwise.

It wasn't that Jason had anything against the man. He was decent enough. Although a bit cagey. It's just that Jason had higher aspirations for himself, and he firmly believed in sticking with the winners. And Jonathan Brighton had ceased being a winner the minute the bullet had entered his brain.

Frankly, if it had been Jason, he'd have wished himself dead. It was a long drop from the top, and he didn't envy Jonathan his fall, but he sure as hell wasn't going to go down with him. He frowned, forcing himself to concentrate on the task at hand. The last time he'd tried this, Jonathan had barged in, spoiling everything. And since then, it seemed that someone was always skulking about. Morbid sons of bitches.

But this time he was all alone. He'd made sure of it. At this hour, he was fairly certain that no one would interrupt. With another cautious look at the door, he reached for the lamp on the credenza and flipped the switch.

Soft yellow light washed across the polished wood, spilling onto the desk. The credenza was a heavily carved affair. The only piece in the room that had actually belonged to Miller. Jason reached under the upper edge, his fingers searching for the tiny indentations. If he hadn't known what to look for, they wouldn't have been noticeable at all.

His fingers found the slots and he pressed sharply, a satisfying click signaling he'd hit pay dirt. The left third of the credenza popped open, revealing a drawer. He reached for the handle, and was starting to pull it open when a noise outside in the corridor stopped him short.

Fumbling to close the opening, he just managed to get it shut when the door swung wide.

The older man in the doorway squinted into the light. "I'm sorry. I didn't know anyone was here."

Jason forced a smile, his heart slamming in his throat. "I'm almost finished. Maybe you could come back in half an hour?"

The janitor shrugged. "Not a problem. Have a good evening, Mr. Pollock."

Shit. The bastard knew his name. He upped the wattage on his smile. "You, too, . . ." He struggled to remember the man's name. Nothing came. He'd never been good at names.

The man waited a beat, and then turned to go, mumbling something foreign beneath his breath.

As soon as the door closed Jason turned back to the credenza. His hands were shaking and his first attempt to reopen the secret compartment failed. He cursed softly and tried again. This time the compartment sprang open, once more exposing the little drawer. Almost home. Just a few more minutes and his ties to Derek Miller would be history.

With a frustrated yank, he pulled the drawer open, his eyes widening in disbelief.

The drawer was empty.

Chapter 13

Katie lay back against the pillows of her bed, and closed the book she'd been trying to read. A comfort thing. A connection to reality. Her reality. But tonight even *Thunder on the Right* wasn't going to do it. She rolled onto her side, and put the book on the nightstand.

Maybe if she closed the curtains.

She crossed the room, stopping at the window to stare out at the glare of the city. It was a familiar glow. Yellows and blues, neon and fluorescent, blending together into a single heartbeat. In some ways all downtowns were similar. Especially at night.

She twisted the latch and lifted the sash, the window groaning in protest. Obviously John wasn't a fan of fresh air. The rush of the warm breeze across her face was almost enough to convince her to close the window again, but the lure of the night was more intoxicating.

The whisper of traffic below her provided an undernote to the other sounds of nighttime activity. The wail of a trumpet, laughing voices, a staccato backfire as base note. The symphony of the city. She rolled her eyes at her own ridiculous ramblings. It was probably best for everyone that she didn't quit her day job.

Although that seemed to be the case in point. She hadn't accomplished anything. Except getting too close to the accused. Which was what she was supposed to do, and yet it wasn't. Somehow she'd crossed the line from a charade to reality and missed the transition altogether. Well, maybe not altogether.

She shivered, the remembered feel of his hand on her breast making her nipples tighten with need. She was in over her head, and she hadn't a clue what to do about it. If she'd been anywhere but here, she could have discussed it with her superior. Maybe even found a way out. But Roswell wasn't a discussing kind of guy, and he was looking for an excuse, any excuse, to send her packing.

And she wasn't going to let that happen. She wasn't about to let Roswell win. It just wasn't in her nature. She was tempted to call her father. But aside from the fact that it was bad karma to mix real world with undercover illusion, she was pretty sure she already knew what he'd say.

Patrick Cavanaugh was a stickler for honor. He came by it naturally. Three generations of policemen before him. One of them, her great-grandfather, had even been the head of Boston's finest.

"Honor and duty, Katie girl." That's what he'd say.

But where did honor lay? With the job? Or with John? The job seemed the obvious choice. And if she had any intention of keeping said job, it was the only choice. She'd already been labeled a maverick, letting herself get involved with a suspect might just seal that fate.

Still, just the thought of him sent white-hot sparks coarsing through her. She closed the window, shutting out the sultry heat. Maybe a shower. A nice cold shower.

The idea held a certain appeal.

"You're awake." His voice washed through the room, reaching out to stroke gently down her spine.

She shivered, turning to face him, his name coming out on a throaty whisper. Almost inaudible.

But he heard her, his slow smile an answer to the invitation in her voice. Like the night before he was clad only in sweats, the soft cotton clinging to the long lines of his legs, the light from the window illuminating him with mouthwatering clarity.

"I couldn't sleep." He held out one hand in a gesture of submission. "I know I probably shouldn't be here, but—" He broke off, the uncertainty in his face heartrending.

She knew suddenly that the rest of it didn't matter. All that was important was standing here in this room. It didn't make sense, and it certainly wasn't practical, but she cared about him in some fundamental way that she couldn't really define.

But then, definitions weren't all that important, were they?

Sometimes it was more important to live for the moment. And he needed her. Really needed her. And she couldn't remember the last time someone had wanted her in that way.

She took a step forward, surprised to find that she was nervous. "I'm glad you came."

And she was. To the very depths of her soul.

Despite everything, she wanted him here, and the thought thrilled her and confused her all at the same time. She'd obviously taken leave of her senses, but just at the moment, she didn't care.

He moved then, his gait slow, but steady. If it was true that still waters ran deep, then John was fathomless. He reached her side, his gaze holding hers, the question there making her breath catch in her throat.

He opened his mouth to speak, and she covered his lips with a finger, unwilling to break the spell. She wanted him and he wanted her, and for the moment that was all that mattered. They could face the rest of it tomorrow. When the magic of the night had faded away.

There would be consequences, but she was more than willing to pay the price.

His good arm encircled her waist, drawing her close. Heart to heart. With a groan that was an echo of her own, he bent to kiss her, his lips hard against hers. Her mouth parted and their tongues met, circling, tasting, each possessing the other. She ran her fingers through his hair, the feel of it crisp between her fingertips.

He stilled instantly, and as her hand touched the ridge of scar tissue above his ear, she realized her mistake. He pulled back, his eyes searching hers, the pain reflected there bringing tears to her eyes.

"It's all right." Deliberately she stroked the scar, her fingers gentle. "Does it hurt?"

"Not when you touch it." He reached up to cover her hand, his gaze still locked with hers. "I don't know if I can do this, Katie."

"But you want to." She held her breath, waiting for his answer, suddenly feeling unsure of herself.

His answering smile sent hot trails of fire curling through her. "Oh yeah, I want to."

"Then don't let anything stop you."

He answered with another kiss, his lips exploring hers, almost as if he were memorizing them. She traced the line of his shoulders, reveling in the feel of his muscles beneath her fingers. He was strong in ways beyond the physical. It was one of the things she loved about him.

The thought drew her up short, and she almost pulled away, but his hand found her breast beneath the silky satin of her nightshirt and with a tiny moan she pressed against him, all rational thought fading away against the power of his touch.

His thumb rasped against her nipple, sending shards of pleasure dancing through her, and she deepened their kiss, breathing in his essence, holding it deep inside her.

His hand moved lower, caressing the skin of her abdomen, soothing and exciting her with one touch.

His lips moved, too, following the hollow of her cheek until he reached her ear, his tongue sending more fire rippling through her as he traced the curve of its shell, his teeth toying with her earlobe, moist and hot against her skin.

His head dropped lower, his mouth trailing along the line of her shoulder, his kisses teasing in their simplicity, his hand continuing to move across her skin. His mouth found the crest of her breast, his teeth grazing against her nipple, the hot, sweet suction tantalizing with its promise of things to come.

Urgency built within her. The need for something more. For connection, belonging. The part of her she kept locked away clamoring for release.

With a gentle tug, she pulled him toward the bed, waiting for him to sit, shivering at the intensity in his dark eyes. She knelt before him, undulating to a rhythm in her head, and slowly unbuttoned the buttons on her nightshirt, each in turn, top to bottom, her eyes never leaving his.

Then with a shy smile, she pushed the nightshirt off her shoulders, letting it fall around her in a pool of pale green satin. Naked now, she knelt before him, praying that he'd still want her. That he wouldn't be disappointed.

His gaze raked across her, sending gooseflesh rippling along her skin. With his good hand he reached out to trace the puckered redness of her scar. She held her breath, waiting.

"War wound?" There was a gentle teasing in his voice. Acceptance. Her heart swelled.

"Car accident." The lie was bitter, but now was not the time for confession.

With a swiftness that belied his own injuries, he closed his arms around her, the contact of her breasts against his chest exquisite, velvet and leather. She closed her eyes, and opened her mouth to his kiss, drinking him in, wanting the night to last forever. Their fervor increased, each touch, each movement raising the stakes, heightening her pleasure.

And his.

Oh, please, God, let her be pleasing him.

He pulled her down so that she was straddling him, his erection hard against her. With trembling hands, she pushed the sweats away, her breath catching at the sight of him. Fully man. Carefully easing the pants away, she lay on top of him, body to body. His sinewy strength the perfect foil for her soft curves. They fit together almost as if it had been preordained.

And for a moment she simply reveled in the contact. Then her need took over. With a passion she hadn't known she possessed, she began to taste him. All of him. The salty skin at the corners of his eyes. His beard-stubbled chin. The softer skin of his neck, and the silky strength of his chest.

She took his nipples into her mouth, caressing first one then the other with her tongue. Delighted when they responded to her touch. Moving lower, she sampled the work-hardened skin of his belly, tracing the line of it with her tongue.

And finally, finally, her lips found the velvety heat of his manhood. She ran her tongue along its length, pleased to feel him tense in pleasure, his hand stroking her hair, urging her onward. With a smile, she took him into her mouth, laving him, sucking him, loving him.

She felt him grow harder, even as her own desire burgeoned, and then he was urging her upward until she was straddling him again, their gazes locked. There would be no turning back. She was cognizant enough to know that. This wasn't a casual dalliance. Whatever they were in the other parts of their lives, they were about to commit to something here that would not easily be broken.

A part of her, the rational, sane side, was screaming a warning, but the rest of her, the part that was Katie, cherished the moment. And the man.

She raised herself slowly, and still holding his gaze, impaled herself on him, the pure pleasure of it threatening to shatter her into pieces.

As if he knew her thoughts, he reached for her, his hands, both of them, settling against her hips. Warm and real. Strong. Whole. And together, they began to dance. Up and down, in and out. Each stroke taking them higher, until she could no longer tell where he ended and she began.

She closed her eyes, letting sensation carry her away. Aware of only the feel of him inside her, filling her, holding her, binding them together with every stroke.

And then there was nothing but the warmth of his touch and light in his eyes, her own joy reflected in the dark mirror of his gaze.

The simple truth was that there were more bills than he could afford to pay. Frank looked at the innocent-looking piles of envelopes. They had the power to topple his world. House payment, car payment, country club, housekeeper. A life suited for the head of a corporation, not a mid-level programmer. But Jessica liked creature comforts, and more importantly, she liked status.

If he couldn't give her the latter, at least he could provide the former. Except even that was a lie. He'd maxed out the credit cards long ago, and their home already had a second mortgage. Sooner or later Jessica was bound to find out.

And when she did—she was gone.

He buried his head in his hands, wishing to hell he didn't care. But he did. Jessie was his whole world. He'd fallen for her all those years ago, and nothing she could do to him changed that fact. So he played the game, hoping that magically he'd wake up one morning and be the man she wanted him to be.

But it wasn't going to happen. Not without money.

And therein lay the problem. He simply didn't have the money. He picked up an envelope from Saint Stephen's. Tuition. According to Jessica, their daughter deserved only the best. And that included private school and all the trappings. All financed to the hilt.

And daddy's little girl couldn't possibly attend school without designer clothes and her own credit card. He picked up another bill. A credit card she wasn't afraid to use. He sighed and wrote a check. One that might or might not bounce, depending on his ability to play the float. He tore the check off with a flourish and stuffed it into the envelope, wondering how he'd managed to sink so low.

Maybe now was the time to come clean. To tell Jessica the truth. Maybe she'd actually understand.

But she wouldn't.

He licked the envelope, sealing his fate. Sooner or later it was all going to fall apart. But not tonight.

Maybe not ever.

Not if Valerie succeeded with her plan.

But that wasn't going to happen as long as Florence Tedesky remained in the mix. She wouldn't vote against Jonathan. At least not without persuasion. She thought of the man as a son.

He'd told Valerie and Jason he'd do something about it. Promised them actually. Which meant he had to follow through. But suddenly he wasn't certain he had the stomach for it. Which made Jessica right about everything. He *was* worthless. Even when given the opportunity to rise to the occasion, he balked.

He sighed. Surely he could do this. All he had to do was reach inside and find the courage. He fiddled with the metal ring on a spiral notebook, his eyes falling again to the stack of bills.

The truth was, he didn't have a choice.

John couldn't ever remember feeling like this. Powerful and submissive all at the same time. It was almost as if she'd become part of him. Joined in some intrinsic way. He held her close, their breathing almost in tandem. She was sleeping.

Their lovemaking had been wild the first time, and languid the second. And now he needed to rest, but he couldn't close his eyes. He wanted only to look at her. As if somehow she could make everything okay—just by being.

It was silly. He knew it. Life wasn't about miracles. Nothing had changed.

And yet everything had.

In the space of a few precious hours everything was different. The world filled with hope.

He stroked her hair, careful not to wake her, reality pushing at the edges of his mind. There was no hope. He was locked in a nightmare of his own making, and he didn't have the key. And despite the fact that she made him feel like anything was possible, it didn't change the facts.

He'd still taken company money and manipulated it for unknown reasons. He'd handed over a tidy sum to a known drug user, and he'd liquidated his assets and headed off for a vacation that evidently had never existed.

So what the hell did it all mean?

He shifted restlessly, and immediately regretted it when her eyes fluttered open.

"You all right?" The question was soft, a whisper.

He thought about lying. About assuring her that everything was fine, but that would be a coward's way out, and somehow he wanted things between them to be based on honesty. "No." He rolled over onto his back. "I'm not."

She reached up to stroke the ridge of scar tissue. "Are you hurting?"

"It's not that. I feel fine." Better than fine actually. For the first time since he'd woken up in a Mexican hospital, he actually felt good. Glad to be alive.

"Then it's Miller."

He nodded on an exhale. "All of it really. I just want to understand. Hell, I need to understand."

"Then we'll just have to find a way to make that happen." She continued to stroke his head, her touch soothing.

"I don't see how. Every step I try to take forward, it seems I end up five paces back."

"Maybe it's a matter of perception. You just need to believe in yourself."

He stared at the wash of light on the ceiling, the shifting shadows making intricate patterns in black on white, their edges fading to gray. "That's not so easily done."

"Maybe, but tell me this." She rolled over on her side, her eyes shining green in the dark. Cat's eyes. "Do you honestly believe you have it in you to kill a man?"

"Under the right circumstances?" His mind turned to the thugs who'd left him for dead. "You bet. But Miller? I honestly can't imagine hurting him."

"Even if he was blackmailing you?"

John thought about it for a moment, picturing the man. He'd been a friend, of sorts, certainly a colleague. "No." He shook his head, suddenly certain, despite the facts. "I wouldn't."

"All right, then. There's one. How about your company. It's doing well, right?"

"Extraordinarily well, under the circumstances." He shifted so that he could see her better, curious to understand where she was going with this.

"Right. And would you do anything to jeopardize that success?"

"No." He shook his head, positive of that much.

"So that means it isn't very likely that you'd have been throwing away the company's money needlessly."

"True. But that doesn't rule out some nefarious reason."

She stared at him a moment, eyes narrowed in thought. "It would if it presented a danger to the company. Besides, we know where at least some of the money went."

"To Miller. Which brings us full circle. There just aren't any answers, Katie."

"We weren't looking for answers, John. We were looking at who you are and what you're capable of."

"The question of the hour." He lay back against the pillow, purposefully putting distance between them. He'd been crazy to think this could work. He had nothing to offer her but an empty head and a murky past.

But she followed him, closing the distance, laying her head against his shoulder. "Stop talking like that. We're going to get to the bottom of this. All we have to do is keep digging."

The word *we,* coupled with her heart beating next to his, was enough to make him want to believe. But he was a pragmatist. He needed something concrete to hold on to. And just at the moment, the only solid things he had all pointed toward the fact that he had been up to something. He'd lied to his brother, to Flo, maybe even to Miller.

And that all led up to the inescapable conclusion that he'd been doing something he hadn't wanted anyone to know about. And no matter how much he believed in himself, he couldn't get around that. No matter how much he wanted to.

"You don't necessarily have to understand something to believe in it." She'd been reading his mind again.

He rolled over to face her again, tracing the soft lines of her mouth with one finger. "You're amazing. You know that, don't you?"

She actually blushed, and for a moment he thought she was going to turn away. But instead she held his gaze, a trace of sadness reflected in her eyes. "I'm just a regular woman, John. Full of faults like everyone else."

"Well, maybe seeing is in the eyes of the believer. And I do know one thing, Katie." He moved closer, until their bodies were pressed together. Two halves of a whole. "I believe in you."

"John, there's something I should—"

He shook his head, covering her mouth with his hand. "Not tonight. Tonight it's just you and me. Anything else can wait until tomorrow."

She nodded, the sadness still there in the crystal depths of her eyes. Maybe she didn't believe in him.

He allowed himself a moment of self-pity, and then he ruthlessly pushed it aside. He needed her. And she was here. That spoke volumes, didn't it?

He pulled her even closer and lowered his mouth to hers, just the taste of her making his senses reel. They'd face the morning together, and maybe, just maybe, find a way out of the nightmare.

But until then, they had each other, and for the moment that would simply have to suffice.

Chapter 14

The first rays of sun danced across the room, their bright color the antithesis to her black thoughts. She'd managed to get herself into one hell of a mess. The kind that had no possibility of a happy ending.

She shifted to look at the man sleeping beside her. In sleep he looked so peaceful. Almost as if he hadn't a care in the world. But she knew better. At the very least, he had to contend with his injuries. And at the worst—well, she wasn't going there. If she had a prayer of making this work out, she had to hang on to her belief that he was innocent.

And despite all the evidence, she did believe that.

The question was, how best to help him.

Her instinct last night had been to confess all—first to John and then to Roswell, but by the light of day she wasn't so certain. If she told John, he'd throw her out. She was certain of that. He believed in honesty above all else. And if she told Roswell, he'd remove her from the case. Maybe even the bureau.

The latter was less upsetting than she'd have thought, but the former had the potential to harm John.

She'd been an agent for a long time now, and part of a law-enforcement family even longer. She knew the drill. Sometimes the ends justified the means to the point that innocence and guilt had nothing to do with it.

There was no question in her mind that Roswell believed John was guilty. But more importantly, he thought that John was harboring information he needed. One way or the other, he needed John convicted. Needed the leverage to get whatever it was he thought John had to give him.

And she was Roswell's hidden arsenal.

She was supposed to dig her way into John's life and find the evidence to serve him up to Roswell on a silver platter. She watched the rise and fall of his chest, the sunlight dappled across him. He trusted her and she was supposed to betray him.

What the hell had she done?

One indiscretion and . . . no, it was more than that. A lot more. She cared about John. Cared about him in ways she wasn't certain she wanted to examine, something in his soul reaching out to hers. Touching her in a way she hadn't dreamed possible.

And her job was to destroy what was left of his life.

A hell of a paradox.

She fought a wave of shame, not for the first time questioning the profession she'd chosen. Lying in order to catch the bad guys had its value, but there was so much of herself she'd lost along the way. And now here she was, wanting to give everything to someone—total honesty. Only all of it was based on a lie.

The ultimate irony. She finally wanted to open up to someone, but he'd never believe her. Not like this. She slid out of bed, grateful when he didn't wake. Part of her wanted to pack her things and run as far away as her credit card would carry her. To pretend that this had never happened. That John Brighton didn't exist.

But looking down at him, sleeping so peacefully, she knew that she couldn't. No matter what the cost, above all else she wanted to help him, to protect him, and there was absolutely no way she could do that from the outside.

And to stay on the inside, she had to continue the lie. Which was like stabbing herself in the heart. Because once he knew the truth it would most certainly be over between them. She reached out and brushed the hair back from his face, wishing she were a normal person, that they'd met in a normal way.

But they hadn't. And nothing she could do would change that fact.

Nothing.

She grabbed her running clothes and walked into the living room, her stomach tightening into a knotted ball. She'd never felt so lost and alone. This was worse than when her mother died, worse than the weeks in the hospital after Priestly's attack.

It was almost as if everything in her life had culminated in last night. As if she'd been waiting for John. Searching for him. And now that he was here, standing in front of her, she'd already lost him. Before anything could truly begin.

Last night she'd taken the easy way out. Let him stop her from telling the truth. If she'd had more courage, maybe there would have been a chance. Maybe she could have explained. But not now. It was too late. She'd lost him. If she'd ever really had him at all.

God, what had she done? Wrapping her arms around her middle, she tried to hold back the tears. She never cried. Never.

Until now.

It was if her insides were being shredded, cut into tiny pieces bit by bit. How had she let this happen? She was always so careful. Keeping everyone at arm's length.

Damn it all to hell.

She was a professional. And this was supposed to be a job. Just a job. But somehow, when she hadn't been looking, things had changed. The stakes were much higher. And now she was locked in checkmate, with no hope of escape. She was supposed to be protected. Insulated. Nothing was supposed to be able to penetrate her fortress.

But he had. *He had.*

And now she was standing here waiting for her world to fall apart. And she hadn't a clue what to do. Life was so damn complicated. Which was exactly why she'd avoided one of her own. Pretending to be other people was much easier. Push come to shove, dealing with the scum of the earth was easier. But that didn't change anything. She was here. Now.

With John.

Maybe that was the truth of it. Life found you. No matter how you tried to hide away, it found you. And the reality wasn't always pretty.

She sighed, rubbing the small of her back, wondering how she'd come to this point. Wondering how she was going to find the strength to continue to lie.

Because that's what she was going to do.

If nothing else, she'd help him out of this mess. He deserved it. Someone had killed Derek Miller, but it wasn't John. And if she could, she was going to help prove that to anyone who'd listen. A last gift.

And then she'd ride off into the sunset—alone. After all, she'd gotten damn good at dealing with things on her own. She'd made her bed.

She'd simply have to lie in it.

Lie being the operative word.

"You're in early this morning." Danny stood in the door to Jason's office, smothering a yawn.

"Just trying to put out a few fires." Jason leaned back in his chair, and reached for his coffee. "You don't look so good."

Danny shrugged, his handsome face splitting into a mischievous grin. "Late night."

Jason returned the smile. There was something disarming about Danny Brighton. Like a little boy lost or something. No matter what he said or did, you still wanted to play on his team. "You still seeing the red-head from Hobson?"

"Rachel?" Danny dropped down into a chair. "Nah. Old news. Been seeing a hot little blonde."

Jason's eyebrows rose in admiration. Danny could really rack up the bonus points when it came to the op-posite sex. Sometimes it seemed all he had to do was wag a finger and they came running.

Even Valerie. Although it had been a long time ago, and their parting had been amicable. "So who's the lucky lady?" He actually thought he knew the answer. But he was curious to see if Danny would admit it.

"You know I never kiss and tell." Danny's grin turned apologetic.

"I can understand that." Jason sipped his coffee, en-joying himself. "It's just that I thought I saw you with someone last week. At Deep Eddy. Looked like Wilson Harris's secretary. Amber or Anita . . ." He trailed off, waiting for the other man's reaction.

Danny's grin faltered for a moment, then regained its wattage. "Angela Thomas? Give me a break, the woman isn't even in my league."

Arrogant son of bitch. Still, there was truth in what he was saying. And the bar had been dark. Besides, what the hell did he care who Danny was screwing? "I really didn't get that good a look." He forced a casual shrug. "It probably wasn't even you."

"What were you doing at Deep Eddy anyway? Not your usual kind of hangout." Danny's grin had turned to a frown.

Shit. When would he ever learn to keep his mouth shut? "It's not. I was just meeting an old friend." Actu-ally, the man had been anything but a friend, but he wasn't about to share that.

Truth was, he was in trouble. Big trouble. He needed cash, fast. Without it, he was likely to be joining Miller at the bottom of Lake Travis. He shivered, imagining the murky water closing over his head.

"You hearing any more complaints?" Danny's question pulled him away from his morbid thoughts.

"I'm fielding two or three calls a day. No one's threatening to pull out yet. But they're worried. How did John's talk with Harris go?"

"As well as could be expected. I think the jury is out, but for now he's hanging tough."

"Well, that's something. I guess we're not going to see an end to this until the police make an arrest."

"Doesn't seem like they're getting any closer. I mean, every new thing that turns up just seems to create more questions." Danny's expression was inscrutable.

"Yeah, but it all still points to your brother." Jason hated to push too far, but Danny's siding with them was a necessity if they were going to push Jonathan out, and this was as good a way as any to try to determine where the younger man stood.

Danny blew out a breath. "I know. It's hard to see it all happening like this. I mean, Jonathan has been through so much. But at the same time, I don't want to see Guardian fall apart because of something my brother may have done."

Jason narrowed his eyes, trying to gauge the sincerity of Danny's comments. The man was a hell of a poker player. "So you think there's a possibility Jonathan is guilty?" He strove to put just the right amount of surprise in his voice.

"Of killing Miller? No. I don't think he has it in him. But I think it's possible he was mixed up in something he shouldn't have been. Jonathan has always liked to push the envelope."

Jason's surprise was no longer an act. "If what you're saying is true, then you have to agree his actions have put Guardian at risk."

"Well now, there's the rub." Danny leaned back, resting his elbows on the arms of the chair. "My brother doesn't remember doing anything wrong. Which means whatever it was, it's permanently in the past. And to my way of thinking, that negates any risk."

Jason tightened his hand on his pencil. The man was enjoying this. "With the police investigating and our names in the papers practically daily, how d'you figure that?"

"There's nothing anyone can prove, is there? Sooner or later the furor is going to die down. And," his gaze met Jason's square on, "if you're doing your job, you'll spin this all to our favor."

"Tall order."

Danny stood up, his smile firmly back in place. "Well, if you can't put it all right, maybe you're not the man for the job."

The pencil snapped in two, and Danny's eyes dropped to the broken pieces. "You'd better be sure of your allies, Jason. If you count on the wrong person, you never know what might happen."

Jason watched Danny walk out of the office. He wasn't at all certain what the hell had just happened. As usual, Danny seemed to be straddling the fence, waiting to see which way the wind was blowing.

But no matter which way he landed, Jason had the distinct feeling that his last words had been meant as a threat. Which could mean a lot of different things— including the possibility that he'd found the secret compartment in Derek's desk.

Jason threw the broken pencil in the trash, then pulled a new one out of his desk drawer, wishing he could handle his other problems as easily.

Running was the perfect cure for everything. For as long as she could remember she'd been running. Which was probably apropos to the way she'd lived her life.

Only she wasn't running this time. At least not figuratively.

Literally, she was running for everything she was worth. It was already blistering outside, but she ignored the cloying heat, instead focusing on the beauty of the trail. The live oaks hung overhead like a living canopy, vegetation parting now and then for a stunning view of Town Lake.

The bright red flowers of turk's cap broke the rolling green of the undergrowth, the upside-down hearts giving it an almost festive appearance. She had passed the occasional jogger, but most intelligent Austinites were already safely ensconced in their office buildings.

Not her. She wasn't sure what that said about her mental state, but surely there was a message in there somewhere. She slowed as she neared the next curve. Roswell was supposed to be there waiting for her, and quite frankly, she could go the rest of her life without having to talk to the man.

And that desire was even stronger when she considered the fact that she wasn't about to win agent of the month with the things she had to tell him. He wanted her to help him nail John. And the truth was, she didn't have anything to give him. Which was a blessing in and of itself, because it meant she wasn't forced to make a choice.

Just a few days ago she'd have sworn that nothing could stop her from making a success of this assignment. Of proving herself to the powers that be, once and for all. Priestly was a mistake in judgment. A righteous one, but a mistake nevertheless.

She automatically traced the line of her scar. She'd been so afraid that John would be repulsed. But it had been a stupid thought. Not John. Never John.

Which made her lies that much more unbearable.

She sucked in a breath and sped up, heading around the bend. Time to face the music.

The bench along the side of the pathway was occupied, just as she'd expected. But instead of Roswell it was Jerome Wilcox. Relief swept through her. Jerome she could deal with. Maybe even convince him she was right about John's innocence. And two arguing with Roswell would certainly be more persuasive than one. Especially when one of them was male.

She stopped running, leaning down to gather her thoughts and get her breath. There was a feeling of déjà vu. They'd been here before, but things were a lot different this time. This time she'd slept with the suspect.

Not exactly the kind of thing you want to confess to a colleague.

So she wouldn't. She straightened, smiling at Wilcox, relieved when the man smiled back. At least her thoughts weren't flashing across her face in neon. "I thought Roswell was coming."

His grin widened. "You complaining?"

"No way." She shook her head to underscore the statement. "I just wasn't expecting you. Things okay with your other case?"

He nodded. "Bastard's in jail. Been a long time coming."

"You make it sound personal."

He shrugged. "It's always personal to some degree, I guess."

Now, there was an understatement. She sat down beside him on the bench.

"You got anything new?"

"Nothing that brings us any closer to resolution of the case, but I think we're barking up the wrong tree."

"What d'you mean?" He frowned, reaching down to pluck a flower growing beside the bench.

"I don't think John's guilty of anything except maybe bad luck."

Jerome twirled the stem between his thumb and

index finger, the red flower twirling in the air. "I assume you have something to back up your conjecture."

"More a lack of anything." She leaned back, crossing her legs, trying to look more casual than she felt. "Everything we've got seems to be contradictory. He pays Miller money, the man winds up dead. Doesn't really make sense to pay someone off and then kill him."

"What about the assets he liquidated?"

"Granted, that's not easy to explain, but there are all kinds of legitimate possibilities. And the fact remains that there doesn't seem to be anything that gives us a motive."

"Maybe you're not looking deep enough." His gaze locked with hers, his dark eyes seeing way more than she wanted him to.

"Maybe. But he's been really forthcoming. And not just with me. He's been totally open with D'Angelo. Even with Roswell."

"Yeah." Jerome grimaced. "I heard he was on-site."

"Son of bitch could have blown the whole investigation." Which turns out might have actually been a good thing. But then, hindsight was always twenty/twenty. "But it worked out okay. And the point is that John was up front with him."

"You know better than I do, Cavanaugh, that some of the best con men in the business can seem like one thing on the surface and be something completely different underneath." His eyes held a warning, one she chose to ignore.

"Of course I know that. But I'm also a damn good judge of character. I have to be."

Jerome flicked the flower across the path. "I'm not doubting your judgment. I'm just saying that you're not presenting any evidence that clears Brighton's name."

Katie fought against irritation. "And I'm saying that we don't have anything that would hold up in court should we try to convict. It's all supposition."

"Which is why you were put on the job in the first place."

"I know that." She pushed the hair out of her face, her gaze meeting Jerome's. "I've just got a feeling about this one."

"Feelings don't count. Especially with Roswell. Bring me something concrete. Something that clears the man, and then we can talk. Until then, we play it Roswell's way."

"Which is?" She already knew, but perversely she wanted to hear him say it.

"Guilty until proven innocent. Miller had something on someone at Guardian. And right now Jonathan Brighton is looking like our man. Roswell certainly believes so. And I trust his judgment." Katie opened her mouth, but Jerome held up a hand to stop her. "Despite his feelings about women in the bureau."

"So I just have to keep digging."

"Seems to be the best plan."

She chewed the side of her lip, trying to decide if she should push some more.

"Maybe you're right about him, Cavanaugh." The man was reading her mind. "But that won't hold up in court either. So one way or the other, you've got to find out the truth. Does he suspect anything?"

"No." She shook her head, unable to keep the sadness from her eyes. "I've done a bang-up job."

Jerome reached over to take her hand. "You asked me earlier if my case was personal. And I said it was. But there are all kinds of degrees of personal, Cavanaugh." His expression held only concern now. "Don't let it go too deep, Katie. It's not worth your career."

She pulled her hand away, and feigned a smile. "Thanks for the pep talk. But you don't have to worry about me. I've been taking care of myself for a long time."

And she had.

But then, maybe that was the problem.

The sunlight slapped him in the face as if it were trying to wake him up. He opened his eyes, at first disoriented, and then smiling as memories of the night came rushing back. He rolled over, reaching for her, only to find an empty pillow.

She was gone.

Irritated, he sat up and immediately wished he hadn't. The pounding in his head had returned and his leg ached. But it had been more than worth it. Truth was, he'd never felt more alive.

He swung out of the bed, careful to support his leg, surprised when it responded almost like normal. Maybe there was hope.

Hell, he'd settle for cautious optimism.

Still, there remained the fact that the woman responsible for his positive outlook was MIA. And right at the moment all that really mattered was finding her. He reached for his sweats, using the bed for support while he pulled them on.

Maybe she was in the living room.

He strode to the door and stopped in the doorway, disappointed. She wasn't there.

"Nice night?" Danny was sitting in the armchair, the shadow from the draperies keeping him almost hidden from view.

"What the hell are you doing here?" he growled at his brother, surprised at the depth of his animosity. He didn't want to talk to Danny. He wanted to find Katie. But evidently his brother had other plans.

"Good morning to you, too, bro." Danny smiled, and pointed toward a pot of coffee on the table. "Maybe a little caffeine will improve your disposition. I take it you had an active night?"

"None of your damn business." He crossed to the

pot and poured a cup, trying to pull his thoughts together.

Danny held up his hands, barely containing his amusement. "I just thought you were going to take it slowly. If this is your idea of slow," he nodded toward Katie's bedroom door, "then I'd hate to see you at full throttle. She in there?"

John fought against an out-and-out scowl. "No."

"Too much of a good thing, huh?" Danny's tone was teasing, but John was still irritated.

"I told you, it's none of your business." He took a sip of coffee and immediately spit it back out, his tongue scorched. "Son of a bitch."

Danny was openly laughing now. "Too hot?"

John wasn't certain whether he was referring to the coffee or his night with Katie, but either way, he wasn't playing. "I'm fine. You gonna tell me what you're doing up here this early in the morning?"

"First of all, it isn't that early." Danny's gaze moved to the clock on the mantel, and John was surprised to see that it was almost ten. "And second of all, unless things have changed since yesterday, this is now your office."

"The *study.*" He sounded crotchety and he knew it. But just at the moment he had more important things to think about than business.

"So I'm not allowed in the rest of the apartment?" Danny's smile broadened. "Things that hot and heavy?"

"God, Danny, get your mind out of the gutter. Of course you're welcome here anytime. I just wasn't expecting to find you here, that's all." He sat down on the sofa, then carefully took another sip of coffee, the steaming brew doing wonders for his head. "So what d'you want?"

Danny's expression grew serious. "I had a little talk with Wilson Harris this morning. I don't think he's satisfied with Frank's involvement in the project."

"I thought we had that all settled. I told him that

anything he didn't feel like Frank could handle I'd see to personally." John felt the now familiar surge of anger. It seemed that every time he thought he'd put out a fire it popped back up again.

Danny nodded. "He mentioned that. And for anything beyond the routine, he's happy to come to you, but my feeling is that he wants Frank off the project altogether."

"Did he say that?"

"Not in so many words, but his message was pretty clear. So I'm thinking, if we reshuffle things a little, I could take over the day-to-day operations."

"Have you mentioned this to Frank?" The man already had an inferiority complex, and being taken off of an account wasn't going to sit well at all.

"No. Of course not. In fact, I didn't make any promises to Wilson. I just told him I'd talk to you." Danny reached for the pot and refilled his cup. "So what do you think?"

John leaned back against the cushions of the sofa, his head still throbbing. "That Frank is going to shit a brick. Still, we can't risk the D.E.S. account just to protect Frank's ego." He closed his eyes, trying to maintain focus. Why was everything so damn difficult?

"Why don't you let me call Wilson. I can even tell Frank, if you want."

He opened his eyes, resigned. "No. We'll split the difference. I'll tell Frank. You talk to Harris."

Danny stood up, looking pleased. "I'll get on it right away, and leave you to," he waved a hand toward the bedroom, "whatever. But remember what we talked about. Until we know what's what, watch your back. Okay?"

Not bad advice actually. Except where Katie was concerned, it wasn't his back that needed watching.

It was his heart.

Chapter 15

Katie watched as John lifted the weight, his bicep straining with the effort. There was something so paradoxical about him. Strength and vulnerability twisted together to make the man. She wondered if he'd been the same before the shooting.

People often changed dramatically after a head injury of that magnitude. But usually not in a Hollywood kind of way. Far more often the changes were not for the better. And although he had complained of increased anger and frustration, she wasn't seeing anything that would indicate he'd gone from hardened criminal to responsible citizen with a bullet.

Under normal circumstances, she was put in place to find evidence that led to conviction, but nothing said that she couldn't use the same talents to find proof that someone was innocent.

The trick was to do it without tipping anyone off.

More lies.

She blew out a breath and stepped into the gym, letting the door swing shut behind her.

He stopped immediately, sensing her presence, and slowly turned, their eyes meeting as Katie's breath caught in her throat. She honestly hadn't known it was possible to feel this way about another human being.

"You were gone this morning." His voice was low, almost husky, and it sent ripples of heat rolling through her.

She nodded, struggling to find the control to speak. "I was running."

"I missed you." His smile was slow and a little crooked, and she thought her heart might just stop beating right there on the spot. So much for cool and collected.

"I, ah, didn't want to wake you." There went suave and sophisticated, too. "I thought maybe you could use the sleep."

His smile widened. "I could think of things I would have preferred."

She felt the heat staining her face and ducked her head so that he couldn't see, not certain why she was embarrassed. Only knowing that she was afraid to meet his eyes, to face the thoughts reflected there.

His hand was warm against her skin, lifting her chin so that her gaze collided with his. "Last night was amazing, Katie."

She nodded again, still having trouble forming words. She'd never met anyone like him. Not ever. And she'd certainly never known anyone who could render her speechless. She opened her mouth, then closed it again, her eyes still locked with his.

There really weren't words.

Thank God he was of the same mind. He bent his head, his lips touching hers, sending sweet fire spreading through her body. She pressed closer, grateful for his touch. Needing it as much as she needed to breathe.

There was something in their joining. A strengthening. A feeling that nothing could happen as long as they were together. The rational part of her brain recognized the fallacy of the thought, but her heart was beyond listening to reason.

Beyond anything but the feel of his skin beneath her fingers, and the touch of his lips against hers, the taste of him spicy against her tongue. His hands were urgent now, kneading her breasts through the thin cotton of her jogging bra, tracing the circles of her areolas, first one and then the other.

She tipped back her head, and his mouth followed the curve of her throat, ending at the sensitive hollow at its base. She shivered with anticipation and delight, her hands curving around the hard planes of his buttocks, pressing him to her, tight against the warm juncture of her thighs.

"Ah, God, Katie, I've never wanted a woman like this." His voice broke on the last, his breath hot against her breast, and she felt tears spring to her eyes.

Slowly, almost reverently, he pushed up the jogging bra, the refrigerated air cold against her skin. Then with a smile worthy of a pirate, he drew her breast into his mouth, the sweet suction threatening to send her spiraling out of control.

They moved backward in a passionate dance, until she could feel the metal edge of the workout bench at the bend of her knees. Pulling him with her, she sat down so that he was standing over her, his legs straddled across her body.

Their gazes met and held, the promise in his taking away what was left of her breath. She wasn't sure how they managed, but somehow, with fumbling hands and shaking fingers, they were skin to skin, his heat filling her. And for a moment they stayed like that, balanced on the edge of the precipice, locked in the magic of each other's eyes.

And then he moved, driving deep, then deeper still, and she rose to meet him, abandoning all doubt, giving herself over to the moment, to the man. They moved together, matching each other rhythm for rhythm, following choreography only they could know.

Higher and higher, faster and faster, until the world began to spin out of control, her mind splintering into shards of crystalline light, and there was nothing but the pleasure of the moment and the touch of his body against hers.

He lay back and let the warmth of her hands seep through him. The massage was meant to be impersonal, their roles as patient and therapist firmly reestablished. But under the surface, the intimacy remained, strung tight, connecting them intrinsically—soul to soul.

"Are you sure you're okay?" Her voice rolled through him, filling him with a sense of contentment, which considering the circumstances was probably ludicrous, but just at the moment felt right.

"I'm fine. More than fine actually. Just not used to the strenuous activity of late." He suppressed a grin when she blushed, instead concentrating on the rise and fall of her breathing, her breasts straining against the thin material of her shirt.

His mouth watered, and against all odds, he felt his body begin to respond. She was one hell of a woman.

"Oh no you don't." She stepped back, her tone brooking no argument. The consummate physical therapist, but her eyes told a different story, and he smiled.

"There's not a lot I can do about it." He reached up to tug on her braid, pulling her against him for a quick kiss. "So I'd say unless you fancy another round, we probably ought to cease and desist with the massage for the moment."

She moved away from him, her expression playful. "If you're sure that's what you want."

He sat up, his gaze locking with hers. "What I want is you. But I think maybe I'd better give myself a little recuperation time."

She bit the side of her lip, her face clouding with worry. "I didn't mean to wear you out."

"You didn't." He got off the bench, laughing. "At least not in the way you mean."

She relaxed a little, the worry not completely leaving her eyes. "I wasn't thinking."

He reached her side, framing her face with his hands, both of them. "Neither was I. But I'm okay. Honest." He leaned forward to kiss her, reveling in the feel of her mouth against his. "Nothing a hot shower won't cure."

She pushed the hair back from his face, her eyes searching his. "I don't want to hurt you, John."

He had the feeling that there was something more to her words, something beyond the physical. "I know that."

She opened her mouth to say something, but a sharp rap at the door interrupted, and they sprang apart, acting for all the world like guilty teenagers.

"Brighton? You in there?"

John blew out a breath and exchanged a look with Katie, regret mixing with irritation. "D'Angelo."

The door swung open, and the detective walked into the gym. "I just had a couple more things I wanted to discuss with you." His smile included them both, and John was struck again with the thought that, had the circumstances been different, he might have actually liked the man.

"I'm all ears." Which actually couldn't be further from the truth, but best he could tell, antagonizing the police wasn't going to get him anywhere.

"Why don't we sit down." D'Angelo nodded toward a small sofa near the window.

John grabbed Katie's hand, and made his way across the room, realizing for the first time just how tired he was. He felt her arm slip around him, and leaned against her gratefully, at the same time wishing he were the one that was supporting her and not the other way around.

Someday.

They sat on the sofa, and waited while the detective

pulled up another chair. D'Angelo flipped open a note-book.

"Do you have something new, Detective?" Katie was watching him through narrowed eyes, her expression masked, but John got the feeling she was preparing for battle. "John's just been through a workout and he's exhausted."

He reached over to put his hand on her knee. "I'm fine." Their gazes met and held. "Really."

She nodded imperceptibly and leaned back against the cushions of the sofa.

"So." He turned to face D'Angelo. "What can I do for you?"

"Well, it's more about clearing things up actually." The detective frowned, all business now. "What do you remember about Mexico?"

John shook his head, knowing his face was filled with regret. "Not a goddamned thing."

"Not even before the shooting?"

"Nothing, Detective."

D'Angelo stared down at his pad for a moment then looked up. "What about after the shooting? Do you have memories of that?"

"Some." It was John's turn to frown. "I remember waking up in the hospital."

"In Mexico?" D'Angelo leaned forward.

"I think so." He closed his eyes, trying to remember. "It's all pretty vague. I was evidently in and out of consciousness a lot. There were nurses and doctors, of course, and I remember talking to a Mexican cop."

"Diego Rodriguez."

He opened his eyes. "That's it. Nice guy. I remember he was trying to help find the bastards who did this." Without meaning to, he rubbed his injured arm.

"Did you talk to him after you got back to the States?"

"No. I never heard from him again." He fought

against frustration, trying to understand where the detective was going with this. Katie covered his hand with hers, her touch centering. He focused on D'Angelo. "Why?"

"I called him today. I wanted to work out a few details timewise, and to understand what exactly happened to you out there."

"I was carjacked."

"Well, according to Rodriguez, that isn't the case. At least in part."

"You're saying he wasn't carjacked?" Katie sounded as bewildered as he felt.

D'Angelo shrugged. "It's not as simple as that, I'm afraid. It seems they caught the boys who stole the car."

"Kids?" Somehow that only made it worse. "You're saying I was shot by kids?"

"No." The detective shook his head. "I'm saying that two teenagers took the car and left you to die out there. But they didn't shoot you. Someone else had that honor."

"Someone who wasn't interested in the car." Katie's entire posture had changed as she digested what he was saying.

John understood the words, but the sum of the parts wasn't turning into a whole. He met D'Angelo's guarded gaze. "So it wasn't about the car."

"Doesn't look like it. The boys swear you were already down when they found you."

"And Rodriguez believes them?"

"Yeah, he does."

"And there's a reason for that," Katie mused. "Right, Detective?"

"Yeah." D'Angelo looked at her with new interest, his gaze speculative. "There is. They might have a lead. The kids got a look at the shooter's truck."

John felt a prickle of fear race across his scalp. Maybe he didn't want to know. "And . . ." He forced the word out, leaning forward, every nerve ending on the ready.

"It was abandoned about thirty miles from where you were shot. Registered to a dead man."

"Convenient." Disappointment washed through him. Disappointment and relief.

"Yeah, but Rodriguez is thorough, and it seems someone saw the truck and its occupants a couple of hours before the shooting. The old man didn't see enough for a positive ID, but based on his description, Rodriguez has a hunch." He paused, looking first at Katie and then at John. "If he's right, Mr. Brighton, your shooting definitely wasn't about your car."

"Okay, you've lost me again." John frowned, struggling to make sense of the detective's words.

Katie's hand tightened on his. "I think he means someone was hired to kill you."

The world tilted on its axis, everything spinning out of control, blackness looming large and welcoming, and John fought against the pull, his stomach tightening, threatening to expel everything inside him.

"John . . ." Katie's voice came from a long way away. "John, are you all right?"

He could feel her hand on his face, and in an instant the world righted, his head clearing. "I'm okay." It seemed he was always saying that. "I'm just having a little trouble processing this."

"I didn't mean to spring it on you. I honestly believed you already knew." D'Angelo's face swam into view, concerned, making him look almost approachable.

"How the hell would I have known?" John shook his head, regaining control, his eyes meeting D'Angelo's.

"Because Rodriguez told the FBI. And it was his understanding that they were going to tell you."

"Well, obviously it was a low priority." He tried but couldn't keep the sarcasm out of his voice. "How long have they known?"

"The FBI or Rodriguez?"

"Both . . . all. Does it matter?" He met the detective's gaze, trying to hang on to some semblance of sanity.

D'Angelo shrugged, his expression sympathetic. "I got the impression that the information wasn't new."

"Son of a bitch." He'd gone through the full gamut of emotions in the last few moments, with incredulous topping the list. "So you're telling me that the FBI has known about this a while, but somehow missed the relevance of sharing the information with me?" Anger was quickly replacing his shock. "Considering the killers didn't finish what they started, it seems like a reasonable expectation to think that someone would have told me what the hell was going on."

D'Angelo held up a hand. "I agree. And believe me, I wouldn't have broken it to you this way if I'd have known."

"You thought I was lying to you?"

He shrugged. "It wouldn't have been the first time a suspect lied to me, Mr. Brighton."

"Shit. I don't fucking believe this." John ran a hand through his hair, fighting to keep his mind clear, to think. "What about the money? Maybe the first guys were after the money."

"They wouldn't have known about it."

"Unless I was meeting them. God, this is like a nightmare I can't wake up from. And with every turn it just gets worse."

"I've got a call in to Roswell. I'm hoping maybe he'll be able to shed more light on this."

"But you don't really believe he will, do you?" John had heard the doubt in his voice.

D'Angelo shrugged again, this time with fatalism. "The FBI aren't noted for their willingness to share information. Even post Nine Eleven. It just isn't the nature of the beast."

John realized suddenly that Katie had grown quiet.

He turned to look at her, surprised to see raw anger reflected in her eyes. "You all right?" It was absurdly nice to be asking someone else the question for a change.

She was silent for another moment, then her eyes cleared, and she smiled at him, a poor attempt to be positive. "I'm just furious that someone could have known about this and not told you. It doesn't seem fair."

Based on her expression, she'd been thinking a lot more brutal thoughts than that, but since they were most likely on his behalf, he didn't want to press. He turned back to D'Angelo. "So you're going to pursue this with the FBI?"

"Yeah. I'll see what I can find out."

"And you're thinking that all of this might somehow tie into Miller's death?"

D'Angelo blew out a breath, shaking his head. "I honestly don't know. I guess I was hoping that you'd be able to give me some answers."

"Detective D'Angelo," Katie's voice was low, her tone grave, "do you think that whoever is behind this—" She shot a look at John, her expression hard to read. "Whoever wanted him dead—do you think they'll try again?"

The thought sent a mixture of rage and fear racing through him, an emotional roller coaster he was beginning to accept as the norm.

D'Angelo frowned, his expression grim. "I think it's possible, but not probable. They haven't tried again and it's been six months. And in addition to that . . ." He trailed off, regret washing across his face.

"I can't remember a damned thing. So you're saying my injuries just might have saved my life?"

D'Angelo shrugged, at least having the grace to look chagrined. "Looks that way."

"But they could still be out there." Katie reached for his hand again, her own cold—clammy.

"Maybe," D'Angelo said. "That's why it's really important that we try and figure out what's going on here."

"So I'm damned if I do and possibly damned if I don't." It was a nonstatement, but both Katie and D'Angelo nodded in agreement.

Son of a bitch.

Why was it every time he began to move forward, to step out of the damn darkness into the light, someone came along and yanked the fucking rug out from under him?

And this time, he wasn't certain there was a floor.

"So where does this leave me?" John was still sitting on the sofa, staring down at his hands.

"I honestly don't know." And that was the key to everything. She hadn't a clue. What the hell was Roswell playing at? He'd never mentioned anything about Mexico. Or the possibility that John had been targeted by a hit man.

He looked up and smiled. "It was a rhetorical question actually."

If he only understood how *not* rhetorical it was. But now wasn't the time to tell him. He needed her protection more than ever, and if that meant keeping her identity from him, then so be it. She was more than willing to pay the price.

"Look, maybe D'Angelo is wrong. I mean, we only have his conversation with Rodriguez. And it sounds like their witness is less than credible. Maybe this whole thing is a mistake." She was babbling, but it was hard to order her thoughts. She needed to get out of here, to confront Roswell, but she didn't like the idea of leaving John on his own.

"You know that isn't the case." His expression was bleak, and she wanted to pull him into her arms and keep him there, safe from all that was troubling him.

She plastered on a smile. "I don't know anything. *We* don't know anything."

"No shit, Sherlock." Again he smiled, this one more of a shadow. "Look, the truth is, I'm obviously involved in something big. Whether I was a willing participant is still out for the jury, but I think that we can safely rule out coincidence now."

She sighed. There really wasn't any point in playing dumb. Even his physical therapist should be able to put two and two together. "I suppose you're right. But I still don't believe you're guilty of anything. And someone trying to kill you seems to underscore that fact."

"You're being optimistic." He reached for her hand. "And I appreciate it. But the truth is, we can't really say that. The hit could have been ordered because I was involved in something up to my neck. There's still the missing money to account for, and Miller's payoff."

She felt as if she were stuck in quicksand, every little bit of progress sucking her deeper and deeper into the mire. "Did you ever see the check?"

He nodded. "Yup. It was clearly my signature."

"And you talked to Andy. What about the broker?"

"On vacation. I'm hoping to hear something soon. I left numbers. But the bottom line is, we've exhausted our options. Unless something else surfaces, I don't know how we're ever going to know what really happened."

She forced a smile. "On the positive side, that means the police are stymied as well."

"I appreciate the thought, but I don't much like knowing that I'm part of why they're stuck. I'd much rather they realized I'm innocent of all this." He leaned back against the cushions. "Unfortunately, I don't even believe that anymore. So I don't see how I can expect them to see it that way."

"Well, I believe in you." The sentiment came from

the bottom of her heart and she meant it. Really meant it.

His answering smile was almost cheerful. "It's nice to know I have one fan."

A fan with the power to find out more about what was going on.

"Are you going to be all right?" It was a stupid question. But she needed to hear him reassure her, even if he didn't really mean it. "I've got a meeting at the hospital."

"Go. I need some time to think anyway." He squeezed her hand, releasing it. "I honestly don't know what I'd do without you here, Katie." His mouth still held the semblance of a smile, but his eyes were deadly serious.

She felt a tremor of guilt rumble through her. "It's going to be okay. I swear. If I have to march over to the FBI and make it so myself."

Which of course was exactly what she planned to do.

John stared at the little phoenix standing on his desk, wondering if he'd been happy before the shooting. He'd had everything. Or at least he'd believed he had. But somehow he couldn't imagine that it had been a particularly satisfying life.

It was funny actually. He was the primary suspect in a murder, he quite possibly had a hit man chasing after him, he'd lost part of his brain, and he wasn't sure anymore who he'd been before the shooting. But he'd never felt so alive.

Part of it was Katie, but part of it was just him. It was like he was seeing the world for the first time. Of course, if he couldn't unravel the mess he was in, he might be viewing it from the confines of prison. Or worse still, six feet under.

He pushed away his morbid thoughts, picking up a bank statement, trying to find a pattern in the deposits

and withdrawals from the account. There didn't seem to
be any rhyme or reason to the withdrawals, but the deposits, transfers actually, seemed to be occurring at regular intervals, four or five times a month.

He flipped to another statement, comparing it to the
first. There was definitely a pattern here. Small amounts
of money transferred into the account monthly. Unfortunately the bank account didn't show where the transfers had originated. He picked up another report, this
one generated by the bank, a list of one month's transfers complete with authorizations.

His.

He turned to the computer and pulled up a ledger.
According to the bank's report, at least one of the transfers had originated from this ledger. He turned to the
proper account and searched for the corresponding
date, but there was no notation of a transfer. He
skimmed the account again. This time he found a dollar
amount that matched. Following the ledger line, he
searched for the payee. The line read "expenses," but
on closer inspection, he realized the account number
matched the inactive account.

Someone had changed the account code. No doubt
the same person who'd authorized the diversion to the
inactive account. Which again, if the bank was to be believed, made him the culprit.

John frowned at the statements. Someone had gone
to great lengths to make sure the transfers wouldn't be
noticed. He turned back to the statements. Copies from
the bank. The originals were conveniently missing.

Since the two accounts used were not currently active, no one would have been looking for statements. It
was simple and well executed. Flawless really. He
wasn't sure it would have been discovered at all if D'Angelo hadn't found Miller's deposit.

Which brought it all back full circle.

Miller was dead. And someone had wanted him to

follow suit. What the hell had they gotten themselves into? He couldn't even begin to guess what he'd done. Of course, if he listened to Katie, he might not have done anything. But if he wasn't involved, then that only made the facts in evidence more puzzling.

And just at the moment he had the horrible feeling that time was running out.

"You wanted to talk to me?" Frank stood in the doorway, shifting his weight nervously from one foot to the other. Sometimes John wondered if the man had any self-confidence at all.

He reached over to turn the monitor off. "Yeah. Come on in."

Frank took a seat in one of the chairs across from the desk, crossing first one leg and then the other, as if he couldn't find a comfortable position. "So what's this all about?"

Best cut to the chase. There wasn't any sense in dancing around it. "I wanted to talk to you about D.E.S. "

"Something up?"

"Not exactly. It's just that I've been talking with Danny, and we think maybe it would be best to let him handle the account from here on out."

"Have I done something wrong?" For a moment his face registered a combination of resignation and resentment, but then almost as quickly it was gone, his expression carefully neutral again.

"No. Not at all. It's just that Wilson Harris is a tough man to deal with."

"And you don't think I can cut it."

"I'm not sure *I* can cut it. You were at the meeting. It's me that Harris distrusts. Since Danny is my brother, we thought maybe the two of us, acting as a team, would help to reassure Harris that we're up to handling his business."

"Was this your idea or Danny's?"

"I don't see that it matters. The point is, we're doing what's best for Guardian."

"What *you* think is best." If it was possible, Frank's tone actually bordered on belligerent.

"I take it you don't agree."

"Of course I don't. You're trying to hold Guardian together by sheer willpower, but the truth is, you can't save it. Not when you're the problem." Frank was standing up now, hands clenched, a vein pulsing in his throat. "You and Derek Miller. I don't know what the two of you were up to. And I'll even accept that you don't remember what happened. But that doesn't change the fact that something illicit was going on and that you were in the goddamned center of it."

"We don't know anything for certain." His voice was deceptively soft, his emotions roiling just beneath the surface.

"You might not know anything for certain, but I'm sure of one thing. Taking me off of the D.E.S. account isn't going to solve any problems. The only way to do that, *John,* is to remove yourself from the equation."

John stood up, too, his fury rising, surpassing Frank's. "I am not resigning. I thought I made that perfectly clear the other day. Guardian is my company, Frank. Mine. And I will decide what's best for it."

"Well, you may not have a choice." Frank's face was flushed, his breathing heavy. "You seem to forget that you aren't the only shareholder."

"But I have a majority."

"Not if everyone else votes together." He somehow managed to sound timid, even in the midst of his anger.

John gripped the edge of his desk with his good hand, trying to control his temper. "You're dreaming, Frank. Danny and Flo would never vote against me."

"Don't count on it. Even they're bound to see that you're determined to drive this company into the ground. You may not want to face the truth, John, but it's out there just the same. And if you aren't willing to do the right thing, then you're not leaving us a choice. In the end, we'll do what has to be done. Either you protect Guardian, or we'll be forced to do it for you."

"Are you threatening me?" John leaned over the desk, his jaw clenched so tightly it throbbed.

Frank started to move back a pace, but checked himself, holding his ground. "No. I'm just telling you how it is. It's time to face reality. Whatever you had going with Derek, you can't allow it to destroy what you've built. What we've built. You owe it to us. And you owe it to yourself."

"Get out of here." The words were spoken on a whisper. All he could manage without saying something he knew he'd regret.

Frank nodded, his face still reflecting his anger. "I'm going. But understand that I'm not backing down. I respect you, Jonathan. But that doesn't change anything. I'm warning you, I'll do what I have to do to protect this company. So please, don't force my hand."

Frank held John's gaze for a long minute in challenge, and then he was gone, leaving only a deafening silence, and a lot of unanswered questions.

John sat back at his desk, his ire evaporating into a sense of helplessness so overpowering it threatened to swallow him whole. He might not remember the past, but that didn't mean it had lost the power to haunt him.

And, perhaps, to destroy what was left of his life.

Chapter 16

"What the hell were you thinking, keeping information from me?" Katie knew she was yelling, knew it because she could see people outside Roswell's office reacting, but she didn't give a damn.

"It was need to know." Roswell was sitting behind his desk, the only sign of his anger the tense line of his shoulders.

"I think I needed to know that someone wanted John dead. It changes everything." She gripped the edge of Roswell's desk, leaning forward, so that their faces were only inches apart.

"It changes nothing. We haven't verified the identity of the shooter, and until we do I can't definitively say that it was a hit."

"But you think that it was."

"It seems probable. But I'm—"

"Not going to commit." She waved him off, interrupting. "I understand that. What I don't understand is why you didn't tell the victim. He could very well still be in danger."

"It seems unlikely, considering his memory loss." He leaned back in his chair, putting more distance between them.

"But there's still a chance." Katie pushed back from the desk, the gesture a reflection of her frustration.

Roswell shrugged, obviously unconcerned. "A small one, maybe. But it was a risk we were willing to take."

"With someone else's life." She fought to keep her voice level.

"He had protection." Roswell's smile wasn't reflected in his eyes.

"Me?" The word came out on a shriek. She gulped in air, struggling for composure. Losing it in front of Roswell wasn't helping anything.

"Yes. In part. Of course, we were also expecting you to come up with something to tie Brighton into Miller's death."

She dropped into a chair, running a hand through her hair. "None of this makes any sense. You're telling me that someone tries to take John out and your reaction is to try to pin Miller's murder on him?"

"We have solid evidence that points to his guilt."

"But it's all circumstantial. It doesn't even add up. And you don't have a motive." She stopped, an ugly thought raising its head. "Unless there's more you haven't told me."

Roswell rested his elbows on the arms of his chair, his fingers steepled, his gaze meeting hers. "A little more. You know that after Miller was arrested he contacted us, claiming he had information we'd be interested in."

"Right. But he died before he could tell us what it was about." She frowned, trying to anticipate where Roswell was going with this.

"What you don't know is that we've been tracking a group of Korean businessmen, a company called Taegu International. We think it's a front. A way for information and certain products to make it out of the U.S."

"Illegally." Roswell nodded, and Katie was intrigued despite herself. "But what's the connection with John?"

"There isn't one. Not directly anyway. The only link we had was through Miller."

"But I thought he disappeared before you had a chance to talk to him."

"He did, but when he made the original call, he said he had information about Taegu."

"Okay." Katie held up a hand. "While I find all of that interesting, provocative even, I fail to see how you made the leap to a connection between Guardian and Taegu. Considering Miller's history with drugs, maybe that's his connection with the Koreans."

"We looked into that, but it didn't pan out."

"Have you definitively connected Taegu to anything illegal?"

"No. It's all speculation at this point. But I believe if we can nail Jonathan Brighton for Miller's death, we can get him to roll on Taegu. And once we have that information, we'll have Lee Jung Hyun."

"Who is Hyun?"

"He heads up the Korean mafia. Or their version of it." He opened a file and pulled out a picture. "This is him. Reportedly he's behind Taegu."

"And you think if you can get him, you can stop the illegal trafficking."

"No. It'll take more than bringing down Hyun to stop this. But it's a start." He slid the photograph back into the file. "And there are other fish to fry. Hyun has a second in command. A man named Kim Soon Hee. He's in charge of security."

"A hit man."

"Something like that. We believe he's responsible for a series of assassinations involving foreign nationals who, shall we say, were friendly to our cause."

"Traitors."

Roswell's smile was cold. "Well now, I suppose that depends on whose side you're on. In this case they were on ours. So from a certain point of view they could be considered patriots."

"It's a fine line, Roswell."

His eyes narrowed, his smile disappearing. "Only if you let it be."

She met his gaze, holding hers steady. He was obviously not talking about Korea anymore. Well, she wasn't playing. Not this time. "So you're looking for Soon Hee."

"Among other things. We think he's in the United States, but we haven't been able to run him to ground."

"Is he here in Texas?"

"I honestly don't know. There's a chance. We think the connection between Guardian and Taegu might bring him here."

"You're thinking he's behind John's shooting?"

"No. It wouldn't be his style to use someone else to do his dirty work. But I think if things have gone bad, and it certainly looks like that's possible, then he'd be the one sent in to clean up the mess."

"So what's the guy look like?"

"That's the question of the hour." Roswell laughed, the sound devoid of humor. "We don't really know what the guy looks like. He's a regular chameleon, I'm afraid." He handed her another photograph, this one so grainy the man was almost indistinguishable from the background.

"This is him?"

"Intel thinks so. But as you can see, it isn't much to go on. That's where Brighton comes in."

"You're pinning a lot on supposition, Roswell. Surely you know that."

He smiled, but his eyes remained cold. "I'm rarely wrong, sugar."

Right, and J. Edgar Hoover never wore a dress.

She forced a smile. "Unless you get something more compelling on the man, you're not likely to find out, are you?"

"That's where I'm counting on you. Of course, if you're not up to the task . . ." He leaned forward, challenge gleaming in his eyes.

She was more than up to the task. She just wasn't

sure she wanted the job anymore. "I don't think there's anything to find."

"Well, we don't pay you to think, Cavanaugh. We pay you to infiltrate the enemy camp. Wherever that might be. So go back in there and find something. It's as simple as that."

"Maybe it isn't." She sounded perverse, but she couldn't help it.

Roswell studied her for a moment, suspicion coloring his expression. "You haven't been made, have you?"

Not in the way he meant. "They have no idea who I am."

"Then all you have to do is go back in there and get the goods on the man." Roswell leaned back, locking his hands behind his head, his smile dismissive.

For a moment she felt a thread of worry, the thought that maybe Roswell was right and John was guilty, but looking at him, sitting there so pompously, she knew she hadn't made a mistake.

And in her line of work, trusting your gut was everything.

"This had better be important." Carrying a cup of coffee in his good hand, John carefully made his way between tables to where his brother was sitting. "Do you have any idea how hard it was for me to get here on my own?"

Danny looked faintly apologetic, but not overly so. "Gotta admit I didn't really think about it."

John set his coffee on the table, and then tested the chair before sitting in it. Austin Java had great coffee, but the old house it was located in had shifted over the years so that its sloping floors could present a hazard for people sitting without a look first to make sure that all four chair legs were well grounded.

"You don't look so good. Bad day?"

It was possible that someone was trying to kill him—

that ought to qualify, but perversely he wasn't ready to discuss it with anybody, not even Danny. He sat down, his gaze meeting his brother's. "I had a little talk with Frank."

"I take it it didn't go well." Danny swirled the tea in his glass absently.

"As well as can be expected, I guess." John reflexively tightened his fingers, grateful when they responded. "He wasn't pleased. In fact, he was downright hostile. He definitely counts himself a member of the John-should-resign team."

"Valerie's always led him around by the nose. But I am surprised he thought he could intimidate you." Danny's tone was derisive.

"Well, in some ways I guess I can't blame him, and to his credit, he's just trying to protect Guardian." John sighed. "Anyway, bottom line is that he's upset and swears he'll force me to resign if I don't do it myself."

"So you going to resign?" Danny's expression was guarded.

"You still think I should?" He was testing his brother and he knew it, but some part of him needed to know where he stood.

"I trust you." Danny shrugged, taking a sip of his tea. "I feel confident that whatever you decide to do, it'll be best for the company."

John felt emotion welling, an absurd sense of gratitude. "I just wish the others had the same faith in me." Hell, he wished he had that kind of faith himself.

Danny shrugged again. "They're not your brother."

John reached across the table to squeeze his brother's hand. Despite Danny's flippancy, at the end of the day, he could be counted on. Blood definitely ran thicker than water—at least for the Brightons.

"Okay." Danny pulled his hand away, obviously embarrassed. "Enough with the loyalty crap. We've got more important things to talk about." He leaned forward, something in his voice sending a shiver of worry chasing down John's spine. "I did a little poking around."

The hairs on John's neck rose, and he prepared himself for the worst. "You're talking about Katie."

Danny nodded, and reached for the file folder laying on the table. "I started at the hospital, and according to her personnel file she checks out." He pulled a sheet of paper from the folder, handing it to John. "Right down to the 'Med' place. Med*field* actually. It says here that Kathleen Alicia Cavanaugh is from Medfield, Massachusetts." Danny pointed to the appropriate blank. "It's just outside of Boston. She went to school in New Adams, at a liberal arts school."

John met his brother's gaze, knowing his face reflected his confusion. "So what's the problem?"

Danny blew out a long breath. "It took me a while to get hold of the hospital record. Red tape. So in the meantime, I did some investigating on my own." He sat back, his gaze troubled. "You'd said Katie was from 'Med' something. That seemed like a good place to start. Only it turns out there's more than one town in Massachusetts with that prefix."

"Meaning?" John could feel his impatience building, and focused on his brother, trying not to let his anger get the better of him.

"That I found another town that fit the criteria Katie gave you. A town called Med*way*. It's right outside of Boston, too. I hadn't seen the hospital records yet, so it seemed as likely as anyplace else. It's a little place. The kind of town where they think everything is news. I found a website, and started digging through the newspaper's archives." He pulled another piece of paper from the folder. "Turns out they had a police chief there by the name of Patrick Cavanaugh."

The niggle of worry was blossoming rapidly. He looked down at the sheet of paper. It was an article about the police chief. Something about his retirement.

He scanned down the page, stopping when he came to the end. The article listed the man's living family.

A daughter and two sons.

"The facts fit." Danny sounded almost apologetic.

John looked up to meet his brother's troubled gaze. "So did the hospital records. Besides, there's an obvious fallacy here." He nodded at the article in his hand. "This man's daughter is named Kaitlin. Not Kathleen."

"You know as well as I do that Kaitlin is another version of Kathleen. Besides, there's more." He handed over another piece of paper, this one a photograph.

It was bad photography combined with an ink-jet printer, but he could see the woman in the picture, recognize the face.

Katie.

He read the caption underneath, his heart constricting, his stomach churning.

Kaitlin.

"She graduated at the top of her law class. Harvard. That's the picture that ran in the Medway paper just afterward. I found it in the archives." Danny's tone was grim. "You agree that it's her?"

"It's her." He stared down at the picture, her green eyes mocking him.

"I'm sorry." Danny's voice was full of regret.

John dropped the photo, his tortured gaze meeting his brother's. "What about the personnel records?"

"I did some more digging. The Kathleen Cavanaugh from Medfield doesn't exist. At least not matching the facts Katie gave you. According to what I could find, the woman lived there, went to college at New Adams, and then for all practical purposes disappeared until she resurfaced a few months ago in the hospital's personnel records."

"And Kaitlin?"

"Was at school in New Adams approximately the same time as Kathleen."

"So she's pretending to be this other woman?" His

heart constricted, the pain more than physical, her betrayal cutting soul deep. "Why?"

Danny took a deep breath, obviously fortifying himself. "Looks like it's her job. After I found this, and then the personnel records, I checked with some other sources I have, and it looks like Katie Cavanaugh is FBI." Their eyes locked, Danny's reflecting his pain. "I really am sorry, John."

The air rushed out of him on a gasp, as if someone had punched him in the gut, the oxygen in the room suddenly too heavy to breathe. His head felt like it was exploding, the pounding making everything else dim to shadows, edges of black framing his vision. She'd lied. All of it, everything—it was a lie.

Rage fought with anguish as he tried to assimilate his brother's words. "You're certain of this?"

Danny nodded, looking as if he wanted to run for the door. "I'm positive. Or at least my source is positive."

"Who the hell is your source?" He hadn't meant to yell, but his mouth seemed to have other ideas, his words spilling out into the coffeehouse, almost tangible things. People turned to look, but he didn't care.

"You don't want to know. Besides, I promised anonymity. But you can believe it. It's all in here." He tapped the file with a finger. "The dying mother, the brothers, father in security. All of it fits. She must have told you more than she meant to."

He thought of the night when she'd first shared a part of herself. When he believed they'd connected. Kindred spirits in the dark. None of it was real. He'd clung to her as bedrock, something to believe in, to hold on to, and it was all an illusion.

She'd taken him for one hell of a ride.

And now he was left to pay the price.

Katie stood in the doorway to John's office, absurdly disappointed. She'd expected him to be here. She'd looked everywhere else, his bedroom, the gym, even the offices downstairs. Jason Pollock had assured her he was in the building. But now he was nowhere to be found.

Which alarmed her more than she cared to admit. Common sense told her he was all right. If someone still wanted him dead, they'd had more than ample opportunity. The odds were that his loss of memory had in fact saved his life.

And, despite the cost to him, she was grateful.

Still, there was danger out there. Danger that circumstantial facts were going to be used to try and create a case against him. A case that could lead to his being charged with Miller's murder. But even that was only a weak possibility at best. Unless something more happened, the facts in evidence simply didn't add up.

So he should be fine.

But he wasn't. And she knew it.

John Brighton was the kind of man who needed to control his world. His injury had robbed him of that. Taken away his sense of self. And if she could, she was determined to help him get it back. To prove his innocence. It was the one thing she could do for him.

Not that it would matter in the end. Regardless of what she accomplished, she'd eventually have to tell him who she really was, and once he knew, everything would change, the connection between them disappearing forever.

Forever.

She shook her head, trying to banish her thoughts. What she needed to do was concentrate on the present. The future would catch up to her soon enough. Right now she needed to find John.

"Perhaps if you stand there long enough you can conjure him out of thin air."

Katie jumped, despite herself, then turned to see Flo's smiling face. There was something comforting about the

woman. Maternal. It had been a long time since someone had smiled at her like that. "I guess maybe that's
what I was hoping. I've looked everywhere for him. So
this was my last shot. Unless you know where he is?"

Flo walked over to the window, leaning comfortably
back against the sill. "I don't know for sure, but if your
face is anything to judge by, I'd say he's on the roof."

"I beg your pardon?" Katie sat down on the sofa, her
puzzled gaze meeting Flo's.

Flo's smile softened. "Ever since he was a little boy,
he's always tried to get as close to the sky as possible. I
used to think he'd become a pilot or something. He was
always climbing up things. Turns out it's just his way of
escaping."

"From what?"

"Everything, anything. Whenever he's troubled
about something, he heads for the tallest place around.
A tree, a roof, Mount Bonnell. Somewhere where he can
rise above it all, I guess. I think that's part of why he
chose to live up here." She waved a hand at the blue sky
out the window.

Katie watched a bird dive past, the sun sparkling off
its wing. Maybe there was tranquillity out there. If so,
John more than deserved it. "It's beautiful."

"But not real. You can't isolate yourself from life,
Katie. There's so much more to it than floating above it
all. Life is about getting messy. Jumping in right up to
your eyeballs, and slogging through it like everyone
else."

"And you don't think John's doing that?"

"Certainly not before his injury. Things have always
come easily to John."

"But he built Guardian from the ground up." Katie
picked up a pillow, hugging it close, trying to see John
the way that Flo did.

"Yes, he did. He put everything into it. But Guardian
is just a company. It can't keep him warm at night, or

hold his hand when things are going badly. It can't even celebrate with him when things are going well." She crossed her arms over her chest, her eyes dark with concern. "There needs to be more to his life than that."

"But you said yourself he cares about others. Look at what he did for Miller."

"He has a wonderful heart, don't get me wrong. But he's afraid to risk it."

"Maybe he has good reason." The statement was out before Katie had time to think about it, and she knew she sounded defensive, but it was almost as if they were talking about her life instead of John's.

"I'm sure he thinks he does. And maybe they're even good reasons. But in protecting himself, he's missing out on all that matters most."

"Even if it hurts?" She met the older woman's gaze, clutching the pillow tightly.

"Hurting is just God's way of reminding you that you're alive. I know it sounds trite, but you honestly can't experience joy if you've never felt pain. It's the contrast that makes it feel so wonderful."

Katie swallowed, pushing back the thoughts tumbling around her head, the emotions roiling inside her. Instead she focused on Flo, and the conversation at hand. "But things have changed, surely, since he was shot. I mean, he's certainly had more than his fair share of pain. And I wouldn't think that's something he can hold at arm's length."

Flo shrugged. "I'd say the jury's out on that one. He's still trying to find his way. And I don't think he's decided what he's going to do. Old patterns are easy to fall into. Especially when the world around you seems to be falling apart."

"But he's not closing the world out. He let me in."

"Yes, he did." Flo stared out the window for a moment, lost in thought, then turned back to Katie. "And in and of itself that says a lot."

She wasn't sure what to say. She wanted to reassure Flo, to tell her that John's faith was justified. But, at least on one level, it wasn't. And to say anything else would be hypocritical. So she settled for a version of the truth. "He doesn't know who I am, Flo."

"Honey, I was married twenty-two years and, there were still things about me that George didn't know. That's part of the attraction."

"Maybe. But there are secrets that can kill a relationship, too. Things that make everything a lie." She was talking too much, she knew it, but her emotions were riding the surface now, threatening to break through and reveal themselves. She knew she should stop. But she couldn't—it was almost as if she needed to talk, to face herself once and for all.

Flo was frowning now. "If there's love, Katie, real love, then I don't think anything can kill it. Damage it maybe. Threaten the trust. But not kill it. Love is amazingly resilient. Even in the face of incredible odds."

"You're an incurable romantic, you know that?"

"Not really. I just believe in magic. And I believe in love. It's rare, you know. That soul-rendering connection between a man and a woman. Most people never find it. So when you do, it's worth taking a few risks to keep it."

Well, she was taking risks. But not the kind Flo meant. She was dancing on a wire so high and so thin that she doubted she'd be able to survive the fall. And once he found out the truth, well, the fall would be inevitable. Her eyes locked with Flo's, the older woman's gaze knowing.

"It's going to be all right, Katie."

"You can't know that." Katie wanted her to deny it. To tell her that somehow, despite everything, things would work out. But she knew it was impossible.

And then, almost as if she'd read her thoughts, Flo crossed the room to sit beside her, taking both Katie's hands in hers. "Sometimes it isn't about knowing, Katie. It's about believing."

"So all I have to do is have a little faith?" The question was tainted by sarcasm, and Katie was surprised that she sounded so bitter.

Flo shrugged. "It sounds cliché, I know. But it's the truth. If you want it to work out, then I believe it will. The connection between the two of you is strong. I've seen it."

Shaking her head, she pulled her hands away. "Some things just aren't meant to be."

"Are you telling yourself, or me? I saw you standing there in his office, remember? And I'm not so old that I can't recognize longing when I see it. I don't know what you're hiding from, Katie. John or yourself. But sooner or later you're going to have to face it. And when you do, I think you'll find that John is still there, waiting for you."

If only that were the truth. But Katie knew better.

She was a fake. Illusive on the outside. Hollow on the inside. And no one, not even John, could possibly love her like that.

Which meant that she was, as always, alone.

Only, this time, she found no comfort in the fact.

Chapter 17

The heat was almost a visible thing, shimmering across the rooftops of Austin. John stood near the edge, a retaining wall the only thing separating him from the twilight sky. There was something freeing up here. Something that made the climb up the last set of stairs worth the effort it had cost him.

He had no doubt he'd regret the action tomorrow, but for now, it was worth the price. He needed to be here. To find solace in the wide Texas sky. The capitol shone white in the distance, the buildings of UT providing a hazy backdrop.

He loved Austin. The juxtaposition of cultures. State government and high tech at one end of the spectrum, the university counterculture and the music scene at the other. And then, of course, there were the icons like Eeyore's Birthday Party and Leslie the cross-dressing mayoral wannabe. Oh yeah, there was something in Austin for everyone. Highbrow, lowbrow, and in between.

Great, he sounded like a fucking chamber of commerce commercial.

He let his gaze fall to the street below, little antlike people scurrying to and fro, each locked into their own patterns. Lives lived without thought or meaning. Everything rote. Every day the same.

He'd become a cynic.

Which wasn't surprising when he considered all that

had happened to him. Most men would have suc-
cumbed sooner. But then, most men hadn't fallen into
Katie Cavanaugh's snare.

He'd always prided himself on letting his brain do
the talking and not his penis. But here he was, gob-
smacked by a woman who'd not only lied to him, but
set out to trap him, using the oldest bait in the book.

And he'd taken it like a fish out of water. He supposed in some psychobabble sort of way, he'd had
something to prove to himself. He'd needed to know
that a woman could find him attractive. That half of
John Brighton was still worth a go.

He'd been so locked in his own need, he'd never seen
her coming. He should have known better.

Bitterness welled inside him, the taste of it foul
against his tongue. He'd actually believed he loved her.
John had never loved anyone outside his family. Never.
It was just too big a risk. Way outside his safety zone.
So it was ironic as hell that when he'd finally decided to
take the leap, it had been for nothing. A con. A game.

His gut tightened, the knot there pressing against his
heart, threatening to unman him. He'd never hurt like
this before. Not even after the shooting. Katie had taken
something from him he hadn't meant to give, and
couldn't possibly take back. And he'd given it for nothing.

Ironic was an understatement.

He was a fool.

"Flo thought you might be up here."

The lilting sound of her voice bit into him like a
sniper's bullet, cutting deep, perversely filling him with
hope. Maybe Danny was wrong. God, he wished it so.
But his mind, the part that was still working, knew that
it was fact. The photograph alone was irrefutable.

No matter how much his heart wanted to believe, he
knew better. She was a liar—a sweet one, but still a liar.

He turned to face her, keeping his expression casual.

Time enough to share the thoughts spinning around in his head. First, he needed to confirm things once and for all. Needed to hear it from her own lips.

"I come up here to think." He forced a smile, his traitorous eyes devouring the soft curves of her face. Whatever else she was, she was a beautiful woman.

"I'm surprised you could manage the stairs." Her voice held nothing but concern. If he hadn't known better, he'd have sworn she was really worried about him.

"I'm not a cripple." Despite his resolve, his words were harsh. "It was slow going, but I did it."

"I guess if something is important enough, one can manage almost anything."

"And what's important to you, Katie?" His gaze collided with hers, her green eyes narrowed in confusion.

"I don't understand what you're asking me." She took a step toward him, and involuntarily he moved back.

"It's not a hard question. What matters most to you?" He leaned back against the wall, the hot breeze caressing his face.

"Until recently I would have said it was my job."

"And now?" He held his breath, waiting.

"And now, I don't know. Some of what I thought was important isn't anymore. I can't really explain it. It's like the things I believed in have been turned inside out. What's black is white and vice versa."

"Because of me." He narrowed his eyes, watching her, wondering if there was any truth at all in what she was saying.

"Yes." The single word hung between them, and he moved forward, lifting her chin with his good hand, searching her face for some hint of truth.

He dipped his head, pressing his lips to hers, the touch fleeting, then dropped his hand and stepped away, his gaze still locked with hers. "Everything isn't always what it seems, Katie."

"Isn't it?" She frowned at him, her beautiful face haunted with something he couldn't quite put a name to. It was almost as if they were preparing to spar, each waiting for the other to make the first move. Neither willing to start the battle.

So perhaps it was time.

"How was your meeting at the hospital?" He moved back to lean against the wall again, waiting to see what she'd say. Everything was riding on whether she would tell him the truth. And even though he already knew that she wouldn't, some part of him prayed that she would. That she'd tell him everything.

She paused before answering, her gaze dropping to her feet. "It was fine. Routine, actually."

And there it was, carved in stone. The truth. She'd lied to him as easily as she'd drawn a breath. The door had been opened and there was no going back. "That's interesting. I called the hospital, and at least according to the woman in physical therapy, there wasn't a meeting scheduled."

She walked over to the retaining wall, looking down at the street. "That's because my meeting wasn't in physical therapy. I was talking to your doctor." She turned around to face him. "Why were you looking for me?"

"I need a reason?" He fought against the bile rising in his throat and forced a smile.

"No, I guess not." She frowned, obviously unsure of where the conversation was going. "I should have left a number."

"It doesn't matter." He moved away from the wall, heading for a group of chairs near a potted tree and some assorted shrubbery. He needed to sit down—his legs were shaking, threatening to give out.

"Of course it does." She followed him, the concern in her voice almost his undoing. "I never want to worry you."

He had to admit she was good, he almost believed she meant it. "Right. That would explain why you lied to me."

She stopped in her tracks, her eyes widening. "What are you talking about? I told you I was meeting with your doctor. If you don't believe me, call him."

"Oh, I'm sure he'll confirm the meeting. But that doesn't mean it happened, now does it?" He was baiting her, and he knew it, but he couldn't help himself. He wanted to know just how far she'd go to protect her identity. As if in measuring he could somehow decide if there had been anything real between them at all.

"John, you're not making any sense." She sounded confused, but a thread of suspicion was there as well, a signal that understanding was dawning.

He fingered a leaf on the mountain laurel, the waxy smoothness helping him stay focused. "Of course I am. You're just not following the conversation." His anger was rising, bubbling to the surface in tangible waves. "We were talking about the hospital. And how you were but weren't there. Just like you are but aren't from Medfield."

"But I am from Medfield."

The branch broke between his fingers, the leaves crushed. "Don't you mean Med*way*?"

"I . . . I don't know what you're talking about." She was fumbling for words, now, her attempt to sound indignant failing miserably.

He fought against his need to go to her, to pull her into his arms and pretend that none of this was happening, to pretend that they were the only two people in the world that mattered. But it was a lie. And unlike Katie, he wasn't going to base a relationship on half-truths and empty promises.

He narrowed his eyes, locking his reservations deep inside. It was time for the final move. "I'm talking about the truth, *Kaitlin*. I think I've been lied to enough."

She blinked, her mouth opening then shutting again, tears glistening in her traitorous green eyes.

Game, set, and match.

He'd won—or lost. Quite frankly, he wasn't sure he knew the difference anymore, and more importantly, he wasn't sure that he cared.

Katie felt the tears welling in her eyes, and fought to keep them at bay. Nothing was ever gained by crying. She'd known the risks when she took this job. Well, maybe not all of them. But she'd known there *were* risks, and that was almost the same thing. The point was, it was a little late in the game to be crying over spilt milk. She'd known this was coming. She just hadn't expected it so soon.

His expression was flat, and if it weren't for the muscle ticking at the corner of his eye, she'd have thought he didn't care at all, but the twitch gave him away, and some silent part of her rejoiced. At least there was emotion left. That was something.

"So you know everything?" It was a silly question, but her brain wasn't functioning, her emotions having taken control.

He shrugged. "I know what's important. I know that you're FBI, and that everything you've told me about yourself is a lie."

"Not everything." Her protest was useless, but her mouth seemed to have a mind of its own. She fought for control. There wasn't any sense in losing it. "How did you find out?"

"Danny." His voice was soft, deceptively soft. "He thought we ought to know a little more about you since I was starting to . . . to . . ." He stopped, his eyes growing hard. "I don't suppose it really matters, does it?"

"Of course it matters." She couldn't keep the need out of her voice.

"No. It doesn't. Not anymore." There was a sense of

futility she'd never heard from him before, and her heart twisted with grief.

If only she could make it right somehow, but even as she had the thought she knew it was hopeless. As far as John was concerned, she'd betrayed him. And in point of fact, she supposed she had.

"So was all of it an act? Just a way to lure me into confessing?" He pulled to his feet, taking a wobbling step away from her. She moved to help him, but he brushed her away.

"No. Of course not. What happened between us was very real. You know that."

"All I know is that you lied to me. And now you're standing here, expecting me to sort out the fact from the fantasy." He gripped the edge of the wall, his knuckles white. "You're not even a physical therapist, are you?"

"No." She shook her head. "I'm not."

"You people have no decency. Did anyone stop to think that I might have been hurt?" His anger was almost palpable.

"Of course they did. We all did. I had extensive training, and I've been in constant contact with your doctor and another physical therapist."

"And I suppose that makes it all better?"

She flinched at the accusation in his voice. "No, of course not. It just means you were safe." She knew her words were ineffectual, but there wasn't anything she could say that was going to make it better.

"Safe from what? Christ, Katie, I almost gave you my heart." His anguish cut through her like a knife, leaving hot, physical pain in its wake.

"Almost?" The word popped out before she could stop it.

"What the hell do you want from me?" He whipped around to look at her. "I'm hanging on by a thread here. And you're looking for confessions of love. Damn it, Katie, you betrayed me."

"I know. But you have to understand it was part of my job. I didn't know who you were when I first came here." She was on the verge of begging, and yet she held herself back, some part of her not capable of dealing with the emotions he pulled out of her.

"Fine. That's a given. I didn't know you either. But later, when we were making love, didn't it occur to you then to tell me the truth?"

"Of course it did." Her own anger rose to meet his. Anger at herself, anger at him, anger at the whole twisted situation. "But I couldn't tell you."

"Because it would compromise your case."

"No." They were standing nose to nose now, eyes sparking with anger. "Because I knew if I told you, you'd throw me out."

"Well, you were right about that." He started to turn away, the muscle by his eye twitching ominously.

She grabbed his arm, forcing him to stop. "If you'd thrown me out, I wouldn't have been in the position to help you."

His face was a play of emotion. Astonishment warring with anger and confusion. "Help me? There's a laugh. You people are unbelievable. You'll stop at nothing to get what you want. If almost killing him doesn't get the job done, then why not seduce the bastard."

"I didn't seduce you." She spoke through clenched teeth, the words coming out on a hiss.

His eyebrow shot up. "Didn't you? You could have fooled me. Is that your specialty, Katie, whoring for the FBI?"

White-hot rage twisted through her, and she swung at him before she had time to think better of it. But he was faster, his left hand closing around her wrist. "I have never prostituted myself for anyone."

"Well, then I'm flattered to know I was the first." His fingers stroked the inside of her wrist, his touch somewhere between sensual and contemptuous.

She jerked away. "You're a jackass."

"Maybe. But whose fault is that?" His smile held no trace of humor.

"No one wanted you to get hurt."

"Oh right. That would explain why you all rushed to tell me my life might be in danger." Sarcasm didn't sit well with him, the sentiment twisting his face in a bitter parody of the man she knew that he was.

"I didn't know about that." She held up a hand. "I swear."

His laugh was harsh. "And you expect me to believe you?"

"Right now I'm not sure I care what you think. But you deserve to know the truth. There's a lot more going on here than you realize."

"Believe me, I'm more than aware of that. The question of the hour seems to be whether I can trust in anything you have to tell me."

"I'm trying to be honest with you."

"Are you? I guess I missed it somewhere between your taking a swing at me and then calling me a jackass."

Her anger evaporated. "I didn't mean that. You know I didn't."

"Katie, what you're failing to see here is that I haven't a clue what you mean and don't mean. So far in our brief relationship, the bulk of what you've told me has been a lie. So why the hell would I believe you now?"

"Because I . . . I care about you." She stumbled over the word *care,* not having the courage to admit even to herself how she really felt about him. Not now. Not like this.

"You certainly have a funny way of showing it." He turned back to the wall, his gaze on the last of the fiery sun riding the horizon.

"John, I know I lied to you." She came up behind

him, laying a hand on his arm. "In the beginning it was part of my job. And then, however misguided it might seem, I lied to protect you."

"Protect me? From what?"

"From whatever is happening here. From whoever it is that's behind all of this. If Roswell's to be believed, we're talking international conspiracy. These people are playing for keeps, John. You need someone on your side."

"I have Flo and Danny."

"But they're as clueless as you are. You need someone with an inside track."

"And so you thought you'd do the job."

"The setup is perfect. I can find out what's happening and hopefully help you head things off at the pass. There's a lot I can do for you, if you'll let me."

He turned to face her, his expression shuttered. "The only thing I want from you, Katie, is for you to get the hell off my roof and out of my life."

"John . . ." She trailed off, hating the note of pleading in her voice.

"Please . . . just go." The words were soft, no more than a whisper, his pain evident in every syllable.

He opened his hand, the crushed leaves of the mountain laurel falling featherlike to the street below, their twirling descent the physical embodiment of her shattered heart.

"Well, you're certainly an improvement over Jason." Frank stood in the door to Jason's office. It seemed that no one worked in their own office these days.

"My computer's down." Florence Tedesky looked up from the computer monitor with a smile. "Jason was kind enough to let me use his. John wanted these reports sent out to D.E.S. tonight."

"Any idea when yours will be back on-line?"

"No. The hardware guys worked on it most of the

afternoon." She tipped her head toward the west wall, the one that adjoined her office. "But it's refusing to co-operate."

He nodded, leaning amiably against the door frame. "The joys of modern technology."

"Damned if we do, damned if we don't." Florence's smile widened. "You looking for Jason?"

"No. I just saw you in here and stopped. Things have been a bit hectic around here and we haven't really gotten to talk about any of it."

"You're worried about John." As usual, Florence managed to cut right to the heart of the matter, and Frank couldn't see any reason not to acquiesce. Might even help them gain ground with her.

"Yeah, I am. Particularly whether he's really up to running Guardian."

She blew out a breath, her expression thoughtful. "I can't answer that. I think he's doing the best that he can, but under the circumstances—"

"It may be more than he can handle?" This might be easier than he'd thought. Maybe he wouldn't need to do anything after all.

"I didn't say that. I just worry that he'll compromise his health to make sure Guardian is protected."

"Protected from him." It came out before he had a chance to think about what he was saying. Which showed just how on edge he really was. He smiled belatedly, hoping it took the sting out of the remark, knowing that it didn't.

Florence's smile was tight. "That's certainly not what I meant. There would be no Guardian without John, Frank, and you'd do well to remember that fact."

He held up a hand in defense. "I didn't mean that the way it came out. It's just that so much of what's happened in the last few days seems to be related in some way to him."

She eyed him speculatively. "I know. But that doesn't

mean there's anything of substance there. The police are grasping at straws, and John is a handy target."

"But the FBI are involved now, Florence. That ups the ante, surely."

She crossed her arms over her ample chest. "It doesn't change anything but the person asking the questions. I'm confident that we'll get to the bottom of all of this. But in order to do that, we have to stick together." She shot him a motherly look, calculated to make him feel guilty.

It worked.

Almost.

"I'm not the one who's been doctoring accounts and withdrawing money."

"No. But you're flirting with the idea of supporting Valerie."

He swallowed, staring down at the tips of his shoes. How the heck had she known that? "I'm not doing anything of the sort."

"Frank Jacoby, don't you dare lie to me."

Why was it he was always on the defensive. With Jessie, with Valerie, and now with Florence. "I'm not lying. I'm not siding with anyone. And Valerie just wants what's best for the company."

Florence's laugh was derisive. "Valerie wants what's best for Valerie. And if you're letting yourself believe anything else, you're setting yourself up for a fall."

He straightened his shoulders, meeting her gaze full on. "I know who Valerie is, Florence. That's not the point."

"So what is the point, then?"

"To do what's best for the company. And as much as you love Jonathan, you have to admit that at the moment he's more a liability to the company than an asset."

Florence shook her head. "That's not true. Even incapacitated, John Brighton is more capable than the rest of you put together. And if you can't see that, then you're not the man I think you are."

He bristled at the statement, his resolve solidifying. He was so tired of people judging him. And Florence Tedesky wasn't even a player. How dare she think she could tell him who he should side with?

At the end of the day, it was all about winners, and if he was going to be one, it was time to start acting like one. No matter what he had to do.

"I think perhaps you're the one underestimating things, Florence. The only thing that matters is Guardian. And that makes everyone expendable." He forced a smile, his hand tightening on the door handle. "Even you."

Chapter 18

"John, when you get the chance, I need to talk to you. . . ." The answering machine warbled on, Flo's voice sounding tinny, echoing through the darkened study.

John reached over and clicked the machine off. He didn't want to talk to anyone right now. Particularly not Flo. She'd see more than he wanted to share, and he wasn't certain he could take that right now.

Maybe later.

Or then again, maybe never.

He'd never felt like this before. So hopeless. It was like he'd sunk into some kind of emotional quagmire and it was sucking the life from him. Now, there was a melodramatic thought. He pushed away from the desk, and struggled to his feet.

Climbing to the roof had been a mistake. The muscles of his right leg had gone beyond aching into some sort of knotted torture. If Katie were here she could massage the pain away. But Katie was gone. Forever.

Good riddance.

He was lying to himself, but for the moment it was the best he could do. There were other things that needed his attention. Little things like embezzlement, hit men, and murdered colleagues. And somewhere in all the questions there were answers.

Without meaning to, he found himself at the door to Katie's room. Hesitating, he peered inside, both relieved

and disappointed to see that she wasn't there. Part of
him was glad she was gone, it followed with what he believed about her, but part of him had secretly hoped
she'd stay. That she'd fight for him.

Stupid thought. She was a federal agent. Nothing
more. She didn't give a damn about anything but her
job. She'd said as much, hadn't she? Nailing him had
been her only concern, the rest of it an act. A charade to
make him confide in her.

He bent to pick up a slip of material. A scarf of some
kind. *Katie's scarf.* He held it to his face, inhaling the
sweet smell of her, his body responding immediately to
the olfactory signal.

With a sigh of disgust, he started to throw it on the
bed, then almost as if his hand had a will of its own, he
tucked the silk into his pocket, his fingers kneading the
material, remembering the feel of her skin.

He was beyond foolish, moving right into moon-
struck lunacy, and he despised the weakness, even as he
accepted it. Some things, it seemed, were inevitable.
And whatever spell she'd cast on him was not easily
broken. Which meant that he had to work all that much
harder to break it.

And, truth be told, he was approaching the task with
something less than enthusiasm.

He walked to the window, the night sky bright with
artificial light. Man's attempt to keep the dark at bay.
Heat lightning flashed on the horizon, a counterpoint to
the flashing neon of the city.

He placed a hand against the window, the glass still
warm to the touch. She was out there somewhere. It
was almost as if he could feel her calling to him. He
closed his eyes, the soft curves of her face filling his
mind. It was almost as if a part of him had been ripped
away. Torn from him. A part that he could never re-
place.

Well, he'd lost part of himself before—and survived.

He'd just have to do it again. Starting now. He blew out a breath, turning his back on the city, the window, Katie—everything.

Things were crescendoing to a climax, and unless he was mistaken, things were going to play out soon. And the only way he could possibly win was if he could figure out the rules of the game. For some people that might present an insurmountable problem, but John had been finding his way around seemingly unsolvable puzzles his entire life.

It was simply a matter of breaking things into their smallest components and then reassembling them in a more reasonable order. And to do that he needed to start at the beginning. Lay out the facts as he knew them.

He walked back through the living room, into his study, the steady blinking light of the answering machine catching his attention. Flo. She'd said she needed to talk. Maybe she'd found something.

And even if she hadn't, two heads were always better than one.

Katie stood by the railing of the bridge, watching the reflection of neon dance in the waters of Town Lake. Pinks, oranges, and blues blending together to form a rainbow in the water. The heat was almost a living thing. It surrounded her, its touch languid, cloying. She felt like she was suffocating. Though if she admitted the truth, she knew it had nothing whatsoever to do with the heat.

Lightning flashed on the horizon, promising everything and nothing—symbolic of her life. She'd always ridden the edge, thrilling in the moment, playing the odds with abandon. And more than once it had gotten her in trouble. First with her family and later with the bureau, Priestly being the last, and worst, of a long line of act-first-think-later situations.

She supposed a lot of it came from being the only girl in a family of boys. When her mother died, she'd been promoted to princess. And more as a reaction than anything else, she'd thrown away the crown and jumped into the testosterone fray.

She'd joined the FBI because she'd wanted to live up to her family's reputation, but she'd stayed because she truly believed that she was making the world a better place. A noble thought. And par for the course for a Cavanaugh. For four generations, her family had been protecting the people. In one way or another.

The family code was, honor and duty above all else. And being female wasn't about to stand in the way of her fighting the good fight right alongside her brothers. Only she was doing it on her own terms.

And quite frankly, failing miserably. If her last case had branded her a maverick, then this operation, coupled with her involvement with John, was going to be one for the books. And the big question was, what the hell was she going to do to untangle the horrible mess she'd made of things?

The fact of the matter was that she needed to choose. John or her job. And while her brain was telling her to cut her losses, her heart was screaming that she go back and beg, on bended knee if necessary, that he take her back.

She bent to pick up a rock and, with a sigh, tossed it over the railing, watching as it tumbled downward, end over end, until it disappeared into the murky water, the traffic behind her muting the splash.

It ought to be simple. But it wasn't. She'd worked for years to make herself something her father could be proud of. Someone *she* could be proud of. And then in one abandoned leap she'd gone and ruined everything, falling in love with a suspect—falling in *love* with a suspect.

The word reverberated through her mind, startling and comforting all at the same time.

She loved John.

Really loved him.

The thought should have been a foreign one, but suddenly she knew with surety that some small part of her had known almost from the beginning, and an even bigger part had recognized the fact the night they'd made love. Dear God, she was in love with John Brighton, and he'd just thrown her out of his life. How was that for irony?

She gripped the railing, her mind churning along with the water below her. She had to help him. It was the only choice really. Job be damned. But how the hell was she supposed to do that when he wouldn't let her near him?

She'd just have to convince him. Make him understand the way she felt. Not an easy task, but then, she'd never shied away from things that were difficult. The greater the risk, the more she enjoyed the challenge. Only this time there was so much at stake.

Almost reflexively, she reached for her cell phone, her fingers closing around the cool plastic casing. She needed to call headquarters. Let them know where things stood. She owed them that much. Flipping open her phone, she resolutely dialed Jerome's number. If she had to confess failure, the least she could do was go through an intermediary. The receiver clicked as an automated voice began its spiel.

He wasn't there. She didn't know if she should be relieved or perturbed. So she settled for accepting. She'd tried. There was something in that. Before she could chicken out, she left her name and number and clicked the phone off, already regretting the call. At least this

way she had a little time to think about what she
wanted to say. If Roswell had his way about it, no
doubt she'd be heading back to Boston on the first available flight.

But she couldn't let that happen. Not now.

No matter what lay between them, Katie wasn't
going to desert John. He might not want her help, but
he needed it, and she wasn't about to let him face
Roswell and his perfect conviction record on his own.

He didn't understand how the game was played. It
wasn't always about finding the right man, especially
when the pressure was on, and she didn't want John vic-
timized by default. She owed him better than that.

She owed herself better than that.

Which left her with only one alternative. She had to
go back. She had to convince him that she could be
trusted. That she was on his side. More importantly, she
had to keep Roswell believing that she hadn't been compromised.

She allowed herself a last look at the reflected beauty
of the lake, and then resolutely started the walk back to
Guardian—to John. Why did everything have to be so
complicated? Just once in her life, she'd like to do something the easy way. Which was a lie, and she knew it. It
was the challenge that kept her going. The adrenaline
rush.

But this time there was something more. Something
she'd never dealt with before.

This time she was in love.

John stood in the living room, confused. It was late,
Flo should be in the apartment somewhere, but she
wasn't. In fact, she wasn't anywhere at all that he could
find. He'd checked her rooms, his rooms, the kitchen,
even her office.

In fact, in a fit of enthusiasm he'd even checked

everyone else's office. Nada. There was no one downstairs but the janitor. So that left the gym and the roof. Neither a likely place to find Flo, her dislike of heights was equal only to her disdain for forced exercise.

He glanced at his watch, surprised to find that it wasn't later. Maybe she was out. She'd mentioned a date. The thought of her with someone besides George was a little more than he wanted to contemplate, but if the guy made her happy, who was he to question the relationship. Hell, who was he to question anything about love.

Which brought him full circle back to where he didn't want to go. What he needed was distraction. As if telegraphing an answer, a muscle in his leg tightened painfully. He'd missed his afternoon workout. Considering his activities of late, a little time in the gym might just be the ticket. The perfect place to release some of his frustration.

He walked out into the hallway and pressed the down button on the elevator.

While he was there, he'd go over what he knew. Try to find some answers. At the moment all he had was a jumble of puzzle pieces, but with patience it was possible he could find a way to put them all together. If only the crucial ones weren't lost forever amidst damage done on a Mexican highway.

The doors slid open with a quiet whoosh, and he pressed the button for the gym, shuddering at the turn of his thoughts. Someone had wanted him dead. Might still want him out of the picture.

He'd never thought about having enemies before. It wasn't as if he'd led an exemplary life. The business world was a tough one, and he certainly hadn't pulled any punches, but that didn't mean he'd done something that would warrant being taken out of the equation permanently.

Of course, there was the little matter of his memory loss. That meant there was a period of time when anything was possible. But Katie had been right about one thing. A man didn't change fundamentally overnight.

Which meant there had to be another explanation.

The elevator bell clanged, announcing the floor, and the doors slid open. He stepped into the hallway, jumping at the sound of something rattling off to his left. He turned, heart hammering, to see the janitor pushing his cart out of the other elevator.

The man looked up, and smiled, his eyes creasing with the gesture. "Hello, Mr. Brighton. Second time tonight." He maneuvered the cart so that he was walking alongside John.

"Yeah. Guess I'm feeling restless." John struggled to remember the man's name. Something Kim. Robert or Richard. He cursed his memory. Even now, he was still forgetting things. "I thought I'd work off some of my excess energy."

The man nodded, his expression thoughtful. "I always find that movement encourages clearer thinking." He stopped the cart.

"You're wiser than you know, Mr. Kim." John stopped, too, his curious gaze meeting the other man's.

Kim's mouth turned up at the corner slightly, but John couldn't tell if he was smiling or not. "I think if you are going to workout, then perhaps I will clean in there later?" His voice lifted at the end, marking his words as a question.

John nodded his acceptance, and watched as the janitor pushed the cart back into the open elevator. He waited until the doors slid shut, then turned to walk down the hall to the gym, his thoughts moving back to his problems.

Everything started with Derek Miller. Or perhaps more accurately, it had all ended with him. Something Miller had seen or done was worthy of getting him killed. And although the man was a junkie, it seemed that his crimes had extended beyond that.

There was, of course, the question of why John had paid him money. Big money. But that could possibly be dismissed as something to do with rehabilitation. Or a payoff. But if it was a payoff—then, why?

His head ached, a vein throbbing in his temple. He drew in a deep breath, and pushed open the door to the gym, still trying to sort out his thoughts. Even if he dismissed the payoff, there was still the matter of the money he'd been moving around and where it had ultimately gone. And of course the large amount of cash he'd taken with him on a vacation that apparently, according to Andy, he hadn't been taking.

He walked into the gym, the room dark except for a swath of light from the window, illuminating the weight machine. The truth was that none of it made any sense at all. Each thing in and of itself could actually have an innocent explanation, but taken altogether it made him look guilty of something.

And all of it left him without answers. Whatever the hell they were. He reached for the light switch, then thought better of it, as bad as his head was hurting, the last thing he needed was bright light.

The weights were in a corner on a rack. He headed that way, trying to remember the last setting they'd used. *They.* One word and he was back to Katie. Her smiling face filled his mind, and his body stiffened as he imagined her hands against his skin. He needed her. She completed him in some way that he couldn't even define.

But she wasn't real.

The Katie he'd fallen in love with didn't exist. He tried to force her image out of his mind, forcing himself to concentrate on the weights. He grabbed two, and then walked over toward the machine, careful to keep the weights distributed to his good side.

A cloud crossed the moon, momentarily casting the room into darkness, he tripped, the weights tumbling to the floor as he fell forward, hands out to protect himself.

He hit hard, his wrists absorbing the impact, sharp pain shooting up his injured arm.

Son of a bitch. Just what he needed.

He pushed himself to a sitting position, rubbing his elbow absently, his eyes searching the shadows for the cause of the fall.

A dark mound off to the left seemed the likeliest prospect. He tried to stand, but the pain in his leg prevented him, so he scooted over instead, reaching out with his good hand to investigate.

His fingers met something soft and warm. His blood ran cold, his breath catching in his throat. Steeling himself, he pushed onward, his hand finding the contour of a shoulder, a neck. His stomach clenched in silent revolt, just as the moon reappeared, its pale beam illuminating a face.

A face he knew.

Florence Tedesky's lifeless eyes stared out at the moonlight, seeing nothing.

He fought down a wave of bile, his fingers groping for her wrist, searching frantically for a pulse.

Nothing.

Kneeling beside her now, he moved his hand to her neck. Not even a flutter. Even as his mind accepted the inevitable, his heart wanted to prove it wrong.

He shook her, calling her name, knowing it was useless, but needing the action. His hands came away sticky. Blood. Her blood. Panicked, he searched the floor, trying to find something anything that would help her—bring her back.

His hand closed around steel, and he held the gun up

to the moonlight, his throat dry, anguish mixing with rage.

Light speared through the room, startling him with its intensity, and he turned, moving slowly, struggling to breathe, to focus.

Frank stood in the doorway, eyes wide, horror etched across his features. "Oh my God, Jonathan, what the hell have you done?"

He tried to answer, but the words wouldn't come. With a sigh, he sank to the floor, the gun falling from his hand, clattering against the tile, the sound chilling against the silence of the night.

Chapter 19

Eric D'Angelo stood inside the doorway to the gym, trying to visualize what had happened. The forensics team was already at work, photographing, measuring, trying to put together the pieces of a very nasty puzzle.

John Brighton was over in a corner, staring into a cup of coffee as if it could predict the future, a paramedic fussing over him, trying to take his vitals. He knocked the paramedic away, moving to stand by the window, the line of his shoulders a testament to his grieving. Whatever had happened here, it was clear that Brighton cared deeply about the deceased.

Frank Jacoby was standing white-faced by a rowing machine, his eyes locked on the body. The little man was doing everything but wringing his hands, the horror of the moment still etched clearly across his face. Every once in a while, he'd shoot a sidelong glance at Brighton, a mixture of fear and sympathy combined with the pallor of a man who was trying very hard not to throw up.

Not that D'Angelo blamed him. The killer hadn't been a professional. There were blood spatters everywhere. Florence Tedesky had made quite an exit. It was almost as if someone had wanted a show.

"Got the weapon here." A tech held up a plastic bag holding a gun.

Eric eyed it dispassionately. It was a thirty-eight, the same caliber used on Derek Miller. But there was a world of difference between this shooting and Miller's. He'd be surprised to find that it was the same gun.

Still, there was no sense ignoring the possibility. "Let's get it over to ballistics. And have them test it against the slugs we got out of Miller."

The man raised an eyebrow, but refrained from comment, instead heading for the door.

"Hanson," he called after the tech. The man turned, the bag with the gun still hanging from his fingers. "Tell them to hurry."

There was no logical explanation, but Eric could sense things about a case the way a reporter smelled out a story, instinct combining with years of police work to make his premonitions hard to ignore, and he had the distinct feeling something big was about to happen here.

With a nod at Tony, who was deep in conversation with one of the forensics guys, he headed over to talk to John. A cursory interview hadn't yielded any useful information, but maybe with a little distance, the man had remembered something that might be of help.

"I came as soon as I heard." Danny Brighton burst into the room, his normally suntanned face red with exertion. "Oh my God." He skidded to a stop, his gaze locked on the body.

So much for containment. "How the hell did you get up here?" D'Angelo's words came out harsher than he'd intended, but there was such a thing as the integrity of a crime scene, and at the very least, his men downstairs should have stopped the man.

Danny wrenched his eyes away from Florence to meet Eric's gaze. "Frank called me." He tipped his head toward the other man, and Frank grimaced, caught in the act, cell phone clutched tightly in one hand.

D'Angelo shot a look at Tony, who shrugged fatalistically. Somebody's head was going to roll.

"Jonathan did this?" Danny's voice was hushed, almost

a whisper. He glanced over at his brother, then back at the detective.

"He found the body, Mr. Brighton. As far as who did it, right now your guess is as good as mine." D'Angelo strove for a reasonable tone of voice. The man wasn't exactly a picture of subtlety.

"Can I talk to my brother?" Danny asked.

D'Angelo waved a hand in John's direction. "Be my guest. But don't get in the way." Probably a pointless statement since the man was already more than in the way. He watched as Brighton made his way over to his brother, then turned to face Frank Jacoby. "Exactly how many people did you call?"

Frank shuffled from one foot to the other, looking decidedly worried. "Just the people that needed to know. Jason, Valerie, and Danny."

"So I should expect two more people to come barging in here."

Frank shrugged.

D'Angelo studied the man, wondering what it was about him that rang false. Something he couldn't quite put his finger on. "Let's go over what happened one more time."

"I walked in on Jonathan kneeling over Florence, holding the g-gun." He swallowed, his complexion moving beyond pasty to a sickly green.

"What were you doing in the building?" Tony walked up, ignoring the pallor of Frank's face. "Seems a little late for business."

"Actually, I was on my way out."

"A bit out of the way, isn't it?" The front door was down the opposite hall, closer to Frank's office.

"I was parked out back. It's safer at night." The man sounded positively insulted, and D'Angelo watched Tony fight against a smile.

"And so you thought you'd stop in for a workout?" He knew that wasn't the case, but if they kept Frank rattled, maybe he'd reveal something he hadn't intended. If there was indeed anything to reveal.

The man's jaw worked for a moment, producing no sound, his pallor changing to an ugly shade of red. "I was walking by here when I heard a noise."

"A gunshot?" Tony's amusement evaporated, his eyes narrowing in concentration.

"No." Frank frowned. "It was more of a thunk. Like something had fallen. Since Jonathan works out a lot these days, I was immediately concerned that it might be him."

"I see." Eric blew out a frustrated breath. Frank's story tracked with Brighton's. According to John, he'd tripped over the body in the dark.

"I pushed through the door," Frank continued, "and flipped on the light." Now that he'd started talking it seemed he wasn't about to be silenced. "At first I didn't see anything out of the ordinary. Just the gym equipment. But then I saw Jonathan over there with . . . with the gun . . . kneeling over Florence, and I thought . . . Oh God, I thought—"

"You thought that John had shot Mrs. Tedesky," Tony finished for him, his voice kept purposefully gentle.

Frank nodded, his expression an odd combination of guilt and fear.

D'Angelo frowned, trying to work out what it was that was bugging him. Nothing tangible obviously, but something in Frank's story felt off. He glanced at Tony to see if he'd picked up on the same thing, but the big man's face showed nothing of what he was thinking.

"Can I take my brother upstairs?" Danny Brighton was back, his tone just this side of civil.

Eric glanced over at John. The man looked physically sick, his face beaded with sweat, his pallor almost as bad as Frank's. "Sure. I don't see why not. Just don't let him leave the building until I give the okay."

He watched as Danny and Frank flanked John, the two of them supporting him as they walked slowly toward the door. A united front.

The big question, of course, was whether they were united in the trauma of the moment, or because they had something to hide.

If he were a betting man, Eric would put his money on the latter. Of course, that still left him with the monumental task of finding out what it was they were keeping secret. But he'd conquered tougher cases, and he'd get to the bottom of this one. Although he couldn't shake the notion that when he did, it was going to be about a hell of a lot more than a couple of dead bodies.

Police cars and emergency vehicles surrounded the Guardian building, and Katie's heart started pounding as her imagination went into overdrive. The forensics wagon could conceivably be there for a number of reasons, but the most likely one meant homicide.

Oh God, what if something had happened to John?

She broke into a run, cold sweat enveloping her body, punctuating her fear. She never should have left him. She'd let her emotions control her actions, throwing years of training out the window at the first sign of hormones, and now it looked like she'd done more than compromise her profession, she'd quite possibly cost someone their life.

A large man in uniform stepped between her and the door, his intention clearly to stop forward progress, but she had adrenaline on her side, and with a forward thrust and a flying elbow, she was past him. There would no doubt be hell to pay for the action, but just at the moment she didn't give a damn.

The hallway was empty, but voices from the gym carried down the corridor. She ran forward, stopping in the doorway, her trained mind accessing the scene. A body sprawled on the floor, the telltale black bag obscuring the identity.

But even at this distance she could tell it wasn't John. Someone smaller.

Female.

The technician working beside the body shifted slightly, the face of the deceased white in the harsh light. *Flo.*

Her stomach clenched and she fought a bubble of hysteria, an emotion somewhere between horror and intense relief tearing through her, leaving her feeling light-headed and weak. She clutched the door frame, using it for support, trying to pull air into her lungs.

The policeman she'd punched arrived behind her, his breathing labored, his red face indicative of his displeasure. He grabbed her by the arms, obviously intent on getting her out of the building. But before words could be exchanged, D'Angelo caught sight of them, and with a wave of a hand, dismissed the officer.

With a look worthy of a seasoned killer, the man released her and walked away, rubbing his rib cage and mumbling something no doubt unflattering beneath his breath.

"Probably not the best way to make friends with the locals, Agent Cavanaugh." D'Angelo raised his eyebrows, working hard to hold back a smile.

She struggled to pull her rattled emotions into control, pushing away from the door frame, eyes locked with the detective's. "How long have you known?"

"I've suspected for a while. Was pretty sure the day Roswell was here. But I really wasn't positive until just now." His eyes still reflected amusement. She'd fallen right into his trap.

"So you were fishing?"

D'Angelo shrugged. "Considering you managed to wind Madison, I'd say it was more of an educated guess."

She nodded, her mind already back on the body. "What happened here?"

"Shooting. She took it in the back. Probably never knew what hit her."

He sounded so impersonal. As if Flo hadn't been a person at all. Which of course was exactly the way he was supposed to sound—the way *she* was supposed to sound. But somewhere along the way things had gotten personal.

Her eyes fell to the plastic-encased body, the remains nothing like the wonderful woman she'd come to know. "She deserved better than this. Flo was a special person." It wasn't enough, but it was meant sincerely.

"So I gather. Brighton's taking it pretty hard."

"John's here?" She pulled her gaze away from the body bag.

D'Angelo nodded. "He found her."

"Oh God." Her mind was spinning with possibilities. "Did he see the killer?"

"No. According to his statement, she was dead when he found her."

Katie frowned. "You don't believe him."

"I'm not making any judgments. But there is conflicting testimony."

She worked to keep her expression bland, her interest only professional. "Such as?"

"Frank Jacoby walked in on Brighton standing over the body holding a gun."

"He probably picked it up on reflex. I've seen it happen a thousand times." Maybe not a thousand times, but it did happen. People weren't thinking in moments like that, and most of them managed to do something stupid. Something that compromised the crime scene.

"We tested for powder residue. We'll know something in the morning."

"That's not conclusive and you know it. If he picked

up the gun just after the shooting, he might still test positive."

"It's possible. But if there's other supporting evidence . . ." He broke off with a shrug, and her heart sank.

"Do you have a preliminary time of death?"

D'Angelo nodded. "The ME estimates she died right around the time Brighton found her."

She fought against a wave of panic, digging deep for control. This wasn't the time to fall apart. "Where is he now?"

"Upstairs." D'Angelo tipped his head toward the door. "He was pretty shaken. Frank and Danny are with him."

"Danny was here, too?"

"Yeah." The cynical smile crossed the detective's face. "It's been a regular circus around here. And I expect there'll be more before it's all over."

"Any other witnesses?" The question was rote, her brain automatically searching for answers.

"The janitor talked to Brighton a few minutes before. Said he seemed really upset about something."

"He say what?"

"No. And he went back upstairs afterward, so he didn't hear anything."

The implication being a gunshot. For all D'Angelo's assertions about waiting for the facts, it certainly sounded like he thought John was the shooter. "What about before. Did he hear anything before he talked to John?"

D'Angelo's eyebrows went up again, as he shook his head. "No. He wasn't on the floor. Came off the elevator to find John in the hallway."

"I see." She chewed the side of her lip, considering the latest revelation. In court, the janitor's testimony could easily be used against John even if in truth it amounted to nothing. "Does Roswell know?"

D'Angelo shook his head. "Haven't heard a peep. I guess I ought to tell him what's up. Or maybe I should leave that to you?"

"I'm undercover, remember?" She hoped to hell that she could convince John to let her keep the charade going. And in the meantime, there didn't seem to be any reason to come clean with D'Angelo. She liked the man, but that didn't make him her confessor. "Besides, I need to get upstairs. They'll be wondering where I am."

D'Angelo's eyebrows drew together in speculation. "Mind telling me where you were?"

"You suspect me?" She was surprised to hear anger in her voice.

"Right now, I suspect my mother. You know the way this sort of thing works."

Her anger dissipated as quickly as it had come. "Yeah, I'm sorry. I guess I'm a little jumpy. I was out walking. Clearing my head, trying to put things into some kind of order." Which was the absolute truth, except that they were talking about two completely different things.

D'Angelo accepted the information without question, his attention focused on one of the forensics folks, a kid with the face too damn young for work so horrific. They conferred for a moment, and the kid returned to the body, zipping the bag shut.

There was a finality to it that hit Katie hard. Flo Tedesky had been so vibrant—so alive. And now she was dead. There would be no more midnight chats. No more tea and comfort.

Flo had loved John like a son. She would have done anything for him. Anything. Even die for him.

Which was exactly what John would be thinking. He'd be blaming himself.

"I've got to go." Katie didn't even try to keep her voice casual. Let D'Angelo think whatever he wanted.

Right now nothing really mattered except getting to John.

John stood in the living room staring out at nothing, emptiness gnawing at his insides. Flo was gone. Dead. Things left forever undone, unsaid. Pain that wasn't truly tangible, yet threatened to eat away at him until there wasn't anything left to feel.

He'd never felt so impotent. So alone.

"I just got off the phone with Dr. Walters. I got him to prescribe a sedative." Danny's voice sounded like it was far away, coming to him through deep water.

He blinked slowly, forcing himself to focus on the here and now. "I don't need a sedative. I'm fine."

Danny came to stand beside him, his face creased with worry. "You need to rest. And you're not going to do that on your own. I know you."

"I'm not going to take anything either. I've had enough things messing with my brain. I'm sure as hell not going to purposefully screw with it some more."

"Come on, Jonathan, it's just a sleeping pill."

"I said no." The words burst from him, staccato in tempo and explosive in tone. "Just leave me alone."

"I don't think you should be on your own right now."

"You afraid I'll do something desperate?" He'd meant it as a joke, something to ease the tension in the room, but instead it came out sounding pathetic. Everything had gone insane—reality turning inward on itself.

"I don't know what to think." Danny looked down at the floor, refusing to meet his gaze, and John's blood ran cold.

"You think I killed her." His pulse pounded against his temples, the cacophonous rhythm almost deafening.

Danny lifted his gaze. "Frank said he saw you."

"He saw me holding the gun." John struggled to maintain control. "I picked it up when I fell. You can't honestly believe I'd hurt Flo."

"You wouldn't have. Not before." Danny shook his head, as if to underscore his words. "But now . . . I don't know. You're not the same anymore. There's so much anger. And there are secrets, John. I see them in your eyes. I don't want to believe any of it, but it's getting to where I don't have a choice."

He stared at his brother's face, seeing far more than he wanted to. Danny thought he'd gone over the edge. He honestly believed that John was capable of murder. There simply weren't words. Nothing he could say that would make it okay.

Nothing he could do that would bring Flo back.

Even if he hadn't pulled the trigger, he was just as guilty of Flo's death. His actions had led them to this place as surely as if he had ordered her murder himself. It was there in Danny's eyes.

"You didn't kill him."

They both swung around, Katie's voice filling the silence hanging heavy between them.

"And nothing either of you say will make me believe that." She walked toward him, her eyes clear, trusting.

But then Katie was a liar.

"You shouldn't be here." Danny took a step toward her, one hand lifted as if to ward her off. "Not after everything you've done."

He wanted to nod, to agree with his brother, but he was simply too tired. All he could see was Flo's face floating through his mind, blood splashed crimson against the pale white of her cheeks. He sank down onto the sofa. "It's too late." His voice cracked, his gaze colliding with hers.

"It's never too late, John. Not if we truly care." There was a plea in her eyes, one he desperately wanted to believe. But he couldn't. She wasn't for real. Nothing that had happened between them was real. And no matter how his soul yearned for her, he mustn't let himself fall into her trap. "John, please . . ."

She took a step toward him, but Danny cut her off smoothly. "Why don't you let me show you the way out." His words were polite, his tone was not.

John summoned his last vestige of strength, and raised a hand to stop his brother. There were still things he needed to know. "That won't be necessary, Danny. There are things Katie and I need to discuss."

"But—"

He waved off both his brother's protest and the flash of hope in Katie's eyes. "She has information that can help us get to the bottom of this. And from where I'm sitting, I think she owes it to me to share that knowledge." His eyes met hers, his gaze impassive.

She nodded once, and moved to sit in the chair across from him. Danny followed suit, heading for a chair by the window, but again John waved him away. "I'd rather we had the conversation on our own."

Danny's eyes narrowed. "Do you think that's wise?"

"Probably not." John attempted a weak smile, but gave up the attempt. It simply required too much effort. "But at the moment, it's all I've got."

Danny shot Katie a venomous look, and walked toward the door. "I'll be downstairs if you need me."

John nodded his thanks, and then turned his attention back to Katie. She looked just the same. No Medusa snakes sprouting from her hair, no traitorous brand on her forehead. Not more than eight hours ago, he'd had such hope.

But hope died easily. Just like Flo.

Their gazes met and held. "I didn't kill her."

"I know that. I said as much."

"Yes. You did. But I needed you to hear it from me."

"John—"

"No." He cut her off with finality. "I don't want to rehash what's already been said. It's over, Katie. I just need you to tell me what you know."

She sucked in a breath, as if for fortification, her expression shuttered. "All right. Where do you want to start?"

"Downstairs." He struggled to maintain clarity, his mind rebelling, wanting only the oblivion of sleep, but he owed Flo more than that. He looked up to meet her gaze. "Are the police still here?"

"Yes, but they're about finished. For now."

He ignored the last remark, pressing onward. "And Flo?"

"They were taking her out when I left."

"I see." He nodded, the finality of it all hitting him hard. "We'll have to make arrangements."

"Not yet. The medical examiner wants to do an autopsy." She sounded almost automated. The consummate professional.

He narrowed his eyes, studying her face. "How about D'Angelo, did he say anything to you?"

"Nothing specific." She held his gaze, her eyes steady. "He took the gun for a ballistics test. Hopefully it'll tell us something. In the meantime, there isn't much else to go on."

"Except the fact that a crazy man was found standing over the body."

"You're not crazy, John. No one thinks that."

"Maybe not. But D'Angelo thinks I killed her."

"I don't know what he thinks, but I can tell you this—the man's a professional. He'll get to the bottom of what happened. The truth will come out."

"And if he doesn't there's always the FBI, right?" He wasn't surprised to hear sarcasm in his voice.

"They're certainly interested in the outcome." She talked as though *they* were a separate entity from her, but he knew better.

"Have you talked to Roswell?" He supposed in some ways the question was a test. Not that her answer would change anything.

"Not since we talked on the roof." She blinked, and

just for a moment he thought he saw tears. But then she shifted, her eyes lost in shadow, and he could no longer be certain. "Under the circumstances, I didn't think it was the best time to tell him you knew about me. There might be things we can accomplish better if I'm still undercover."

"*We* meaning the FBI." At least now she was admitting it.

"*We* meaning us, John—you and me." The hint of pleading was back again.

He ignored it. "There is no you and me, Katie. You killed that with your lies."

She flinched at the anger in his voice, but continued to hold his gaze. "I can help you if you'll let me."

"The only help I need from you is the truth. Earlier, on the roof, you said something about international conspiracy. Something Roswell told you."

She sighed, her expression so lost and sad he wanted to pull her into his arms and make it all right. But he couldn't. Some things just couldn't be fixed.

She settled back into the chair, her face devoid of expression, emotions firmly back in control. "Roswell thinks there may be a tie-in between what happened to Miller and a Korean company called Taegu. It's one of those nebulous companies with obscure origins and purpose. Supposedly it's a front for the Korean mob. We've apparently been watching the company for some time. There is evidence that supports the idea that Taegu is dealing in trade secrets."

"International espionage." He tried but couldn't keep the incredulity from his voice.

She nodded. "According to Roswell, when Miller contacted the FBI he mentioned Taegu. And because of the kind of work Guardian does, Roswell thinks maybe there's a connection."

"You're telling me he thinks that I'm selling information to the Koreans?" Anger pooled in his gut, hot and heavy, the pounding in his head intensifying.

"I'm not telling you anything definitively. It's just a possibility. And only because of the evidence."

"Evidence that just keeps mounting." He fought for control and won, forcing his breathing back to an even keel. "What about the hit? Surely that negates my involvement. If I was working the wrong side of the street, why would someone try and take me out?"

"I don't know. What we have are a lot of puzzle pieces with absolutely no sense of order. Every time we fit some of them together, a new piece comes along and throws it all out of whack again. The truth is, this isn't an easy case, but that doesn't mean there isn't an explanation."

"Well, for the moment, I seem to be everyone's odds-on favorite." He rubbed the bridge of his nose, the tension on the bone easing his headache a bit.

"Maybe. But there are other suspects. D'Angelo was even questioning me."

"Does he know who you are?"

"Yeah. He guessed. I'm afraid I took a swing at an officer when he wouldn't let me in the building."

"And you won."

She shrugged. "D'Angelo already suspected, and after putting two and two together, he trapped me into admitting the truth."

"You said yourself he's good at what he does."

She stared down at her hands, silence stretching painfully between them, and despite himself, he let his eyes devour the soft waves of her hair, the curve of her chin. He reached out with an open hand to touch her, caress her, but at the last moment drew back, closing his fingers into a fist instead.

"Why did you come back?" The words came of their own volition, without so much as a by-your-leave.

Her head jerked up, their eyes locking together, communicating on a level that had nothing whatsoever to do with reason and logic. "I was coming to tell you that I was sorry."

"You'd have been wasting your breath."

Her eyes were full of tears now. He hadn't been imagining it. "What we had was special, John. Something worth fighting for. You can't just throw it away."

"I didn't throw it away, Katie." He stood up, certain that his heart was crumbling to dust. "You did."

She was making a habit of standing at this window. The skyline was muted, the city at sleep, but moonlight more than made up for the loss. It slashed across the living room, the light clear and white, washing away the shadows of gray.

If only it would work on her life.

She'd made a hell of a mess of things. And her attempt to fix it had been too little too late. Not that she blamed John. His reaction was more than understandable. If she'd been in his place she probably wouldn't have handled it as well as he had.

But then, he did have a few other things on his mind. D'Angelo was gone. The crime scene reduced once more to a gym. A gym with blood spatters for decoration. She shivered. Roswell had been there. Jerome, too. But there hadn't been time to talk about anything but the murder.

Roswell had asked her to stay and watch over John, although his intent had probably not been altruistic. D'Angelo had seconded the idea, and even Danny had grudgingly accepted her presence, heading for home shortly after the police packed it in. Of course, there were still cops out there somewhere, keeping watch, but they held their vigil from outside the building.

For the time being she was on the front line. She patted the service revolver tucked in the back of her jeans. A loaner from Wilcox. The cool steel was comforting in a way only someone from law enforcement could understand. As if a missing part of her had been restored. An old friend, of sorts.

John was sleeping. Which was a blessing, for any number of reasons. Mainly because it meant he didn't know she was here. He wouldn't want her watching over him. Wouldn't want her anywhere near him.

But he didn't have a choice. He might not be able to forgive her now, but she'd find a way to make things right between them, if she had to die trying. And in the meantime, whether he liked it or not, they were in this together, and nothing, not even his stubbornness, was going to prevent that.

Life was so damn complicated. One moment everything was clear and simple and the next it was tangled into an inextricably complicated mess. The simple truth was that she loved him, and somehow she had to prove it to him. She had to prove that there could be trust again. But it was a tall order, and even if she succeeded, she knew the final choice would have to be his.

And in the meantime, she had to concentrate on the events at hand. John may not have killed Florence Tedesky, but somebody certainly had, and odds were that whoever was behind it was probably behind everything else that was happening.

She needed to get to the bottom of it before the powers that be tried to hang it on John. Roswell was already gunning for him, and D'Angelo hadn't sounded convinced of John's innocence either. And she had the distinct feeling that her window of opportunity was closing.

Someone out there was getting panicky. They'd tried to kill John once, and she had the horrible feeling that despite his memory loss, if things continued to spiral out of control, they'd try again.

And this time they wouldn't miss.

Chapter 20

The answering machine.

John sat up, immediately regretting the action. His head spun, the blackness threatening to overtake him again. Gritting his teeth, he closed his eyes, and waited for the world to still. Then, confident that he was in control, he swung his feet over the side of the bed, relieved when his right side obeyed the command.

He needed to get to the study.

Flo had left a message on the answering machine. He'd turned it off, not wanting to listen. But now he needed to hear what she'd had to say. Something about needing to talk.

He pushed off of the bed, shifting so that his weight was supported more on the left side. The moonlight was faint, but there was enough illumination to see. A soft sound broke through the stillness, and he spun around, surprised at his agility, wishing he had a weapon of some kind.

Light from the window spilled across a chair near the bed, and despite his pounding heart, he smiled. Katie was curled up in the chair, fast asleep. His own private guardian angel. Only she wasn't much of an angel. His smile vanished. They'd said it all. There wasn't anything left.

Yet here she was.

God, he wished things were different, that they'd met some other place, some other time. But they hadn't. And the sooner they both accepted the fact the better. And just at the moment he had more important things to think about than the inviting curve of her lips.

He needed to find Flo's killer. And, innocent or guilty, he needed to find the truth.

And the best place to start was with the answering machine.

He made his way down the hall and into the living room, turning toward the study, moving slower now, automatically listening for intruders. Stupid, of course, the police were probably watching downstairs, but despite that, the quiet felt ominous.

He moved across the room, stopping at the door to the study. It was darker here than in the bedroom, pinpoints of light from various machines shining green in the dark.

Green. He felt the pull of panic at the edges of his consciousness. The answering machine light should be red. He hadn't listened to the messages. It should be red. He rushed over to the black box, hitting the play button, already knowing what he was going to find.

Silence.

The messages were gone. Erased.

Someone had beat him to the punch.

Again.

"We shouldn't be meeting without my brother."

"There wasn't an option, Danny, and you know it." Jason sat back, watching his friend, trying unsuccessfully to read his expression. "We have to come up with a strategy before morning. Any chance we have to control this thing is over as soon as the news breaks. You know that as well as I do."

"Especially in light of the fact that it looks like John has totally lost it." Valerie's statement sounded almost gleeful, and Jason found himself despising her for it.

"No one has been accused of anything at this point."

Jason ran a hand through his hair, grateful for the anonymity of the restaurant. The clientele of Magnolia Café tended toward students and die-hard Austinites. People who had thrived during the seventies and stayed there, despite the passing decades. This time of night it was still hopping, providing a perfect place to disappear into a crowd.

Not that he had that option.

With everything that was happening, he had the feeling his time in the spotlight was only just beginning. Which, under normal circumstances, wouldn't have bothered him at all, but with things the way they were, frankly scared him to death.

"Jason? You're not listening." Valerie's hand was warm against his skin, and he forced himself to pull away. This certainly wasn't the time to reveal their relationship.

"I'm sorry, there's just so much to think about." He waved at a passing waiter, who stopped to refill his coffee cup.

"Which is the whole point actually." She sat back, her eyes narrowed in thought. "We were just saying that even if no one is pointing fingers yet, it doesn't look good for Jonathan. I mean, he was found holding the gun, standing over the body."

"He was kneeling actually." It was the first time Frank had said anything, his voice so soft it was almost a whisper. "And according to him, he only found the body."

"I hardly think he's likely to admit shooting the old girl." Valerie drummed perfectly manicured nails on the scarred tabletop.

"Christ, Valerie. Have a little respect." Danny choked on the words, emotion obviously getting the better of him.

"Well, if he didn't do it, then who did?" She fixed

Frank with a stare worthy of a judge or jury, and he
squirmed under the inspection.

"I haven't the foggiest notion." Frank stared into his
cup, his face pale. "I . . . I just walked in on the man."

"You haven't said why you were in the office in the
first place." Jason watched the little man, wondering if
he'd been behind Florence's demise. There was something pathetic in the thought. And tragic. Her death had
the power to bring down Guardian. No matter who was
behind it. Truth be told, the microscope they'd all be
under had the potential to bring down more than just
the company.

He shivered, wondering how in the world he'd let it
all get to this point.

"I came back to finish something." The sound of
Frank's voice pulled him out of his reverie.

"And just happened to walk in on Jonathan?"
Danny's skepticism was clearly visible, reflected in the
lines of his face.

"Look, it doesn't matter why he was there," Valerie
interrupted, her eyes on Frank. "It doesn't even matter
who killed Florence. What matters is how it's going to
impact the company."

Jason sighed. "She's right. It isn't going to be pretty.
There have already been calls."

"Clients or press?" Danny leaned forward, his hands
clenched around his coffee cup.

"Both. And this is only the beginning." He reached
into his pocket for his Filofax, and flipped it open. "So
far I've diffused the worst of it, but tomorrow, when the
story hits the paper, all hell is going to break lose, and
we need to be ready."

"What do you suggest?" Valerie reached into her
purse, producing a pack of cigarettes. Lighting up, she
sat back, inhaling deeply.

"First off, there's no more room for debate. Jonathan
has to resign. No matter what the police ultimately find,

he's at the center of all of this. He's got to distance himself from the company. There isn't a choice anymore."

"I think he'll agree to it." Danny's voice was soft but resolute. "He loves Guardian more than anything."

"Except maybe that therapist of his." Valerie blew a smoke ring, the casual gesture at odds with the intensity in her voice.

A shadow crossed Danny's face. "She's FBI."

"What?" Jason fought against a wave of pure panic, struggling to remember everything he'd said or done when she was around.

"Undercover." Danny blew out a breath. "I did a little investigating for Jonathan, and stumbled on the truth."

"Does she know?" Frank looked up from studying Jason's Filofax, his face if possible was even whiter.

"Yeah, Jonathan confronted her with it. Threw her out." Danny waited a beat, his gaze locked with Jason's. "But she's back."

"With Jonathan? Why?" Valerie stubbed out the cigarette, her eyes reflecting her anger. "Surely he's not that addled."

"Orders. Or at least I think that's all it is." Danny shrugged. "Frankly, I don't know what's going on between them."

"At this point, it may not matter." Jason leaned back in his chair. "The damage has been done. The only thing we can hope for is that the police have a killer by morning."

"They recovered the murder weapon, right?" Valerie asked. "That ought to tell us something. Maybe even put an end to this nightmare."

"What if there isn't an end?" Frank looked up, his eyes full of something that looked suspiciously like regret. "What if it's just going to continue until it destroys us all?"

"Oh, there's a positive thought, Frank," Jason

snapped, trying to ignore the remark. But he couldn't. There was too much truth there. Frank couldn't know it. Couldn't begin to have an idea.

But Jason was suddenly certain that the words were prophetic.

John stood in the doorway to Flo's office, his stomach clenching at the familiar smell of her perfume. It was probably too soon for him to be here. But time wasn't a luxury anymore, and he needed to know if there was something here that might help him—help Flo.

He crossed the room and sat down at her desk, opening the top drawer. A picture of him and Flo smiled up at him, their laughing faces testament to happier days. He swallowed, dangerously close to losing it altogether.

He'd loved her so much. Loved her still.

And just at the moment, he couldn't imagine his life without her. She'd been his safety net. Someone who'd always believed in him. No matter what. She'd run buffer between him and his father, keeping them from fracturing their relationship, and she'd managed to keep him and Danny friends as well. Helping him to understand that his brother's way of dealing with life was dramatically different from his own.

He picked up the picture, tracing the lines of her smile, accepting somewhere deep inside that he'd never see it again. To lose her was bad enough. But to lose her like this was almost beyond comprehension.

He sucked in a breath, knowing that he couldn't help her if he gave in to his grief. There'd be time for grief later, but right now was a time for vengeance. And if he had his way, Florence would get hers.

A sound outside in the hallway drew his attention. The building was supposed to be deserted. He grabbed a letter opener from the desk, well aware that it would offer little protection against a gun. Still, it was better than nothing.

He edged around the desk, moving toward the door, straining into the silence, listening for another sound. Reaching the doorway, he paused, relaxing a little when he didn't hear anything more. Obviously he was overreacting. Although under the circumstances he figured overreacting was better than the alternative.

Just as he turned to go back, a light cut across the hallway. Someone was in his old office. Clutching the letter opener in his left hand, he inched forward, stopping when he reached the edge of the doorway. He could hear someone inside, and with a deep breath, he stepped over the threshold, the blade of the letter opener gleaming in the light.

Frank Jacoby jerked upright, his eyes glued to the blade, his face going a funny shade of green. "Don't hurt me."

John lowered the letter opener, his breath coming out on a whoosh. "What the hell are you doing in here, Frank? You scared the shit out of me."

The little man took an involuntary step backward. "I could say the same about you."

"I live here, Frank." He was surprised to hear exasperation in his voice, although he supposed it was par for the course.

"Not down here."

"I was going through Flo's things." He sat down, his leg throbbing from the exertion of creeping down the hall. "I thought maybe there'd be something to help."

"I see." Frank leaned back against the desk, his stance far from relaxed.

"You haven't told me what you're doing in here. Last I checked, this was still my office."

"I was trying to find a file."

"It's three o'clock in the morning. You expect me to believe that?"

Frank stared down at his shoes as if he were memorizing the laces and then looked up, his expression regretful. "I was looking for some sort of evidence."

"To incriminate me." John knew he ought to cut the man some slack. If the situation were reversed, he'd probably be doing the same thing.

"Yeah." Frank was kicking at the ground now, resembling a schoolboy caught red-handed doing something wrong.

"And did you find anything?"

Frank's head jerked up, a flash of anger cresting in his eyes. "No. There's nothing in here. But you know that."

"I don't know anything anymore." He ran his good hand through his hair, feeling suddenly tired. "If you find answers, I wish you'd share them with me."

"Even if I find something that hurts you?" It was a test, and John immediately recognized it as such, grudgingly admiring Frank his fortitude.

"Even then. I just want to get to the bottom of whatever is going on and put a stop to it."

Frank frowned, studying his face. "You really mean that, don't you?"

"I do. I don't remember what I did the months before I was shot, but if it was something that started all of this, then I want to know about it."

"Are you going to step down?" There was no segue, but John didn't pretend to misunderstand the man.

"I think I have to. At least until after all of this dies down."

Frank nodded. "It's what's best for Guardian."

"Yeah. And for all of you. I owe you that much, Frank."

The other man looked away, staring out the window. "I believe you, Jona . . . John. And I'm sorry I didn't trust you from the beginning."

"No harm done." He forced a smile. "I wouldn't have trusted you had the situation been reversed."

Which was more than the truth. Because he wasn't all that certain he trusted the man now, and although he thought Frank was basically harmless, he wasn't certain he was capable of resisting temptation if it were placed within his grasp.

Hell, he wasn't certain anyone was.

Which led him back full circle to the question that frightened him the most. Had something fallen into his path he couldn't resist? Something that had led to Miller's death? And more importantly, to Flo's?

There was no answer. At least not yet.

But before he was done, he was going to find the truth.

No matter who it hurt.

Frank pounded on Valerie's door, the Hyde Park bungalow rattling from the pressure. He knew she was home. Her car was in the driveway. And despite the fact that is was barely after dawn, he needed to talk to her. To tell her what he'd discovered. She hadn't seen fit to respond to his call. And he wanted to know why.

The world was coming apart and no one seemed to care.

He walked across the porch, framing his eyes with his hands so that he could peer into the front window. The living room was empty, Valerie's perfectly appointed furnishings mocking him.

Where was she?

Angry now, he stalked toward the back of the house, his feet crunching against the gravel driveway. This was not the time for a disappearing act. Things were happening fast, and he needed to talk to her. Devise a plan.

They'd figured John all wrong. He was going to do the right thing after all. Which meant everything was different. At least he thought it did. Truth was, he was confused. But at least he still had his ace in the hole. He just had to figure out how best to use it. Which, frankly, wasn't his strong suit. So he needed Valerie.

And he needed her now.

The back of the house wasn't quite as pretty as the front. The paint peeling in places, the old detached garage threatening to tumble down. Sort of like Valerie herself. He peered into the back window. Valerie's bedroom was all pink and mauve, like an overtrussed valentine, but worse still was the fact that her bed obviously hadn't been slept in. Despite the car in the driveway, Valerie obviously wasn't home.

The hum of tires against asphalt alerted him to the car in the alley behind the house. The engine faded as the car rolled to a stop, and Frank ducked back behind a yew tree, straining to see through the hurricane fence that surrounded the property. Probably nothing to do with Valerie, but best to be certain.

Besides, he didn't relish the idea of being caught trespassing.

A car door slammed and then the back gate creaked as it opened. The hairs on his arms stood up as Valerie and a companion came through the gate, lips locked in obvious seduction.

He pushed back against the wall of the house, shifting the branches of the tree with one hand to better hide himself. He certainly didn't need to be caught hiding in the bushes like some lecherous voyeur.

He started to step back, to head for his car and forget the whole thing, but curiosity got the better of him, and he leaned forward instead, determined to catch at least a glimpse of Valerie's latest paramour. Her laughter rang out as the couple turned, the pale morning light hitting Jason Pollock square in the face.

Frank fought against a wave of nausea. Jason and Valerie. The thought was almost more than he could handle. She'd played him for a fool. Used him to get what she wanted, all the while laughing about it with her lover, and he'd fallen for it like a lovesick idiot.

Inching sideways, he managed to duck around the corner, out of sight, the thorns of a rosebush ripping across his face, clinging to his clothes. With a muttered oath, he tore himself free and ran for his car, clutching his side. Sliding to a stop, he yanked the door open as he fumbled one-handed for his keys, his only thought escape.

Once again he'd let himself be manipulated, and once again he'd chosen the wrong woman. But he still held his trump card, and he'd be damned if he'd play into their hands. He wasn't out of the game yet. He just needed to think, and to do that, he had to get the hell out of there.

John stared at the computer screen, willing it to tell him something. Anything. But it remained stubbornly unhelpful. Just like the answering machine and Flo's office. Every step forward, two steps back. Meanwhile, someone out there was watching. Knew his moves. His thoughts. Which was more than he could say for himself.

And to top it all off, his own employees were beginning to watch him, too. Frank had driven that point home nicely. He honestly believed that John had killed Flo. Believed it strongly enough to have been searching for evidence.

John closed his eyes, fighting against exhaustion. His body couldn't handle much more. He knew that, but he didn't have a choice. He had to push onward. Everything in him urged him forward. He owed it to Flo. He owed it to himself.

His glance fell again to the answering machine. Why hadn't he listened to the message when he'd first seen it? If he had, Flo might still be alive. But she wasn't—she wasn't. And nothing he could do was going to bring her back. So it was up to him to avenge her death.

But good intentions weren't enough, he needed evidence, something tangible that could provide answers. And what he had was nothing. He slammed his hand down on the desk, the gesture testimony to his frustration. He'd checked Flo's office after Frank had left, searching through her things for something to explain why she'd called him.

But there was nothing out of the ordinary. He'd even done a cursory search of her room, again coming up empty-handed. So the only thing he had left was her computer. But so far, he'd found nothing that seemed unusual. Nothing that pointed to why someone would want her dead.

She'd said she'd wanted to talk. In and of itself, that could mean anything. But taken in consort with the fact that she was murdered only hours later, he had to believe that she'd discovered something.

He studied the computer screen, the log from Flo's computer taunting him. There was nothing here that he didn't already know. For the last few days, Flo had spent the bulk of her time examining financial records. At his request. The rest of her time had been spent dealing with routine Guardian business. The only thing at all of interest was the fact that for most of the day yesterday her computer had been out of commission.

According to the log, it hadn't been put back on-line until sometime just before her death. He pounded the keyboard in frustration.

"You don't look so good." Katie stood in the doorway, her concern obvious.

"Surprise, surprise." He narrowed his eyes, glaring at her. "You may not have noticed, but I'm the primary suspect in a murder investigation."

"I'm aware of that." Her voice was soft, cajoling.

"But there's no sense in putting yourself back in the hospital."

"Oh, come on, Katie, you can give up the playacting. I know Roswell left you here to spy on me."

"I don't give a damn what Roswell wants, and you know it. I'm here to make sure you're safe. In case you've forgotten, someone out there wants you dead."

"I haven't forgotten. It's just getting a little hard to tell the good guys from the bad guys."

She flinched. "I guess I deserve that, but it doesn't change the fact that I'm on your side."

"Well, you've certainly got an odd way of showing it." Despite himself, he felt his anger dissipating. There was something disarming about her. He supposed it was what made her good at her job.

"So have you found anything?" she asked, obviously trying to change the subject.

"You expect me to tell you?" The words were out before he could stop them, exasperation mixing with indignation.

"If it helps you, yes, I do." She sounded earnest now, and he almost believed her. Or maybe it was just that he wanted to believe her. Everything was so damned confusing.

But she was right about one thing. He did need help. And quite honestly, there was nothing damning in what he'd found, and there was always the chance she'd see something he'd missed. There might be an emotional gulf between them, but that didn't mean she was out to railroad him.

He sighed, resignation replacing confusion. "Flo left me a message. On the answering machine." He tipped his head toward the offending black box. "I'd forgotten about it, with everything that happened. But when I came in here to check it, it was gone."

Her eyebrows shot up. "Someone erased it?"

He nodded. "And if I had to call it, I'd say it was

someone here at Guardian. No one else would know there was a machine up here. Much less that Flo would use it."

"Unless she told them." Katie frowned, her eyes narrowed in thought.

"Either way, we still have nothing." He tried but couldn't keep the bitterness out of his voice. "I searched her office last night, while you were sleeping. Ran into Frank while I was down there."

"What was he doing out that late?"

"Trying to prove I killed Flo." He was used to the idea, or at least he thought he was, but saying the words out loud made it seem so irrevocable.

"Oh, John." The compassion in her eyes was almost more than he could bear.

"I'm fine. Really. I don't give a damn what anyone thinks about me. All that matters right now is finding Flo's killer."

"So what did you find when you searched her office?"

"Nothing. Hell, I even searched her computer, but according to this," he tapped the monitor, "it was down all day. It wasn't back on-line until shortly before her death."

"Wait a minute. Maybe I have something." She moved toward the desk, frowning in concentration. "On my way out of the building last night, I saw her. She was working in the office next door—Frank's office."

Despite everything, John felt a surge of excitement. "Which means anything she did would be in his log, not hers." He started to type, his good hand moving faster than his bad one, making a jumble of the effort. He forced himself to calm down, typing one-handed instead.

Katie had moved to stand behind him. "But if it's Frank's computer, you won't be able to tell the difference between what he was doing and what she was doing, right?"

He shook his head, intent on the files he was pulling up. "No. Each computer in the system is password protected. Only the principal user knows the password."

"So she'd either have to have the password or she couldn't get on. Same problem."

Again he shook his head, moving down the file list, selecting the log. "I'm the administrator. Which means my password overrides everyone else's."

"And Flo had your password." She leaned closer, her hair brushing against his shoulder. "But I still don't see how that would allow you to differentiate between activities of the user and the administrator on the same computer."

"I set up the system so that it tracks users by individual password." He clicked again, then waited while the computer whirred into action. The file opened, a string of new files displayed. "Got it."

"Let's hope it's something to prove your innocence, Mr. Brighton. Because from where I stand, you're going to need all the help you can get."

John looked across the desk to meet the chilly gaze of Edmund Roswell, and automatically reached over to turn off the computer. Whatever was there, he had no intention of sharing it with Roswell. He didn't like the man on principle. No matter who he worked for.

Eric D'Angelo strode into the room on Roswell's heels, his expression grim. John fought against a shiver of dread. Whatever was happening, it wasn't good. "We got the ballistics report back."

"What did you find?" He choked out the words, not certain he wanted to hear the answer.

"The gun we found on the scene is the same one that killed Miller." D'Angelo's gaze collided with his, and John wished it hadn't. There was recrimination there.

Recrimination and disgust. In all his years of business dealings, no one had ever looked at him with disgust.

"And it only gets better." Roswell's smile was slow, totally devoid of humor. "You see, we ran the serial number on the gun, and guess what, turns out it's registered to you."

"But I don't own a gun." John fought against his anger. This was a setup, he could smell it coming. And Roswell was enjoying himself entirely too much.

"The records don't seem to agree with that." D'Angelo handed him a report.

He scanned the paper, his anger dissipating, replaced with a drowning sense of inevitability. He felt Katie's hand on his shoulder, and looked up at her, needing something, anything, to hold on to. Her eyes were on Roswell, her face a mask, emotion locked tightly away. But he knew her well enough to recognize the taut line of her shoulders, the tiny twitch at the corner of her mouth. She was angry. More than angry, she was furious.

And in some absurdly surreal way he felt comforted.

He returned his gaze to D'Angelo, Katie's hand still warm on his shoulder. "So what happens now?"

"We take you in." D'Angelo lifted a pair of handcuffs, his gray eyes unreadable. "You're under arrest for the murders of Florence Tedesky and Derek Miller."

Chapter 21

"Come to gloat?" John watched her from a corner of the cell as the guard let her in, the door clanging shut ominously behind her.

"I thought we had a truce."

His laugh was dry, not much more than a hiss of air. "I think, considering the circumstances, all bets are off."

She crossed over to him, lifting a hand to touch his cheek. "On the contrary, I'd say they count now more than ever."

He waited a beat before pulling away, and Katie counted it a small victory.

"So what's the situation?" John looked out of place in the jail cell, like a cartoon version of reality, and she wished she could reassure him, but the news wasn't good.

"Besides ballistics and the gun registration, they've got prints." She sat down on the cot, tipping her head back to look at him.

"I picked up the gun. Of course there are prints." He sounded angry and hopeless all at the same time.

"There's more." She sighed, realizing there wasn't anything to do but tell him the truth. "The first shooting, Miller's, was right-handed."

"And the second?" She could see in his eyes that he already knew what she was going to say.

"Left-handed. It's circumstantial, but considering you

were right-handed before Mexico and left-handed after-ward, it fits. And when you combine that with the prints and registration, it's pretty damning."

"I didn't kill her." The words were low, almost forced.

"I know that, John. But unfortunately they've got a lot against you." She stood up, searching for words. Things were strained between them at best, and his arrest only amplified their differences. At least for the moment, they appeared to be on opposite sides of the fence.

Literally.

But she wasn't letting him go. And she wasn't letting him take the fall for something he hadn't done. "How're you holding up?"

"As well as can be expected, I guess. In light of my condition they expedited the arraignment. Fat lot of good it did me." His bitterness was raw, almost a tangible thing.

"No bail."

He shrugged, the gesture telling. "They seem to think I'm a flight risk."

She struggled for something more meaningful to say. But there simply weren't words. "You've got an attorney?"

"Yeah. Anson Carabello. He's supposed to be the best. Not that it seems to matter. He pretty much said what you did." He walked to the tiny window, leaning his head against the bars.

"We'll find a way out of this."

He turned to face her, the shadow of his beard making his teeth shine white in the dark of the cell. "I don't see how."

"Well, first off, I'm going to check that computer."

"For the FBI?" His brows lifted, his expression harsh.

"No." She met his gaze unflinchingly. "For you."

He sighed, resignation coloring his expression. "You'll need the password."

She nodded, her gaze still locked with his. "Shouldn't be a problem, I used to have an in with the boss." So much said, in so few words. She waited, not certain that he'd trust her this far.

"They won't want you on the computers." He didn't have to say who. Considering the circumstances, she wasn't exactly a welcome fixture at Guardian.

"I'm not planning to ask for permission." She hoped her face reflected more confidence than she was feeling. "I'll be back as soon as I can."

He nodded, and whispered the password.

Resurrection.

She bit back a smile, thinking of the misshapen phoenix. Jonathan Brighton certainly had a knack for rising from the dead. She just hoped he could manage it one more time.

Frank paced the confines of his study, trying to decide what to do. He could leave things the way they were, and most likely he'd get what he'd been promised. But somehow the idea didn't sit well with him. Valerie and Jason had lied. Played him for a sucker. And quite possibly set John up to take a fall. He didn't think they were killers, but suddenly in light of what he'd discovered, he wasn't so sure.

He needed to talk to someone. Someone he could trust. Unfortunately, the only man he'd ever truly trusted was behind bars. Guilt washed through him. If he'd turned over what he'd found . . .

But he hadn't. Although that didn't negate the fact that he'd sided against John, and that in doing so, he might at least partially be responsible for the situation at hand. The idea made him physically sick. He'd let his ego get in the way of good judgment. Let Valerie Alejo charm him into treasonous thoughts.

So the question of the day was what he was going to do about it. He'd skated along to someone else's tune for far too long. It was time to stop being everybody's doormat.

Enough was enough.

The moment had come to stand up and be counted. He either stood with John or continued to cast his lot in with liars like Valerie and Jason. Put like that, the choice was easy. He'd just needed to face himself to recognize the truth of it.

He'd stand with John. No matter what happened.

Even if Jesse didn't get everything she wanted.

The thought was freeing. And for the first time in a long time Frank smiled, certain of what he was going to do. If he couldn't talk to John, he'd do the next best thing. He'd talk to Katie Cavanaugh. John trusted her, and she was with the FBI. She'd know what to do.

Now all he had to do was find her.

Guardian was quiet, considering the excitement of the night before, although Katie had taken the service elevator just to be safe. John's apartment was shuttered and still, the dark shadows giving it an almost sinister feel.

Despite herself, she shivered, wondering if there was really a way out of this nightmare. She forced herself to abandon her dark thoughts, and instead concentrate on the computer in front of her. She'd followed John's instructions, and through the miracle of modern technology had accessed the computer log on Frank's machine.

The problem was that there was nothing on it to indicate that Flo had used the machine. According to John, she should be seeing a list of activities. Things Flo had done the day of her murder, but there was nothing. The only person who'd used Frank's computer was Frank.

And just at the moment, that didn't help her one lit-

tle bit. She leaned back in the chair, closing her eyes, trying to remember seeing Flo. Her thoughts had been on
John, so her powers of observation hadn't been the best,
but she clearly remembered seeing the woman sitting in
Frank's office.

Or at least she thought she did. It had all happened
so fast. She'd been running away from John's recrimi-
nations, and Flo had seen her and called out, but not
from her office. She'd been in the office next door,
working at the computer.

If things hadn't been so dire, Katie would have
stopped to talk, but under the circumstances she'd only
waved, intent on escape. The only reason she remembered it at all was that it had seemed odd to see Flo in
the wrong office.

Frank's office.

Katie's mind obediently trotted out the image, except
that it was wrong. The image reversed. Right on left.
Understanding dawned and she opened her eyes, fingers
flying over the keyboard.

Flo hadn't been in Frank's office at all. She'd been in
the other office, the one on the left of hers. It had been
Jason's office—Jason's computer.

She entered the commands again, consulting John's
notes, this time using Jason's ID, and John's password.
The computer whirred for a moment, as if thinking,
then beeped insistently, informing her that her password
was invalid.

Frustrated, she repeated the commands, with the
same result.

She banged the keyboard in frustration, and tried a
third time, this time typing slowly, making certain each
letter was correct. After all, three times was the charm.

Not.

Again the computer beeped at her, this time in suc-
cession, its patience obviously wearing thin. Which was

par for the course. Katie ran a hand through her hair, studying the error message.

Incorrect password.

Either Jason had a different setup than Frank, or Jason's ID had been changed. Either possibility had merit, but the latter meant that it was possible someone knew she was in the system. Instinct made her move quickly, shutting down the computer, moving from behind the desk.

The door squeaked as it opened, signaling her instincts had been dead-on.

"What are you doing in here?" Danny's voice was way beyond anger.

It crossed her mind to try and confide in him. To tell him what she was looking for, but she hesitated. It wasn't her story to tell, and if John wanted Danny to know, he'd have told him himself.

She turned slowly, schooling her face into what she hoped was placidity. Truth was, she didn't do vapid all that well. "I was looking for this." Her hand closed around the little phoenix and she held it out for Danny to see. "John wanted it. And since I was going to be here packing up my things, I offered to bring it to him."

Danny eyed the little statue, then lifted his gaze slowly to meet hers. "You've no right to be in here. Not unless you've got a warrant."

"For a statue?" She raised an eyebrow, hoping she didn't look as transparent as she felt.

"I don't give a damn about that piece of crap and you know it, but I don't like your sneaking around John's office without him being here. How do I know you aren't procuring evidence?"

She held out her arms, allowing her rancor to show. "So search me."

His eyes narrowed. "Don't tempt me."

She glared back at him, her ire raising the ante on his anger by more than a little. Where the hell did he get off questioning her? She sucked in a deep breath, striving for calm, reminding herself he was only trying to protect John. "Look, Danny, whether you believe it or not, we both want the same thing. I want to help John as much as you do."

"And why should I believe that?"

"Frankly, I don't care what you believe. I care about your brother, and I intend to help him any way I can. So you can either work with me or work against me, but before you decide, you might want to remember that I've got the full weight of the law on my side. And people tend to take FBI agents seriously. Am I making myself clear?"

A muscle in his jaw signaled his agitation. Danny Brighton didn't take well to being told what to do. Which was something they obviously had in common.

Finally, with a glare worthy of an inquisitioner, he nodded. "You do what you have to do, *Agent* Cavanaugh, but you do it with a warrant. If my brother needs anything else, I'll see that he gets it. In the meantime, you have fifteen minutes to get your things and get out of here. If you're not gone by then, I'll call security and have them throw you out. Am I making *myself* clear?"

She opened her mouth to argue, then closed it again, turning heel to go get her stuff. She couldn't really say that she blamed the man. After all, as far as John and Danny were concerned, the FBI was the enemy. And for all Danny could see, despite her protestations to the contrary, she was a bona fide player on the enemy's side.

She'd have thrown her out, too, had she been in his position. Besides, the man was a zealot when it came to protecting his brother. She'd seen it from the first time she'd met him.

Moving quickly, she stuffed the rest of her clothes into her duffel and zipped it closed. The little statue was lying on the bed, one eye staring up at her balefully.

With a tiny smile, she picked it up and tucked it into her pocket. She hadn't meant to take the thing, but now that she'd lied about it to Danny, she could hardly put it back. Picking up the duffel, she walked into the living room, surprised to see it empty, evidently Danny's bark was worse than his bite.

Quickly, she walked to the study, poking her head inside, relieved to see that it was empty as well. John's laptop sat in the corner, and without stopping to consider ramifications, she grabbed it, turning back to the desk for a last look. If nothing else, she'd have a way to access the company computers if John thought of another way in.

If Danny had a problem with it, he could take it up with his brother. The outside door opened with a creak, and she stuffed the computer bag into her duffel as she walked into the living room. Maybe Danny had called the guards after all.

She held up a hand, ready to acquiesce, but dropped it in surprise when Frank Jacoby rounded the corner.

"I'm glad you're still here." His voice was softer than a whisper, his eyes darting about the room as if he expected someone to jump out at him. "I need to talk to you."

"All right. Have a seat." Katie frowned, and waved toward the sofa, trying to sort out what in the world had the little man so spooked.

"No." The word came out a staccato burst. "Not here. Meet me in half an hour. The Starbucks on Congress and Sixth." He shot another look around the empty living room, pivoted, and practically ran from the place.

All thoughts of Danny and his threats fled as she turned her mind to Frank and whatever it was that had him running scared. She just hoped that whatever it was, it changed things for the better, because, honest to God, she wasn't certain it could get any worse.

* * *

"What the hell is going on?" Jason stood in the doorway to Danny's office, his fears manifesting themselves in anger.

"I'm not sure I'm following, Jason." Danny swiveled his chair so that they were eye to eye. "I realize that things have been hairy of late, but what specifically seems to be the problem?"

"Don't patronize me, Brighton." He swallowed back further retort.

As if reading his thoughts, Danny raised a hand in placation. "I'm sorry. Tempers are running high around here. I didn't mean to snap. What's up?"

Jason swallowed a lungful of air, letting the influx of oxygen soothe his frazzled nerves. "I can't get onto my computer. Damn thing says my ID is invalid."

"Yeah. They all say that. I'm trying to restructure the system."

"What the hell for?" He immediately regretted his outburst. No sense letting Danny realize how upset he was.

"Seems like the wise move. We don't want any unauthorized entry into the system. And until this is over, there's no way to know who to trust."

"Something happened." He waited, already knowing the answer, but was curious to see where the newest danger lay.

"I caught the FBI bitch upstairs in John's office."

"She was on the computer?"

"Not when I walked in. But I see no point in taking chances."

"So when am I going to be able to access the files?"

"Later this afternoon. You'll have limited access restored." Danny sat back, steepling his fingers. "But until we get to the bottom of what's happening, I'll be the only one with full access."

Jason frowned. "Under whose authority?"

"Mine. Jonathan isn't here, and according to the corporation bylaws, I'm second in command until he re-
signs or is replaced."

"I see." So much for Valerie's coup. "And after
that?"

"Let's cross one bridge at a time. Right now, it's
going to take all the skill I have just to get around
Jonathan's security. The man is obsessive about protecting files. I'm going over there in a little while to get the
rest of the codes. We'll be off-line until then."

No sense in creating problems where there were
none. If no one was on-line, then things were safe—for
the time being. He'd just have to be patient a little while
longer.

"I, ah . . . found something." Frank stared down into
his latte, looking like he wished he were anywhere but
here.

"Something that can help John." She tried to lead
him, resisting the urge to scream at him instead. Scaring
a witness had its uses, but not in an instance like this.

"Maybe." He laid a small black notebook on the
table. "This was in Derek Miller's desk."

"You took it?"

"I found it, in a hidden compartment, and I thought
it was important, so yes, I took it."

She flipped open the book. Columns of numbers
were neatly listed, along with dates. Each entry followed by the initials *JB*. John Brighton. "Do you know
what these are?"

"I'm not sure. But I think it's a record of transfers
and withdrawals. Jonathan mentioned the money he
paid to Miller. I think it's there at the end." He reached
for the book, flipping to another page, pointing to the
number.

The date was accurate. The initials damning. John

had recorded his crimes with the diligence of an accountant. "I thought you said this would help him."

Frank's smile was only a shadow, but it was there nonetheless. "You're seeing it the way I did. I thought it was Jonathan at first, too. But look at this." He reached into his pocket, pulling out a folded piece of paper.

Katie unfolded it, and stared down at a page from a day-planner. The appointments initialed in the same way as the black book's entries. She looked up, to meet Frank's gaze, puzzled. "I don't see—"

"It's Jason's. I took it out of his Filofax. The initials are *JP*, not *JB*. It's just the way he writes. John didn't pay money to Derek, Jason did—because of this."

Katie felt a small stirring of hope. "But I saw the check, Frank, it had John's signature."

"I've got an answer for that, too." He reached in his pocket again, this time producing a rubber stamp. "It's Jonathan's signature. I found it in Jason's desk."

She looked back at the book, the stirring blossoming into something more. "How long have you had this?"

"A while. I wasn't sure what to do with it. At first I wanted to keep it quiet for Jonathan's sake, and then," he looked down at his hands, obviously unwilling to look her in the eyes, "and then I decided to use it against him."

"But you didn't." Despite the implications of what he'd been going to do, Frank was here now, and in her book that counted for something.

"I tried. I planted it in his old office, figuring someone would find it. That's what I was doing last night— when I found Jonathan and Flo." He looked up, his eyes begging her to believe him. "Then later, I met with Valerie and Danny and Jason. To talk about what happened and what we were going to do."

"And that's when you saw the Filofax?" She frowned, trying to sort through the new information, to put it in context with Flo's murder.

"Yeah, and I decided to go back and get the book."
He shrugged, still looking uncomfortable. "I . . . I
thought it might be useful."

"To blackmail Jason." He was easy to read, his
thoughts practically telegraphing themselves to her.

"I considered it. For a moment. But I couldn't go
through with it. Not if there's a chance this can help
John. Not if Jason's the one who killed Florence."

She reached over to cover his hand with hers. "You
did the right thing, Frank. You should be proud of yourself. It took courage to come to me with this."

"Will it help?" His face was so hopeful, she wanted
to lie to him, to make him believe everything would be
okay.

But there was nothing to be gained in doing that.
Jason Pollock might be an embezzler, and he might even
have written the check to Derek Miller, but that was still
a long way from proving he killed the man.

"I don't know. But it certainly can't hurt. I'll get this
to my boss, and then we'll take it from there. At least it
creates reasonable doubt. In the meantime, you be careful, Frank. Two people are already dead. Watch your
back."

He nodded, straightening his shoulders. "I'll be okay.
You just take care of John. He's been through enough."

"I will. You take care of you."

He nodded, and stood up, beginning to make his way
out of the crowded coffee bar. Allies came from the
most unlikely places.

She closed the little book and tucked it into her
pocket along with the stamp. She'd take it to Roswell,
but before she did that, she was stopping to make a
copy. One for John's lawyer and another for Eric D'Angelo. If things played out the way she expected, she
wanted to cover all her bases.

She *was* going to help John. And to do that, she
needed to plan her strategy carefully, make every move

count. One mistake, and she was out of the game. And she simply couldn't afford that.

Despite his misgivings, John was counting on her, and she wasn't about to let him down again. This time she was going to prove she was worthy, not only of his trust, but of his love. There was going to be a happy ending if she had to sweat blood to make it so.

He deserved that. *She* deserved that.

And Jason Pollock deserved to be strung up by his balls.

Chapter 22

"Hey, bro, not exactly the Savoy, huh." Danny's attempt at humor elicited a small smile, despite the circumstances. "I thought I ought to check in and see how things were going."

"I've been better." John watched his brother enter the cell. Comrades in arms, at least for the moment. "Phones ringing off the wall?"

"About as you'd expect. Jason is handling it. How'd the meeting with Carabello go?"

"Lawyerly. Basically he told me to hang in and keep my mouth shut."

Danny walked to the hole that passed for a window, making a play of looking outside. "It doesn't look good, John."

"I know. That's why I'm going to have to resign. I don't see any way around it. You all can't fight my battles and keep the company alive at the same time. If I distance myself, maybe you can still salvage something."

Danny's expression was grim. "I guess it can't be helped, but I don't have to pretend to like it. Guardian is your company."

"Yours, too, and that's why I'm trusting you to take care of it for me until I can work this thing out."

"No worries. You can count on me." Danny's smile was halfhearted, but well meant. "Along those lines, I need to get some passwords from you. I'm restructuring the computer system so that I have administrative access."

"There's a list of passwords in the safe in my study."

Danny shook his head, frowning. "They're not there. I looked this morning."

John repressed a smile. "You had my combination?"

"For a hacker you can be a bit obvious, Jonathan." He shrugged. "You always use Mom's birthday when you need a numeric password."

"I might be predictable, but I'm not stupid. There's another safe. Hidden inside the first one. And the password isn't mother's birthday."

"So what'd you use? Dad's birthday?"

"Converted to hex."

"You converted Dad's birth date to hexadecimal?" His brother's expression had changed to astonishment. "Very James Bond."

John shrugged. "It made sense at the time. Anyway, the lock is behind the metal backing. It just pushes aside."

"Right." Danny was all business now. "I'll get the passwords and get to work. I'm assuming all the account passwords are there?"

"You should have everything you need." John's head was beginning to pound; he hadn't really slept since finding Flo.

"You look tired. I wish to hell I could get you out of here."

"I know, Danny. But right now there's nothing we can do. Just keep things running and help Carabello." He stood up, stretching his muscles. "He's going to find the truth."

"Even if it implicates you?"

It seemed to be the question of the hour. Frank last night, and now Danny. "Yeah. Even if it proves I'm guilty. I didn't kill Flo, Danny. Not with a gun anyway.

But if I had something to do with it, then I want to know. She deserves that."

Danny shook his head, his expression back to grim. "You're a better man than I am, Jonathan."

There'd been a time when he'd actually believed that was true, but if he was honest, he'd have to admit that he just wasn't certain anymore.

And not knowing was far worse than whatever the truth might be.

"I don't see how this changes anything." Roswell eyed her with something akin to the way a man looked at an imbecile, the overdrawn patience in his voice making her want to scream.

"Are you kidding?" She fought to keep her tone on an even keel. "This changes everything. If this book is right, Jason Pollock was operating one hell of an embezzlement scheme."

"But it doesn't prove he murdered Florence Tedesky, and we've got Brighton dead to rights for that. Miller, too."

Katie fought against her anger. "But if Pollock was behind the money, then wouldn't it follow that he was behind the killings?"

"Not necessarily. I told you we think this involves industrial espionage. It seems to me that what we've got here is two different crimes. Simple embezzlement, and treason. Let's see . . . treason or embezzlement? I'll take treason for five hundred, Alex."

"You're a bastard, you know that don't you?"

"I'm good at what I do. And I'm a month from retirement. So are you asking if I lead with my heart? Hell no. I've learned that fucking lesson more than once. Give it up, Cavanaugh. There's no such thing as an innocent man. Everyone has his demons. And it's our job to find them. If that doesn't sit well with you, then perhaps you're pursuing the wrong profession."

She narrowed her eyes, wishing once again that she had the courage to deck him, but leveling him wouldn't solve anything, and quite frankly it was likely to land her in jail. For the moment, she figured one of them in jail was enough.

"I'm fine. I'm just not into witch hunts. No matter how it affects my career."

He glared at her a moment, but when she didn't continue with anything more pointed, he obviously chose to ignore the barb. "The indictment stands. As far as I'm concerned, Brighton killed the woman. The evidence supports it."

"But what if it doesn't? What if the gun registration was forged?" She waved the stamp at him for effect.

Roswell frowned. "It wouldn't explain the fingerprints. Or the left/right manipulation. You're whistling in the dark, Cavanaugh."

"Inquiring minds want to know." She strove for intimidating, but based on Roswell's smile she wasn't getting the job done.

"Fine, we'll look at the application. Anything to get you off my back. Just so happens D'Angelo sent over the files a little while ago."

"So let me see it. Let me see the signature." She grabbed a pad of paper and stamped it, John's signature stark against the white sheet.

Roswell reached for a manila folder and handed it to her. "It should be in here."

She flipped through it, resisting the urge to read. There'd be time for that later. She found the registration and laid the signature line alongside the stamped paper.

Roswell's smile cranked up a notch, and her stomach sank. Although the signature was similar, it wasn't a match. The registration signature was larger, loopier, and quite obviously blue. Clearly not a stamp at all.

"Well, I guess that shoots your theory to hell, sugar." Roswell's tone was just this side of taunting.

"Not necessarily. What about the money Jason paid Miller? Surely that's reason enough to suspect him of Miller's murder?"

"Possibly." Roswell fingered the file, his eyes glittering with self-satisfaction. "If we didn't already have the killer in custody. Give it up, Cavanaugh, you're trying to make the facts fit your theory. It's a rookie mistake and you know it."

He was right and it really didn't sit well with her. She'd never been good at taking direction, trusting her own instincts more. Still, she couldn't argue with the facts in front of her, but that still didn't make John guilty. Despite the evidence.

"I'm trying to save an innocent man. I'd think you'd be interested in seeing that justice is done."

"You're trying to justify the fact that you've taken a personal interest in the man, sugar. And I'm telling you that's the fast road to failure. The fact is that Jonathan Brighton is guilty, and as far as I'm concerned, that's just where I want him. Or have you forgotten that?"

"I haven't forgotten anything. But it seems to me you have. Our job is to make sure that we have the right man, but all that matters to you is your precious record." She'd tried to keep her disdain private, but she couldn't help herself.

"You're missing the big picture, Cavanaugh. We're interested in something more important than Jonathan Brighton. And if he takes a fall to get us there, so be it."

"God, you're a sanctimonious son of a bitch. Any means to justify the end? Roswell, we're talking about a man accused of a murder he didn't commit. I've just brought you supporting evidence, and you're blatantly ignoring it. I'm telling you, John didn't kill anyone."

"Wishful thinking, Cavanaugh."

"If you won't listen, I'll take this over your head."

His eyes narrowed to slits, sparks there threatening

to ignite into full-blown rage. "If you do, I promise you'll regret it."

They were standing face-to-face, her anger matching his in tenor and velocity. "What I regret is standing here talking to you." She reached for the black book, but Roswell was faster.

"I'll make sure this gets into the right hands."

"Buried, don't you mean?" It was the first thing that popped into her mind, and she immediately regretted it.

His face turned an angry red, a vein throbbing in his temple. "I'm going to pretend you didn't make that remark, Cavanaugh. I don't know how *y'all* handle things up in Boston, but down here in Texas, we don't accuse each other of misconduct unless we're pretty damn certain we're right."

"I didn't mean it." There was a code in law enforcement, and she'd just stepped over the line. "I was angry. I'm sorry." She choked on the last words, the apology bitter.

Roswell studied her for a minute, his own anger fading. "Fine. But you'd better work on that temper, sugar. It's going to get you in some serious trouble one of these days."

She nodded, feeling all of about twelve. Her father had spent most of her childhood telling her exactly the same thing.

"From here on out we'll proceed on the facts of the case, Agent Cavanaugh. Are we clear on that?" There was a touch of sarcasm in his voice, but also a note authority she couldn't ignore.

So she nodded again, admitting grudgingly that Roswell's logic was solid. She'd counted on the information about Jason clearing John, but it hadn't. If anything, it had only muddied the water more, and despite her instincts, the notebook didn't negate the ballistics findings, or the gun registration.

Which left them with nothing but John's word, and

considering his state of mind, she wasn't sure a jury would buy it.

A tough spot if ever there was one.

And damned if she knew how they were going to get out of it.

"I won't let this happen. Do you understand me, Jason? I won't." Valerie wasn't happy. She'd made that abundantly clear, but Jason wasn't certain she realized that she didn't have the power to do anything about it.

They'd planned for this, been ready to take advantage of it, but they'd made a crucial error in calculation. Danny Brighton was standing with his brother. Which meant their shares carried the day. More importantly, it meant that Danny was head of the company. Their attempted coup had amounted to nothing.

"I think you'd do best to go with the flow, Val. There's not a lot we can do about it. And there's no sense in pissing Danny off."

"I don't care who I piss off, Jason. I want control of the company. I deserve it. Danny Brighton couldn't run a taco stand, let alone a business. Who the hell do you think has been keeping things going all these months?"

Actually, if he had to call it, he'd say Frank had been the one holding things together. The guy was a little odd, but he knew his stuff, and without his organizational skills they'd have been stuck with Danny's and Valerie's posturing, none of which had resulted in anything tangible as far as business was concerned.

Not that he was going to share that thought with Valerie.

"It's not about what you deserve, Val. It's about how the company is structured, and whether you like it or not, Danny is the legal heir to the throne, so to speak."

"Wonderful." She threw up her hands, eyes flashing behind her glasses. "This is all Frank's fault anyway."

"How do you figure that?"

"He was supposed to make certain Danny was on our side." She sat on the edge of her desk, crossing one long leg over the other. "Face it, he fucked up."

"It wasn't Frank, Val. It was Florence. Her death united Danny and Jonathan in a way that never would have happened if she'd stayed alive."

"Then that makes him even more guilty. He said he was going to do something about Flo. Remember?" Valerie glared at him, stabbing her finger into the air to underscore the point.

"You don't mean to imply that Frank killed her?" Jason tried but couldn't keep the shock from his voice. The idea was ludicrous.

"That's exactly what I'm saying. Frank is always trying to prove himself. And he did say that he'd take care of things."

"He meant he was going to talk to the woman, not blow her brains out."

"You don't know that. Frank walks a fine line. It wouldn't surprise me at all to find out that he has sociopathic tendencies."

"You're spouting garbage. Frank wouldn't know the butt end of a gun from the barrel."

"It's pretty straightforward, Jason, you just point the thing and pull the trigger." She demonstrated the action with her hand, her index finger pointing at him. "Bang. You're dead."

"I still don't buy it. Killing Florence wouldn't accomplish anything except what it did—uniting the Brightons. Strategically, it would have been a colossal mistake. Frank may be desperate at times, but he isn't stupid."

"I hope you're right."

"Of course I am. Besides, even if I could accept the idea of Frank as the shooter, he couldn't possibly have managed to frame Jonathan. And then there's the whole issue of Derek Miller. The same gun was used to kill him, which, if you'll pardon the pun, shoots a hell of a hole in your theory."

"I suppose so." Valerie's eyes were narrowed in thought. "But if Frank didn't kill Flo, then what do you suppose he was planning to do? I know he had something. He was too certain about his ability to solve our problems."

"I haven't a clue. And the truth is, I don't think it matters anymore. The game has been played and we lost. The thing to do now is to try and work with Danny to keep Guardian viable."

"Wonderful." She stood up, her sigh filling her room. It was the first time he'd ever seen her look defeated. "Business as usual."

He held back a smile. "Something like that. Has Danny given you any of the new passwords?" His hand tightened on the arm of the chair as he worked to keep his voice casual. "I'm trying to tie up a few loose ends and I need to access some files that aren't on my computer."

"I've only got access to my stuff. He's still working on everything else. I think there was a problem with getting around some of Jonathan's safeguards. Danny's gone to see him."

"Well, I hope he hurries. I don't like having my hands tied."

Which was the understatement of all time. Someone out there had his book, and he needed to find it before things got any further out of hand. Despite the fact that Jonathan was in jail, he had the feeling this thing was far from over. If he wasn't careful, he was bound to be caught in the backwash.

And that simply wouldn't do at all.

Police stations were all alike. Voices mixing together in a cacophonous symphony as people tried to argue their way out of the mess they'd made of their lives.

There was even a particular smell. Antiseptic mixed with stale coffee and human fear. A heady combination.

One she'd been attracted to since she'd been old enough to go with her father to work. She'd sat at his desk more times than she could count, watching humanity filter in and out like ocean water on sand.

And she'd known right then that this is where she belonged. Chasing the bad guys, avenging the good ones. Making the world a better place. Noble crap like that. Except that the line between good and evil wasn't always discernible. There was bad in good people and good in bad people. The trick was to measure the degree, and sometimes the difference between black and white got all mucked up.

Which left one in a hell of a mess.

Case in point. She tightened her fingers around the manila envelope she held in her hand, and, shoulders squared, walked up to the desk sergeant. "FBI, Agent Cavanaugh." She flashed her badge. "I'm here for John Brighton."

She needed to explain things to him, and to let him know about Jason Pollock. Then she was going to give a copy of the notebook to D'Angelo. It wasn't exactly proper procedure, but she didn't trust Roswell to expedite the matter, and she couldn't just sit around and wait. It wasn't her style.

"Sign here, please."

She took the clipboard the sergeant was offering and scribbled her name, her thoughts still centered on John. Everything was happening so fast. As far as Roswell was concerned, John was already convicted, and as much as she despised the man, she couldn't completely discount his logic. The evidence was damning. Without something more, even the best of lawyers wasn't going to be able to get him off.

She needed time, and that's exactly what she didn't have. Maybe, if she was lucky, D'Angelo would take an

interest in the Pollock case, but even if he did, she
wasn't certain it would necessarily translate to John.

It was a conundrum, and since she couldn't access
John's computer files, she wasn't certain there was anything she could do to help. Truth was, she needed John.
Needed his knowledge of his system, and, quite possibly, his hacking abilities. Somewhere in the Guardian
computers there had to be a clue, but the way things
stood, they had a ice cube's chance in hell of finding it.

She slid the clipboard back across the counter, pushing away her fears. It wouldn't do for John to see her
like this. He had enough problems without her adding
to them. She was supposed to be helping him. Not increasing his burdens.

A noble thought. Despite the severity of the situation,
she bit back a smile. The door to her left opened and a
uniformed officer led a handcuffed John into the room.
He looked up, his gaze meeting hers, his expression anything but welcoming. "You."

"Me." Her answer was automatic and not particularly enlightening. Still trying to sort out this newest de-
velopment, she shot a look at the sergeant, who was
examining papers on the clipboard.

He ripped the top copy off, holding it out to her.
"Everything's in order, Agent Cavanaugh. He's all
yours."

She frowned at the officer, trying to make sense of his
words, and then reason hit her square in the face. John
was being transferred to federal authority, and the sergeant obviously thought she was here to collect him.
She hadn't signed a visitor's log at all. She'd signed the
transfer papers. Providence, or temptation? She wasn't
going to think about it. At least not now.

"Thanks. We'll take good care of him." She smiled
and took the sheet. "Oh, and Sergeant, could you see
that this envelope gets to Detective D'Angelo? Just some
information I promised I'd bring him." She laid the

envelope on the counter. Hopefully D'Angelo would take it for what it was—a little bit of an explanation for what she was about to do.

A burly man in overalls pushed his way past her, already grilling the sergeant as to the whereabouts of someone. She turned to John, and with a nod at the officer, took his arm. "Let's go."

"What the hell is going on?" The words came out on a hiss, something less than a whisper even, but he still managed to convey his anger.

Keeping a hand firmly on his elbow, she started forward, heading for the front door. "You're being transferred, Mr. Brighton." She pitched her voice louder than necessary, using a flat tone she hoped conveyed routine disinterest.

"Transferred where?" He jerked his arm away, his dark eyes sparking with anger.

"Federal prison. You'll stay there until your trial." She glared at him, trying to telegraph her thoughts, and not getting anywhere. So much for cosmic connection between lovers.

"You need help, Agent Cavanaugh?" The officer had obviously overheard their conversation, his steely-eyed gaze locked on John, a hand resting casually on his holster.

She smiled at him. "Thank you, but I'm fine."

He frowned down at her, his eyes assessing. "You certain a little thing like you can handle him?"

Gritting her teeth, she upped the wattage of her smile to beauty-queen level. "I'm positive." Returning her hand to John's elbow, she reached behind her, drawing her service revolver. "But if I have any problems, I'm sure that this will give me the advantage I need."

He looked from the gun to John and then back again, his skepticism still apparent. Stupid Neanderthal.

"I'll be fine. Now, if you don't mind, I'd like to get

him out of here." Before Jerome or Roswell showed up
to collect him.

The man shrugged and started back for his desk, and
she sighed with relief. One man under control. Now if
she could just do something about the other one.

She glanced up at John, propelling him forward. His
jaw was locked, a muscle in his cheek ticking in anger.
Not exactly a warm welcome. But then it wasn't every
day he was accused of murder and then sprung from jail
by his undercover FBI girlfriend. All in all, it would
probably make even the most flexible of men a little
testy.

And John wasn't exactly known for being flexible.

Chapter 23

"This is insane. You know that, right?" John was pacing around the motel room, his gait slow, but nevertheless agitated.

"I know that if we don't find a way to get to the bottom of what's happening, you're going to wind up on death row." Katie yanked the phone cord out of the socket, replacing it with the modem line. "You need access to your computer, it's as simple as that."

"Surely there is some legal way we could have accomplished that." He stopped pacing to glare at her.

"We tried that, remember? But I couldn't get in."

"So you could have asked me for more instructions. Or asked Danny to help you. I don't think it warranted a jailbreak."

She stopped messing with the computer, turning to face him, meeting his glare with one of her own. "It wasn't a jailbreak. You're still in custody—technically. We're just having a bit of a detour, that's all."

"Somehow I don't think Roswell is going to see it that way."

"Maybe not. But if we can prove you're innocent, it'll be worth the heat."

"I'm assuming you don't mean that literally." He grimaced as he turned the nonfunctioning air conditioner all the way to high, the tepid blast of air only making the room seem hotter.

"Come on, it's not that bad." As if to refute her statement, sounds from the highway filtered through a gap under the front door, the roar of a passing semi making the walls rattle. "Look, I know it's not the Four Seasons, but it's good cover. I figure there's no way Roswell's going to look for us this close to the police station." She turned back to the computer. "So how do I make this thing connect?"

"I'm still not convinced I wouldn't be better off just turning myself in."

His tone was stubborn, and she fought to keep from exploding, only half succeeding. "You really don't get this, do you? Roswell doesn't give a damn about you, John. For all he cares, you can spend the rest of your life on death row. You're a means to an end. Nothing more. He believes you can roll on Taegu. It's as simple as that."

"But I don't know anything. Surely that has to count for something." He sounded so certain, so positive that right would triumph. She wished there were some way to make it true.

But there wasn't.

"It means absolutely nothing. If Roswell's gamble doesn't pay off, you'll simply be a casualty of the system, and Roswell will move on to the next option."

John stood by the window, rubbing the bridge of his nose. "So it's a lose/lose situation."

"It doesn't have to be. That's why we're here. To change the odds. If we work together, maybe we can find a way to prove your innocence."

"Together." He said the word like a curse, the doubt in his eyes cutting through her like a knife.

"Unfortunately, I'm all you've got."

Their gazes met and held, communicating on a level far beyond words. There was a connection between them that even her betrayal hadn't broken. If only he'd trust it—believe in it.

"You're asking for a lot, Katie." He turned away from her, staring out the window.

She sank down onto the bed, anger giving way to despair. "Look, I didn't plan this. The opportunity just presented itself, and I think we're being fools if we don't make use of it. It's like a chess game. Up until now, Jason, or whoever is behind this, has had all the advantages. Every time we moved forward, he was ready with a countermove. It's almost as if it's all been choreographed. Prearranged. But this move is unexpected. So maybe it's the break we need." Her eyes met his, willing him to understand.

He held her gaze for moment, and then with a sigh he walked over to the computer. "There's a code box in the right-hand pocket of the case."

She reached into the computer case, her hand closing around the little phoenix. She'd forgotten putting him there for safekeeping. "I brought you something."

He swiveled to look at her, curiosity mixing with impatience.

She held the little bird out to him, a mute offering.

"You took it from my office?" He reached out for it, his thumb stroking the clay feathers lovingly. It might not be much to look at, but it was a powerful reflection of John's courage and fortitude.

"It was when Danny caught me on the computer. I said you'd asked for it."

He carefully put the statue on the table by the laptop, the little bird acting sentry. She swallowed back tears, and reached back into the computer case, pulling out a rectangular box about the size of a pack of gum. "This it?"

"Yeah." He glanced up from the computer, then went back to typing, the telltale hissing from the speaker indicating the connection was going through. "I need the displayed number."

"Ninety-six . . . sixteen . . . fifteen." She read the

numbers again to be sure she'd called them out right. "This is some kind of security code?"

"Right." He sat back for a moment, waiting, then resumed typing. "It changes every few minutes or so."

"How come I didn't have to use it?" She stared at the screen over his shoulder, praying that the code was still good.

"Because you weren't accessing via a modem." The computer beeped and a new screen appeared, this one asking for a user ID and password. "Okay, Danny, let's see how thorough you've been."

She frowned. "Danny did something to the computer?"

"Yeah, he's changing the passwords, limiting access until we get some sort of resolution to my predicament."

"So you're not going to be able to get in?"

He smiled up at her, the first one she'd seen since she'd liberated him from the police station. "It's my system. I can get in. It's just a matter of how hard it's going to be." He typed in a name and then a password, the password showing up as stars. The computer beeped angrily and a message box indicated the password had been refused. He entered another password and ID, and again the computer refused access.

"That's what happened to me."

He nodded, already typing something new. The computer beeped its disapproval again, but this time before the message window could appear, he typed another string of commands. With a whir, the computer sighed, the screen signaling his entry into the system.

"Will anyone know you're in there?"

"It's possible, if they're looking for me, but the odds are against it. It's already past five, most everyone is gone, and as you said, no one is expecting to find me on-line. So I think we're okay."

"So what are we looking for?" She watched over his

shoulder as he manipulated the keyboard, tapping out commands.

"An audit trail of sorts. We're trying to find out what Flo was doing just before she died. There's a possibility that whatever she found was on the computer, and so if I can re-create what she was accessing, then maybe I can figure out why someone would want her dead."

The screen displayed a table, the columns alternating in blue and green. The headings indicating the same kind of log as the one she'd accessed earlier on Frank's computer. "Is this Jason's machine?"

He nodded, his eyes narrowed as he studied the displayed information. "And from the looks of it, Jason's the only one who has been using it. Maybe you were mistaken about seeing her in there."

"It's possible, I suppose. I had a lot on my mind." He looked up at her, their gazes locking, their eyes saying things that neither of them were ready to put into words. She broke contact first, moving to sit on the bed. "It's also possible that someone cleaned up the log, right?"

"More than possible. I'd say likely, considering they found and erased Flo's message. I guess I just hoped that with Danny pulling the passwords, there wouldn't have been time to access the logs. This is what happens when you employ a bunch of hackers."

"Is Jason as good at hacking as you are?"

"No." He tapped out more commands, the computer buzzing with activity. "His forte is strictly PR, but he obviously knows his way around the system well enough to divert funds. So I wouldn't put it past him to be capable of cleaning up his mess."

"There's still got to be some part of this we're missing." She lay back on the bed with a sigh. "If we assume that Jason paid the thirty-five thousand to Miller—which seems like a fairly solid assumption based on what we know—we're left with the same problem we had when we thought it was you."

He stopped typing and turned to face her, his eyes narrowed in concentration.

"Why would Jason have paid Miller all that money and then turned around and killed him? It just doesn't track."

"There could be a million reasons. Maybe Miller was supposed to do something specific with the money and instead blew it on drugs. Or maybe he was blackmailing Jason and got greedy and wanted more."

"Yeah, but under any of those scenarios, you'd think Jason would have cleaned out the records. And he didn't. The embezzlement activity was hidden, I'll grant you that, but if you'd killed someone over it, wouldn't you want all evidence gone?" She frowned.

"I suppose so. I mean, now that you say that, it was almost too easy to find, wasn't it?"

"Right. As if someone wanted you to find it. We were just too surprised to see it at the time."

"Okay." He ran his good hand through his hair. "So how does that translate to what we know?"

"I'm not sure. But it seems like everything centers around Derek Miller. Maybe we've been looking into the wrong files. Have you looked at Miller's computer?"

"No. It wasn't in his office, I just assumed it was at home. He used a laptop, that way he could have everything with him all the time. He had docking stations at home and at work. I meant to follow up on it, I just didn't." His eyes telegraphed his regret.

"Hey," she sat up, intent on reassuring him, "it's not like you haven't had a few things on your mind."

"Thanks for that. I feel like I'm always a beat behind. Like you said about the chess game. I've been playing defense rather than offense."

She stood up, walking over to him, looking down at

the computer. "So what do you say we start fighting back. Can you access Miller's computer if it's at home?"

John was already working away at his computer, entering another ID and password. "No. The only way that would work is if it happened to be logged on to the network."

"So we pray you were mistaken and it's at the office."

He frowned as a message box beeped onto the screen. "It's not there."

"Damn. Do you remember seeing it earlier?"

He shook his head. "Not the actual machine, no. You're thinking someone could have taken it."

"Anything is possible. If we had the time, I could have D'Angelo check the police inventory."

"But considering the situation," he'd already turned off the computer and was packing it into its case, "we don't. Besides, we're being proactive not reactive, remember?"

She allowed herself the smallest of smiles. "So we're going on a road trip?" She was already reaching for the car keys, adrenaline pumping.

"Yeah. And hope to hell that Derek Miller's computer is still in his house."

"So why do you think she gave you the information?" Tony propped his feet up on his desk, his jacket slung across the back of his chair, his shirtsleeves rolled up, the ever-present hamburger in hand.

"I haven't a clue. But they're copies, so my guess is that she took the originals to Roswell." Eric stared down at neatly written columns, his mind churning with possibilities. "And from what I've seen, I'd say he told her to forget about it. The guy's got a one-track mind."

"A good one, Eric. I mean, you saw the evidence, he's got Brighton. So either this Pollock fellow is an accessory of some kind, or not related at all. Wouldn't be the first time that working on one case inadvertently led to another."

"Maybe." He picked up the papers, thumbing through them. "But I had our Ms. Cavanaugh checked out. And according to the boys in Boston, she's really good. An almost perfect record."

"Almost?" Tony raised an eyebrow, obviously intrigued.

"There was an incident about three months ago. Evidently she blew her cover going after a murderer. Almost lost her life in the process. Pissed off her superiors, but the guy I talked to was pretty damned impressed. Bottom line is, push come to shove, Cavanaugh is well respected. And according to my source, usually dead-on. So if she thinks there's something here, then maybe there is."

"If it's so goddamned important, why didn't she hang around to tell you in person?"

Eric shrugged. "Maybe she had another assignment. For all we know, she could be on her way back to Boston. Wouldn't surprise me at all. There was certainly no love lost between her and Roswell."

"You're not exactly a fan of the man yourself."

"No, I'm not. Which makes me wonder what I'm missing in all this."

Tony's face split into a smile. "And you're thinking maybe we can do a little snooping around?"

"Couldn't hurt."

"But the Brighton case is officially FBI now, and as far as they're concerned they've got their man."

"This is totally different, Tony." He shot his partner a crooked smile. "You said it yourself, one case leading to another. And I'd hate to think that an embezzler was allowed a walk just because his boss has been indicted for murder."

Tony leaned forward, hamburger forgotten. "So where do we start?"

"You start by telling me where Jonathan Brighton is." Roswell strode into the office, his voice harsh, his face ruddy with anger.

"He's with you." D'Angelo purposefully worked at keeping his face neutral, his gut reacting with a powerful lurch. "Desk sergeant said one of your boys picked him up this afternoon."

"Well, since I'm the 'boy,' I'd have to say he was mistaken." Roswell's fist was clenched so tightly, his fingers were white. "Who signed him out?"

Eric exchanged a glance with Tony, and quietly slid the copied notebook under another file. "I have the record here somewhere. Hang on a minute." He moved slowly, purposefully keeping Roswell waiting, already fairly certain he knew the answer.

He pulled a sheet of paper from a file on the desk, but before he could look at it, Roswell grabbed it, the old guy's jaw working in fury as he read the signature. "Cavanaugh." The name might as well have been an expletive. Hell, in Roswell's mind, it probably *was* an expletive. "Why the fuck would you have let her take the prisoner?"

"Because she's an FBI agent?" Tony's lower lip was quivering, as he tried to control his laughter.

"She's not the agent of record, Detective. She's . . . she's UC, for God's sake, and she's not even from Texas." Which in Roswell's book was obviously right up there with heaven.

Originally hailing from Jersey, Eric wasn't as convinced of the connection. "I can't imagine what the desk sergeant was thinking, Roswell, releasing the prisoner to a *Yankee*. An undercover one at that. Must have just been a bad day."

"I want an APB out on Brighton this minute, and I expect the full cooperation of this department in finding him."

"Not that I want to quibble, Roswell, but if I recall

correctly, you made it more than clear that this is your case, and that you wanted the Austin PD to stay out of your way."

"This is your fuckup, D'Angelo, and I expect you to fix it, before Brighton manages to get out of the country." Roswell was yelling now, others in the squad room glancing over at them with curiosity.

"I haven't fucked up anything, Roswell." Eric stood up, anger replacing his disdain. "You've done that all by yourself. Besides, if I had to bet on it, I'd guess that Cavanaugh and Brighton are holed up somewhere here in Austin. He doesn't strike me as the type to run away."

Roswell's eyes narrowed, a pumping vein in his throat signaling he was close to apoplexy. "What do you call Mexico? He's run before, and thanks to that bitch, he's running again. I guarantee it."

"Have you considered that maybe Cavanaugh isn't to blame here?" Tony held up a hand, the gesture meant to ease the tension, but accomplishing just the opposite.

"Of course she's to blame. She's got the hots for the bastard, and we all know how women are when they're like that." Again with the disgust. Despite the gravity of the situation, D'Angelo found himself wondering how long it had been since Roswell had gotten himself laid.

"Kill the anger, Roswell. I'll see what I can do to find them. In the meantime, I suggest that instead of wasting your time here yelling at me, you head back to your office and see what the FBI can do to find them. Unless, of course, you've got a reason for not wanting them to know you've misplaced an agent and a suspect all in one fell swoop."

Roswell stood for a moment, his angry gaze locked with Eric's, then without another word, he turned and walked out of the office.

"Well, I'll be damned." Tony's smile was slow, his expression reflecting Eric's, their thoughts obviously in tandem. "You were right."

* * *

"This is a bad idea." John stared up at the house, wondering what the hell he was doing. Derek Miller lived in an Enfield bungalow. Small square footage, big price tag. The paint need refreshening, but the lines of the house were good, the small yard the perfect frame for it, pecan trees arching gracefully over the roofline. The quintessential yuppie fixer-upper.

Except that there was police tape across the entry-way.

Wonderful.

"Come on." Katie grabbed his arm. "We need to get out of sight."

They'd left the car in Pease Park, making their way on foot from there, using the evening shadows for cover. Pulling him forward, Katie ducked under the yellow tape, maneuvering her way past the porch swing to the front door.

"Okay. Now that we're here, how are we supposed to get in?" He couldn't help the skepticism in his voice. "I might be an expert at hacking into computer systems, but I'm afraid physical breaking and entering is not on my résumé."

"Well, first we try the obvious approach." She reached out and turned the doorknob. It rattled ominously, but refused to open. Stepping back, she studied the front of the house, her expression hard to read among the shadows of the porch.

"That window's our best bet. See, the screen's busted." Without waiting for an answer she crossed the porch and pulled off the screen, peering in through the dusty window glass. "It's not latched."

The window groaned in protest as it lifted, and with a mischievous smile, Katie disappeared through the resulting black hole. Wonderful, they were adding breaking and entering to their repertoire.

"In for a penny . . ." He muttered to himself, surprised

at his own reticence. Still, they'd come this far. He threw his leg over the sill, stopping almost as quickly as he'd begun.

Katie was standing off to his right, equally still, her gaze locked on the chaos around them. The house was a mess. Papers strewn everywhere, the couch cushions ripped, shredded actually, their stuffing spilling out onto the floor, white against the dark wood of the floor.

"When the police use the phrase *toss a house*, they aren't kidding, are they?" He dropped to the floor, but Katie grabbed his arm, halting forward progress.

"The police didn't do this." Pulling her gun, she edged in front of him, her eyes scanning the room, the doorways, looking for motion of any kind. Back to the wall, she motioned for him to stay put and then disappeared into the next room.

It was a side of her he'd never seen. The real woman. The FBI agent. Proof that the Katie he'd fallen for really didn't exist. The thought hurt more than he cared to admit.

She came back into the room through another doorway, her gun arm relaxed. "Whoever did this is gone. There's nobody here."

He released a breath he hadn't realized he'd been holding. "Did you find the computer?"

"Yeah. It's in the bedroom." She tipped her head toward the door on the right.

He headed through the door, ignoring the chaos of the room, focusing instead on the oak desk and the computer, safely tucked into its docking station. Righting an upended chair, he powered the computer on, waiting as the machine booted up.

"Why do you think someone would leave the computer?" Katie's breath brushed against his cheek, almost a caress.

"I don't know. Either they didn't find what they wanted, or—"

"They erased it." She finished his thought for him, bending down to stare at the machine.

The computer beeped, and the operating system started with Window's musical refrain, the sound jarring against the silence of the house. He clicked explore to pull up a list of directories. Nothing happened.

"Shit." Katie's expletive echoed his thoughts perfectly as he tried again. The computer screen remained blank.

"It's all been erased." He slammed his hand against the docking station.

She sank onto the unmade bed, her expression bleak. "Checkmate."

He sat back, rubbing his temples with his fingers. His head wasn't hurting as badly as it had been, which should have given him hope, but it didn't. Considering the circumstances, his injury was suddenly the least of his concerns.

Be careful what you pray for.

The phrase ran through his head like a litany. How many nights had he prayed for it all to just go away. For something to come along and take his mind off his problems. Prison wasn't exactly what he'd been hoping for.

Guess he should have had a backup prayer—something along the lines of a miracle or two.

"John, are you all right?" Katie was kneeling beside him, her expression clouded with worry.

He dropped his hands, his eyes on the computer again, the word backup singing through his brain. "I'm fine. Couldn't be better. Help me look for a tape drive."

"You think he had a system backup?" She was already moving, pushing aside books and papers on the desk.

"I know he did. Miller was anal to a fault. We break into other people's systems all the time, which means we know the havoc that can result when someone gets in.

Tends to make a guy overly cautious." He started yanking open drawers, disappointed to find most of them empty.

"The tape drive's here. But no tape." Katie pointed at a shelf near the desk, her tone bordering on despondent.

"See if you can find the tape, maybe it's on the floor somewhere. I'd do it myself, but crawling isn't on my dance card at the moment. I'll search the bookshelf to see if there's anything else."

"Secondary backup." It was a statement not a question, and he was grateful for her continued hope.

He reached above the desk, pushing aside the books that littered the bookshelf. "Whoever preceded us at this didn't give a damn if anyone knew he'd been here."

Katie crawled along the floor, pushing aside wires and other discarded junk. "The stakes seem to be pretty high here. My guess is that destroying evidence was a lot more important than tidying up."

"What about the police, why wouldn't they have taken his computer?" He reached for a stack of magazines leaning drunkenly against the far side of a shelf.

"Unless they thought it would be useful in the investigation, they wouldn't have looked at it too closely. And when this first happened they thought it was drug related, remember?"

"Yeah. Wish it had been that simple." He pushed the magazines aside, his hand shaking. "Hang on, there's a zip drive here." The magazines had hidden it. He hit the eject button, heart hammering. A disk popped out, the black casing looking like manna from heaven. A bona fide miracle.

With a quick look heavenward, he smiled down at Katie.

"Looks like we aren't out of the game yet."

Chapter 24

"Not a damn thing." John pounded a hand against the computer screen, his voice reflecting his frustration. Her frustration, too, for that matter.

They were safely back in the motel room, which meant that for the moment they were still undetected. They'd brought Miller's computer with them, and John had successfully imported the backup files from the zip disk, but so far they hadn't found anything helpful.

"Have you checked his email?" She was sitting cross-legged on the floor, the meager remains of their dinner spread on the floor beside her.

John was braced against the end of the bed, the computer in his lap. "What, you think he emailed somebody with details of why someone would be out to kill him?"

"No. But people do discuss their lives in emails. It's possible there's something. It's not like you've come up with anything spectacular." She reached for her Coke, letting the fizzy liquid cool her throat. Despite the late hour, the heat hadn't abated at all, the humidity making her hair curl around her face. Her clothes were stuck to her body, and her temper was just barely in check.

"Sorry," he offered mildly. "I wasn't trying to pick a fight. It's a good suggestion. Let's see what we can find."

They'd fallen into a truce of sorts, ignoring the undercurrent between them in favor of concentrating on the task at hand. It was the right decision, but the building tension mimicked the palpable heat, its power allusive, like heat lightning, a harbinger of things to come.

She shook her head, clearing it of romantic notions. This wasn't the time. Scooting over beside him, she chewed on the corner of her lip, staring at the screen, willing it to yield Miller's secrets.

"There's a lot here. Looks like he kept just about everything." Thankfully, he seemed oblivious to the turn of her thoughts. "Why don't we start by looking at the emails around the time of his death?"

"All right. Look for things from you or Flo or Jason to start with."

"Me? Still thinking I'm in on this?" He frowned, and the tension between them ratcheted up a notch.

"No. I'm just trying to be thorough."

He glanced over at her, his expression inscrutable, and then turned back to the computer, reordering the list of emails. "Nothing to or from Flo. Not surprising really."

"How about Jason?"

"There's a couple." He opened an email dated the day before Derek's disappearance, scanning the contents. "Just a request for some promo material. Pretty routine."

"What about that one?" She pointed to another one dated the day of his murder. John clicked on it, and she read the brief missive. "This guy isn't big on words, is he?"

"He was always the cryptic type. Sort of a social misfit. Incredibly bright, but not too adroit at dealing with people. It was sad really. I think that's where the drug use came from. His way of leveling the playing field."

"Something to make him feel more normal."

"Exactly." He opened another email and they read through it. It was a thank-you note, of sorts. Something about securing the horse with the purloined groat.

"What the hell is he talking about?" She stared at the words, as if by doing so they'd suddenly make sense.

"Heroin. He's talking about buying heroin. The groat is an old English coin. He must have used the thirty-five thousand he got from Jason to feed his habit."

"Wonderful. So we've got vague confirmation he received money from Jason, but nothing that gives us anything new."

"Hang on." He moved up the alphabetical list to the J's. "Maybe there's something to your idea about me."

She looked at the list, short but sweet. Only two emails corresponded with their time period. One that John had written to Miller, and another that Miller had written back. John sucked in a breath, a sure sign that he was as nervous as she.

"Okay, here goes." He clicked on the email. It seemed John was no more inclined to wordiness than Jason.

"Thanks for the info on D.E.S.," she read out loud, trying to find meaning in his words. *"Keep hunting. There have to be answers somewhere."*

"Well, that's wonderfully cryptic." Her frustration was reflected in her voice. "Maybe there's more in his email." She reached over to move the cursor, clicking on the email to open it. They read it in silence, and despite the ambiguity, a chill chased across her spine.

Problem solved. Evidence secure. Per your email. Reference phoenix file.

"Clear as mud." John sounded more disgusted than anything.

"Wait a minute. There's something to this. First off," she pointed at the date, "this was written just after you left on your vacation. Which goes a long way to proving you didn't kill the man. I mean, he's writing, so he's obviously alive."

"But if Miller found the evidence, where the hell is it? Certainly not in my email."

"The phoenix file . . ." She trailed off, her eyes locking on the little statue. "Oh my God, John. You knew about this."

"What? I thought you just said you believed me." There was hurt mixed in with anger.

"No." She shook her head. "Not that. I mean the statue. It was your brain's way of trying to send a message. Remember the movie *Regarding Henry*?"

"Unfortunately, I do." He winced, the memory obviously hitting too close to home. "But I don't see—"

She cut him off with the wave of a hand. "Your bird is like Henry's painting. His mind was sending him a message. Telling him that Ritz was important somehow. So he painted a box of crackers, but the message short-circuited somehow. He thought it was crackers, but it was really the hotel."

"And you think it's the same with my phoenix?" He looked over at the statue, incredulity washing across his face.

"Yeah. Same short circuit, only in your case, it's the file that's important, John, not the bird. Miller's file. You take your computer, I'll search his."

She grabbed the laptop and entered the find command, typing the word *phoenix* into the blank. The computer whirred and began its search, and she waited, watching as John ordered his computer to do the same.

Hers finished first. "There's nothing on this computer by that name."

"Nothing here either, so far." John shook his head, his eyes glued to the screen. "But there's more to search. I want to look at the router logs as well, in case something came in or went out with that name."

Katie frowned and called the emails back to the screen, something tugging at her brain. The first email, John's, mentioned D.E.S., hunting for information and answers that needed to be found. Miller had obviously continued the hunt, found the answers, and put the evidence somewhere secure.

Per John's email.

She stared at the machine. The only physical thing mentioned in the email was D.E.S. But that didn't make sense.

"Katie, I think maybe I've found something."

She broke away from her train of thought. "A reference to phoenix?"

"No." His tone was regretful. "There was nothing in the system with that name. But it looks like just before Miller emailed me, he accessed the D.E.S. system. There's a reference to it on the log."

"That's got to be it." She jumped to her feet, coming to stand beside him. "He must have hidden the phoenix file, whatever it is, in the D.E.S. computer system. Then he emailed you, and in his own obtuse way told you where to look. A blinding glimpse of the obvious." She gripped his shoulders, excitement building. "So all we have to do is get into the D.E.S. system and find the file."

"Easier said than done."

"What do you mean? You've been telling me what a fabulous hacker you are. Now's your opportunity to prove it."

"I can get in, but not from here." He sat back, rubbing his temples again. "When I was injured, Wilson Harris was worried about security. He's always been a bit obsessive about it. Up until then I was the only one allowed full access to the system."

"But we're assuming Derek got in. In fact, the log says so."

"I could have given him the access codes. If I thought it important enough. They could easily have been changed again later if I wanted to keep him out."

"So what happened after you were hurt?"

"Harris blocked access altogether. Frank was working on the account, and anything he did, he gave to Harris and then he added it to the system. I'd already put most everything in place. There was very little that needed to be done. More maintenance than anything else."

"So we're out of luck?"

"Maybe not. If I can get access to the actual D.E.S. computers, I should be able to get in." He frowned up at her. "I wrote a back door into my program. So that I could get into the system if there was an emergency."

"Well, I'd say this qualifies as an emergency."

"Yes, but in case you've forgotten, I'm on the lam. I can hardly just walk up to the door and request a little computer time. Besides, it's the middle of the night, and while I think I handled breaking into Miller's house with aplomb, I don't think I'm ready for breaking into a department of Defense contractor's corporate headquarters."

"Department of Defense? I thought D.E.S. produced engines."

He shot her a look, as if debating what to tell her, and she lost it, the pressure of the day suddenly more than she could bear.

"Look, Jonathan," she stretched out his name, each syllable punctuating her anger, "you're not the only one with something at stake here. I've put my job on the line for you. This operation was supposed to be about proving myself, and aiding a suspected murderer isn't exactly the way to do that. So make up your mind right now. Either you trust me or you don't. It's as simple as that."

He moved with a quick grace that belied his condition, one finger covering her lips, his gaze colliding with hers. "I know you're on my side. I shouldn't have hesitated. I'm sorry."

They stood for a moment, as if the touch of his hand

held them together, linking them in some deep intrinsic way, then he dropped his hand, stepping back, purposefully reestablishing the distance between them.

She fought against the tide of emotions threatening to engulf her. John might believe that she was on his side, but that didn't mean he truly trusted her, and without trust, there certainly could be no love.

Ruthlessly she pushed away her disconsolate thoughts. Now was not the time. Instead, she forced herself to concentrate on the situation at hand. John needed her help, and for the time being that would simply have to be enough. "So tell me about the connection between D.E.S. and the Department of Defense."

"They're developing the guidance system for the weaponry aboard the U.S.'s newest bomber. The whole plane is classified. I had to get all kinds of clearance to even be able to work with them. That's why I was the only one with total access."

"That certainly explains why the Koreans would be interested. Schematics of something like that would be worth a fortune on the open market. Roswell was right." She frowned, trying to assimilate the newest piece of the puzzle.

"We can't know that for certain. At least not until we get our hands on the phoenix file." He blew out a long breath. "Which brings us right back to square one. I need a way to get into the D.E.S. system."

She tipped her head back, rubbing the small of her back. "Well, you're right about one thing. We can't just break in. It's doable, of course, but not without careful planning. And we don't have time for that. We'd be far better off to simply walk in tomorrow."

"We'll be recognized."

"No we won't. Pretending to be something I'm not is what I do for a living, remember?"

*   *   *

"It was you, wasn't it?" Jason strode into the office, his face pink with anger. "You found my book."

"What do you mean?" A curl of fear traced its way up Frank's spine, but he fought it down, forcing nonchalance.

"Don't play dumb with me. I found a page missing from my Filofax, and couldn't figure out what the hell had happened to it. But then Valerie remembered seeing you take it. At the Magnolia Café, the night Flo was killed. It wasn't hard to put it together after that. You needed proof it was me. So you took the page. And now I want the book back." He held out his hand, his eyes telegraphing his fury.

Frank's fear increased a notch. "I don't have it."

"I know that you do. So stop lying about it."

Anger mixed with the fear, making him feel a little light-headed. "I gave it to the woman from the FBI. I thought it might help John."

"What?" The word came out on a whisper, his face going from red to white in an instance, his anger dissipating like smoke in the wind.

"I said, I gave it to the authorities." His breathing was coming more normally now, his fear subsiding. "So there's no point in hurting me, Jason. I've already told what I know."

If possible, the other man looked stricken. "I'd never hurt you, Frank. Surely you don't believe that I . . ." Jason broke off, understanding dawning. Understanding and horror. "You think that I killed Derek and Florence."

Frank shrugged. "It fits the facts."

"I never . . ." he sputtered, then tried again. "I didn't kill either of them."

"Derek was blackmailing you, wasn't he?"

Jason sat down, burying his face in his hands. "He figured out about the money. Said he'd turn me in if I didn't give me a cut of the profits."

"You were embezzling from Guardian."

Jason nodded. "Yeah. I owed some less than savory people money. It was supposed to be a one-time thing. The next time I'd come out on top."

"But you didn't." The truth hit Frank square in the face. "You lost the money gambling."

Jason's laugh was bitter. "I never met a bet I didn't like. Football, horse racing, you name it. Only I always seem to wind up on the wrong end of the game."

"So you used Guardian funds to support your habit." Frank wondered how he could have missed the signs. He thought he knew Jason, but obviously he'd been wrong.

"You make it sound like I'm a drug addict." Jason lifted his head, his eyes imploring. "It isn't the same thing."

"Isn't it?" Frank wished there were some way to sugarcoat the words, but there wasn't.

"Maybe. I don't know. Derek certainly saw it that way. And I can't say that I was sorry when he disappeared. But you've got to believe me, Frank, when I tell you that I didn't kill him. I'm not that kind of man."

"Well, neither is John Brighton." He was suddenly certain of that fact. "So the first thing you're going to do is turn yourself over to the FBI. Maybe there's something you know that will help."

"It may be too late." Valerie walked into the room, her face crestfallen.

"What do you mean?" Frank stood up, the hairs on the back of his neck rising to attention.

"I just got off the phone with Danny. It seems that John has gone missing. Katie Cavanaugh signed him out of jail, but the two of them never showed up at the federal holding cells."

"Do they think something's happened to them?" Frank felt his stomach sink. It seemed his efforts were too little, too late.

"He doesn't know. The Feds seem to think that they've run off together, but according to Danny, the police think it's more likely they're holed up here somewhere, trying to find answers." Valerie looked less authoritative somehow, and certainly less alluring. Or maybe his perspective was what had changed. Either way, he almost felt sorry for her.

"Where's Danny?"

"He's at the police department. The call came from that detective who's been hanging around here. Apparently, the FBI didn't think it was worth the time to let Danny know."

"How's he taking it?"

"He sounded all right, but Danny never shows his emotions. I've tried to call John, but he isn't answering his cell phone. I'm sure Danny's tried, too." Her face reflected her worry.

"Valerie, just because he isn't answering his phone doesn't mean he's been hurt. If he's on the run, he's not very likely to answer his phone, now is he?"

She nodded, her expression relaxing. "So what do we do? I feel helpless standing here. The company is certainly not going to survive this without a lot of damage control." Now, there was the old Valerie. Frank was almost grateful. Too many things had changed. He needed something he could rely on, even if it was only Valerie's unabashed self-interests.

"Well, for starters, I think Jason has a date with the FBI." He shot the other man a pointed look. "It's past time to tell the truth, don't you think?"

"I don't see what good it would do." Jason narrowed his eyes, daring them to argue. "Not with Jonathan on the lam."

"So, what, you're going to wait for them to come to you?"

"Maybe they'll lose interest." His self-justification was just this side of pathetic.

"It's the FBI, Jason. They don't lose interest. They'll get you now or they'll get you later. It's that simple."

"Unless he runs." Valerie's eyes were thoughtful behind the lenses of her glasses.

"You knew about this?"

She shrugged. "I suspected."

"And you didn't say anything?" Frank tried but couldn't keep the derision out of his voice.

"I wasn't sure, and I didn't see how it could help Guardian. So I didn't press the issue."

"Meaning you wanted John to fall so badly that you were willing to let Jason get away with murder."

"I told you I didn't do it." Jason's retort hung between them in the air.

"*She* didn't know that." Frank felt sick. These people were supposed to be his friends.

"Well, I do now." She shot them both a sanctimonious look.

Frank ignored her. "What matters now is doing the right thing. How about it, Jason?"

Jason's face suddenly looked haggard, and he sighed in defeat. "I don't see that there's any other way." He shrugged, his gaze meeting Valerie's. "I'm not the running type."

The clouds cast dancing shadows across the motel room, light feathered against dark, creating patterns on the floor and walls. Lightning—the real kind—flashed intermittently, the smell of rain comforting, the touch of the breeze cool against her face.

John was sleeping, his soft breathing rhythmic against the night. Katie leaned against the window, looking at the play of light against the sky, the reflection like a fractured mirror in the water below. With the exception of the circumstances, this was life as it was supposed to be. Two people alone, sharing the intimacies of the night.

But the truth was, they were only together because of the circumstances, and she wasn't sure if there would be anything left to build on when the dust settled. If it settled. Everything depended on tomorrow, her skills at passing unnoticed and John's skills with a computer. If all went as planned they'd have answers, and hopefully a way out of this mess. But nothing would ever be the same, for either of them.

The reflection in the water was dancing now, raindrops distorting color like an impressionist painting. When she was little, her mother had woken her when it rained like this—soft rain, gentle rain—and the two of them had snuck from the house, reveling in the sweet fall of water, the midnight hour bewitching them. It had been magical. A moment captured forever in her heart.

And here it was again, far from home.

Midnight rain.

"You're awake." He'd come to stand behind her, his big body warm, familiar, his breath teasing her senses as it brushed against her cheek.

"It's raining." The words were stark, devoid of magic, but she had no way to tell him, to explain her memories.

Silence stretched between them, accentuated by the soft patter of the rain. Finally, with a sigh, he moved to stand beside her. "We need to talk."

"About tomorrow?" She knew that wasn't it, but some perverse part of her wanted to hear him actually say it.

"No." His dark eyes met hers, the intensity there robbing her of breath. "We need to talk about us."

"Is there an us?" She turned to search his face, uncertainty mixing with fear. There was so much between them. So much at stake.

"I honestly don't know. There shouldn't be, but somehow I can't seem to let it go—to let you go." The words were what she needed to hear, but there was so much anger behind them. Anger and doubt.

"Flo told me once that real love can survive anything. If that's true, then—"

"Flo is dead." He cut her off with a wave of his hand. "And I don't know if I even believe in love anymore. At least not the kind that conquers all."

He looked out at the rain-swept night. "When I woke up in the hospital after the shooting, I couldn't remember much of anything. I mean, I knew who I was on a technical level, but a lot of the emotion surrounding the memories was gone. And even though eventually most of it came back, I never lost the feeling of disenfranchisement. It was as if I'd lost my way somehow, and couldn't get on track again. And to make it worse, everybody kept telling me how I was supposed to feel.

"It was like I was only pretending to be me. Only that's not even a good way of explaining it. Mostly it was like being alone in a room full of friends. Danny, Valerie, all of them. They said the right things, and I could see that they cared, but they couldn't understand that I was different from before. They refused to allow me to change. Everything was about regaining what I'd lost. When in reality, I wasn't certain I wanted it back.

"Then you came along, bursting into my life with no knowledge of me as anything other than the man I am now. You accepted me as is—no questions asked." He tipped back his head, sighing. "You even made me believe in myself again. Somehow, you became my talisman against the dark. I thought that with you by my side, anything was possible.

"And then Danny told me who you really were." His gaze met hers, pain etched across his face. "And I died all over again. The only thing I thought of as real turned out to be a lie."

"How can you say that?" She wanted to wipe the anguish from his face, to take away his pain, but she wasn't certain she could find the words. "There were lies surrounding it, certainly. But the night we made love, that was real, John. *I* made love to you. Me. Katie. Not the FBI agent. And not some physical therapist. *Me.* The real me."

"I want to believe that. But how can I?" He studied her face as if he were memorizing it.

"You listen to your heart." She touched a finger to his chest. "And you step out on a limb. No one is perfect, John. You of all people should know that. People make mistakes."

"And they live with the consequences."

"I know that. But does that mean we have to lose everything? Look, I should have told you who I was the night we made love. I wish I had. God knows, if I could go back and change it, I would. But if I'd told you, it wouldn't have changed the outcome. You'd still have felt betrayed, and we'd still probably be standing right here."

"So what do we do now?"

Wordlessly she held out her hands, not knowing what it was she wanted exactly, but certain that she wanted it with him. He allowed her to pull him through the sliding glass door and into the night, the rain falling around them, like fairy mist—and just for the moment she let herself believe that anything was possible.

Anything.

He framed her face with one hand, his fingers strong and sure, and she reached for the other, the weaker one, kissing first one finger and then the next, loving each one as a part of him. And when she'd finished, she kissed his palm, the feel of his skin against hers lighting something deep inside her.

A candle in the window to lead him home.

There was magic afoot tonight.

With a groan, he pulled her close, his mouth finding hers, his kiss gentle, yet possessive. But she wanted more, wanted to taste him, to brand him with her heart and mind. To show the world that he was hers. Now and forever.

No questions asked. No matter what happened.

His tongue met hers, and they dueled together, an ageless battle fought since the beginning of time. Giving and taking, melding together, one body, one soul. His hand found her breast and the touch sent fire dancing along her synapses, pooling hot and heavy, deep within her. She pushed against him, wanting more, wanting him.

He pulled her nightshirt off her shoulders, his kisses hot against the curve of her neck and shoulders. She shivered from the touch, waiting, waiting, until his mouth, hot and hungry, closed over her breast, her nipple held captive with tongue and teeth.

She writhed against him, moaning with joy, the cool rain a constant counterpoint to his touch—his heat. He tugged at her breast, teasing, loving, the low sound in his throat a testament to his fever.

She arched back, closing her eyes, offering herself in a way she never had before. Offering her spirit as well as her body. And he accepted her gift, his hands and mouth caressing, honoring—their coming together a commitment neither could ignore.

He pulled her upright, his eyes meeting hers. "This is for keeps, Katie. If we make love here, now, it's forever."

She shivered against the rain, and pressed against him, letting his warmth seep into her. "I want you, John. I've never pretended otherwise. I . . . I love you. And nothing that happens is ever going to change that fact. Nothing."

The words came out of her of their own volition, and she was surprised at how easily they came. Painless. Joyful. A promise made. A promise to be kept.

He tilted his head back, the lightning illuminating his

face, raindrops clustering on his eyelashes. "Then let me show you how much I love you."

She nodded, and wordlessly let him lead her inside to the bed. With gentle hands he pulled off the nightshirt, kissing her skin as he bared it, licking away the remnants of rain, replacing its cool moisture with the heat of his tongue.

His hand dipped lower, past her abdomen, to the soft skin of her inner thighs, caressing, teasing, the tension at once wonderful and terrible. Her legs were shaking. Her breath ragged. His touch driving her closer and closer to the edge.

And then, just when she thought she would explode, his hand moved, inward, upward, thrusting, stroking deep inside her. His mouth found hers, his tongue matching his fingers stroke for stroke. She pressed hard against him, needing more.

With fumbling fingers, she pulled at his clothes, sliding off the sweats, needing to feel his skin against hers, his heat joining with hers. She stroked the work-hardened muscles of his back as they fell onto the bed, their bodies locked together in a passionate embrace.

He shifted his weight, moving to place a knee between her legs. She opened for him, wanting him deep inside her. And she murmured her protest when he pulled back, bracing his elbows on either side of her, his gaze locked on hers.

"We belong together. Two halves of a whole."

She nodded wordlessly, tears filling her eyes, her love for this man bigger than anything she could possibly have imagined. With a slow smile, he slid inside her, his strength becoming hers. The two of them intrinsically linked.

They began to move together, establishing their own special rhythm. Each stroke taking her higher, faster, until she felt like exploding, like screaming, and then she lost all control, the world splintering into brilliant color.

The canvas of their love. She locked her legs around him, holding him close. Trying to bind them forever.

This was different from before. As if they'd crossed some sort of bridge, reaching the other side not as two people but as one. She'd never felt like she belonged anywhere. Always uncomfortable in her own skin. Always searching for something indefinable.

She knew the magic would end at morning. Knew that reality held threats they might never overcome. But right now, here in this room, she knew that she had found where she belonged—in a most unlikely way, in a most unlikely place, in the middle of a midnight rain.

"So how much of what you told me about yourself is actually true?" They were nestled together in the bed, energy spent for the moment, and John felt more content than he'd ever dreamed was possible. Especially when one considered the circumstances.

Katie raised up on an elbow, her long hair swinging over her shoulder. "Pretty much everything, except the physical therapy part, and my name." She blushed and ducked her head, and John reached over to smooth her hair back.

"So why the FBI?"

"I wanted to do something with law enforcement." She smiled at him. "It's in my genes. Four generations' worth. But my father had decided notions about what his baby girl was to do with her life."

"I take it kicking in doors for a living wasn't part of the plan."

"Exactly. And he had my brothers for moral support. So I took the easy way out and got a law degree."

"But you didn't take to the bar?"

"Something like that. I guess the need to be part of the action was more powerful."

"So why didn't you become a cop like your father?"

She laughed, and the sound warmed him inside and

out. "It would have been the kiss of death. My father's reach is long, and if I'd even tried to join the force, he'd have had his cronies assigning me to permanent desk duty before I could have graduated from the academy."

"I take it he isn't as well connected with the FBI?"

"Oh, he has friends, but for the most part they stay out of my way. Something to do with being UC, I think."

He pulled her close, nestling her into the curve of his arm. "You said something earlier about my case being a chance to prove yourself. What did you mean by that?"

She was silent for a moment, her breath warm against his chest, and he wondered if she'd share. Or if she was still keeping secrets. With a sigh, she tilted her head so that she could see him. "My last assignment was a RICO case. We were trying to nail a man suspected of involvement with the mob. In Boston. As part of the operation, I went undercover in one of his strip clubs."

"As a stripper?" He fought against an irrational wave of anger, his mind conjuring up visions he'd just as soon not have seen.

"No." Her laughter vibrated against his chest. "I worked the bar. Among my other talents, I make a mean cocktail. Anyway," she continued, her tone more subdued, "while I was working there, one of the strippers, a girl named Stacey, had a bit too much to drink, and insisted that she was being stalked by an old boyfriend. The club's manager. A guy named Walker Priestly." She paused, and he stroked her hair, not certain where the story was going, but sensing it was a difficult one for her to tell.

"I blew her off. She was drunk. She was a stripper. I don't know, maybe I was just worried about screwing up the assignment. Anyway, two days later, a customer finds her out back, her skull cracked open."

She rolled onto her back. "It was my fault. If I'd listened to her, if I'd done something, she'd be alive." She looked over at him, tears glistening in her eyes. "She was just a kid trying to find her way in the world, and when she reached out to me for help, I refused to listen."

He cupped her face in his hand, his eyes meeting hers. "You couldn't have known."

She shook her head. "That's just it, John. I should have known. It's my job to protect innocent people." She blew out a long breath, the act seeming almost cathartic. "Anyway, after they found her, I went to my superior and told him what I knew. Asked him if I could go to the police. But he was afraid it would compromise the investigation. He arranged for another source to get them the information, but they didn't take it seriously."

"So you decided to do something on your own."

The ghost of a smile played about her lips. "Yeah. I was so angry at myself, I wasn't thinking clearly. I went after the bastard, without a plan, and without backup. Just waltzed into his office and told him what I knew. Threatened to share it with the police if he didn't turn himself in.

"I had a gun. But I hadn't counted on his knife." Reflexively she ran her hand along the ridge of scar beneath her breast. "He threw it before I realized what he was doing. And I guess he'd have killed me, except I managed to get off a round."

"You killed him."

She nodded. "And blew the operation in the process. Needless to say, the powers that be weren't all that pleased with me. I spent three months on leave. Recuperation, they called it. And I spent most of it listening to my father tell me a hundred different ways how stupid I'd been. Which of course was entirely on the money. I let my heart get in the way of my head."

"I don't think that's such a bad thing." There was a

world of meaning in his words, and he felt the sharp intake of her breath.

"Well, you're the only one who thinks so." There
was resignation in her voice, and something else—hope.
Maybe he wasn't the only one who needed to be res-
cued. "This assignment, your case, was supposed to be
a new leaf. An opportunity to prove that I could follow
directions, do as I was told, but—"

"But I came along and messed all that up."

Her smile was weak, but genuine. "Something like
that. The truth is, I think maybe I confused honor with
duty. Sometimes the two aren't the same. And in the end
it's got to be about honor. About doing what's right.
Even when it goes counter to what you've been told
to do."

"Heavy thoughts." He pulled her on top of him, rel-
ishing the feel of her skin against his. "But good ones."
His smile was slow and sure. "Especially for me."

She leaned down to kiss him, her hair dropping like
a curtain around them. His lips captured hers, and despite all the danger that lay ahead, he felt absurdly at
peace with the world, everything that he wanted right
here in this room.

If only he could hold this moment captive forever.

As if she'd read his mind, she pulled back, her gaze
locking with his. "We'll find a way out of this, John.
We're together now, and that means we can do anything."

He prayed to God that she was right. Because tomorrow, come hell or high water, they were jumping
into the fire.

Chapter 25

The elevator doors slid shut with an almost silent whoosh. John pulled off his cap, and unzipped the coverall he wore, revealing pressed chinos and a dress shirt beneath. They'd made it past the first hurdle, walking past the building's security guard with little more than a nod. She'd been right, no one paid attention to repair people.

He hadn't even asked where she'd gotten the coveralls. He wasn't really certain he wanted to know. She'd woken him this morning with hot coffee and a kiss, already dressed, her plans for getting into the D.E.S. computer room complete.

He watched now as she slid out of her coveralls, her movements quick and efficient, the pants suit beneath black and nondescript. He marveled at her composure— the elevator floors were sliding by, and she hadn't even broken a sweat.

She smiled at him in silent reassurance, and grabbed his coveralls, tucking them along with hers under a panel in the roof of the elevator. Taking a pair of glasses from her pocket, she handed them to him, the black frames a contrast to his carefully grayed hair.

With a quick flip, and the snap of a barrette, she pulled russet hair into a neat chignon, her smiling green eyes now brilliant blue. Briefcase in hand, she waited for the elevator doors to open.

Stage one completed.

The next round depended on him. And on whether the codes he'd liberated last night were still valid. They stepped into the hallway, grateful to find it deserted. It was still early, and not too many people had arrived.

Walking with purpose, they turned right, and headed for the computer room. If nothing had changed it should be unoccupied for the next couple of hours. Small beads of sweat broke out along his hairline, and he tried to tell himself this was no more than a physical hack, but the danger seemed more real.

And the stakes were certainly higher.

Last night had changed everything. Until that point, he'd been playing the game for himself. Now suddenly he was playing it for her, too. No, he corrected himself, they were playing it together. There was a difference. One that he wanted to adhere to. *Together*.

What a wonderful word.

He reached out to touch her hand, needing the momentary contact to bolster his courage. His leg ached, but he was determined to keep his limping to a minimum, even if it meant pushing his muscles farther than they wanted to go. Katie'd promised that no one would notice, that lots of people had awkward gaits, but he was still concerned that, despite their disguises, it would mark him for who he really was.

A door opened down the corridor, and he held his breath, his heart rate increasing incrementally with each passing second. A man in jeans and a T-shirt, carrying a steaming cup of coffee, came out into the hallway, his attention on the papers in his other hand.

Katie nodded almost imperceptibly and they kept walking, keeping their pace slow, almost leisurely. Which wasn't an easy task when his instinct was to run. He wondered if she was feeling any of his fear, but a sideways glance confirmed that she was fine. The smile on her beautiful face as natural as if they were taking a stroll in the park.

The man passed them by with barely a glance, intent on his paperwork. John released his breath on a slow hiss. "I don't know how you do this all the time."

"It just takes practice. You're doing fine. We're almost there."

He nodded, hoping his face didn't reflect the racing fear inside him. They continued down the hallway, taking a right at the first intersection, the double doors at the end of the corridor their immediate goal. Just a few more steps.

"Can I help you?"

He turned around, smile firmly in place, his heart threatening to break out of his chest. An older woman in a paisley suit stepped out of her office, staring at them politely over the tops of her glasses, waiting for an answer.

"We're due in the conference room for a presentation." Katie's voice was perfectly composed, just the right degree of pleasant. "My colleague is a little nervous, so I thought the walk might do him good."

The woman nodded, her eyes softening. "I hate speaking in front of people. Especially if I'm trying to sell something." She met his gaze, her smile understanding.

John blew out a nervous breath, forcing himself to return the gesture. "I'll be fine. I just need to pace a little."

"Don't worry." She gave him the once-over, her eyes reflecting her approval. "You'll do fine." With a last smile, she went back into her office.

Two for two.

Katie's hand on his arm signaled it was time to continue the gauntlet. The doors loomed large in front of him, the big test still to come. Checking behind him to make sure the woman hadn't reappeared, he opened a keypad near the doors, two red lights glowing ominously in the dim hallway lighting.

He entered a series of numbers, and waited with baited breath until the first light beamed green, then he entered a second string of numbers, followed by a third alphanumeric code.

The second light flickered and turned green, the sound of the doors unlocking seeming unnaturally loud.

"We're through." Katie was already moving through the doors, and John was quick to follow. Another hallway stretched out in front of them. "Where's the computer room?"

"Third door on the left."

She nodded, and they moved forward in tandem, stopping when they reached the proper door. Another key panel waited, and John dispatched this one with the same efficiency as the last, the final green light a signal that they'd reached their goal.

Stage two completed.

The computer room was cold, kept that way to protect the hardware, the floor raised, the walls specially designed, configured to protect the dollars invested here. This was his purview, and almost before the door closed, his confidence returned. Conversely, Katie seemed more nervous, peering through a crack in the door to the hallway beyond.

"Turnabout's fair play." The words were pitched low, but he couldn't keep the smile from his voice.

"I'm fine," she lied, "just get it done. We don't have much time."

He turned back to the room, searching for the right terminal. It had been a while since he'd been here, but fortunately everything looked the same. Finding the machine he wanted, he pulled a chair over in front of it, and began to type.

Five false starts and eight minutes later he was in. The trick now was to find the file, copy it, and get the hell out of here, before someone noticed there was an unauthorized user in the system. He'd designed the back door so that he'd be virtually undetectable, but nothing was perfect, and with everything that had been happening, he had no doubt that Harris had his people on alert.

"Are you in?" Katie's question was terse, her eyes still trained on the door.

"Yeah. No problems so far. But I still have to find the file."

She nodded. "So far there's no one out there, but I don't like staying in one place too long."

"I'm hurrying." He typed in a series of commands, using the word *phoenix*, initiating a systemwide search for Miller's file. The computer moved with an agonizing slowness, every passing minute a risk of detection.

Finally a beep signaled that the search was finished. No sign of Miller's file. He stared at the screen, his mind trying to think of another approach. The beginnings of a headache threatened to interfere, but he ignored the pounding, trying instead to think like Miller.

For a moment he could see the man's face clearly, hear his laughter. It was almost like he was there with them. And in that moment, John knew what to do. His lips quirked into a half smile as he entered more commands. What better place to hide a Guardian file than on the Guardian system within the D.E.S. framework? Miller at his most ironic.

The computer hummed as it accessed his system, and when the appropriate box appeared, he typed in a series of numbers. Then before the code could be rejected, he typed another set of commands, and the computer grudgingly let him in. The search itself took only minutes. The file was buried in a series of subdirectories, but with the proper commands, it presented itself obediently when requested.

"I've got it," he called over his shoulder, his eyes never leaving the monitor.

"Great." Katie's voice was calm, but there was an undernote of urgency. "Can you copy it?"

"Hopefully. I'll need to see how big it is first." He clicked on the file and was surprised to see that it in fact contained a series of files, each containing documents and shortcuts to other existing files. "Shit."

"What is it?" She moved away from the door to stand beside him.

"This is way too much to copy. Some of these are links to logs, from the look of them. I suspect to a particular part of the log. But I can't copy all of it on a single disk."

"So use more than one." She sounded impatient, her eyes cutting back to the door, obviously listening for sounds in the hallway.

"It doesn't work like that. All this stuff is linked together. It's almost like he didn't want anyone to be able to copy it to disk."

She blew out a breath, her mind obviously considering this latest turn of events. "All right, then, we'll just have to look at it. And hopefully you can copy enough to give us some sort of proof. Assuming, of course, there's something there that can help us."

It was the first time she'd sounded negative since they'd started the operation, and he reached out to squeeze her hand, trying to offer reassurance, wishing he'd never gotten her involved in any of this. Their eyes met and she offered a weak smile, squaring her shoulders, moving back to the door.

He returned his attention to the computer and began to examine Miller's files.

D'Angelo hung up the phone with a decided bang, his temper rising. Edmund Roswell was a pain in the ass. Still, he'd called, and Eric had to admit that was something.

"What's up? You look like your mother died." Tony stood by his desk, coffee cup in hand, looking more rumpled than usual—but then, looks were deceiving.

"Just got off the phone with Roswell."

"They find Brighton?" He sat down, and began the ritual of adding sugar and prepackaged creamer to his coffee.

"No. But Jason Pollock turned himself in last night."

Tony's eyebrows disappeared into his hairline. "He give it up?"

"About the murders? No. Swears he had nothing to do with them. But he did admit to embezzling money. He's got a gambling problem. And he also admitted that he paid Miller off. Seems Miller got wise to Pollock's less than noble antics and demanded his fair share."

"Sounds like reason enough to off the guy."

"Probably, but he didn't. At least not according to Roswell."

"So you thinking Brighton *is* guilty?"

Eric shook his head. "Can't say for sure, of course, but my instinct still says no. This thing is starting to smell like a setup."

"What'd Roswell say?" Finally satisfied with the amount of chemicals in his coffee, he took a slurping sip.

"That they had their man in Brighton, and nothing Pollock said had changed the fact."

"He's one cocky son of a bitch, you gotta give him that, but I tend to think you're right about Brighton. Unfortunately, the poor bastard doesn't stand a chance if they find him."

"And they will."

Tony shrugged philosophically. "At least it's out of our hands. Maybe if he's lucky he'll find something out there to clear his name, and if he doesn't there's always the courts."

"Oh yeah, there's a comfort. The laws these days are more about protecting the guilty than the innocent. I know I sure as hell wouldn't want to be in Brighton's place."

Tony drained the last of his coffee. "You know what your problem is, Eric. You care too damn much. You can't let it get personal. Look what happened to Cavanaugh."

"Who's to say she isn't right?"

"Hey, D'Angelo," another detective called from across the office, his hand over the mouthpiece of his phone. "Looks like I might have a lead on your man."

The hairs on Eric's arms prickled to attention. "John Brighton?"

"Yeah. Maybe. I'm talking to dispatch and they just got a call from a guy who says he saw him about an hour ago."

"Where?" He was standing up now, already reaching for his jacket.

The detective consulted the person on the other end of the phone, then looked up. "Dispatcher says the guy works at D.E.S."

Tony was grabbing his coat, too. "Looks like Brighton may have found his answers."

"Or he's walking into a trap."

Miller's files were like a puzzle, and putting the pieces together was taking longer than he liked, but the picture that was emerging was far more disturbing. So far he'd uncovered at least fifteen unauthorized entries into Guardian clients' files. Each entry cross-referenced with the appropriate log index.

Miller had been exceedingly thorough.

From the look of things, Roswell was right. Someone had been using the Guardian system to access and extract sensitive information from their clients.

The big question was, who?

"Are you finished yet? We've been here almost half an hour." Katie had been alternately hanging over his shoulder and watching the door, her face growing more concerned with every passing minute.

"I'm working on it. This is the last file."

He clicked on the icon, and waited while the computer pulled up the file. At first, the columns of numbers meant nothing. He frowned, frustrated, and switched over to an earlier file. Looking for a link between the two.

"John, we've got to hurry."

"I know. Just one more minute." He looked at the last file again, smiling this time as his beleaguered mind finally registered what he was looking at. The file linked each of the random IP addresses assigned to the illegal entries with another log that listed the actual machine in use. He clicked on the link to the secondary log, and his stomach sank.

He clicked again on another entry, with the same result. Bile rose in his throat, the reality of what he was reading almost more than he could bear. It couldn't be true, but Miller's evidence was methodically relentless, and John realized there was no escaping the truth.

His brother was using Guardian computer systems to steal information from the company's clients.

"John?" Katie's voice seemed to come from far away, a rhythmic whooshing sound obstructing his hearing. He felt her shake his arm, and struggled back from the blackness of his thoughts, the sounds fading as his blood pressure resumed normal levels.

"I'm here." He tried to focus on the sound of her voice, but disbelief was warring with horror, the combined emotional impact leaving him numb, incapable of contemplating the reality of the situation. Even without his handicaps, he'd have been blown away. As it was, he wasn't certain his mind was capable of processing the information, let alone accepting it.

Danny. Holy Mother of God—*Danny.*

Katie was kneeling beside him now, her face full of concern. "John, tell me. What is it? What did you find?"

He drew in a breath, fighting for clarity. This wasn't

the time for an emotional breakdown. "Roswell was dead-on. Miller documented everything. Someone has been stealing secrets." He reached for her hands, needing to feel the warmth of human contact, his mind still rebelling against the truth.

Katie's gaze met his, the anxiety reflected there mirroring his own. "Does Miller identify the thief?"

He nodded, his heart threatening to explode from his chest. "It's Danny."

"No. There's got to be some kind of mistake." Her hands tightened on his, anxiety changing to shock.

He shook his head, wishing there was some way to make it a mistake. But Miller had been too thorough. There was no escaping the truth. Danny had betrayed him. "It's all here. He's been doing it for years."

"Does Miller mention the Koreans?"

"No. But it fits, doesn't it. I mean, Danny had to be selling the information to someone. Why not the Koreans?"

"You realize what else this means, John. It could have been Danny who—"

"No." The word came out more explosively than he'd intended, but he wasn't going to allow the thought to be put into words, as if by saying them they became true. "He wouldn't do that, Katie. He wouldn't."

Her voice was gentle. "John, you can't know that."

"I have to hold on to something or this is going to eat me alive. Can't you see that?"

She reached out to touch his face, her eyes filled with regret. "We'll work this out, John. I promise. But not now. There isn't time. What we have to do now is get this information to Roswell. It's our best chance of getting you cleared, and right now that's got to be our priority. All right?"

He nodded mutely, forcing himself to the here and now.

She searched his eyes, and evidently satisfied with

what she saw, stood up. "Can we take any of the file with us?"

"No." He glanced back at the computer screen. "It's too interdependent. But I've changed the name of the master file. That ought to stop anyone from finding it before we can get it back."

"All right, then, let's get out of here." She was all action now, ready to go. She'd already lost the suit, her biker shorts and braided hair, changing her appearance yet again. "You go first, and then I'll follow in about five minutes."

Their plan was to leave the building separately and meet at the Schlotzsky's across the street. From there, they'd head to Roswell's office. He pulled off the glasses, and peeled off his pants and shirt. The jeans and T-shirt beneath making him look much like the man they'd met in the hallway. "I'm ready."

She took the clothes from him, and stuffed them into a gym bag. No doubt she'd dispose of them on her way out. There wasn't time for conversation, so he pulled her to him roughly, pressing his lips against her hair. "I love you."

She nodded, and pushed him toward the door. "John?" He swung around to look at her, letting his eyes linger on the soft curves of her face. "What did you name the file?"

"Redemption."

She resisted the urge to follow him out the door. This was an operation just like any other, and despite the fact that she loved her partner, she had to keep her emotions under control. Five minutes, and then she'd follow him. Ten minutes tops, they'd be together.

Worst-case scenario, they'd be discovered and taken in. All that meant was temporary separation. The hard part was over. The evidence they needed was safely hidden on the computer. Once it was turned over to the proper people, everything would come right in the end.

Or at least she hoped so.

She walked to the door, peering out through a crack, in time to see John reaching for the release button on the entry doors. He paused for a moment, turning to look back, his gaze meeting hers as he signaled okay with his fingers.

She released a breath she hadn't realized she'd been holding. Everything was going to be all right. It had to be. She turned away from the door and walked back to the computer, bending to pick up the duffel bag. Standing on a chair, she pushed back a ceiling tile next to an air duct and shoved the duffel through the resulting hole. She'd retrieve it when they came back for the files.

Or leave it be. It really didn't matter.

All that mattered now was getting the evidence of Danny's betrayal to the right people and clearing John's name. There was still more they needed to prove, but with the information here, even Roswell would have to give it all a second look.

She slid the tile back into place and dropped down off the chair, moving cautiously toward the door. They'd made it this far, no sense in screwing it up in the final minutes. With her back flat to the wall, she inched the door open, peering out into the hallway, her heart lurching to a stop.

John was still out there, flanked on one side by his brother, and on the other by what looked like the Guardian janitor. Except that the janitor held a gun. Her heart resumed beating, at a rate that would rival a racehorse's, and she dropped to the floor, scurrying across it as fast as she could.

Based on what she'd seen, she had about two minutes. She hit the chair on a dead run, grateful that it wasn't on wheels. Her breathing coming in shallow gasps, she pushed aside the ceiling tile once again, this time pulling herself through the gaping hole, praying the ductwork would support her weight. Praying even harder that John had the foresight not to mention her presence.

The ceiling held, and she slid the tile back into place, just as she heard the door slam open.

Chapter 26

John stumbled into the room, his eyes automatically searching for Katie, surprised and relieved to find no one there. The only sign at all of activity was a chair standing in the middle of the room. Glancing up, he thought he caught a modicum of movement as a ceiling tile slid back into place.

Jerking his vision back down, he pretended to fall, knocking the chair over in the process, the clamor hopefully covering any sound from above.

"Get up." A dispassionate Mr. Kim motioned John with the gun.

"I can't, I've hurt my leg." He rubbed it for emphasis, his eyes locking on his brother. Danny refused to meet his gaze, his attention centered on the floor.

"Help him." Again it was Kim who issued the order, and with a belligerent look, Danny complied, helping him up, then moving back, leaving Kim's line of fire clear.

Ever the brave one, his brother.

"Where's the girl?" Kim's eyes shot around the room, looking for hiding places.

"She's not here." John worked to keep his tone even, determined not to give Katie away.

"Don't be foolish, Brighton, I saw you walk in with a woman."

"It wasn't her, I swear it. It was a woman who works here, Evelyn." His mind scrambled for a plausible explanation. "I used to date her. You remember her, Danny? She's a technician for D.E.S. That's how I got in. Look, Kim, you said you saw her. She doesn't look anything like Katie."

"Is this true?" Kim turned to Danny, his gun still pointing at John. "Is there an Evelyn?"

Danny shuffled nervously, as if he was afraid to answer, then finally shrugged. "There was a woman here that John was seeing. But I can't remember her name."

Kim frowned, turning his attention back to John, eyes narrowed in thought. "If Agent Cavanaugh isn't here, then where is she?"

"I'm afraid I had to incapacitate her. It was the only way to escape. I needed to clear my name and she wasn't exactly a team player." He shrugged, hoping for nonchalance.

"So you're on your own?" Kim didn't look as if he was totally buying the situation, but he seemed to be on the verge.

John struggled for something to say that would seal the deal, praying that Katie was headed for help. "It seems these days I'm always on my own, Mr. Kim." He shot a look at his brother, having no problem at all adding the necessary touch of cynicism.

Kim nodded in acquiescence, and moved toward the door. "Your brother will explain to you what we need, while I secure the corridors." He slipped from the room, his movements silent, almost catlike.

John spun around to face his brother, his intent to convince Danny that they could act together against Kim, but the look on Danny's face put an abrupt end to the thought.

"I need the blueprints, John. And you have the codes." The words were simple, their meaning quite clear, but some part of John's mind refused to accept them. Refused to accept the fact that his brother was his enemy.

He took a step toward Danny, not really sure what he intended to do, his mind still resolutely avoiding the reality of the situation.

"Stop." Danny stepped toward the door. "You can't take me. Not with your leg like that. And even if you could, you'd still have to get past Kim. And believe me, he wouldn't hesitate to kill you."

"It doesn't have to be like this. Together we could stop him." John hated the note of pleading in his voice, but Danny was his brother. Surely that still meant something.

"Don't be obtuse. I'm not interested in changing sides." Danny's words were harsh, driving reality home.

"So you'd just let him kill me?" John knew the answer, but perversely he needed to hear Danny say it.

"You haven't given me any choice, Jonathan. I thought I had it all worked out, you know. With your memory loss, you weren't a risk anymore. I hoped things could go back to the way they were, but then you started nosing around again, and everything escalated out of control."

John stared at his brother. Danny looked the same, even sounded the same, but the words belonged to someone he didn't know. "So you're blaming all of this on me?"

"In a way. If you could have just left well enough alone, then Miller would still be alive and none of this would have had to happen."

"I don't understand." He thought maybe he did, but the idea of it was so repulsive he couldn't find the strength to accept it as truth.

Danny blew out a breath, his eyes hardening. "Of course you don't. How could you? For all your ramblings about walking on the edge, you haven't really got a clue what it's like to take a chance. I mean, really step out on a limb for something. There's a rush, Jonathan.

An amazing high that comes with taking that kind of risk."

"Is that how this started? As a game?" He tried, but couldn't keep the incredulity from his voice.

"Something like that. At first I just wanted to prove I could do it. In fact, in the beginning I actually put the information I 'borrowed' back again. But as Guardian grew, so did the opportunities to take the game to a new level. The things our clients were asking us to protect were worth more and more money, and that meant the risk of stealing them was exponentially higher as well."

"So you did all of this for the thrill of it?"

Danny shrugged. "There was money, too. And after I got involved with the Koreans, a certain degree of threat." There was a note of regret in his voice that hadn't been there earlier. "I suppose it's possible that I got in over my head, but once it was done, there was no going back. And at least in the beginning, our association was a good one. Until you managed to mess everything up. You and Derek Miller. When Miller found out someone had been selling secrets, he didn't realize at first that it was me, that came later, but in the meantime, being the overzealous employee that he was, he took the information he had to you. And *you* came straight to me."

"Because I trusted you." John felt physically ill as he realized that he'd been right all along. Inadvertently, he *had* been responsible for Miller's death.

Danny actually looked apologetic. "I didn't mean for you to get hurt. You have to believe that. But ultimately it was my only way out. When Miller figured out it was me, he came to me wanting money. At first I refused. But then he threatened to go to the Feds and tell them everything." He sounded like a little boy trying to justify the mischief he'd caused. Only they were talking about murder. "He left me no alternative, Jonathan."

"So you shot him."

"Yes. And arranged for you to take the fall."

"Why didn't you just come to me, Danny? I could have helped you."

His brother shook his head, his expression sorrowful. "It had gone too far. As I said, the Koreans were threatening me. And in truth, you knew too much. You were going to die one way or the other, Jonathan, but if I wanted to live, I needed a cover, and you provided the perfect out. It was down to you or me." Danny struggled for breath. "And as hard as it was to do it, I chose me. So I shot Miller with a gun I'd registered in your name. I've been forging your signature forever. Don't you remember when I signed you out of the hospital?"

The memory came flooding back. Danny laughing as he signed the papers. Pretending concern. Promising it would be all right. John swallowed the bile rising in his throat.

"I'm sorry, Jonathan. But the setup was too perfect. I'd already arranged your vacation, so that I'd have an opportunity to get into the D.E.S. system."

"That's why Andy didn't remember my agreeing to take the villa. It was you." John's mind was spinning, frantically trying to remember things that were forever gone.

Danny's laugh was without mirth. "You believed what you were told. But yes, I convinced you to go, and promised to tell Andy. And I would have. At that point I just wanted you out of the way. But then Miller started making noises. So I was forced to change plans. I conveniently forgot to tell Andy, and off you went. All that was left was to arrange for your death."

"And the money?" John leaned back against the computer desk, his head pounding, his knees weak.

"I played with your computer records." Danny met his gaze, regret still reflected in his eyes. "Made it look like the money had gone missing. Just a matter of changing numbers here and there."

"But it was all for nothing—I didn't die."

"No. You didn't. And whether you believe it or not, I was glad. You're my brother, for Christ's sake. I wouldn't have ever even considered the idea if things hadn't gotten so desperate."

John ignored the platitudes, choosing instead to face reality head-on. "And since my memory was shot to hell, there was no need to follow through on the botched attempt. Only, then Miller's body surfaced."

"It still might have been all right. But you started digging again. You and Flo. She figured it out, Jonathan. I don't know how. But she figured it out." Another flicker of regret crossed Danny's face. "She came to me that night. Confronted me with the truth. Our Flo never lacked courage. I didn't know what to do. She thought she could get me to turn myself in. But I couldn't. I knew too much. They'd have found me and killed me. I didn't have a choice. Surely you can see that." Tears glistened in his eyes. "I loved her like a mother, but I had to kill her. I had to."

The door creaked as it opened, and Kim stepped back into the room, his gun trained on the two of them.

"Where have you been?" Danny snapped.

"There was a complication, I was detained." The man wasn't exactly a font of information. "Time is running out. We need the documents."

"Jonathan hasn't exactly been forthcoming." Danny's tone was harsh, all evidence of remorse gone, and John realized that the man he knew as his brother was gone as well.

"Give me the codes." Kim's voice was as cold as the barrel of the gun in his hand.

"I don't have them." John narrowed his eyes, his gaze unflinching.

"Then you're of no use to me." Kim raised the gun, the metallic click of the hammer echoing through the room.

*   *   *

The air duct was narrowing, which meant forward momentum had slowed to a crawl. Katie inched forward, using her elbows and knees to propel herself, careful to keep from banging against the metal walls.

She'd stayed above the computer room long enough to determine that getting help was their best alternative. Leaving John had been wrenching, but she hadn't seen another choice. Now, however, she was beginning to regret the decision. Having crawled fifty feet or so without so much as a vent, she was becoming more and more convinced that the airway served only the computer room.

She bit back a curse as her T-shirt snagged on a weld, the material holding her back as she tried to move ahead. Reaching back with her right hand, she struggled to dislodge the shirt, but only succeeded in getting it more tangled. Gritting her teeth, she used her legs to push forward, the material straining and finally ripping free.

With a surge of irritation, she conceded defeat. The duct was simply too narrow for her to continue, and even if she could manage it, odds were that she wouldn't find a way out anyway. Which meant that instead of providing the cavalry, she'd only managed to waste precious time.

Wriggling her body, and using her toes, she began to inch her way backward. It was too dark in the duct to see her watch, but she estimated about ten minutes had passed, which meant that it would take at least that long to get back to John.

John.

Just the thought of his name sent her heart racing. He was back there dealing with God knew what. Her stomach twisted as guilt washed through her. She should never have left him alone. If something had happened to him . . .

Panic gripped her, threatening to cut off rational thought. Breathing deeply, she forced herself to calm down. To think clearly. She'd taken a chance and unfortunately it hadn't panned out, but that didn't mean she was out of the game. There had to be something she could do. Something to help John. She just had to think of it.

And in the meantime, she had to get back to the computer room.

Inch by inch by inch . . .

"Wait." Danny eyed his brother, his expression shrewd. "Even if he doesn't know the codes, he'll have left a back door. My brother is nothing if not thorough."

"Is this true?" Kim's voice was calm, almost dead, but his eyes were alive, watching, planning.

"Even if it were, I wouldn't use it to help you." John spit the words out, anger giving him courage.

"Brave words." Kim's smile was a poor imitation of the gesture. "But I do not think you're a fool."

John's courage evaporated. It had been a foolhardy thought anyway. Danny could most likely figure out the way in. And his death would have meant nothing. Better he stay alive and try to stall things. He sat at the computer, and began to type the appropriate codes. "I'm in, but I'm not certain I'll be able to find what you want. And even if I do, I sincerely doubt it'll fit on a disk."

"Just find the schematics. I'll take care of copying them." Kim moved so that he was watching over John's shoulder.

"I'll try and find the phoenix file." Danny was sitting at another terminal, typing commands at a rate faster than John's injured fingers could follow.

"You know about it?" John looked up at Kim, unable to contain his surprise.

"Thanks to your brother."

John looked to Danny for an explanation.

"Miller was more than happy to tell me all about it when he tried to blackmail me. Except of course I couldn't get the bastard to tell me where the file was hidden. So for six long months I've known the damn thing was out there, I just didn't know where."

"And you think it's here?" John strove to keep his voice level, disinterested even.

Danny continued to type, his smile lacking humor. "Oh, I know it's here. It took me a while, but I finally found Miller's trail. That, compounded with the fact that you're here, makes it pretty damn certain. Besides, we've looked everywhere else."

"You're the ones who ransacked Miller's house." John looked from Danny to Kim, helplessness mixing with anger.

The older man nodded once.

"Too bad you missed the zip drive." Despite the absurdity of the notion, he felt as if he'd won a point.

"I wondered how you figured it out." The man's calm was becoming annoying. "I thought perhaps your memories had returned."

"No such luck."

"There's nothing here." Frustration, laced with anger, colored Danny's voice. "Nothing called phoenix. I'll bet he renamed it."

"I think perhaps you'd better tell us the name." Kim moved closer, and John felt the cold muzzle of the gun against his neck.

He considered not telling them. Just throwing shit to the wind, and letting the chips fall where they may. But a tiny noise from the ceiling reminded him that he wasn't alone in this. And that miracles were indeed possible.

He looked over at his brother, and making no attempt to conceal his animosity, told him the name of the file.

* * *

Katie stared down through the vent, her heart pounding. Danny was typing furiously now, forcing the computer to yield its secrets. He was going to delete the evidence and there didn't appear to be a damn thing she could do about it.

Without a weapon, the odds were not in her favor. Damn D.E.S. and their security. This is what she got for acting without backup. *Again.* But it wasn't like she'd had a choice. She'd tried to tell Roswell, but he'd refused to listen.

With a shake of her head, she abandoned her regret, focusing instead on the scenario playing out beneath her.

"I've got it, Kim." Danny hit a key, his voice triumphant. "I'm deleting it now."

"Excellent." The janitor moved away from John, his interest centered on Danny and the computer monitor. "Now perhaps you can speed your brother's search along."

Holding her breath, she slowly began to inch the vent aside, trying to estimate the distance between her and Kim. If only he'd move back a bit, she'd have a clear shot at him. As if he'd read her mind, John stopped his typing, pointing at the screen. "I think maybe I've got something."

Kim turned, the movement placing him almost directly under the vent.

Launching herself with her feet, Katie came flying through the hole, taking part of the ceiling with her, she hit Kim with the full force of her body, knocking them both into the wall, the gun clattering as it spun from his hand to the floor.

He was strong, but she had the element of surprise, and with a swift elbow to the chin, she knocked his head against the wall, his body slumping forward as he lost consciousness. She swiveled, eyes to the floor, searching for the gun.

It lay in the corner, only the muzzle showing, the rest of it underneath a bookshelf. Danny and John were already in motion, the two of them colliding in their effort to reach it. She started forward, then stopped as Danny's hand closed around the steel cylinder.

He rolled to his feet, his eyes wild. "Get back."

Despite the command, she took a step forward, her eyes locked on John, his body sprawled on the floor.

"I mean it. Get back." Danny waved the gun at her, panic making his voice sound hoarse.

She held up her hands, feigning agreement, years of training kicking in to keep her steady. The rise and fall of John's breathing meant he wasn't dead. Which meant there was still a chance.

"It's too late for escape, Danny." She kept her voice low and even, trying to remember everything she'd learned about negotiations. It hadn't been her strong suit. She'd never had the patience.

"There's always a way out. I just have to think of it." His gaze careened wildly around the room, finally landing on Kim. "Is he dead?"

"No. But he won't be waking up any time soon." She held her ground, keeping her voice soothing. "Which means you're on your own."

"I've managed to turn things around before. I'll just have to do it without Soon Hee."

Soon Hee. *Kim Soon Hee.* Katie shot a look at the janitor. Roswell had been right. The Koreans were behind everything. Mind spinning, she shifted her focus back to Danny. "It won't work. Even if you do get away, you know too much. Which means that sooner or later Kim's men will find you."

"And I suppose you think you can protect me." The words were meant to be sarcastic, but his hand was shaking, the gun swaying with the motion.

"I can't, but the FBI can." She edged a little closer, and he waved the gun, shifting away from her, his back to John now.

"If I testify. But that would mean incriminating myself. I can't do that." He backed away from her, his eyes darting around the room, looking for an out.

"We're not interested in the little fish, Danny. We want the Koreans. And you can deliver Kim."

He considered her statement for a moment, then shook his head. "It's too dangerous. You said it yourself, I'd never be safe again."

Behind Danny, John shifted silently, slowly rising to a crouching position, his eyes cutting toward his brother, signaling her. She caught her breath, praying that he had the necessary strength, and deliberately stepped forward. Danny jumped, trying to cock the gun, but John was faster, ramming into his brother from behind. Danny twisted, so that they were facing each other, bodies locked together, the gun jammed between them.

They struggled, first upright, and then rolling on the floor. Katie edged closer, grabbing a folding chair, waiting for a moment when Danny was turned toward her. The two men broke apart slightly, and with a deafening clang she brought the chair down, the metal crashing into Danny's back, sending him sprawling, the action dislodging the gun.

It slid across the floor and Katie dove for it, but Kim was awake and faster, scooping up the gun, aiming it directly at her. With a cry to rival a banshee, John launched himself toward Kim, the momentum of the hit sending the two men across the floor, John sprawled over Kim, the gun's report reverberating through the room.

Time seemed to slow to a crawl, her heart pounding like a drum in her head. Hardly daring to breathe, she took a step forward, her eyes locked on John. A low moan preceded motion as he pulled himself off of Kim.

Blood stained his shirt, but the lifeless eyes of Kim Soon Hee were testament to the fact that it wasn't his blood. Relief washed through her so powerfully it weakened her knees, and she reached out to steady herself on the computer console.

"You're all right?" The words were no more than a whisper, but he heard her, his blood-spattered face cracking into a weak grin.

"I'll live. How about you?" His eyes covered the distance between her head and feet, not once but twice, as he searched to make certain she was unharmed.

"I'm okay." She reached out and touched his face, if only to make certain that he was indeed standing in front of her. She wanted to wrap her arms around him and never let him go. But there was still Danny to deal with.

She turned to find him sitting up, rubbing his head, his expression dazed, almost vacant. "What happened?"

"Kim is dead."

Danny's face crumpled then, as if the enormity of what he'd done had finally hit home. He looked like a little boy lost, and John hesitated only a moment before he crossed the room to his brother's side, just as D'Angelo and Haskins burst into the room, guns drawn.

D'Angelo's gray eyes calmly took in the battered computer room, the dead man, the two brothers, his gaze finally settling on Katie. "What happened here?"

"A war, of sorts, I suppose." She couldn't tear her eyes away from John's anguished face.

"And the winner?" D'Angelo asked.

Katie swallowed back her tears. "No one. Absolutely no one."

John fought against fatigue, concentrating instead on the sounds of activity around him. Danny had been sedated and taken away, and Kim's body had been removed. D'Angelo and Roswell were talking to Katie, questioning her about everything that had happened. He knew he should be participating, but he simply couldn't seem to summon the energy. Every muscle in his body hurt.

Despite all that Danny had done, some bonds were not easy to sever. He knew that Danny would recover from his shock, and most likely try to rationalize all that had happened. And he also knew that his own emotions were stunted, shock taking precedence over the anger and hurt that were certain to follow.

But right now all he was concentrating on was the soft cadence of Katie's voice. Like a lifeline, he held on to the sound, knowing that as long as they were together, he could handle anything.

"But I told you, we found proof." Katie's tone was indignant.

"Yes, but that proof has conveniently been destroyed. So we've only got your word that it ever existed. And frankly, Agent Cavanaugh, at the moment your word doesn't mean shit."

Roswell's slam against Katie was like a bucket of ice water. John's lethargy dissipated in an instant, leaving red-hot anger in its wake. "Her word means more than yours, Roswell. She doesn't use innocent citizens as bait."

"I certainly don't have to explain my motives to you, Brighton, but for the record, I believed you were guilty." Still believed it, if John was reading him right.

Which made it all that much more pleasant to burst the bastard's bubble. "Sorry to disappoint you, Roswell, but I am innocent. And even better than that, I can prove it."

Roswell's nostrils flared, a definite sign of displeasure, but he made no comment.

John suppressed a smile. Obviously Edmund Roswell

had severely underestimated his opponent. "You see, in my business, backups are everything, and so I made a copy of Miller's file. It's right there on the computer."

D'Angelo was already moving toward the keyboard, Roswell close on his heels. In the end, it seemed, Roswell *was* interested in truth—as long as it got him where he wanted to go. "What's it called?"

John's smile was slow, the gesture meant for Katie alone. "Kaitlin. I called it Kaitlin." His gaze locked with hers, and he waited for her reaction, everything but the two of them seeming to fade into the background.

"My name." She whispered the words, her breath warm against his cheek.

"I thought it was symbolic. A new beginning."

"You and me, together?" He heard the trembling in her voice, and realized that even Katie had fears. The thought was comforting. And liberating.

"Two halves of a whole." He pressed his lips against hers, the kiss a covenant. "Always."

Epilogue

Rain fell in buckets, filling the rivers and streams until they were bursting, threatening to break through their boundaries and swallow everything in their path. But safe at the top of their canyon, Katie and John didn't care. It was all a part of living in the hill country. Nature taking and then giving.

Opposite extremes.

John stretched in the warmth of their bed, listening to the sound of rain against the roof. It was a magical sound. One they'd always cherish. Katie sighed, and curled into him, his wife still craving his warmth, the feel of her burrowing against him kindling a depth of emotion he'd never dreamed possible.

Life was good. He'd probably always have headaches, and he'd always walk with a limp, but overall he was healthy, inside and out, and building a future with Katie was far more important than dwelling on the past.

Her eyes flickered open. "You're not sleeping."

He pulled her even closer, his body already responding to the proximity of hers. It was a wonder he ever got any sleep at all. "I was listening to the rain."

"Our song." He could hear the sleepy smile in her voice.

"So you don't regret moving to Texas? The bride of a reinvented businessman?" Guardian had perished with the revelations of Danny's deceit, but from its ashes, John was building a new company, Phoenix. It catered to law enforcement. A way for them to stay on top of technology. Sort of a detective agency on disk.

"You're doing what you always do, John. Finding a path to the top. This is just a new challenge, and if you'd admit it, you'd rather be forging a path than sitting on your laurels."

He laughed. She knew him well. "Frank says you're too good at reading my mind." The man had proved a stalwart in everything they had been through, and though Valerie had moved on, he'd stayed with John, his loyalty proving invaluable.

"He's right, you know." There was a definite smile in her voice now. One he was learning to recognize. "And that's not the only thing I can read." Her hand found his hardness, caressing his strength.

"You're sure this is where you want to be?" He asked the question again, certain he'd never tire of the answer.

"Positive. Although I have to admit, I'm craving release from my desk job." She'd been given a reprimand and limited to desk work for six months, but the time was fast drawing to an end. With Roswell's retirement, Wilcox had been promoted, and he was chomping at the bit to have her back on the team.

"Jerome has no idea what he's in for." He received a punch for his remark, followed by a kiss. A long, slow, burning kiss that filled him with desire. He'd never get used to having her here. His prayers were daily and devout. Only a man truly blessed could be as fortunate as he was.

With a possessive groan worthy of a man with a treasure, he braced himself on his elbows, his eyes devouring hers, his body sliding strong and sure into her heat—uniting them as one. The sound of the midnight rain surrounded them, it's incessant rhythm a counterpoint to the power of their love.

Read on for a sneak peek at the next chilling novel
of romantic suspense from Dee Davis

DANCING IN THE DARK

Coming in Fall 2003

Chapter I

Austin, Texas

The shrill sound cut through the night.

It reached deep into Sara Martin's subconscious, jerking her from sleep, vanquishing her dream like smoke on the wind. Angrily, she pushed upright, reaching for the phone.

"Hello?"

The line was silent, except for the soft hiss that meant someone was there.

"Hello?" She wasn't certain why she asked again. He never answered. Just waited, listening. As if he knew what he was interrupting—but that was impossible. With a release of breath, she slammed the receiver into the cradle, dismissing the prank. It didn't matter.

Nothing mattered.

Not anymore.

Moonlight, filtering through the curtains, cast intricate shadows across the room, and she watched as they danced across the ceiling. Closing her eyes, she tried to recapture the dream, but as always it was illusive, coming only when it chose, never on demand.

Tears welled, and she pushed them away. Time, it seemed, did not heal wounds. It only left them to fester, the memory of all that was good tantalizing in its obscurity. Here in the dark, reality seemed a cruel joke. A punishment for a crime she'd never committed.

Still fighting tears, she reached for the lamp, and with the flick of a switch banished the shadows back into the night. Reflexively she turned, her eyes searching the pillow next to hers. Wanting to find an indentation, a scent. Anything.

She traced the contours of the pillow, letting her imagination remember other times. Better times. But they were gone, along with her husband and son. Forever. Squeezing her eyes shut, she rolled over, fighting for control. It was always worse at night.

Maybe it would be best if she'd just stop dreaming. At least that way the past would stay where it was supposed to be. But even as she had the thought, she knew she didn't mean it. The dreams were all she had left.

No matter how much they hurt.

After all, it was the hurting that reminded her she was still alive.

The smell was the first thing he noticed, and it wasn't as if he was new to crime scenes. But this one was bad. He could tell just from the sickly, sweet stench of decaying flesh. With a sigh, Eric D'Angelo pushed past the gathered crowd of homeless people and ducked under the yellow tape, steeling himself for the task at hand.

No matter how many murder scenes he worked, it was always one too many.

"Wondered if you were going to grace us with your presence." Tony Haskins ambled over as if it were Sunday at the park. His partner's girth and slow gait hid an astute mind and a quick wit.

"I was across town, and there were a few things I had to handle before I could leave."

"Right." Haskins' eyebrows rose, not missing a beat. "Anyone I know?"

"No." The single word brooked no further discussion. "So what have we got here?"

"Dead female. Caucasian. Looks to be somewhere

between sixteen and twenty, and based on the clothing, I'd say she was a little bit more than just the kid next door." Tony shifted so that Eric could see the body.

A woman was sprawled beside a Dumpster, refuse scattered around her like a picture frame. Even without Tony's caustic comment, he'd have guessed at her profession. The gold lamé halter combined with the micro-mini skirt could have been considered chic, if it weren't for the fact that they were about two sizes too small. A smear of lipstick marred one cheek, blood staining the other, the two reds at odds with one another, the effect garish.

"She was left like this?" D'Angelo frowned, trying to visualize the situation.

"No." Tony shook his head. "The guy over there found her. Evidently he pulled her out of the Dumpster to get at the stuff underneath, and then couldn't be bothered to call it in."

"Or wasn't able to tell the living from the dead." Eric shot a look at the old geezer. Between the grime and the layers of clothing it was hard to tell what he really looked like, but the vacant gaze was apparent even from here. He'd seen it a hundred times over the years.

"Well, fortunately for us, he wasn't the only one digging in the garbage." Tony nodded toward a woman sitting on a crate, huddled over a Styrofoam cup of coffee. "She's the one who called. From over there."

Eric looked across the alley to the open door of a club, light slashing across the pavement like a rip in the asphalt. "How long since she called it in?"

"A couple of hours. Took the uniforms a little while to locate the woman."

"So what else do we know about the vic?" Eric walked over to the body, his seasoned mind already absorbing details.

"Not much. There's no ID. Although they haven't finished searching the Dumpster. There's no sign of struggle and very little blood. Which sure as hell isn't consistent with her wounds. This woman was stabbed repeatedly, and unless I've missed something, that isn't easy to accomplish without leaving one hell of a mess."

D'Angelo bent down for a closer look. "There's blood all over the body, but most of it's dried." He frowned, reaching out to carefully touch her cheek. "Rigor's set in. And the smell alone indicates she's been dead more than a few hours."

"Wouldn't be impossible for her to have been in the Dumpster a while."

"Not impossible." Claire Dennison joined them, her eyes narrowed in thought. Claire was a forensics specialist—a damn good one—and Eric was glad she'd responded to the call. "But not the case here. There's no blood in the Dumpster, either. And even without an autopsy, it's fairly clear she bled out."

"So where's the blood?" Eric stood up, his gaze meeting hers.

"Hard to say. Truth is it could be anywhere." Claire studied the body with the cool eyes of a professional. "If we're lucky we'll find something to tie her to the killer. If not, maybe a fiber or two will at least give us a location."

Eric nodded, turning his attention to Tony. "So why were we called in?" They were technically off duty, and under normal circumstances, the murder should have fallen to someone else.

"The woman was raped."

"Kind of hard to tell with a hooker, isn't it?"

"Not when someone leaves their bat behind." Tony tipped his head toward a bloody piece of wood protruding beneath the skirt.

"Jesus." Eric forced his gaze away from the body, frowning up at his partner.

"It gets worse. The guy took her fingers."

His eyes were automatically drawn to the hand

folded against her breast. The lamé hid part of it, but now that he was looking—really looking—he could see that all five fingers had been cut off.

A quick glance at her other hand confirmed that it too had been altered.

"Son of a bitch." He swallowed a mouthful of bile, his gaze locking with Tony's. "He's back."

The soft sound of music filled the air, and Sara let the notes wash over her, the rhythm carrying away some of her tension. Taking a sip from her wine glass, she let the dark smoky taste of merlot run down the back of her throat. Drinking alone was a dangerous luxury. One she seldom indulged in.

But tonight, she needed it.

She took another sip, and stared at the phone. It would be so simple to pick it up, to call Ryan or Molly. But that would mean confessing her state of mind and to be honest, she wasn't certain she had the energy. Besides, she was a firm believer in maintaining a stiff upper lip. A throwback to her days in foster care.

Never let 'em see you sweat.

She smiled despite herself. The music and the wine were working, the shadows that haunted her life withdrawing. She looked around the living room, pleased with the soft colors and fashionable antiques. Her home was almost a diametric opposite to the house she and Tom had shared.

Tom had loved the sleek and modern. An architect, he delighted in simplicity. Form and line. Their house had been beautiful. Perched on a cliff, soaring above the treetops, it had been like living in a fantasy of glass and light. After the accident, the house had become a horrifying symbol for all she'd lost.

So she'd sold it, and moved to the center of Austin. As far away from the hills as she could get without leaving the city all together. The Hyde Park Victorian was a far cry from Tom's designs, but it suited her somehow. And with time, she'd actually grown to love it. There was something cathartic in making a place for herself. Almost as if the walls themselves had the power to heal her.

The doorbell rang, breaking through her reverie. Frowning, she set the wine glass down, wondering who could possibly be visiting so late. Cautiously approaching the door, she grabbed an umbrella from the stand, and stood on tiptoe to peer through the peephole.

Releasing a breath, she replaced the umbrella and unlocked the door, swinging it open. "Damn it, Ryan, you scared me half to death. It's the middle of the night."

Ryan Greene smiled, his eyes crinkling with the gesture. "Sorry. I was on my way home and saw the light."

Sara moved away from the door, gesturing for him to come in. "It's awfully late to be working. Looming deadline?"

"No." He shrugged sheepishly. "Actually, I was following up on a story."

Ryan was the editor in chief for *Texas Today*, a weekly magazine with a large regional reader base. But despite the fact, he'd never been able to totally give up the thrill of chasing a lead.

Case in point.

"So what's the story?"

He crossed over to the wine bottle and poured himself a glass. "There's been another murder."

A chill chased down her spine. "The same guy?"

"They're not saying. There's a press conference scheduled for tomorrow. Until then, we won't know anything for sure. But the M.O. is similar. The main difference seems to be that the body was left in a trash bin."

"Where?"

"Downtown. In an alley behind a bar."

The press had been consumed with the brutal murders of two prostitutes over the last eighteen months.

Speculation was that the deaths were the work of the same man. But two cases weren't enough to establish a pattern. Three on the other hand . . .

"Were you there?"

"Yeah." His eyes darkened, his features harsh. "It wasn't a pretty picture."

"You should have called me. I could have gotten some shots." Although she didn't normally photograph murder scenes, she'd done it several times over the years. Usually when she was nearby or there wasn't anyone else available.

Ryan's gaze met hers, his expression softening. "I wouldn't subject you to that."

"I'm tougher than I look."

"I don't doubt that. But considering all that you've been through, I didn't think it was appropriate. Besides, I can pull pictures off the wires." He took a sip of wine, studying her over the rim of his glass.

"You're staring."

"Sorry. I was just noticing the circles under your eyes." Ryan frowned, his eyes reflecting his concern. "You've been having the nightmare again, haven't you?"

She shook her head, trying for nonchalance and failing miserably. "It's just a dream."

"It's more than that and you know it."

"Right. It's a manifestation of my grief. A normal part of the healing process." She mimicked the doctor perfectly, unable to keep the bitterness out of her voice. "Well, I, for one, would like for it to manifest itself into oblivion." She picked up the glass again, swallowing the contents in one gulp.

"You don't mean that."

"Yes, I do." But she didn't—and therein lay the problem.

"Damn it, Sara." Ryan leaned forward, his hand covering hers. "Why didn't you call me?"

Gently she pulled away, leaning back on the sofa.

"Because I'm a big girl, Ryan. I can take care of myself."

"Right." He sat back, his concern still evident. "And that would explain the merlot at midnight."

"Look, I'm fine. They're just dreams. It's not like they cause me physical harm. So I lose a little sleep. It's not such a bad price to pay."

"I know you miss them, Sara. But you've got to move on. You can't keep living in the past." He ran a hand through his hair, his look beseeching. "You know as well as I do that Tom and Charlie wouldn't want that."

"Sometimes I don't think I know anything anymore." She rubbed the gold of her wedding ring, wishing it were a magic lamp. A way to change time. To change fate.

"Don't say things like that." He looked so earnest, she almost laughed.

"I'm sorry. I didn't mean it. Honestly." She stood up, smothering a yawn. The wine had done its job. "It's just that it's late and I'm tired."

"You want me to stay?"

She smiled, shaking her head. "I'll be fine. It's almost morning anyway. You go home and get some sleep." She reached up to lay a hand on his cheek. "Thanks for watching out for me."

He covered her hand with his. "That's what friends are for, Sara."

She stepped back, embarrassed suddenly. She wasn't usually given to outbursts of emotion. In fact she prided herself on maintaining control. It's just that sometimes it was so damn hard. "You want me to try and get some photos at the press conference tomorrow?" She walked with him toward the door, firmly steering the conversation back to business.

He shook his head. "I already called Satchel. But I do still need you at the mayor's office. He's not an easy man to photograph, and I'm counting on you to pull the best out of him."

"I'll do what I can."

"That's my girl." He walked out onto the porch. "Try and get some sleep. I'll see you in the morning."

Nodding, she lifted a hand to wave, then shut the door, throwing the deadbolt. Turning around to face the empty room, her eyes were drawn to a picture on the wall. Tom and Charlie smiled out at her from the frame and her heart twisted with longing.

Reaching over she traced first her husband's face, then her son's, her mind conjuring the feel of Charlie's baby-soft skin, the smell of Tom's aftershave. She knew it was time to move on. Time to make a new life. But somehow she couldn't let go. Couldn't find the courage.

Or maybe it was just that she just didn't know how.

Eric D'Angelo stared down at the pictures on his kitchen table. He'd arranged them side by side so that he could examine each victim in context with the others, hoping that one of them at least would have something to tell him.

But so far the ladies were being stubbornly silent. The differences between the three women were as numerous as the similarities. Location had varied, although, until the last one, the body had been found at the site of the murder. One was a confirmed prostitute, and another had been known to sell her body when she ran out of drug money. The third looked like a member of the same sisterhood, although the fact had not yet been confirmed.

None of the ladies were exactly cream of the crop. But that didn't mean they'd deserved to die. Not like this. Hell, not at all. He picked up the picture of the first victim. Laurel Henry was well over thirty, and she'd obviously lived a hard life. Her cheeks were pockmarked, and a tiny scar ran from the corner of her mouth down her chin.

She had a rap sheet a mile long. Everything from solicitation to petty larceny. Like the other two, she'd been raped repeatedly, then stabbed, and left to bleed out.

She was also missing an ear.

His stomach twisted with revulsion. He saw the results of humanity's inhumanity every day, but something like this still had the power to shake him.

He picked up the second picture, studying the lifeless black woman. Candy Mason was the diametric opposite of Laurel, her curly dark hair and chocolate skin a tin-type negative of the older blonde woman. She had also been stabbed, after an umbrella had been used in ways he didn't even want to contemplate. Like Laurel there'd been angry wounds, and blood everywhere.

But this time the killer had cut out her tongue.

He picked up the last of the photos. The latest victim was nothing like the other two. Younger by maybe ten years, she couldn't be more than eighteen. Her over-mascaraed eyes stared vacantly up at him, her hands crossed almost virginally across her chest.

Another kid on the streets with nothing to lose— except her life. The body appeared to be the least marked up of the three, but that didn't negate the horror.

Even in death, pain seemed to radiate from her. As if her soul was still there, calling to him from the photograph.

He put down the picture, rubbing the bridge of his nose. It was late, and he wasn't getting anywhere. Tomorrow, after the M.E. was finished with her, they'd know more. Like her name. And why she'd been dumped there.

Maybe her murder wasn't connected to the others. She was younger, softer somehow. And the others had been found at the scene. This girl had obviously been moved. Still, there were commonalities between the three. The use of a knife, the missing appendages, and the impersonal savagery of the rape.

But there was one major difference.

The music.

When the first two women had been found, there'd been music playing, an endless recording of soft swelling notes, a love song forming a poignant counterpoint to the brutal violence that had ended their lives. He looked down at the picture of the third woman.

There'd been no music—at least not in the alleyway—but then she hadn't actually died there, and D'Angelo had the feeling that when they found the murder site, they'd find the music. It was a signature of sorts, the reason the press had dubbed the perp the Sinatra Killer.

He blew out a breath, and leaned back in his chair, closing his eyes. One thing was definitely for certain; there was twisted logic in every move a guy like that made. Which meant he was still out there somewhere, waiting, watching, and sooner or later, he was going to strike again.

The only real question was when.

Don't miss these
exciting novels of suspense
by Dee Davis

DARK OF THE NIGHT
*Deadly secrets reveal a nightmare
of blind ambition. . . .*

JUST BREATHE
*Loving him could be
a lethal propostion . . .*

AFTER TWILIGHT
Everyone walks with a shadow . . .

Published by Ivy Books.
Available wherever books are sold.

Subscribe to the new Pillow Talk e-newsletter—and receive all these fabulous online features directly in your e-mail inbox:

♥ Exclusive essays and other features by major romance writers like Linda Howard, Kristin Hannah, Julie Garwood, and Suzanne Brockmann

♥ Exciting behind-the-scenes news from our romance editors

♥ Special offers, including contests to win signed romance books and other prizes

♥ Author tour information, and monthly announcements about the newest books on sale

♥ A Pillow Talk readers forum, featuring feedback from romance fans...like you!

Two easy ways to subscribe:
Go to **www.ballantinebooks.com/PillowTalk**
or send a blank e-mail to
join-PillowTalk@list.randomhouse.com.

Pillow Talk—
the romance e-newsletter brought to you by
Ballantine Books